Crow
Hollow

Crow Hollow

MICHAEL WALLACE

LAKE UNION
PUBLISHING

Text copyright © 2015 Michael Wallace
All rights reserved.

Published by Lake Union Publishing, Seattle

www.apub.com

Amazon, the Amazon logo, and Lake Union Publishing are trademarks of Amazon.com, Inc., or its affiliates.

ISBN-13: 9781477828014
ISBN-10: 147782801X

Cover design by Laura Klynstra

Library of Congress Control Number: 2014953298

Printed in the United States of America

CHAPTER ONE

Boston Harbor, December 16, 1676

James Bailey stared down from the main deck of the *Vigilant* as it eased up to the wharves, a knot of excitement forming in his belly.

Twenty men armed with muskets waited for him along the shore. A short man stood at the front of the formation, staring up at the ship with sharp eyes. A strong wind snapped in off the North Atlantic, blowing his shoulder-length blond hair around his face. He rested a hand on the pommel of his sword.

James met the man's gaze. After eight weeks at sea, he was anxious to get off this rickety, barely seaworthy barrel and set about the king's business. If that meant confrontation with a colonial welcoming party, he relished it.

The ship made contact with the pier, groaning as it heaved against the wooden pilings. Sailors scrambled off the decks like so many bilge rats, leaping to the pier, tossing ropes, and hauling the gangplank into position.

Peter Church stood at James's side. The older man wore the same serene smile that seemed fixed to his face at all times, whether he was about to say one of his curious Quaker prayers or was staring into the driving rain of an ocean gale.

"I had supposed we had sailed from Weymouth in secrecy," Peter said. "Yet it seems our reputation precedes us."

James looked around at the forest of masts that dotted the harbor. "Did you see that pinnace when we were heaving to? I swear it's the same ship we saw off the Cornish coast."

On the first full day out of port, a full-rigged pinnace had overtaken them while they were still in sight of land. It swooped in until it lurked a quarter mile off starboard. The *Vigilant*'s captain had cursed, thinking they were about to be attacked by pirates out of Dunkirk. But the other ship had continued past them without sign or signal. James had spotted two men on deck watching them through spyglasses. After that, he noticed several suspicious characters among the crew and passengers of the *Vigilant* itself. Men who seemed to watch him when he came onto the deck, or sat too close when he and Peter took their supper.

"Did the Puritans send spies?" Peter asked.

"Why not?" James said. "*We* certainly did." This was largely bluster. No more than a handful of royal agents operated between Quebec and the Province of Carolina.

"But who sent them?"

"Hard to say. These stiff-necked fools have plenty of friends in Parliament. Any one could have sent word." James eyed the older man. "And when they hear you're on board, we're bound to attract a special flavor of vitriol."

By now, the immigrants crowding the deck were making such a noise in anticipation of landfall that the two men had to raise their voices to be heard.

Peter Church chuckled. "Which will upset them more? That I'm an Indian or that I'm a Quaker?"

"Let's see if you live long enough to find out."

The gangplank fell into place with a thunk. Passengers lined up to file off the boat that had held them prisoner for eight cold, wet weeks. Sailors grabbed trunks and muscled into the fray. Any longer and the two men would be caught in the crush.

James reached into his cloak to verify that he hadn't left the king's commission in his sea chest. He had left his pistols and sword behind and carried only a small hidden dagger that had served him well in Paris and London. Also in the chest, a tidy sum in silver coin, plus the money he had on his person.

The air smelled of brine and fish guts. Seagulls wheeled overhead, crying. All around, men shouted. Sailors, fishermen, immigrants on the deck yelled back and forth to people waiting on the shore.

James cleared a path through the passengers and seamen and clomped down the gangplank, with Peter following. A rime of sea ice encrusted the wooden pilings and the surface of the pier itself. James made sure of his footing before stepping off the gangplank.

For a moment he thought the pier was floating, because everything was still swaying. Even the ramshackle wooden buildings that lined the harbor seemed to be rocking from side to side as if carried by the waves. Further into the town, everything wobbled: the crowded brick buildings, the chimneys, even the smoke trailing into the cold December air.

Eight weeks crossing the vast ocean, and his head could no longer tell the difference between the swell of waves and the solid feel of rooted timbers beneath his feet.

James had been to sea before, of course, had traveled a dozen times across the Channel to Holland or France, sometimes openly, other times on clandestine business for the Crown. Pockets full of silver to bribe French officials, or carrying secret treaties to negotiate with avaricious Dutch merchants. But he'd never before lost sight of land for more than a day or two.

The seas had turned angry west of the Cornish coast, and he'd spent a week spewing his supper over the rail until he wanted to throw himself into the ocean to relieve the misery of it. The swaying wharf reminded him of that awful stretch.

"Art thou feeling well?" Peter Church asked.

"Well enough. You?"

"In good health, praise be."

"Of course you are." James looked down the pier to the armed men standing on the shore. "This is delicate business. Can you hold your tongue?"

"I speak as the spirit urges. As thou knowest, James."

"That's exactly what I mean. This business with Christian names, all of your thee-ing and thou-ing—you'll get us flogged and thrown into the pillories. If they don't hang *you* outright."

"I don't fear death."

"No? Well, I do."

Peter's smile broadened slightly. "And what about the king's commission? Doesn't it offer thee protection?"

"Yes, and no."

James had orders to do the king's bidding, but not the power to do so without subterfuge and outright deception. And yet, didn't that give him *more* freedom? *More* latitude to use whatever means and measures he saw fit? He'd vowed before leaving English soil that he would return in triumph, take the prize that was waiting for him in London.

"You'll have plenty of time for Quaker nonsense," James said. "When the time comes, I'll even encourage it. For now, patience."

The Indian didn't answer. In James's experience, that meant he intended to obey but did not consent.

A small crowd had gathered on the wharf near the armed men James had already identified. They were mostly strong, sober-looking fellows in leather breeches, with heavy woolen cloaks and short-brimmed caps with the flaps pulled down against their ears. They wore wooden clogs over their felt shoes as they stood in the freezing mud. A few boys and women waited among the men, but there was none of the rabble James was accustomed to seeing. In England or on the Continent, any harbor was infested with pickpockets, drunks, and other shifty sorts looking to separate the travel-weary from his possessions. Boston, with all of its cold, huddled look, also had a certain tidiness about it.

James and Peter strode down the pier toward dry land. James thought briefly about calling for the dockers now unloading trunks from the *Vigilant*, retrieving his possessions, and then forcing his way past the men with their muskets. But these men were staring with such hard expressions that it would be openly disingenuous to pretend he didn't see. And so he led Peter right up to the short, blond man at their head.

"Well?" he demanded. "What is this?"

"Are you James Bailey?"

"Aye."

"You are ordered to return to your ship and remain there until she puts out to sea. You are not to set foot in Boston or anywhere else on the New England coast."

James drew up to his full height and looked down at the man. He kept his voice cold. "And who are you, sir?"

"I am Samuel Knapp."

"That name means nothing to me. Who?"

"I'm a servant of Governor Leverett and a constable of Boston Town."

"And I am in Massachusetts on royal business."

"Royal business?" Knapp's eyes widened slightly. His tongue passed over his lips. "I was told you were hired by Sir Benjamin's heirs."

"For what purpose? To confirm his death? That's stale business, Master Knapp. His death is confirmed and his estate settled, both in England and the colonies. I am here on orders of His Majesty King Charles."

Knapp looked at Peter Church, then glanced at his men, who still clenched their flintlocks but with markedly less certainty.

"What kind of royal business?"

"Samuel Knapp, did you say?"

"Captain Samuel Knapp. Yes."

James snapped his fingers, as if it were just now coming to him. "Wait, I *do* know that name. From the war. You chased King Philip through the wilderness. An Indian fighter."

"Indian *killer*," Knapp said with a glance at Peter and an expression approaching a sneer. "Yes, I put down plenty of heathens in the war."

King Philip—or Metacomet, as he'd been known before adopting an English name—had raised so many tribes into war that the whole of New England had been threatened with destruction. Suspicions had been growing in London that much of the fault of the war lay with the colonists themselves.

"What do you think of that?" James asked his companion. "This man delights in the Godly work of killing your brethren."

The placid smile never left the older man's face. "If this man is a killer, then we're fortunate peace has returned, praise be." He met Knapp's gaze. "But I'm no heathen, Samuel."

Knapp sputtered at the use of his Christian name. "Who the devil do you think you are? Blasted Praying Indian, have you no shame?"

James allowed himself a smile. Here in Boston, even mild cursing could land one in the pillories. One of James's delights was seeing a rival lose his temper, and it had scarcely taken two minutes to goad Samuel Knapp sufficiently.

"Forgive my friend," James said. "He's a Quaker."

"A *what*?"

Now Knapp looked ready to burst, like a tick engorged on blood. The men around him muttered darkly.

"Wretched business," James said. "I don't care for it either. In the Church of England—I'm still faithful to the mother church, of course—we'd be happy to drive the Quakers to Holland or some other godless cesspool. But His Majesty has ordered the peace be kept. So I endure. As will you."

"Now, you listen to me—"

"No, sir, I won't," James interrupted. "I have no time for it. My duty is to the Crown, not to your seditious orders."

At the mention of sedition, Knapp and the others fell silent. These were dangerous times, with the Crown restored and the last memories of the Puritan violence in England moldering along with Oliver Cromwell's head, which rested on a spike on the roof of Westminster Hall, where it had remained since 1661. Yet more than fifteen years later, when peace had descended upon England herself, a rabble of dissenters and separatists sneered from their supposed safety on the edge of the American continent.

That would soon change.

By now there was considerable traffic to and from the ship. Dockers, the immigrants, and waiting friends and family from shore hauled out trunks, furniture, carts laden with household items, and anything else the travelers had brought from home. In addition, the dockers unloaded goods from England: nails, glass windows, linen cloth, paper, crates of pewter and iron manufactures, and every other necessity that wasn't produced in New England. Soon other goods would be packed into the *Vigilant*'s hold for the return journey: dried fish, barrels of grain and cheese, and, of course, furs worth hundreds of pounds.

Plenty of these people coming and going were openly eavesdropping as they passed Knapp and his armed men. Knapp scowled at one ugly docker who was gaping at them, until the man looked away and continued past with his burden, breath billowing in the cold winter air.

"There's no sedition here, Master Bailey," Knapp said, his tone more conciliatory. "But we're cautious of strangers. And Indians." Another glance at Peter. "Hundreds fell to the heathens. Nearly every family was cursed by the devilry of our enemies. And people in England have delighted in our troubles."

"Nobody delights in the death of good Englishmen." James took out the king's commission and showed the wax seal marked with King Charles's emblem. "For Governor Leverett. I demand an audience."

"The governor is in Hartford and will be gone at least another week."

"I don't believe it."

Knapp's face reddened, but talk of sedition seemed to have bridled his tongue for the moment. "It's the truth, Master Bailey. The last of the Nipmuk fled north, looking to the French and Abenaki for protection. That leaves us virgin land to settle, and a disputed border between the two colonies. Leverett went to Hartford to settle it."

James rubbed his thumb over the wax seal on the paper before tucking it back into an interior pocket. This was unexpected and unwelcome.

"Why don't you share it with me?" Knapp said. "I'm commissioned by the General Court to keep order in Boston."

"I didn't know Boston was in *dis*order."

Knapp gave a sad shake of the head. "It's these wretches left destitute by the war. The town is full of them. They're resettling, but slowly."

"Who commands Massachusetts in the governor's absence? The General Court?"

"Aye, the court. And William Fitz-Simmons, the deputy governor." Knapp frowned. "If it's not Sir Benjamin's death that brings you, then what?"

"It is his death, in part. But not in the way you suppose."

Knapp continued, as if he hadn't been listening. "The sachem who ordered his murder was put to death, his entire tribe shipped to Barbados and sold into bondage. And Sir Benjamin's estate is settled, as you said." Knapp looked at Peter Church. "Why are you traveling with a Praying Indian? Which tribe gave birth to this man?"

Knapp's questions risked exposing James's real purpose in entering the Bay Colony, so he deflected. "If Leverett is in Hartford, I have no choice. Take me to Master Fitz-Simmons."

"You won't see him today. It's almost sundown, and he'll do no business on the Sabbath."

"Very well. I'll wait until Monday."

"You have lodging? Or shall I arrange it?"

"I thought to stay in the Windlass and Anchor. It's on the waterfront, isn't it?" James scanned the wharves for sign of the inn.

"A sinful place, fit only for sailors and Dutchmen."

"Then find me a suitable establishment."

"Reverend Stone has a room he lets to visiting ministers for a modest sum. You may stay there."

Sir Benjamin Cotton—the king's dead agent in the colonies—had mentioned a minister by the name of Henry Stone in his reports. James would have to double-check the papers in his trunk, but if memory served, Stone was a dissenter whose father had come over during the migrations of the 1630s. Better still, he had some sort of connection with Benjamin Cotton's widow. An uncle? Cousin? This might be a way to get to the woman. James had read her account of captivity during the war and thought she might have useful information.

"About this Stone fellow," James said. "How will he feel about an Anglican and a Quaker lodging under his roof? Is he one of these thin-lipped fellows who stands like he's got a blunderbuss up his bunghole?"

The men grumbled at this. These Puritans were priggish.

Knapp looked like he'd had a drink of sour milk. "Hold your tongue. Reverend Stone is a Godly man and I won't have you abusing him."

"No abuse intended. I merely inquired after his nature. Is he of good humor?"

"He is a sober man who does his duty," one of the other men spoke up.

It was the first time any of the others had addressed James directly, and he sized the man up. The speaker was an older man with long, graying hair, tidily kept. Like the rest of them, his clothes were clean and in good repair. His voice was clear and proud, but the man didn't sound particularly hostile, either.

"And you are, sir?"

"I am Reverend Stone."

"Oh, I see. Well, I suppose your lips don't look overly thin. May we rent lodging for the night?"

"You may, if you behave in a sober manner," Reverend Stone said.

"Both of us? Including the Quaker?"

Stone's jaw tightened, but he nodded without comment. The effort must have cost him, given the strict laws against Quakers in the Bay Colony. But James had his papers, and though none of these men had seen them, the fear of royal power was sufficient to cow them. For now.

"Good," James said. "Ah, here are our sea trunks and other personal effects."

He paid each of the dockers two shillings. He let everyone present see how full his purse was before tucking it back into a pocket in his cloak, where it would be safe from cut-pockets and greasy-fingered urchins. Then he spoke to the dockers about hiring them to haul the goods through town to the reverend's home. According to Stone, it lay a half mile up the muddy alley from the waterfront. Given the generous pay, the dockers readily agreed.

When that was arranged, James turned back to Samuel Knapp. "It seems that I am in the capable hands of Reverend Stone. Good day to you, sir."

A look passed between Knapp and Reverend Stone. Then, without comment, Knapp led the other armed men into town, while Stone remained behind.

"Churlish fellow, isn't he?" James said.

"Pray keep a temperate tongue," Stone said. "Especially when you reach the house. My wife has a delicate and righteous temperament."

That *was* the temperate version. Heaven forbid if James had voiced what he'd really been thinking about Knapp.

"Apologies, Reverend," James said. "Of course I will."

James and Peter followed the reverend at a languid pace as they stayed with the dockers hauling the heavy oak chests. The waterfront was littered with refuse: broken barrels; rotten, barnacle-covered planks stripped from the keels of boats as they put in for repair; sodden ears of Indian corn, their kernels gnawed away by mice and rats. Bits of rope and scraps of nets washed against the dock pilings or gathered onto the shore. Gulls lurked overhead, eager to plunder the fishermen hauling their catch from the holds of two-masted doggers.

The wooden shacks and log houses closer to the waterfront gave way to sturdier homes, packed shoulder-to-shoulder, as the men climbed into town. Some of the newer buildings were timbered with greater care, and some were even made of brick. Most were small, square structures, but a few boasted a second floor.

The sodden ground near the waterfront turned to hard, frozen mud. Reverend Stone's clogs clomped noisily with every step. There were a surprising number of people in the streets, hauling handcarts or leading horses that pulled wagons. Some of them seemed to be loading up from houses and moving out.

"It's *Henry* Stone, isn't it?" James asked. "Born in England, if I remember."

Stone glanced at him with a curious expression. "That's right."

"And you know Sir Benjamin's widow? Is she a relation of some kind?"

"She is in mourning. And not your concern."

"My concern is what I make of it," James said sharply.

"I haven't seen your commission, Master Bailey. Until then, I will reserve judgment."

"Hmm. Very well."

"There will be no strong drink under my roof," Reverend Stone said a moment later as they stepped across a rare cobbled street and passed down a lane so narrow that a man living on one side could have opened his shutters and shaken hands with the fellow in the opposite house. "And you will not speak in a loose way to the unmarried servant girls."

"Of course not," James said. "Who do you take me for?"

"And this Indian is forbidden to speak his heresies. That I will never tolerate."

Peter spoke up. "My name is Peter. Not *the Indian* or *the Quaker*. And I'm not fond of *the heretic*, either."

"I can't simply call you Peter, Goodman—?" Stone began.

"It's Peter Church," James said. "But he won't answer to Goodman or Master. He prefers 'friend,' or his whole name, if you can't bring yourself to call him by his Christian name alone."

"I will not hold the Indian part against you, Peter Church. That was your birth, but not necessarily your nature. Your parents were simple people, but you were introduced to the truth."

"That I was," Peter agreed.

"But why, having seen this truth, did you embrace the Quaker heresy?"

"The Lord spoke to my heart, friend. He shall speak to thine own heart, if thou wilt open it."

"What makes you think He hasn't?"

"Hast thou felt the inward light?" Peter asked.

"I have been convicted. I am attentive to the will of God, and He has chosen to save my sinful soul and gather me into the body of visible saints. Can you say the same, Goodman Church?"

Peter looked away.

"I told you," James said, "he won't answer to titles."

"That's hardly a title."

"It is to him."

Stone let out a long-suffering sigh. Ahead of them, two of the dockers heaving trunks flashed each other grins.

"The body of saints is the church of all believers," Peter said after a moment of sufficient duration to emphasize his peculiarity with names and titles, "be they English or Indian, bonded or free. Any man—or woman—can be called by the Lord. There is no need to prove ourselves before such abominations as popes, priests, bishops, or ministers."

"Enough." Stone's voice was harder than the frozen mud at their feet.

"Can I note, Reverend," James said, "that *you* initiated the theological dispute, not the Quaker?"

"And you brought him to our shores."

"I was *born* on these shores," Peter said.

Reverend Stone stopped in front of a sturdy two-story house, square, with good windows and straight lines. It was wood but had a solid brick chimney and was painted gray with a red door. The bit of color gave it an unexpectedly whimsical air. A small brass bell hung from a chain next to the door.

Stone lifted the wooden latch and pushed the front door open. As he did so, he gave the bell a chime. "What cheer! I have returned."

The voices of women and many children sounded from inside. Before they appeared, Stone said to the dockers, "Set down your chests. I won't have you in the house." The reverend turned to James and Peter. "Remember what I said about the servant girls."

James opened his mouth to protest, but then two beautiful young women emerged. He couldn't tell if they were the reverend's servants or his daughters, and at the moment he didn't care. The first was a comely lass of sixteen or seventeen, her chaste clothing—head rail tied over her head and under her chin, woman's doublet, and looped petticoat—doing little to conceal a voluptuous figure. Blond hair and large green eyes. The second woman was several years older, perhaps early twenties, and similarly dressed, except she wore a laced bodice instead of a petticoat, and a bit of green ribbon at her throat that stood out all the more against the blacks and whites of her clothing. She was even more striking, with raven-black hair, curls bursting out from beneath her head rail, and dark eyes.

Peter looked off to one side, as if taking no notice of the young women, but after eight weeks at sea, James couldn't tear his gaze away.

"Alice, Prudie," Stone said in a sharp voice after casting a hard glance at James, then an even more severe look at the dockers, who were gawking behind them. "Fetch the boys. Ready the attic room. We have lodgers."

James knew he looked and smelled a fright. He was unshaven, and his clothes were dirty and reeked of the close living quarters below deck. But both women looked at him a moment too long before they turned away to do their master's bidding. The younger woman touched her tongue to the corner of her mouth, while a hint of a smile crossed the face of the older one. Interesting.

You will not speak in a loose way to the unmarried servant girls.
Had he promised that?

Chapter Two

James and Peter waited upstairs while Stone and his family ate their supper.

"Is that beef I smell?" James asked. "And onions too. Fresh bread, no doubt slathered with butter. It's torture."

"All the more satisfying when it's our turn to eat," Peter replied. He sat on a raised bed with a mattress on drawn ropes. The bed had several blankets and two large goose-feather pillows.

James sat on a smallish stool by a tiny, rough-hewn desk, where he was shaving and washing up. "Are you sure they're going to feed us? Maybe we're expected to gnaw on hardtack from the ship."

The guest room apparently doubled as a study room for children. One of Stone's many young sons had cleared the desk of a primer, a children's Bible, and papers and ink, while a girl of eight or ten had brought in a wooden pitcher of water, a basin, and a pair of chamber pots. The pitched ceiling was child size too. James could only stand upright next to the door.

Below came the muffled sounds of Reverend Stone saying grace, then the clank of dishes and murmured conversation. The other voices hushed as a child spoke up in clear, even tones. No way to parse out the words through the floor and walls, but it sounded like she was reading from the Bible.

"A fine, disciplined family," Peter said when she'd finished. "And Stone is a righteous, Godly man. It's a pity he's living his life in error."

"Were those older girls his daughters? Or servants?"

"I did not pay them particular notice. Mayhap one of each." Peter said this as if it were the least interesting subject imaginable.

"Better a servant than a daughter," James said. "Assuming she is discreet."

"Put those thoughts out of thy head, friend."

"The flesh is weak, and the Lord forgiving. Moreover, you don't know what it's like. You're older, never married. Have you even been with a woman before?"

Peter said nothing, but looked uncomfortable.

"Oh, I'll wager you haven't, have you?"

"That would be a faulty assumption, friend."

James brightened. "Pray tell."

"That would be loose talk."

"I won't touch the servant girls," James said in answer to Peter's disapproving expression.

And he meant to keep that vow. He would leave for England within the fortnight, triumphant and ready to claim the newly opened position of chancellor of agents for foreign affairs and internal dissent. It was a great prize—and he was the youngest, strongest man reaching for it. But it was only his if he avoided stumbling here. That meant no entanglements of any kind.

Peter kept staring at him, the frown deepening. "I don't entirely believe thee."

"I'm not a fool, Peter. They hang fornicators in Massachusetts. Or force them into marriage." James leaned back in the chair. "I don't know which is worse."

The door swung open, and Reverend Stone stood in the doorway. He was frowning as if he'd heard some of the conversation, and the grin died on James's lips.

"I dismissed the children," Stone said. "There's room for you at the table. Come."

Downstairs, it occurred to James that Reverend Stone might have kept them upstairs not through lack of hospitality so much as for lack of space at the table. He had eight or nine young children running about, all seemingly healthy and bright eyed. The youngest three had long, curly hair and wore wool biggins to keep their heads warm, and because they all wore doublets and petticoats, it was impossible to tell the girls from those boys who were not yet breeched.

Some of the children were leaving the table as James and Peter came in. Others were helping the servant girl clean the table under the direction of Stone's wife, a handsome woman of about forty whose hair had not yet started to gray. She kept things moving in a firm but gentle manner as dirty plates left the table and clean ones appeared. The family ate on pewter, with fine spoons and knives. Enough of it that they had sufficient for the servants and guests without washing those already used by the family. Several pale-green bayberry candles burned with a cheerful light and smell. The hearth gave off additional light, plus a fine heat for such a dark, cold December evening.

A few minutes later the family had departed, leaving James and Peter at the table with three servants: an older man and two girls. The man sat next to the newcomers, while the women sat at the far end. One of the girls was the pretty blond who had greeted them at the door. The other looked so similar that she had to be the first one's sister, perhaps two or three years older. Both girls were comely, with healthy skin and shiny hair. No sign of the dark-haired girl from earlier. The girls conversed in quiet, breathless tones, occasionally glancing at James and sharing secret smiles. He was certain they were talking about him.

Peter bowed his head in silent grace, then hefted his spoon. James was already eating.

The meal was a rich, meaty pottage. This being America, the bread was a golden color, apparently made from Indian corn, and there was an enormous corn pudding as well. James cut a hunk of the crumbly corn bread and slathered it with butter, then ladled the pottage into a pewter bowl. He lifted his mug, filled with small beer, wishing Reverend Stone hadn't proscribed stronger drink.

"To the end of a long sea voyage, and the first good meal in months."

"It is sufficient for our needs," Peter said, mouth full.

"It's a good sight more than that or you wouldn't be stuffing your face like a starving goat." James waved his mug at the girls. "To your good health, my ladies." They giggled and looked down at their food. He nodded at the old man. "And to you, sir."

The old man cupped his hand at his ear. "Eh?"

"He's quite deaf," the younger girl said.

"And not much use around the house," the other said.

"But he has served with the family these thirty years," the first one added. "Since England. They won't turn him out now."

James said the toast again, louder this time and mouthing the words clearly. He clapped the old man on the shoulder as he said it. The man roared back. "AND TO YOU, SIR!"

"Where's the other woman who greeted us at the door?" James asked the girls. "I didn't see her leaving the table. Is she one of the reverend's daughters?"

"James . . ." Peter warned, with a nod toward the door. Two of the Stone boys stood there, looking in with curiosity at the two strangers. "Loose talk."

"My apologies, good mistresses. I misspoke." James considered the subjects he might legitimately broach. "Do either of you know Goodwife Cotton? Sir Benjamin's widow?"

The girls looked at each other and giggled. Then they turned their attention to their food, and James did the same, disappointed. These two might have breasts as ripe as fresh peaches, but they seemed to lack any other distinction. Only pure animal instincts kept him interested in them at all.

The pottage was delicious, made with beef, barley, peas, leeks, and plenty of savory spices. The corn bread was even more divine after weeks of stale, moldy biscuits. And the butter so good. He considered the pewter and the brightly burning candles. This Henry Stone was a prosperous fellow.

James could think of nothing else but eating for a stretch. When he dished up the corn pudding, he'd gathered his wits enough to consider his strategy. He had only a short time before he was in bed, then rising early to attend services with the Stones.

He'd glanced through his papers before coming down. He now removed a few sheets from a breast pocket. It was Prudence Cotton's captivity story, from her time with the Nipmuk Indians during the war. Sir Benjamin's widow enjoyed a certain fame in both the colonies and England for the hardships she'd endured at Winton and Crow Hollow and the masterful way she'd written about them.

He looked at the old man, who was gumming his food. Convinced he was indeed deaf, James lowered his voice so neither the servant girls nor the eavesdropping Stone children could hear.

"What about services in the morning?" he asked Peter. "Will you go?"

"That is the law in Boston. Everyone must attend."

"It's also the law that Quakers not enter the Bay Colony under pain of death. If you feign illness, nobody will drag you to the church by one ear."

"As a point of fact, I am feeling a little strange." Peter gestured with his spoon to the pottage, which was only half-eaten, though he had downed his beer and poured himself more from the pitcher. Then he shrugged. "Everything is still swaying from the ship."

"You too? I can still see the heaving deck when I close my eyes. Should be gone by morning, I'll wager." James mopped up the last bit of broth with a hunk of crumbling bread. "My question is what you'll do when you get there. Disrupt the meeting again?"

Quakers had been known to stroll naked into the services of other congregations, be they Anglican, Papist, or dissenters. More likely, they'd interrupt the sermon to argue scripture with the dumbfounded minister.

"I have no intention of doing so. But I speak as the spirit prompts, friend. As thou knowest."

"Well, if you must, you must."

Perfect. An Indian at services, when the wounds of the brutal war against King Philip and his fellow sachems were still fresh. And a Quaker too. It would take little to foment chaos. Perhaps James could make contact with Sir Benjamin's widow if he could identify her at services. He glanced down at the widow's tale to see what else he could glean from the pages.

Peter made a sound deep in his throat. "I truly feel ill. 'Twould be strange if I'd crossed the ocean in all that filth only to breathe bad airs on my first day in Boston."

"It's probably the rich food. You'll feel better after some sleep."

James wasn't particularly worried. True, Indians were even more susceptible to agues, fevers, chills, and poxes than Englishmen, but Peter was no ordinary Indian. He'd lived more than a decade in England, come over with three other Praying Indians to study with a Puritan minister in Tonbridge. The other three Indians had died of European illnesses within three years. Peter claimed he'd never once fallen sick. Except for the spiritual plague of the Society of Friends, that was.

Of course, James hadn't recruited the man for his health or his religion. No, it was his ability to speak Abenaki and Nipmuk. Still, he'd worried how the man would fare in the cramped, unhealthy quarters of the *Vigilant*.

James had soon had other worries. Two hours out of Weymouth, the waves were already so choppy that he was heaving up his breakfast. The seas surged for the next ten days until almost every passenger was ill, together with several members of the crew. Not Peter Church, though. The man's guts were made of iron.

Somewhere in the middle of the ocean, the waves had calmed. Then disease swept through the passengers. They were mostly farmers and craftsmen from Lincolnshire, strong and hale, not sickly—yet they'd proved helpless against the bloody flux that roared through their midst. James had counted himself fortunate not to fall ill, but he was more worried about his companion. Still, Peter remained healthy.

They'd come into no contact with any disease or bad air since coming off the boat. No illness or death. No, James wasn't worried about Peter.

"It seems to me," Peter said, "that thou art the one planning to disrupt the Puritan services, not I."

"Why would you say that?"

"Friend, after all of our discussions, thou remainest suspicious, thy heart hardened. Thou stopped me three separate times when I tried to testify on board the boat. So why allow me to speak now if not to put my plain speech to thine own purposes?"

James kept his face blank. Peter was so sincere in his misguided faith, and it was a hard thing to purposefully manipulate a man to one's own means. Especially when it might put him in danger. But that's what it meant to serve the Crown. It justified hard measures.

"You know what I think of your heresies, but they're harmless enough. These Puritans, on the other hand—Cromwell and his ilk—nearly destroyed the Church of England. They'd overthrow every bishop and tear down the cathedrals if they could."

"As would I."

"Aye, but don't delude yourself. The Quakers are small and powerless."

"Power is an earthly term."

"Exactly. And you have none here, regardless of where you stand in the eternities. So go ahead and disrupt, should you feel so moved."

"Thou art scheming, my friend."

"Of course I am," James said. "That's my sworn duty."

Peter studied James's face, and it was all the Englishman could do not to turn away from the Indian's piercing gaze.

"When do we leave Boston?" Peter said at last.

"As soon as I present my commission to Fitz-Simmons. Of course, I want to speak to Widow Cotton first, if possible."

"Then ask to see her. She's probably here in Boston."

James made sure he kept his voice low and avoided looking at the servant girls. "You know what will happen. As soon as I express interest to Reverend Stone, it will turn out that the widow had pressing business in Hartford or Providence."

Goodwife Stone appeared in the doorway, and the two servant girls rose to their feet and began to clear away the dishes. The old man tried to do the same, but the mistress shook her head, pulled up a chair next to the fire instead, and handed him a whetstone and a pair of knives to sharpen.

"YOU ARE TOO KIND, MY MISTRESS."

The old man lit a long-stemmed pipe. It dangled from the corner of his mouth while he slowly pulled a knife back and forth across the stone with his gnarled hands. The scrape, scrape, scrape joined the crackle of the fire. Goodwife Stone snuffed all the candles but two. She moved the hanging candleholders to the hearth, above a double-wide wooden bench. Here she sat to mend stockings. A few minutes later, Reverend Stone came in without a word, carrying a big Bible, and took his place next to his wife.

The sight of the reverend reading his scripture had a predictable effect on Peter Church. He fetched his own, smaller Bible from upstairs, and the two holy strivers sat across from each other, reading almost competitively by the light of the bayberry candles. James tried to study Prudence Cotton's captivity story but was too distracted by trying to make sense of everything he'd seen and heard so far. Instead, he smoked his own pipe and watched the reverend and his wife. No sign of the children; they must be in bed already.

A few minutes later one of the blond servant girls filled a fire scoop with glowing coals and carried it upstairs, while the other followed with a pair of brass bed warmers. At the thought of climbing into a freshly warmed bed, a deep, wearying exhaustion washed over James. He yawned and tied off the papers with a bit of twine. Then he emptied his pipe into the hearth.

"I'm going upstairs," he told the others. "Goodnight to you, Reverend. Goodwife Stone."

"God rest you," Stone said.

"I'll be up shortly," Peter said.

Doubtful. Once the man started in with his Bible, he'd be engrossed for a good stretch. Probably until the candles burned down or Goody Stone snuffed them. And James doubted the reverend would leave off until Peter did. Heaven forbid.

James was climbing the stairs when he heard movement in his room. Alarmed, he reached for his knife, thinking that someone was inside trying to force open his sea chest. But of course it was only the older of the two servant girls from supper. She bent over the bed, thrusting with a bed warmer up and down the mattress. Her blond hair spilled from her head rail. Her bottom stuck out toward him and jiggled with every movement. He stood in the doorway and stared.

When she finished, she straightened, then gasped when she saw him. "Pray, pardon me, Master Bailey. I didn't realize you would be back so soon."

Her face was flushed and invigorated from her labors. James was invigorated in his own way. His earlier resolve seemed suddenly foolish.

He only just remembered his purpose in Boston. "You ignored me at supper. Will you tell me now? At services tomorrow—where will the Widow Cotton be seated?"

"Next to Goody Stone, of course. The reverend's family always sits together. Is that why you've come, to marry the widow?"

"Good heavens, no." He let his eyes range up and down the girl's body. "I have no interest in the widow."

She smiled at this. Emboldened, he shut the door quietly.

Her smile turned uncertain. "Master Bailey, the door. You closed it."

"Do I unsettle you? Shall I open it again?"

"If the mistress sees . . ."

"She's mending stockings. The reverend is reading his Bible. As is the Indian. Nobody will know, except perchance your sister. Can you trust her?"

"I suppose a few moments wouldn't be a sin."

That was all the invitation James needed. Almost overcome with passion, he closed the distance. She didn't resist as he took the bed warmer and set it aside, then pressed her against the wall. Her mouth fell against his. Her kisses were clumsy but eager.

"*Master Bailey.*"

"Call me James." He smothered her mouth again, then drew her neck back to kiss it.

"Yes, James. Yes."

"What is your name?" he said, voice husky.

"Lucy Branch."

"Lucy. Oh, you're beautiful. The most heavenly thing I've seen in ages."

"Do you truly think so?"

He pressed into her. One hand reached for her breast. The other lifted her petticoat and stroked along her inner thigh. Lucy let out a little moan.

"James, no. Please."

"You don't like it?" he asked between kisses on her neck.

She was panting, her breast heaving up and down. "Yes, yes. But . . ."

"But what?"

"If they find out, I shall be whipped. And then thrown into the street."

James had taken greater risks in the past. That time at Versailles, for instance, making love to the mistress of the Marquis de Prouville, while the man argued a treaty with an English diplomat in the next room. But Louise-Colette had been the one pushing herself on him. This was different.

"James, please. I am helpless."

He tore himself free. He drew back a step, then another. His body was throbbing, and from the way the girl was plastered against the wall, her hands flat against the timbers, her eyes closed and her mouth open, he could tell that she was throbbing in her own way. She didn't want him to stop, not really.

He was convinced they had time, that the danger was slight. And if he pressed her, he knew she would not resist much longer. And if she did truly want him to stop, then what? Would she cry out? Of course not.

Damn you, James. Don't do it.

With effort, he backed toward the door. His hand found the wooden latch, and he lifted it slowly, quietly. Then he stepped to one side to let her go.

Lucy looked at the open door, looked back at him. Her gaze continued to smolder. She opened her mouth, and he knew she was going to tell him to shut the door again. If he did, he would take her. He was not so strong as that. But she gave a tiny shake of the head and straightened her clothing. She bent for the bed warmer, which presented another view of her glorious bottom. She made her way to the door.

"Talk to the mistress first," she whispered as she brushed past him.

"What?"

"If you ask the reverend, he'll say no. But the mistress holds no hatred of Anglicans. And if she talks to him on your behalf, he'll agree to whatever she suggests."

"Oh." Then again when he understood fully. "*Oh.*"

An impish grin crossed her face. "Then you may have me all you want, James Bailey." She pushed past him into the hall.

James leaned out to stare after her as she lifted her petticoat with one hand and held the smoking bed warmer with the other. She hurried down the hall to the stairs.

Good Lord, that was a disaster averted. If he'd had her, the girl would have expected him to marry her and seen to it that he'd done so.

He stripped off his boots, but he'd already changed his shirt and breeches before supper, and he kept them on. He climbed beneath the blankets. The bedding was still warm from Lucy's work.

He was too aroused to sleep and could do nothing but listen to the wind howling around the roof until Peter arrived about an hour later. The older man knelt to pray in silence before climbing into bed next to him.

James sighed. At least the man would help conserve warmth. And yet.

Blasted Praying Indian. Cursed Reverend Stone. Quakers and Puritans, damn them. Would the heavens really shake if James made Peter swap beds with Lucy Branch?

CHAPTER THREE

Prudence Cotton stood in the chilly, moonlit corridor with one hand on the wooden latch to the guest bedroom. Her other hand gripped five sheets of paper, folded and tied with twine.

She listened. From inside came a gentle snore, followed moments later by a higher whistling sound. When she was certain that the two strangers were asleep, she lifted the latch slowly. It creaked, and she froze, wincing. A snort, a mumble, someone turning.

When the noise settled, she pushed the door open. The barest stream of moonlight seeped into the room, like a reflection of a reflection. Her eyes adjusted to the dark shapes within. The bed held two lumpy figures sleeping peacefully, not so different from the children tucked into bed down the hall.

Master Church, an Indian and a Quaker. Master Bailey, some sort of agent or spy from London. One provided spiritual danger, the other carried violence in his posture and had stared at her earlier with lustful intent. Yet thinking of them as sleeping children softened them in her mind. Not Church and Bailey, but Peter and James.

Prudence peered into the dark corners of the room. There, draped over a chair, James's cloak.

She'd gone barefoot to quiet her movements, but the cold planks still creaked with every step. What if James sat up and challenged her in that arrogant tone she'd overheard downstairs? What would she say? Would he wake the house? She was in enough trouble as it was.

The cloak was like none Prudence had ever encountered. Instead of a single, great pocket on the outside, the inner lining held sewn-up folds of cloth, others with buttons, and even a pocket inside of a pocket. One pouch held a purse, fat with coins.

Silver was scarce in the colonies. Seemed each time a ship dropped off its goods, every shilling in Massachusetts departed with it. Even her husband had quickly found himself short of silver, although he'd arrived with a small fortune.

Other pockets held lumpy objects, papers, even rings and medallions. All of it made her burn with curiosity, and she only just resisted the urge to take some of the items with her to examine later. Instead, she found a deep inner pocket, empty, and tucked her papers inside. With all the other things in the cloak, he might not notice it until he was on the road, riding west toward Winton. Good. Then he would take them out and read them when he was long gone from here.

The men were still sleeping when Prudence backed her way into the hallway. She pulled the door shut until it snicked into place, then turned toward her own room.

A dark shape stood waiting. Prudence gasped.

A hand closed on her wrist. It wasn't the reverend, thank the heavens, but his wife—Prudence's older sister, Anne, in her nightgown and cap.

"What madness is this?" Anne hissed.

"Shh."

"What were you doing in there? Those men—have you no shame?"

"I swear, it was nothing like that."

Anne looked back up the hall to her bedroom, where the reverend would be sleeping. Then, still gripping Prudence's wrist, she dragged the younger woman toward the stairs. The younger sister let herself be pulled along.

Moments later, the two women sat opposite each other in front of the dying embers of the fire. It reflected off the pewter mugs hanging from their hooks, but did little to cut the chill in the room. Prudence shivered and looked at her feet rather than meet Anne's glare. Prudence was twenty-five years old, but her sister's disapproval could still pierce her breast with shame.

"Well?" Anne said.

"I wasn't doing anything shameful. There are two men in there. What could I have done?"

"Then what, rummaging through their possessions? Stealing?"

"No!"

"Then what?"

Prudence didn't answer.

"One would think you were five years old, Prudie. Am I to paddle you until you spit out the truth?"

"Why not? You used it often enough when we were young."

"That's unfair."

"Is it?"

"I didn't ask to be the oldest," Anne said. "And I didn't ask for seven younger sisters."

"And I didn't ask to have seven *older* sisters, either. And I certainly didn't ask you to lord it over me." Prudence didn't like the way she sounded when interacting with Anne, but she felt helpless not to slip back to their childhood roles. "Anyway, I'm an adult now, I've been married and had a child of my own. And I don't answer to you."

"But I have to answer for whatever happens under my roof. Am I to tell Henry I caught you sneaking out of that room? What would he think?"

That question didn't need an answer. Prudence had heard plenty of the reverend's ranting sermons about fornication. And he seemed even more worried about his sister-in-law than about the unmarried girls in the house. After all, she knew, and presumably had enjoyed, sexual congress with her husband before he was killed. Maybe she still lusted after it.

"I told you, it wasn't that," Prudence insisted.

Anne's expression hardened. "I'm losing my patience. It wasn't that, and you weren't stealing, either, because I can see now you've got nothing on you. So what?"

It would be easy to say that she'd spotted something in James's cloak, had heard rumors he was a spy for the Crown, and had been torn with curiosity. There was at least a partial truth hidden in that claim. But her tongue felt oily at the very thought of lying to her sister.

"I slipped the missing chapter into a pocket in his cloak," she said.

Anne's expression softened. She put a hand on Prudence's knee. "Oh, Prudie. You didn't. What good would that serve?"

"He's going to Winton. Then maybe north. If he does, he'll be speaking to the Abenaki and Nipmuk."

"He wouldn't do that. There's no reason. The war is over, the matter settled."

"Settled?" The bitter laugh that came up tasted like gall. "It has been scarce nine months since my captivity."

"Time enough to put it behind you," Anne said firmly. "Yes, to see matters settled. God willing, to never think of them again."

How could matters be settled, when every time Prudence closed her eyes she could see the murdered English at Winton, hear the harsh cawing as flapping black wings settled blanket-like over the slaughtered Nipmuk warriors at Crow Hollow?

One particular image never ceased its torment. A crow had buried its beak into the eyeball of a dead Indian and worked it back and forth like a child trying to twist a green apple from a tree. The bird came up with the eye in its beak and cocked its head at Prudence, as if concerned that she would try to take its prize. The eye had stared mutely, accusingly, in her direction before going down the crow's gullet.

My daughter . . .

"Prudie?" Anne said, worry touching her voice.

Prudence gave a shudder, fighting to recover her wits. "For what other purpose would Master Bailey bring an Indian if not to meet the Nipmuk and Abenaki? Peter Church knows the tongue."

"He didn't bring an Indian, he brought a Quaker. To be a thorn in our side. Master Bailey is here to disrupt and agitate. He's not here out of concern for your husband, believe me."

Prudence had no doubt some of that was true. The Crown had ever chafed at New England's liberties. There were some in London, she knew, who blamed the colonies for the war with the natives, and suggested that King Charles should appoint a royal governor to prevent future conflagrations.

But James had known her husband. The two of them were apparently confidants. Benjamin had mentioned the man on several occasions—the two of them had served the king together while in France—and she'd once caught a glimpse of a letter back to London addressed from her husband to Master Bailey.

"I have to take a chance."

"I wish you wouldn't agitate yourself."

"They never should have made me take that chapter out. It was the truth."

"It was speculation," Anne said. "Later proven false. Men saw your daughter dead—they reported the sad truth."

"Those men were Nipmuk. They were in turn killed, and we have their testimony from white men."

"How does that make a difference?"

"If Mary is dead, then what happened to her body?"

"I don't know. You know how the savages behaved—your own words are testimony enough. They tortured and maimed. Even ate them, the brutes."

"They tortured men," Prudence said firmly, "never children."

"You're telling me they didn't kill children?"

"Well, yes," Prudence admitted. "But not like that, not once they'd taken the children prisoner. That isn't their way."

Anne fixed her with a look, and Prudence closed her mouth. Her memories of captivity were brutal, horrific, but occasionally mixed with moments of surprising kindness, even civility. She'd tried to call forth that contradiction with her weak, imperfect writing, a narrative that had gripped the colonies. But what the people read eagerly by candlelight, shared from home to home, was not her full story. Men—the reverend, the printer in Boston—had taken out parts. They didn't fit, didn't make sense. Those things, the men presumed, were the product of a fevered mind, confused into error by the horror of her experience.

"Is it your only copy of the missing pages?" Anne asked at last.

"Yes. I have never copied them."

"Then that will be the end of it."

"You think so?"

"Master Bailey is a servant of the Crown. Even if he believes you, he has no time or interest in chasing down the fancies of a grieving widow and mother."

"I hope you're wrong. I hope he's not so mercenary and unfeeling as that. But if you're right, if he tosses them in the fire with a laugh, it's still all here." Prudence tapped her head. "I'll write it down fresh."

Anne sighed. "Prudie, it has been almost a year."

"Make it ten," Prudence said stubbornly. "I don't care."

"A year is enough. You're still young and pretty. There are men in Boston in want of a wife. Good men, strong men. Some even strong enough to rule you with a light touch."

Anne said it with a smile in her voice. Surely, she meant no malice, only to gently point out what they both knew already, that Prudence was headstrong and stubborn to a fault. But the younger sister bristled nonetheless.

Anne put an arm around her shoulder. "Don't be angry. I know what you've lost. The Lord has blessed me beyond measure, but even I lost two little ones to the pox. I ache for them every day. But don't let the loss of one child keep you from the blessings of many."

"This is different. Mary is still alive."

Anne started to say something else, but the stairs creaked. Reverend Stone appeared on the other side of the room.

"What is this? Why aren't you in bed?"

Prudence couldn't answer that without lying, so she shut her mouth and braced herself for another interrogation.

"Prudie couldn't sleep," Anne said with scarcely a second of hesitation. "She's troubled by thoughts of the war. I heard her and came to offer comfort."

"Very well, but it's cold down here, and we rise early for the Sabbath. To bed, both of you."

He turned and creaked his way back up the stairs. Anne kissed Prudence's forehead. "Time for bed, little sister."

The younger woman followed, shock warring with elation that her sister had lied to her husband to keep Prudence's secret.

Chapter Four

James stood in front of the meetinghouse with his cloak held tight against the cold, but his hood swept back so he could get a full view of the people filing in through the wide wooden doors. He leaned against the pillory—empty, of course, because of the Sabbath. Next to it were stocks and a whipping post. A few blocks away, the town bell rang solemnly through the cold morning air, calling people to services.

A sober crowd filed past. Men and women with hoods, wool caps, felted hats, and heavy overcoats made their way through the wide wooden doors into the meetinghouse. And children. So many children. They carried muffs and wore thick mittens, with almost every inch covered.

The men, women, and children gawked at the two strangers by the door. They stared especially hard at the Indian.

It was a prompt crowd, and shortly the steady stream of people had ended, save for a few stragglers. The deacon at the door gave them a look. James held up a finger to urge patience.

"That was a spectacle thou madest of us," Peter said as the deacon turned away.

"I'm an agent of the Crown. I won't skulk around in secret."

"Purposefully courting danger, 'twould seem. Especially for me."

"A risk you accepted when I hired you. Too late for regrets now."

"Nay, I have no regrets. But I cannot help but feel trepidation as I enter the house of mine enemy."

"Fatalistic nonsense," James said, but good-naturedly. "You won't be murdered in church."

"Art thou ready to enter?"

"One moment."

The Third Church meetinghouse sat on a hillock overlooking the Boston Harbor. It was a simple square box, with only its greater size and the modest steeple setting it apart from the dozens of block-shaped houses around it. A road cut down the hillside toward the harbor, where dozens of ships swayed against a brutal wind that knifed off the North Atlantic. The Charles River flowed to the northwest, bisecting fields and pasture. A narrow neck held Boston itself off from the mainland, which from this height and distance presented a vast forest, broken here and there by small villages.

James studied the last few people entering the meetinghouse. He'd spotted several of the other men who had confronted them yesterday at the wharves, but no Samuel Knapp. He must belong to another parish, unless he'd arrived early.

James and Peter entered to find the members crowding the pews. The women and young children sat together on one side of the chapel, the men and boys on the other. The better sort of men sat up front, including several tall fellows with flowing hair and clothing that was a little neater, a little newer. Magistrates, merchants, and deputies. Members of the General Court. Many servants stayed together, while others sat with their respective masters and mistresses. A dozen or so slaves and indentured servants—mostly, but not all, Africans or Indians—sat in a knot at the back of the room.

"The Lord sorrows at the folly of His children," Peter said with a sigh.

James didn't know which of the many curiosities had aroused the Indian's pique, and he didn't care. Instead of questioning the man, he found a place directly across the aisle from Goodwife Stone and her daughters and forced his way in. There were already men there, but he urged them aside. They complied with some grumbling.

Reverend Stone stood at the pulpit. He was dressed no differently from his parishioners. The man watched James and Peter until they'd settled in, then nodded to the deacon, who closed and barred the doors against further entry.

Stone prayed with the congregation, then called up the deacon. This was a young man in his midtwenties, about the same age as James, but he carried himself with a stiff air like one much older. James pegged him as a self-important windbag. The members sat up a little straighter, and the children stopped fidgeting and whispering. Something interesting was about to happen.

Now that their attention was gathered up front, James no longer faced the surreptitious glances of half the assembly, and he took the opportunity to look around. Lucy Branch and her sister sat with several other servant girls a few rows behind and to the side. She stared at the deacon and licked her lips as if nervous.

He scrutinized Goodwife Stone and her family. A younger woman sat to the left of the goodwife, one of the Stone toddlers on her lap, her finger in the child's mouth to pacify him. On first glance, James had taken her for a servant, but now he was less certain. Who was she? Too young to be a sister. Too old to be one of the Stone daughters.

She turned her face slightly, and James got a better view. It was the beautiful young woman with the raven curls who had appeared with Lucy's sister yesterday when James and Peter first arrived. Of course. That was Widow Cotton. She had to be.

The deacon cleared his throat. "Goodman Miller, please rise."

A man rose from the congregation. Across the aisle from him, a woman looked down at her lap. Half a dozen children with her gaped across at what could only be their father.

"You were reported drunk last Tuesday. Have you anything to say for yourself?"

"No, Deacon. I was weak and fell into error."

"Two hours in the pillory." A note of triumph in the deacon's voice. "Goodwife Brockett. Rise."

A woman rose, but, unlike Goodman Miller, she seemed confused as she looked across at her husband. The man stared back at her, brow furrowed and worried.

"You are accused of idle gossip."

James suppressed a snort. Gossip? May as well pillory every woman in the building.

"What gossip, Deacon?" Goodwife Brockett asked.

"About a stolen chicken. You know the incident and the conversation. It was reported by two other women."

"Goody Thompson and Goody Hooper? But they were a party to the conversation."

"Aye, but they confessed. You didn't. You are being called to stand, apparently without contrition. Twenty lashes."

"Twenty lashes? *Twenty?*"

Reverend Stone was standing behind the deacon's shoulder. He'd winced visibly at the pronouncement, but now he said, "Goodwife Brockett, are you disputing the punishment or the accusation itself?"

For a moment it looked as though she would argue. Then she bowed her head. "I accept the punishment, and beg forgiveness for my error."

Twenty lashes for gossiping about a chicken? Heaven forbid it had been a cow; they'd have given her the gallows!

James shot a glance at Peter to see if any of this was inspiring the Quaker to disrupt the meeting, but Peter only wore a neutral expression, none of the glowing fervor that James had seen on board, indicating that the inward light—or whatever it was called—was working its power.

There were five more accusations. One man, a widower, was accused of improper advances toward his servant girl—here James glanced at Lucy to see her eyes widening in a guilty way, as if she were expecting to be called up herself—but the wrongdoer only got three hours with his legs clamped in the stocks and a fine of ten shillings to be paid directly to the aggrieved girl. His confession seemed to be the deciding factor in the lightness of the sentence.

Two men stood accused of Sabbath violations, and another woman of gossip. Unlike Goodwife Brockett, she suffered nothing more than a public denunciation, perhaps because she was an unmarried girl, or maybe simply because she seemed fully contrite. The harshest punishment fell on the last man, who was accused of profanity, apparently muttering, "The devil scald you!" to one of the deacons of the church. Most damning of all was that he was not present at the meeting. This earned him twenty lashes, four hours in the pillory, and a nasty fine to boot.

James's English sensibilities had been shocked by the licentious French court, but this was shocking in a more disturbing way. Ah, to be in Paris or Versailles again. Preferably in spring, when the flowers were in bloom. Instead, he was stuck in this coldest, most stiff-necked English outpost in the darkest time of the year.

After that bit of excitement, the Puritan meeting settled into a tedious affair. There was none of the beauty and majesty of an Anglican service. Instead, a lot of parish business, some psalms sung without accompaniment, verse, or even someone to keep time, just a lot of warbling out of tune, and then an interminable sermon. Even the building itself was dull. No crosses, no stained-glass windows, no beauty to the vaults. All strictly functional.

Reverend Stone began his sermon with an anecdote about a man who paid his tithes, who kept the Sabbath, who didn't blaspheme or bear false witness or commit adultery. Yet he was speedily on his way to hell nonetheless. For you see, in his heart he was a secret whoremonger, committing every crime from buggery to blasphemy.

Some twenty minutes later, James was dozing off, idly daydreaming about getting his hands on Widow Cotton, when Peter stiffened next to him. James's eyes opened, and he was instantly alert. The Indian gripped the pew in front of him, knuckles white. A peculiar light had entered his eyes.

This was it. The disruption James had been seeking.

Reverend Stone continued. "These troubles with King Philip and his savages are a warning voice from the Lord. We set ourselves to be a city on a hill, yet Boston Town—the entirety of New England, even—has become no more holy, no more Godly, than any other blighted corner in Christendom."

Peter rose to his feet. "You are wrong, friend!"

A gasp and a visible shudder worked its way through the congregation as dozens of heads turned to stare. Seemingly stunned, Stone could only gape.

James had known Peter's reputation before hiring the man to return to his native New England. He'd even seen it on the ship, when Peter had interrupted the services held for the crew. But to see it here, in the midst of so many sober and devout Puritans, was staggering. An Indian and a Quaker—and in the aftermath of the Indian war too.

"Pray sit down," Reverend Stone said, recovering. "There shall be no contention here."

He sounded remarkably calm, considering that angry mutters were passing through his flock and a few men rose tentatively to their feet.

"God's judgment is upon these people, that much we agree on," Peter said. "But not for backsliding. Not for secret whoredoms or witchcraft."

"Both of which you are well accustomed to, I am sure," a woman said.

Angry assent mixed with scattered, nervous laughter. The speaker was Goodwife Brockett, the one so recently condemned for her gossiping.

"Thou hast cast out the servants of the Lord," Peter said. His voice was strong and unwavering and easily cleared the growing noise. "The Society of Friends came to share with thee truth and light. Thy people, proud and hard of heart, have put these Friends to death, driven them from New England." Peter's expression hardened. "And thou hast defrauded and persecuted the native sons of this land. Those who hunger and thirst for truth have been given gall to drink and hot lead for their supper. Their blood cries up from the soil against thee."

"Have respect, Master Church," Stone said. "Men in this room have lost brothers to the savages. Women, their sons. Entire families murdered in Medford, Andover, Winton, Sudbury, their children cruelly tortured and killed."

"And entire nations lie slaughtered under your swords," Peter answered. "Families burned alive in their homes. Is there a soul in this room who doesn't know the fate of the Narragansett? The Nipmuk? Are there not men present who did the killing at Crow Hollow? Let them answer now for their crimes."

"And I'd do it again!" a man shouted. It was Samuel Knapp, now rising from the front pews. "Bring me a pistol and ball, and I'll see one more Indian put down like a mad dog."

"You are a heretic and a savage," another man cried at Peter.

"Please!" Stone cried. "All of you, be calm."

The reverend waved his hands and called the people to restrain themselves, but his words drowned under a rising tide of shouting men, and children now bursting into wails.

It was all working better than James had hoped. As Peter continued to call the Puritans to repentance, and the accused shouted back and shook their fists, James edged out of the pew, though not without a twinge of guilt at abandoning Peter.

Cooler heads—mostly women—hustled children out of the meetinghouse. James helped Goodwife Stone get her youngest children out of the pew, then caught Sir Benjamin's widow by her sleeve as she brushed past.

"Prudence Cotton?" he said, struggling to be heard over the tumult.

She turned to him, startled. "Master Bailey."

"I must see you, alone."

"Let me go."

"Meet me at the Common at dusk. You must be there, do you understand?"

"No, I won't do it. Unhand me."

She jerked free and hurried off after her sister and the little ones. Damn. Well, it had been worth a try.

A scuffle at his rear drew James's attention. Two men had climbed over the pew and were struggling with another man, who was trying to protect Peter from violence. Or no, he was trying to get at the Indian himself, trying to tear loose Peter's grip from the pew in front of him. Peter stood with a placid look, doing nothing more than trying to hold his ground while continuing to argue in a loud tone. His words were incomprehensible through the din.

More men forced their way into the fray. They finally knocked Peter from his feet. A man rained blows on the Indian's face.

"Get off him!" James roared.

He reached into his jerkin and drew his dagger. A woman screamed.

A man reached for him, but James slashed at the man's chest and drove him back. He threatened and waved the dagger until he had forced his way to Peter's side. He grabbed the jacket of the man pummeling the Indian and tore him off. He swung an elbow to shove another man out of the way. Soon he had the pew cleared. He lifted Peter to his feet. Blood streamed from the man's nose, and he looked shaken.

Half the congregation had fled the building, but the remainder gathered in an angry mob, shouting and waving fists. It was precisely the disturbance James had been hoping to cause, yet the savagery of it left him stunned. He struggled to recover his wits.

"Quiet, all of you! I am James Bailey, and by the authority of His Majesty, by the grace of God your sovereign and king, I order you to disperse."

They did not disperse. They did, however, ease off with the shouting. It was enough for Peter to start up again. He lifted his hands, palms up, like a prophet. Or a madman.

"Good folk of Boston—"

"Be quiet, you fool," James said.

Peter fell silent. Thank God for that.

"Now listen to me," James said to the crowd.

"No, we will not," Reverend Stone said. "We have listened quite enough."

Stone pushed his way through the crowd. Samuel Knapp was with him, the short man red faced and huffing. A taller man with long, flowing hair came in behind them. As Knapp and Stone cleared away the mob, this man approached.

"Goodman Knapp says you have papers, a commission from the king," the man said. "Do you have them on you?"

"Who are you, sir?" James said in as cold a voice as he could manage.

"I am William Fitz-Simmons, the deputy governor. And as God is my witness, if this commission from the king is false, I shall see both of you hanged."

CHAPTER FIVE

James stood in front of the three men with his hands bound behind his back. They'd taken his dagger and stripped open his jerkin and undershirt, then groped him from head to toe to check for other weapons. He had none. They had not rummaged through the pockets in his great cloak, thankfully.

The three men—Reverend Stone, Deputy Governor Fitz-Simmons, and the self-proclaimed Indian killer Samuel Knapp—sat together in the front pew, while James stood where Stone had been delivering his sermon less than an hour earlier.

Peter remained unbound and sat two pews back. Knapp had argued strenuously that they should tie up the Indian too, but he was overruled by Stone and Fitz-Simmons. Apparently they believed that Peter's Quaker pacifism would master his savage nature.

Fitz-Simmons laid the king's commission, still unopened, across his lap. He wore a gold signet ring on his right middle finger, twisting the ring back and forth while he stared down at the king's wax seal.

"Why haven't you broken the seal?" Fitz-Simmons asked.

"Why should I?" James asked. "That is King Charles's emblem. Nobody else has questioned my orders. Or are you claiming that it's a forgery?"

"What else would we expect from the likes of you?" Knapp said.

James gave him a withering look. "You, sir, are a fool."

Fitz-Simmons stroked the seal with one finger. "It's not a forgery. But it may well be a fraud."

"How so?" Reverend Stone asked. He looked less angry than the other two, more thoughtful, though it had been his services that James and Peter had disrupted.

"For all we know," Fitz-Simmons said, "it's an order to buy a thousand hogsheads of barley in New York. Or letters of marque to attack Spanish shipping. It could be anything, or nothing at all."

James snorted as if that were the most ridiculous thing he'd ever heard. Inside, he was pleased. After the initial threat, the seizure of his weapon, the way they'd rudely tied his hands and groped him, he'd wondered if he'd underestimated the boldness of these Puritans. They acted as if monarchy had never been restored, as if the Roundheads still held sway over England.

But the way the deputy governor fondled the orders, but didn't dare break the seal, was emboldening.

"The point is," Fitz-Simmons continued, "you carry secret orders and rely on their secrecy to work your purposes. I say there's nothing here."

"Then go ahead, defy me. Defy the king. Break the seal. If you are right, if the orders amount to nothing, what risk do you face? But if you're wrong . . ."

"He's bluffing," Knapp said. "I can see it in his face."

"What do you know of bluffs?" James said.

"I know plenty."

James raised his eyebrows. "Why, are you a card player? What is your game, Knapp? All fours? Pharaoh? I thought gambling was illegal in Boston. I thought this was a Godly land."

Knapp sprang to his feet, eyes bugging. Fists clenched, he made as if to spring at James, but Fitz-Simmons and Stone grabbed his arms and forced him back to his chair.

"Let him come," James said. "I'll smash his face in."

Knapp strained against the grip of the other two men. "With bound hands? Hah!"

"I don't need hands. Your head is so low to the ground I'll use my knees."

"Peace, friend," Peter murmured from his pew. "Must thou goad them so?"

James had almost forgotten about his companion. The Indian was sweating in spite of the chill inside the unheated meetinghouse, the residual warmth of the parishioners almost completely bled away in their absence. The man should be in bed, not here listening to James arguing.

He was about to suggest they release Peter when he glanced behind the man. A woman stood quietly at the back of the meetinghouse by the door.

It was Prudence Cotton, her expression unreadable, her hands clasped in front of her. What was she doing here? And how long had she been standing there?

James didn't want to stare and draw the others' attention to the widow, so he strode up to Fitz-Simmons. "Untie my hands, sir. I'll break the seal and show it to you."

"You will?"

"If you promise to obey the king's commission, yes. Can you do that?"

Fitz-Simmons glanced at Stone.

The reverend furrowed his brow, then nodded. "We'll obey any command that does not contradict a higher law."

"There is no higher law than the rule of your sovereign."

"Who is not a despot, as he is anxious to remind us," Fitz-Simmons said. "Very well, let us see what you have. Untie him, Goodman Knapp."

Knapp had stopped straining, but now, as he rose and approached, he got a nasty look on his face that only James could see. James braced himself to be assaulted, vowing that he'd make this arrogant little twat pay dearly, bound hands or no. But Knapp came around behind without further ugliness and untied his hands.

James rubbed his wrists, laced up his jerkin, and took the sealed paper from Fitz-Simmons. "I was only waiting for some civility. Was that too much to expect?"

He broke the seal and handed the paper to the deputy governor. Fitz-Simmons and Stone read it at the same time, and then Fitz-Simmons handed it to Knapp.

"This is meaningless," Knapp said. "Vague words about passing unmolested through the colony."

James took the paper and read it as if seeing it for the first time. The wording was hardly a surprise; he'd been in the king's antechamber when it was written by Lord North, and then taken it in himself to be signed by the king.

"And so you *have* molested me."

"Only when you disrupted services," Fitz-Simmons said.

"I was saving my companion from violence. Peter Church is mentioned here too. Men were attacking him. They might have killed him if I hadn't intervened."

"What is it that you intend to do in the Bay Colony, Master Bailey?" Fitz-Simmons asked.

"Not be hanged, for a start. Nor trussed up, nor put in the pillories, nor suffer any other indignity."

"So, to live peaceably?" Fitz-Simmons said. "Any man may do that. You don't need the king's signature and seal. So what brings you?"

"First, I demand respect as the agent of the king. So far I have been treated with hostility by the likes of this man." James nodded at Knapp, who glared back.

"You ate at my table," Stone said. "You slept under my roof. That's hospitality, not hostility. No, I wasn't pleased that Master Church spoke his heretical views in a most odious manner, but I would have treated it with forbearance if you had not drawn arms."

"He was about to be killed!"

"The reverend is more forgiving than I am," Fitz-Simmons said. "I think you purposefully disrupted our services, although to what end, I cannot fathom."

"That's preposterous. I had no idea. Peter was so well behaved on the *Vigilant* that I forgot about the peculiar habits of his sect."

"What do you want, Master Bailey?" Fitz-Simmons asked again.

"I want to know what happened at Winton."

"Are these details unknown in London?" Fitz-Simmons asked. "The Indians of Sachusett swore they would remain neutral in the war. Then they fell like wolves upon the innocents of Winton and slaughtered Sir Benjamin and others to whom they had pledged peace and friendship."

"Many details remain unknown," James said. "And I want justice for Sir Benjamin."

"He had his justice," Knapp said. "The savages who did it are dead. They are quite extinct in these parts."

The deputy governor nodded. "Goodman Knapp speaks truth. We punished the Indians of Sachusett for their villainy. Drove them into the wilderness and pursued them without remorse. When we overtook them at last, we freed the Widow Cotton from her captivity, and then, when the natives refused generous terms, finished matters at Crow Hollow."

James resisted glancing at Prudence Cotton. He assumed she was still there by the door. "So I have heard," he said, leaving a note of skepticism in his voice.

"What more evidence do you need?" Knapp demanded. "I rammed the sachem's head on a spike myself. It sits outside the Winton meetinghouse next to the heads of wolves and other vermin. I hanged three of the murderer's sons and two of his brothers. I burned the savages' village to the ground."

"Who is the savage?" Peter said in a quiet voice.

Knapp whirled. "Good men are dead because of them, you son of the devil. Either you hold your tongue, or so help me I'll—"

He stopped and his eyes widened. "Widow Cotton!"

CHAPTER SIX

Prudence froze at the door as the five men bored into her with their gazes.

What are you doing? Go, run.

Reverend Stone looked stern and disappointed, Deputy Governor Fitz-Simmons more annoyed than anything; Knapp stared. She didn't meet his gaze. Knapp had bought her husband's lands in Winton, and rumor had it he wished to plow more than the dead man's fields. In that, Prudence had no interest whatsoever.

As for the strangers, James looked momentarily concerned, before his expression changed to calculating, scheming. He may not welcome her presence, she decided, but now that she'd supplied it, he meant to turn it to his advantage. Peter Church barely glanced at her and looked pale and sickly, as if he'd eaten a bad piece of fish.

"What do you want?" Fitz-Simmons asked. The annoyance deepened on the deputy governor's face.

"I heard what you were saying," she began, faltering.

"And what business is that of yours? Reverend, have you no mastery within your own household?"

Stone sputtered at this but fixed his anger in Prudence's direction, not at the man who'd challenged him. "You weren't invited to this meeting. Go home."

"I want to know what she's doing here first," Fitz-Simmons said.

"She suffers from childish curiosity, that is all. I'll see that she's disciplined later. My wife will get to the bottom of it."

Why *was* Prudence here? After the evacuation of the meetinghouse following Peter Church's outburst and the subsequent scuffle, she'd had no intention of hanging about to find out what they intended to do with the two strangers. Only on her way home did she remember James's shocking suggestion that she meet him at the Common at dusk.

No, she would not. She wasn't Lucy or Alice Branch, the servant girls, who had been whispering breathlessly about James when they thought nobody was listening.

The lady doth protest too much, methinks.

The words from her husband's Shakespeare folio had seeped into her conscience as she had approached the Stone house with her sister's children in tow. And then she had another thought—and almost cursed herself for her foolishness.

James didn't want to meet her on the Common to satisfy his lusts. He'd read her pages, that's what. The chapter about her daughter. He wanted to help. So she'd entered the house and immediately slipped out the back door as if going to the privy, but really to hurry back up the hill to the meetinghouse.

Except now that Prudence was here, facing these men in defiance of clear rules about a woman's place at a man's council, she felt frozen, unable to respond.

"Master Fitz-Simmons asked you a question," Knapp said, his tone demeaning. "Are you going to answer or stand there in contempt?"

Knapp's rudeness brought Prudence's courage to a boil. She walked down the aisle until she stood between James and the men seated in the pews. "I'm here because of Winton and Crow Hollow."

The scowl on Fitz-Simmons's face turned to confusion. "What do you mean?"

"I heard you talking. Master Bailey said something about going west, about finding out what happened."

"We know what happened," Knapp said. "I was there, remember?"

She turned on him. "So was I. You seem to forget that."

"Prudence, please," Stone said. "I beg you. Now is not the time."

"And at Crow Hollow," she continued, "when you were as brutal as the savages themselves. How about the Nipmuk village? What did you do there? That's the part they wouldn't let me see."

"Do you want particulars, is that it?" Knapp said. "I can share every ugly detail, though it would make you faint from the horror of it."

Her fists clenched. "I don't easily swoon, Goodman Knapp."

He snorted. "You're a woman. You have no idea."

"Leave her be," James said.

Knapp glared at him. "You know nothing about the war, so I would suggest that you shut your mouth."

"I've read the widow's account, and that's more than enough. The hardships she endured while you strutted around, ordering men about, slaughtering unarmed Indians—you are a coward in comparison."

"This man is a knave," Knapp said. "Bind him, stick him in the pillory. Then flog him and send him back to England on the next ship."

"Will you guard your temper, for heaven's sake?" Fitz-Simmons said to Knapp. He turned back to James. "We've all read the widow's account. What of it?"

"You haven't read it all," Prudence said, "so you don't know everything. The reverend does, though he refuses to accept it. And now Master Bailey knows too. That's why I came back."

"I do?" James said. He glanced at Peter, who was wiping the perspiration from his brow with a handkerchief. The Indian gave a confused shake of the head.

An ugly misgiving settled into her belly.

"The papers. The missing chapter from my narrative. Didn't you read it?"

"I don't know what you're talking about."

The worry in her belly became a writhing mass of snakes. She had mistaken his message during services. Her pages must still lie undisturbed within the pockets of his cloak. He had not invited her to meet him on the Common because he had read her narrative. Rather, for some other reason she couldn't guess at.

James's cloak was lying on the pew between Stone and Fitz-Simmons, with the man's dagger sitting on top of it. If she pressed the matter, had him bring out her unpublished chapter, one of them would surely confiscate the pages.

"Then why are you going to Winton?" she asked.

"I'm not."

"I thought you said—"

"I said no such thing. I said I need to know what happened, but I have no intention of setting off into the godforsaken wilderness myself. Boston is cold and dreary enough as it is. No, I intend to speak with knowledgeable parties, yourself included, and get to the truth that way. Then I'll return to London."

But . . . but then why did he have the Indian with him? It wasn't so Peter Church could speak directly to the Nipmuk? Was it only to goad the good folk of Boston with Quaker heresies to trump up grounds for the Crown to interfere, as Anne had claimed?

"So you see, it was a simple misunderstanding," Stone said. "Now run home and help Anne with supper. There's a good girl."

"Before she goes, I want to see these papers Widow Cotton mentioned," Fitz-Simmons said. "What are they?"

"It's nothing," Stone said, his tone a little too dismissive to be believed. "The records of a nightmare she suffered in her captivity. Not fit for publication."

"Nevertheless."

"I don't have them anymore," Prudence said. "I got rid of them."

"That's the truth?" the deputy governor asked her.

"Aye, Goodman Fitz-Simmons. As the Lord is my witness. I got rid of them."

"I am relieved to hear it," Stone said. Then, to his two companions, "I told her and told her. Burn them, I said. They're only causing you trouble."

"Again," Fitz-Simmons said. "You are the master of your own house, are you not? You should have cast them into the fire yourself."

Prudence tried one more time. "Master Bailey, please. My daughter was taken from my arms."

"How terrible to suffer the loss of a child," James said. "I am truly sorry."

"But she's still alive. The Indians have her, and I need her back."

He frowned. "Your account made no mention of it. I'd assumed that once she'd been taken—"

"I tell of it in the missing chapter." If only he had checked his pockets. Prudence's voice rose in despair. "Don't you see?"

"Don't listen to her," Stone said. "The babe is dead."

"She's not!"

"Dead or alive, it doesn't matter," James said. "I'm not here to look into the disappearance of children in the war, only to confirm the honorable death of Sir Benjamin. I am sorry, good woman, I really am."

He didn't sound sorry, he sounded indifferent. Just like the rest. Either they thought she was deluded, or they didn't care.

Knapp looked triumphant, Stone and Fitz-Simmons relieved.

"Go on," Stone said to Prudence. His tone was gentler than before. "Tell Anne I'll be home shortly."

Utterly defeated, Prudence turned to obey.

"Well, then," James said. "Give me my commission. And may I have my cloak? It's wretched cold in here."

"Very well," Fitz-Simmons said. "You are dismissed. And your heretic companion as well. Neither of you may speak to the widow without either myself or the reverend present."

"Understood."

Prudence slipped out the door. She drew her cloak against the cutting wind, sharp as a blade, that came in off the harbor. It had gained strength and swept the smoke of a hundred chimneys west, toward the bare winter forests. The air tasted clean with a hint of brine.

So that was that. She'd lost her recollections about the fate of her dearest Mary. And not only was James oblivious to her need, he seemed not to care.

Her daughter would be almost three now (she refused to consider the alternative possibility) and speaking only Nipmuk. No matter. Prudence had learned enough of the tongue in her captivity to say the most important thing. She had learned the words in captivity and practiced them daily in the months since she'd escaped to freedom.

Dearest child, I have come for you. I am your mother.

CHAPTER SEVEN

Later that afternoon, Prudence couldn't help but glance at the thick, blown-glass windows as the shadows lengthened outside. Almost dusk. No sign of the two strangers from England. Not for hours.

The days had drawn short with the coming of late December, and it was only a few hours after the lighter midday meal when the women of the Stone household began preparing for supper. Children lit tallow candles and tended the fire while Prudence and Anne slid loaves of bread into the oven, together with a pair of large corn puddings to bake.

Reverend Stone sat at the table, penning letters to the ministers of congregations in Gloucester, Plymouth, and Roxbury. He looked up only to dip his quill or to blow on his hands and flex his fingers.

Anne and Prudence went to the pantry to fetch the Dutch oven. The two servant girls were chopping turnips to add to the two whole chickens, plus peas, carrots, and onions to cook in the broth.

"Will Master James be at supper?" Lucy asked.

Anne gave her a sharp look. "Don't you worry. I'm sure *both* men will sup with us."

"I meant the Indian too," Lucy said quickly with a glance at her sister. Alice covered her mouth and turned away, as if suppressing a laugh.

"Are they out?" Prudence asked innocently as she helped Anne carry the Dutch oven into the front room, each woman gripping one of the iron handles. "I thought maybe they were upstairs, resting."

"You know good and well that they're out. I've seen you watching the door, looking out the window when you think I'm not paying attention."

Prudence glanced at the reverend, but the man didn't look up from his work. His brow furrowed and he touched at his forehead with an ink-stained hand, leaving smudges. Then the words seemed to come to him; he brightened and went back to forming his smooth, even letters, lips moving.

Prudence used the iron shovel to clear a space in the hearth. With tongs, the women eased the oven in and shoveled coals over the top. Anne made a notch on a candle to mark the time when she'd need to check the oven.

"What do you suppose they're doing, anyway?" Prudence asked.

"Vexing the good folk of Boston, no doubt."

"On the Sabbath?"

"It's the devil's work they're about, and make no mistake."

Was Anne right? Or was James even now in the Common, waiting to meet her? It was dusk already. Much longer and it would be too late.

Old John Porter came into the front room and made a show of looking at the wood box. It was still half full, but bringing firewood in from the shed out back was one of the few things the deaf old fellow could still do—his hands were too unsteady even to split kindling anymore—so he grabbed his cloak from its hook and made for the back door.

Prudence touched his shoulder to get his attention. "It's icy out there. Let me help you."

A smile brightened his aged face. She put on her cloak, and she took his elbow when they reached the wooden stairs out back, which were slick with ice.

When they came to the woodshed, she loaded his arms with split logs from the older, dry pile.

"I'm a grown woman. I kept my own household before Benjamin died."

Old John turned. "Eh, what?"

Now was the time, but she hesitated, torn with guilt. "I don't need anyone's permission to come and go. Let Anne scold me when I return—what does it matter to me?"

He cupped a hand at his ear. "Speak up, child. These old baskets don't gather like they used to."

She only smiled at him, then helped him back up the stairs without bothering to gather wood herself. When he was inside, she pulled the door shut and walked quickly around the side of the house to the lane.

Her clogs clacked on the cobbles as she hurried up the lane, and she shortly regretted not having put on her good boots. It was at least a mile to the Common; her feet would be sore and cold by the time she arrived. But boots would have looked suspicious. Already she could picture Anne's disappointed expression, see the judgment in the minister's eyes.

"Let it be," she said aloud.

How easy to falter, to doubt. It was like a blemish in the skin, and picking at it would only make it bleed, and then there would be a pock. Enough guilt and you could cover yourself with scars and blemishes. Her husband had told her that once, when she'd been worrying over some piece of gossip she'd idly passed along, and the more she'd thought about it since, the more true it seemed.

Sir Benjamin had been a nominal Puritan—perhaps not a true dissenter, but no friend of the Papist trappings of the Anglican Church, either. He was twenty-seven years old and handsome when he died. He owned a share in a small merchant fleet trading in furs from New England and sugar from the Indies. A fine house in Boston and six hundred acres of rich land in Winton, plus more land outside Springfield. By all accounts, a good husband.

But in the two short years of their marriage, Prudence had not been a very good wife, she now realized. Instead, she found fault with his lax ways and too often tried to correct him, attempting to make him as devout as her own father.

And why beholdest thou the mote that is in thy brother's eye, but considerest not the beam that is in thine own eye?

Benjamin had thawed her, little by little, but more so, the birth of her daughter taught Prudence that not all things could be planned. You couldn't perfect another, make him or her free from error. You couldn't even do the same to yourself. And God, she was convinced, didn't expect it.

Her blood was pumping, her heart pounding by the time she reached the top of the hill to High Street. The movement warmed her, inside and out. She'd shed her guilt and was now filled only with purpose.

Beacon Hill rose to her right, filled with a growing number of houses clustered around narrow streets. To her left, Fort Field, and the Great Cove below it, crowded with swaying ships. More houses lined High Street, but they thinned as she continued west toward the Common. She was high enough to see the Neck and the town gate, a couple of miles distant through the gloom.

A bell chimed and lanterns moved along the gate as it swung shut. Within the past two years the gate had been fortified with iron bars and a watchtower of cut stone. During the low point of the war, there had been talk of the entire population of the Bay Colony taking refuge on the peninsula until the militias could put down the Indian insurrection. An incident over guns and the death of a Praying Indian had led to war between Plymouth and King Philip of the Wampanoag, and then the conflict had quickly spread from tribe to tribe, colony to colony, until all of New England was in flames. Only by the grace of God had the English been preserved in this land.

Prudence soon reached the Common, which stretched from High Street toward the bay on the north side. It was a flat plain, studded with the rotting stumps of trees, still standing as mute witness to the forest cut down more than forty years earlier. Given the lateness of the season, the Common lay empty of animals, save for a lone hog, a big boar rooting in the snow along the rail fence. It came grunting toward her when she approached.

"Get along, you filthy thing, or I'll call the hog reeve and you'll end up in someone's pot." She kicked at it until it went away.

The last light was fading, and the moon wasn't up yet. Lights twinkled from the town at her rear, and, more faintly, from Cambridge and Charlestown, north across the mouth of the Charles River, which twisted like an inky ribbon as it thrust westward into the interior. There wasn't enough light to see clearly across the Common, but perhaps James was crouched at one of the stumps, waiting.

She watched for the pig, then climbed the fence and trudged through the snow. It was only an inch deep, but a fair bit ended up inside her shoes, melting through her woolen stockings. The wind pulled her hair from her head rail and whipped it around her face.

"Is anyone there?" she called. "Hello?"

She inspected the stumps one by one. Nothing. She'd almost crossed the field to the farmhouses on the opposite side when the clop of hooves reached her ears. A team of four horses came down High Street from the direction of town. They pulled a coach that jerked and bounced as it hit the frozen ruts in the mud surface. A driver sat on the perch, flicking a whip to drive them on. Two lanterns hung on long poles over the team. Their flames cast flickering cones of light that cut the gloom ahead.

Prudence's first thought was to duck behind a stump and hide. By now they would be looking for her back at the house and probably organizing a search. But that would bring people on foot or horse, not a coach. This was someone hurrying to the gates to leave Boston at dark. Who had reason to sneak out? Who would break the Sabbath to hire a team?

James and Peter. It must be. But why?

Prudence sprang to her feet and ran across the snowy pasture to intercept the coach before it passed the Common. She scrambled over the rail fence and came into the road waving her arms as it approached.

The horses were snorting, pulling already, nervous at being out in such poor light. When they saw her emerging from the darkness, they reared and snorted. The driver cursed and cracked his whip. He hadn't yet spotted her. In a moment they'd be past.

"Over here!"

"What the devil?" The man jerked back on the reins, dropped the whip, and fumbled in his cloak to remove a pistol, which he lowered when she came into the circle of lantern light.

"What is it, man?" a voice called from inside the coach. It sounded like James.

"A lady." Then, to Prudence: "Out of the way, good woman. We're in a hurry." He groped around for his whip, but by the time he found it, tangled in the horses' harness, she'd stepped in front of the coach to block it.

"Master Bailey!" she cried. "Where are you going?"

The coach door swung open and he leaned out. "You! What are you doing here?"

"You told me to come!"

"Oh. Well, you said no, so I supposed that . . . Anyway, matters have changed. Out of the way."

"You're leaving Boston, aren't you? You're going to Winton! You . . . you *lied* to me."

"Oh, by all the saints—of course I did. Don't you want me to find out who killed Sir Benjamin?"

"I know who killed my husband. I want you to find my daughter."

"Not my business. Now clear off."

"Is Peter with you?"

"Driver, move! Throw her from the road if you must."

The driver lifted his whip to drive the horses forward, but before James could pull the door shut, a bell clanked from the direction of the town. Dogs barked. A man's shout carried through the air, then swept away in the wind.

James leaned out and craned back toward the town. "Damn. How did they know?"

"As I warned thee," Peter's voice spoke from the darkened interior.

The driver cupped a hand to his ear. "'Tisn't the general alarm."

The man was so bundled in cloaks and scarves that she hadn't recognized him, but she knew his gravelly voice. It was Robert Woory, an unmarried man who kept stables in the North End and ran an overland transport service to Gloucester and Plymouth. His custom had been devastated by the war with King Philip, which explained why he'd break the Sabbath to carry James and Peter out of town.

"Well if not that," James said, "then what—"

"It's the *initial* alarm," Prudence cut in. "Soon they'll have twenty armed men on horse. Then they'll sound the general alarm."

Woory grunted. "Eh? What is that you're saying?"

What it was was a lie of the worst kind, and she burned with shame to utter it. But James had started it, lying to her first. And she was desperate.

Before Woory could overturn her story, she rushed around to the coach door and blocked James from closing it. "Take me with you. I know a side road through Cambridge that will get you off the highway. I'll show you."

"What kind of road is that?" Woory said, thankfully put off the subject of the bells for the moment. "Never heard of it."

"And I can get you through the gates." She didn't speak to Woory, but directly to James. "But you must hurry."

James grabbed her wrist and pulled her up to the coach. He stared hard into her eyes, and she thought he'd throw her aside, calling her a liar and a wretch. Instead, he nodded.

"Get in."

Chapter Eight

James checked the load on his flintlock pistols as the coach approached the gates. He was almost, but not quite, certain the widow was lying to him about the bells raising the general alarm. But if she had told the truth, he might have to blast his way out. The men at the gates would have heard the alarm as well and would react appropriately.

Woory slowed the coach. James tucked his pistols into his breeches and got out the king's commission. He wished Fitz-Simmons had not forced him to break the seal. It had carried more weight sealed and full of mystery.

"Tell them—" Prudence began.

"Quiet, you. I have the king's commission."

"Art thou too proud to listen to a woman?" Peter asked.

It was too dark to see the Indian's face, but he sounded weaker. He'd stumbled earlier getting into the coach, and when James had steadied him, Peter's hand had been damp and clammy. Sweat steamed on his forehead. He was now wrapped in two blankets but was still shivering and cold, compared to Prudence's warmth.

"Tell them you received a signal from Charlestown across the bay," Prudence said. "They sometimes flash messages when they need help. Then show them the commission and refuse to provide details, except to say that Charlestown needs you."

Outside, the men at the gates shouted an aggressive challenge to the driver. Woory shouted back, told them his master would be out shortly.

"That's a clever lie," James told Prudence.

"May the Lord forgive me."

"I didn't mean it as an insult. It's a compliment."

"That makes me feel even more wretched," she said.

He allowed a smile at her labored innocence. The lie had come easily to her lips, as had the one that got her into the coach in the first place. He was more certain now that she'd attempted to deceive him.

James got out, not so anxious about drawing his pistols as he had been. And a good thing too. The men in the squat tower held out a pole from the window with a lamp on the end so they could get a better look at him, but otherwise they stayed well protected behind their stone wall. One of them had a musket, which he aimed down at James. There would be no winning a shootout with these two.

So he followed Prudence's advice. When they asked exactly what kind of signal he'd received, he refused to answer but held up the king's commission and said he needed to get to Charlestown. They had apparently heard of him already and didn't come down to inspect it. He put it away.

"Why not send a boat across?" one of the men asked. "You'd get there in half the time."

"In this wind? I tried to hire a boat, but nobody would risk the swells at this hour, and on the Sabbath too."

"Goodman Woory, is this true?"

"I know nothing but what this man tells me," Woory said with a grunt. "'Tis the king's emergency, he says, and I seen his papers. Couldn't very well blame the wind and waves to keep me indoors. Heaven knows I don't care to ride on the Sabbath, but what choice did I have?"

Woory had balked, it was true, but only until James shoveled silver into his paw. Then he was off to the stables like a hound after a rabbit.

It went back and forth with more pointless arguing, but neither of the guards took notice of the occasional clanking still to be heard in the direction of the town. James wouldn't be able to relax until they got well clear of Boston, but he no longer expected to be shot down.

At last the guards came down to unlock and open the gates. The moment they were open, James hopped back inside, and Woory had the horses moving down the darkened highway. The gates closed behind them, severing the last light of town, and soon they were clomping across the Neck, then onto the mainland by what little light was cast by the lanterns. Inside, James dropped the curtain for warmth, plunging them into darkness.

"Now, where did a Godly woman such as yourself learn to lie so prettily?" James said to Prudence.

"Pray don't remind me," she said. "I know it was wrong to deceive those men."

"I'm talking about the lie you told to get yourself onto the coach."

"What do you mean?"

"I've been lied to in Paris and London. Faced French spies and assassins sent by the Vatican. Did you think a devout Puritan from Boston could deceive me so easily?" When she didn't answer, he added, "Those bells weren't for me, they were for you. I'll wager you ran off, didn't you?"

"I had no choice." She took a deep breath. "Pray, pardon me. You're angry, aren't you?"

"Not at all. I'm delighted. I thought I'd be traveling all night with this dour Quaker. Now I've got a beautiful, charming woman, instead."

"If I thought you were serious, I would be highly offended."

He laughed. The situation was delightful, or would be, if not for the increased danger he'd put himself in.

The coach hit a rock and would have thrown them from their seats if they hadn't been packed in so tightly. Peter let out a small groan as he resettled himself.

"Are you all right, Master Church?" Prudence asked.

"Call me 'friend,' please. And lying is never right. Let thy language be plain, thy words unadorned and without deception."

"No, he's not all right," James said. "He's very ill."

"Then why did you take him out?"

"To save his life. Someone is trying to kill him. Maybe me too."

"But aren't we in danger breathing his bad air?" She stopped. "Wait, what do you mean?"

"He was fine until we got to Boston. Suddenly, he's taken ill? I asked in town this evening. There's no fever in Boston at the moment, no plague or pox."

"Maybe he picked it up on the ship and it's only manifesting itself now."

"No. We lost several souls on the journey, but nobody for weeks."

"But he's an Indian," she protested. "You know how they suffer our ailments."

"Ten years in England without so much as a cough, isn't that right, Peter?"

Peter groaned.

"There were two others with him, a Pequot and a Narragansett," James continued. "They both died in England. But not Peter. He even survived the miasma of London. Then the crossing. Still nothing. So now, we arrive under the Stone roof and twenty-four hours later he's dying."

"Oh, please. Don't say that. I couldn't bear it."

Prudence fumbled in the dark and a moment later had her cloak off, which she reached over James to wrap around Peter, who slumped against the door on the opposite side of the coach.

Now she was shivering too. James opened his overcoat and offered to share it with her.

"No, no, I couldn't. That's not proper."

"As you wish."

"But how will getting him out of Boston save him? If he took bad airs under our roof, it's in him now. He'll either fight it off or die."

"He didn't take any bad airs. He's been poisoned."

Prudence stiffened. When she spoke, it was in a low, chilly voice. "You are mistaken, sir."

"Give it some thought, you'll see."

"No, it's impossible."

She fell silent after that, resisting James's attempts to draw her out. So much for his hopes of improved company.

Peter slipped into a delirious sleep, where he muttered in what must be his native tongue. Once, he said something and Prudence drew in her breath, and James realized that she understood at least some of what the Indian was saying. He wondered how much she'd picked up in her captivity.

They continued in silence for a good stretch, the coach rattling down the bone-shaking road, a little faster than a man could walk. James tucked his head against his shoulder and tried to sleep. A few minutes later, Prudence slumped against him. She was icy cold and didn't resist this time when he shared his overcoat with her, making sure not to touch her more than necessary. Silly woman, he should let her freeze if she was that offended by the contact.

It was after midnight when Woory banged on the door and told James to come out. The coach was stopped, the horses stood blowing and snorting. Woory said they'd hit a deep rut while going up a hill and become stuck. He'd already tried to push, but without success.

"Can't scarcely believe you slept through it," Woory grumbled.

James climbed over Prudence, who groaned and shifted as she came awake. He closed the door behind him. Outside it was brittle cold of the kind where every breath stole heat from his lungs. The forest rose dark and forbidding on either side.

He eyed the coach by the light of the moon. Didn't look too bad. If they hadn't been going uphill, he doubted they'd have even got stuck.

"I didn't even realize we'd stopped."

"What about them wolves?" Woory asked.

"Wolves?"

"About an hour back, they paced us for a stretch. Bloody vermin—I thought you'd be checking your powder."

James was alarmed. "No, sorry."

"No sign of them now, but you never can tell. Let's get her moving again."

James pushed from the rear, while Woory pulled up front and slapped at the haunches of the four horses. The wheels rocked back and forth in the ruts but didn't come loose. Moments later, Prudence came out, yawning and stretching. James gave her his overcoat.

Woory had them untie the trunk from the back and put it in the road, then he opened the coach door. "Get out, you. You're weighing us down."

"Leave him be," James said. "He's deathly ill."

Then, to his surprise, Peter came out, still bundled in blankets and with Prudence's cloak wrapped around his shoulders. He leaned against the side of the coach.

"I feel improved. I think it's passing."

"Really? Wonderful." James gave Prudence a sharp look. "Well? What do you think now? If he wasn't poisoned, why is he improving so quickly?"

She turned away.

Peter staggered off the road to take a piss, but James didn't want him pushing anyway. Together, the burden lighter, the three others rocked and heaved until they got the coach clear of the rut. Woory led the team ahead ten or twenty yards until he found an even stretch where the horses could get a good run at it. Then they loaded up the coach again and a few minutes later were off.

Again they traveled in silence for a spell, but while Peter slipped back into sleep, Prudence stayed upright. James could almost feel her thinking.

"People do recover miraculously at times, God willing," she said at last.

"He was fine yesterday morning. He first complained of illness after he entered the reverend's house. We ate and drank nothing but what Stone provided until this evening, during which time Peter grew progressively worse, meal by meal. Now that we're away, he seems to be recovering."

"The reverend is a God-fearing man."

"As are many men who kill in the name of God."

"But he's gentle, peaceable. He was against the war, tried to calm the bloodlust. When he heard that one of Philip's sachems could read and write, the reverend wrote him letters to seek a negotiated peace. And he has never hanged an adulterer or burned a witch. He would never murder a man."

"It must be someone in your house, then. One of the servants?"

She let out a harsh laugh. "Old John Porter? He's a gentle sort, and quite deaf. Lucy and Alice Branch are silly, light-minded girls, without an original thought between them. They know little of the world and care less. Half their life is spent giggling about handsome young men they spy around town. The sooner they marry, the better. They are one stray glance from falling into sin."

James thought of his own interaction with Lucy and was glad Prudence couldn't see his face in the darkness for fear of what it might give away.

"Well then," he began cautiously. "That leaves your sister."

"Bless me, no!"

"She had access to Peter's food and drink."

"My sister is the wisest, most upright person I know. I was the youngest of eleven children, and Anne the oldest. She practically raised me herself. I have never seen her shirk her duty. She would accuse her own husband if she thought he was guilty of such an odious crime. Not that he would ever do such a thing, either," she added quickly.

Then who? Unless it had been one of the Stone children—highly unlikely—there had been one other person in the house, James realized, and she was sitting next to him. Prudence had lied before. No doubt she was capable of more lies.

"It had to happen under your roof," he said. "If not, others would have sickened as well."

"Then you must be wrong. It wasn't poison."

"Hmm."

Liar or no, Prudence might be useful on the journey. If he remembered his maps, it would take at least two days to reach Springfield, depending on the condition of the roads. Then another day to Winton. He could harvest whatever information he could extract from her about the death of Sir Benjamin, use her to ease their passage through the more prickly Puritan towns ahead, then leave her in Winton if he and Peter needed to continue beyond that. Into Indian country.

The road opened up as the first light began to filter around the curtain. James drew it back to look past Prudence and through the tiny window. The landscape had turned from black to gray.

No sign yet of the sun, but it would soon rise. They were passing through an area of overgrown pasture and ruined farmhouses, reduced to chimneys and charred support beams. Destroyed in the war, Prudence said.

After studying the terrain, she declared that they were west of Waltham.

As it brightened, Peter woke and licked his lips. He drew open the curtain on his side and looked out the window.

"'Twould seem," the Indian said at last, "that I have survived the night."

CHAPTER NINE

"How are you feeling?" James asked Peter.

The Indian rubbed at his chin, as if considering. "Somewhat improved."

The coach hit a rock and the three of them jounced about. The road was growing worse. Nevertheless, Woory picked up the pace now that there was light to see by.

"I'm glad to hear it," James said, encouraged by the strength in the Indian's voice. "I was worried that we'd arrive in Winton with a half-frozen corpse."

"A cheery thought," Peter said. "But no, it would seem that the Lord has preserved my life for some purpose or other."

"That almost passes for idle chatter," James said. "You *must* be feeling better. How about you?" he asked Prudence. "Do you need to stop to stretch your legs, relieve yourself?"

"No, I'm all right for now."

"Good, I'd like to put some more distance between us and Boston."

"So you're going to Winton after all?"

"Aye, and Crow Hollow, if necessary. That nonsense in Boston was only to put them off the trail. I intended all along to inspect the site for myself. Do you have family there? Somewhere to stay?"

"Nay, I have no family in Winton. One of our servants lives there still—Goody Hull. But she lives in humble circumstances. Her cottage could scarcely accommodate us all."

"It only needs to accommodate you," James said. "Peter and I will continue on without you."

Prudence crossed her arms. "I'm going with you."

"You're a fugitive—that makes you a risk. At the moment, your usefulness outweighs your danger. After Winton, that arithmetic changes. I don't need a search party tracking us into the woods."

"Don't be so confident," she said. "They must know that I've gone with you. They might have sent someone already."

"Oh, I would certainly hope so. Your sister will be worried about your safety."

"Quite frantic," Prudence said. "But as worried about my soul as my body. The first thing she asked when I escaped from the Nipmuk was whether they had insulted my virtue."

"Not about your daughter?"

"No. She was presumed dead." Prudence paused. "They didn't, you know."

"I would not think less of you if they had."

"I saw all sorts of atrocities. Believe me, an Indian at war is as savage as any other man. No offense, Master Church. I mean . . . Peter."

Peter turned with a smile. "No offense taken, friend. Most men are brutes at heart. My people are no exception."

"But they never laid a hand on me—not in that way. The other things I saw . . ." Her voice trailed off.

"I read your account," James said.

"As I said in the meetinghouse, that wasn't the whole of it. If you had read it all, you'd know why I intend to travel with you beyond Winton."

"Yes, I recall. You spoke of your daughter being yet alive. Is your narrative incomplete in some other way?"

But Prudence didn't seem to have heard. Her eyes had taken on a glazed, distant expression. Her brow furrowed, and her mouth pinched tight. It was a dark look, and James wondered if some wretched memory had clawed its way free and taken possession of her.

"Art thou well, friend?" Peter asked.

Prudence shuddered, as if trying to clear her head of a nightmare. "Pray, pardon me." She turned to James. "What is in the pockets of your overcoat?"

"Pistols, paper cartridges with balls and powder."

"Not those ones. The inner pockets. Where you keep your coins, your secret messages. The vials and things."

He started. "Did you go through my possessions while I was sleeping?"

"No," she said. "I mean, yes, but not last night. It was the first night you arrived. I entered your room when you were sleeping."

That was fairly alarming. The weeks on the ship must have dulled his senses. He'd slept while wolves stalked the coach, and now it appeared that this woman had groped his belongings while he lay sleeping, as dead to the world as a hibernating bear. His suspicion of the widow was growing.

"About the poison," James said. "Where were you when we were eating? Back in the kitchen, was it?"

"No, I—wait, you can't believe that. Peter, tell him. I would never! Please, you have to believe me."

"Gentle, friend," Peter told her. "He's trying to rile thee into making a mistake. He doesn't actually believe that thou art guilty."

"Will you let me do my job, you silly Quaker?"

"Thou attempted to deceive this good woman."

"The devil take you," James said irritably.

Peter shrugged and looked back out the window.

"Very well," James said to Prudence. "Then what were you doing in my belongings?"

"Look in your pocket. You'll see."

He reached into the pockets one by one. There were so many things there, things he didn't trust to his trunk, that it took a moment to figure out what she meant. Letters of credit and introduction. Rings with hidden compartments. Invisible ink for delivering secret messages. A list of French and Dutch spies and their aliases. The names of the other agents of the king currently stationed in New England and New York, written in numbered code. How to find his associate in Springfield, and another man in Hartford, these instructions also written in a cipher.

At last he found it, an unfamiliar sheaf of papers tied together with twine. He took it out, slipped off the twine, and unfolded the papers. There was writing in a fine, feminine hand, but it was still too dark to read easily.

"What is it?"

"The story about my missing daughter."

"I see."

"I want you to find her."

"Where do you think she is?"

"In the northern forests, with a tribe of Nipmuk and Abenaki. The land of Verts Monts—French-claimed, but wild."

"So the frozen, hostile wilderness. With Indians who killed hundreds of English and suffered near extermination by their hand. Yes, I'm sure they'll welcome us. You don't have some secret French map of the waterways and Indian trails, do you? No? I didn't think so."

"I'll pay you handsomely."

"How? From what I understand, your brother-in-law was given stewardship of Sir Benjamin's estate until you remarry."

"That is true, but—"

"It doesn't matter. I'm a servant of the Crown. No bribe will turn me from my purpose."

"James, please."

He raised his eyebrows at the use of his Christian name, and it was light enough now to see her flush.

"I am not heartless, *Prudence*, but I must do my duty to the king."

"Which is what?"

"My own business. Anyway, I will help if I can, but I'm not wandering into the north country to get myself killed. You don't even have evidence that your child is alive."

"Mary. Her name is Mary. She will be three years old, with blond ringlets and fat cheeks—assuming they have fed her properly."

He tried not to wince. It was more than he wanted to know. Anyway, he'd as good as invited Prudence to argue that her daughter was still alive, which was irrelevant.

"Read my account, please. Then you'll see what I mean."

"I don't want to read it. I don't want to take responsibility for this thing." He lifted his hand when she started to protest. "No, I mean it."

He dropped the papers on her lap. She didn't pick them up.

"What harm could it do?" Peter said. "Either thou canst be dissuaded from thy purpose, or not. If not, there's little harm in reading the pages—thou mayest even learn something new about Sir Benjamin, whether thou believest Prudence's claim or not."

"It is a waste of time," James said.

"Time is something we possess in abundance, friend. It must be three days to Winton by coach. What else wouldst thou do, engage in idle chatter the entire journey? Read her account unless thou art worried."

"Nay, I'm not worried," James said. "They're only words. What would possibly cause me worry from that?"

"That thy conscience may be pricked."

Prudence looked at James hopefully. She held out her papers. "It's dawn," she said. "There's enough light to read now."

"Very well, hand it over." James untied the twine. "Now let me move so I can sit next to the window."

Once he was next to the window, he turned his back to her, partly to get away from her prying gaze, but also to get as much of the light coming through as possible. Their breath had frozen on the pane, so he scraped it away with his fingernails.

The road was emerging from a marshy stretch that might be impassable in spring but was flat and hard at the moment. A forest of bony, leafless trees rose beyond, with hills rising behind them, and even taller hills—almost mountains—beyond that. It was a strange and terrifying landscape.

This wasn't the pastures and fields of England or France, with their neat stone walls and hedges, every inch measured and owned for centuries. This was wild, the realm of wolves and savages. Never tamed, never cleared, never manured. Never brought under the civilizing influence of plow or ax.

A few score miles deeper into New England and even the scattered roads and towns would disappear. What lay beyond these huddled communities clinging to the edge of a vast, impenetrable wilderness? Could be anything. For hundreds upon hundreds of miles. The very thought made James want to leap from the coach and run toward Boston.

Instead, as if the devil were whispering James's fears into Woory's ears, the driver cracked his whip and shouted for the horses to pick up the pace. The coach lurched forward, carrying them ever deeper into the interior of the continent.

James looked down at the first page of Prudence's account.

March, 1676

I lost track of the precise date as the tribe marched into the wilderness. Even to this day, my memories of those hungry, exhausting weeks of fleeing hither and yon remain muddled.

We walked and walked and walked. There was little rest, and less food. Soon I could scarcely feed my little one. My milk was drying. She cried most piteously, but there was nothing I could do to give her succor.

The war was lost for the tribes and they knew it. With every bit of news, the situation grew more desperate. The Narragansett were annihilated in the Great Swamp—the attack on Plymouth had failed. King Philip had attempted to enlist the Huron and Iroquois, but those powerful tribes rebuffed him. A French trapper came through and promised to take word to Quebec, but there was little hope that the French would intervene.

As we fled north, a Praying Indian caught up with us—a deserter from the English forces—to warn that Captain Knapp and two hundred men had marched from Springfield. The English had won a fierce battle with the Wampanoag, and now vowed to exterminate the Nipmuk.

Traveling with so many women, children, and elderly, it was clear that we would not outrun the English militia. One morning, as I lay weak, unable to feed my babe, Laka, the sachem's wife, entered. She offered me a corn meal porridge and a roasted thrush.

I devoured the food. It was scarcely a mouthful, but was the largest meal I'd eaten in several days. Laka watched me eat with a sharp expression. When I'd finished, she told me she had a message from her husband, and I understood why I'd been fed so well.

Captain Knapp and his men were scarcely five miles behind. Praying Indians from Natick were helping the English track us. They would catch us by nightfall.

My heart pounded. I was elated that my ordeal might be over, yet terrified that I might be killed by my captors. And afraid too, that Knapp would put these people to the sword. His reputation among the Nipmuk—even if half were true—had made me think of him as a demon of bloodshed and death.

But the sachem had an idea. He wanted me to return to the English and beg them for a parley. The Nipmuk wanted no more of the war. They would even quit New England. Only let them escape into the wilderness and they vowed to disappear forever.

Yet even after so many months, the Nipmuk did not trust me. Laka told me I must leave my precious Mary behind until my task was accomplished. If I betrayed them, my child would die.

Yes, I said—If it is the only way to end the war and save the lives of these people. I will do it.

James glanced back to the beginning. March 1676, scarcely nine months ago. He'd forgotten how recently Prudence had suffered at the hands of her captors. Instead, his thoughts had been on the earlier events at Winton, as Sir Benjamin was tortured and killed. But when that happened, Prudence's nightmare had just begun.

He better understood the terrible look that had swept over her face when she'd asked if he'd read her account.

"You suffered so terribly at their hands," James said. "Yet you were worried what would become of your tormentors. Why?"

Prudence was no longer studying him. Instead, she carried a worried expression. "Something is amiss."

The coach was moving too quickly, jouncing through ruts and over rocks. They'd traveled most of the night. Why the devil was Woory driving the horses so hard? They might hit a rut or a stone heaved up by the frost, and the carriage would be tossed from the road.

Another whip crack, then Woory's shouts. "Ha! Ha! Faster, you brutes!"

James opened the door and leaned out of the coach. The horses snorted and blew. Steam rose from their haunches. They stumbled with exhaustion, only minutes, it seemed, from collapse.

Woory leaned forward on the perch. He glanced over his shoulder at the road behind, even while rearing for another crack of the whip. James turned to look at the road behind, wondering what had the man so spooked. More wolves?

No.

It was half a dozen men on horse. They came riding two by two down the narrow strip of dirt and frozen mud that divided the forest. Trotting, not galloping, they were still a hundred yards back. Perhaps Woory knew something, but James didn't initially note a hostile intent. Rather, he saw a group of men on fresher horses, soon to overtake the coach, yes, but no threat.

Then James took a closer look. His heart leaped into his throat.

They wore scarves tied around their faces. Hoods drawn over their heads. Some men carried muskets laid across their saddles. Others held drawn swords. Their posture, tense and leaning forward in their saddles, spoke of violence.

CHAPTER TEN

James ducked back into the coach. He drew his pistols and tucked his dagger into his belt.

"What is it?" Prudence demanded.

"Armed riders. Six of them."

James checked the powder in the pans, to make sure the pistols were ready to fire.

"Reverend Stone must have sent them," she said. "Tell Master Woory to stop. I'll talk to them. They'll see I've come of my own free will."

"You're wrong. They're not here to bring you home. They're masked. Whatever it is, they don't want to be recognized."

Peter rubbed at the window on his side to clear it of frost, then cupped his hands and peered through. There was no door on his side. "I can't see behind us. Are they highwaymen?"

"Could be," James said. "I waved around plenty of silver in Boston. Word might have got out when I was hiring the coach that I carried a goodly sum."

"That's impossible," Prudence said.

"How so? There'd have been plenty of time to outfit riders and come after us."

"There are no highwaymen in New England. No thieves of any kind. We are a lawful, Godly people."

"A hungry man has no religion," James said. "Half the western settlements burned. There must be a thousand desperate men roaming about."

"I'm telling you—"

He cut her off. "Whatever it is, they won't find me easy prey. I mean to fight back."

She looked alarmed. "Against six men?"

"Six cowards and bullies. And you say they're not thieves. Fine, then they're murderers. If I surrender, they'll kill me anyway."

"There are no murderers in New England, either."

"Give them what they want," Peter said. "Whatever they ask, it isn't worth spending thy God-given life, my friend."

James said nothing to either of their ridiculous assertions. Instead, he went back to preparing himself for a fight. His heart pounded in his chest and he forced himself to remain calm. He had faced cutthroats and assassins before. Highwaymen among them.

The coach began to slow. Woory cracked his whip, but nothing he did could keep the team racing forward. They'd spent their strength. Two horses came by outside the door. More figures darkened the other side a moment later. The coach jerked to a halt.

"Stand and deliver!" a voice shouted.

Indeed, highwaymen.

Maybe Peter was right. James could turn over his purse while keeping the half crown and several shillings he'd sewn into the lining of his cloak. Enough money to hire a room in a tavern while he sent back to Boston with a letter of credit to raise more funds.

"What is this?" Woory cried. His voice was high and panicked.

"You heard me. Your goods, your arms, your money. Now."

"Wait, I know you. What are you doing here? Goodman Wal—"

A musket fired and cut him off. Woory cried out. Then someone jumped from a horse and grabbed for the coach door.

"Out, all of you!" a man boomed from outside.

James leaned back onto Prudence and drove open the door with his legs. The man on the other side fell backward. When James jumped out, the man was on the edge of the icy road, fighting to regain his balance.

The man held a sword in hand. His eyes were tired, bloodshot. His kerchief had slipped down, revealing thick, almost feminine lips that were red with cold. Stubble stood out on his cheeks. He looked well fed, not thin and desperate like other highway robbers James had faced in England and France.

The man pulled back his sword to take a swipe at James's head. But he was moving too slowly, and he'd need two steps to close with his weapon. James lifted one of the pistols, took steady aim at the man's face, and pulled the trigger.

The flint in the cock struck the frizzen, which sparked the powder in the pan. The muzzle of the gun discharged with a woof of fire and smoke. The man's head jerked back, and he fell with a scream. Blood sprayed across the snow. He lay writhing on the ground. James dropped the empty pistol and snatched the man's sword.

The sword in his right hand, the remaining pistol in his left, James whirled as a second man came up behind him on horse. The rider lifted a musket.

James dropped to the ground and rolled against the back wheel. Hooves pranced around him. The man tried to aim down at him, but there was little room for the horse to maneuver between the coach and the tree roots that snatched at the edge of the road. His gun went off, but the ball slammed into the ground almost a foot clear of James's head.

Unable to get a clean shot himself, James sprang back to his feet when the horse passed. He thrust with the sword. It pierced the man's cloak at his lower back. The man reached around for the blade with a cry as James pulled it free.

Conserving his second pistol, James slashed again with the sword, but this time the blade got caught in the man's cloak, then hooked under his belt. James jerked it free, cutting loose the man's powder horn. It fell, hit the ground, and spilled a fat black line of powder across the snow as the cap dislodged.

Meanwhile, the rider had recovered from the stab to his back. He fumbled for a pistol of his own, turning stiffly in the saddle as he tried to take aim.

James fled around the back of the coach before the man could bring it to bear. He came around the opposite side to discover three of the remaining highwaymen in front. Two had dismounted and stood over the prone, groaning form of Robert Woory. They thrust their sword tips into his belly.

The remaining man spotted James. He dropped the reins of his horse and lifted his musket.

But once again James had a chance to aim his pistol and take a calm, measured shot. He was farther away, so he aimed at the chest this time. The pistol kicked in his hand. The man fell from the saddle.

James had already dropped his discharged weapon and was charging at the two men standing over Woory. They came up with sword tips dripping blood. Woory was no longer moving. The villains had murdered him in cold blood. James brought the sword around from his shoulder to swing at the nearer of the two men.

The man lifted his sword and deflected the blow, but James had delivered it with such fury that it forced him to take two stumbled steps backward. James pressed his advantage. But his thrusts and stabs were parried aside. The second man circled and came charging in from James's left.

This man was all aggression and no skill. James turned the initial thrust and swung around with his blade as the man rumbled past. His sword caught the man at the neck, and he fell.

But now the first swordsman was after him again. He had much more skill, and it was all James could do to fight him off. The two men were soon circling each other, trading ineffectual blows.

James gave a frantic glance to his rear. He'd shot two men with his pistols and cut down a third. That left this man and two more riders. Where were they? That stab wound hadn't done enough to disable the first, and James hadn't seen the other man since his initial glance out of the coach. Both men should be coming around to ride him down.

"Friends!" a familiar voice cried from the other side of the carriage, the speaker concealed by the snorting team of horses.

It was Peter. He came around the front of the coach with his hands held out beseechingly. He took in the carnage and his face slackened with dismay.

Go back, you fool!

"There has been enough bloodshed," he said. "All of you, put down your weapons. Let us speak plainly one to another."

A rider came up behind Peter. It was the man James had stabbed in the back earlier. He held himself stiffly in the saddle but had otherwise recovered. His sword gleamed in the bright light of dawn, reflecting off snow. As he came up behind the Indian, he leaned out.

"Peter, look out!"

The Indian turned toward the rider, but he didn't cry out or throw himself clear. Instead, he stood in place while the man swept forward with his sword. It slashed him across the upper breast. Peter staggered but didn't fall. He bent over with a cry, clutching at the wound as the rider turned his horse to renew the attack.

James tried to fight his way toward his companion, but he was hard pressed by the swordsman still coming at him. His opponent was an older man, and beginning to tire, his initial advantage dissipating. Had it been the two of them, James was confident he could hold the man off indefinitely until exhaustion settled the fight in his favor.

If only Peter would have the sense to throw himself from the road before the rider could get turned around to finish the business. The horse was having a hard time getting its footing on the snow and ice.

But then came the second missing rider. He must have been lurking behind the coach, perhaps watching the road. He brought his sword down from the shoulder as he overtook Peter. It struck the Indian across the neck. Peter fell. When the rider rose in the saddle, blood drenched his blade.

No!

This brutal attack had taken no more than a few seconds, but by the time James turned back to face his attacker, the man was already climbing back into the saddle of his horse. Meanwhile, the other two remaining riders spotted James and yanked on the reins to come at him.

James tried to shield himself with the edge of the coach. He didn't stand a chance against three men on horse.

A pistol fired. The man who'd struck down Peter slumped in the saddle with a cry. His horse reared, snorting, and the man fell hard to the frozen ground. His horse galloped down the road without him.

What the devil?

Then James spotted Prudence standing calmly, holding James's pistols. Smoke leaked from the muzzle of the gun in her right hand. She dropped it and shifted over the second pistol.

The two surviving enemies exchanged a glance. Without a word they turned after the fleeing, riderless horse and galloped away.

CHAPTER ELEVEN

The instant the men turned to flee, Prudence's hand and wrist began to tremble violently, and she thought she would be sick. She dropped the gun. It was unloaded; she'd not had time to load them both. She doubled over, her head light, and her knees buckling.

James flinched when the second gun hit the ground, as if expecting it to go off, but he quickly came over to catch her arm and steady her. "Where are you injured?" Worry pinched his voice.

The sharp tang of black powder filled the air, and a cloud of smoke hung around her head. She stepped away, into cleaner air. When she did, she felt a little stronger.

"I'm unhurt. Pray, pardon me, I—"

But James was already releasing her and pulling away. He whirled about, his sword outstretched, as if searching for remaining enemies. The tip was slick and red.

There were none who could fight. Only men groaning in various states of death.

They might have won, but at a terrible cost. Woory lay dead in a bloody puddle, shot through the shoulder and then stabbed to death. So much blood—it was hard to believe it came from one man.

Peter lay curled on his side, gasping, clutching at his neck, which was streaming blood. A second deep wound cut across his chest. Prudence took the kerchief from one of the wounded enemies and pressed it to his neck. James sat behind Peter's shoulders and lifted his head.

Peter's eyes moved slowly to James's face. "I shall soon see my savior."

James gave a hard, visible swallow. "Thou art brave and strong, friend."

"Search for the inward light. Both of you. That is the way."

There was too much blood seeping through the kerchief and into Prudence's hands. Again, she felt lightheaded. The blood, the violence—suddenly she was back in Winton, on that awful day when the Indians overran the town. A child screaming, the smell of fire.

Not now. Please, not now.

With effort, she fought down her panic.

Peter's eyes rolled back in his head. His breathing turned shallow and rapid. "Mother, please. I am here," he muttered in his native tongue.

During the night, when he'd been struggling with his fever (or poison, as James claimed), he'd spoken in his sleep. It was nothing—something about digging for clams—but she'd been shocked by how well she'd understood. Not just Nipmuk, but the same dialect spoken by the tribe that had taken Prudence hostage.

"Peace, friend," Prudence told him in Nipmuk.

"Mother. Are you there?"

"What is he saying?" James asked.

"He is asking for his mother."

Peter shuddered and fell still. A final sigh leaked through his lips, and his body went limp. James set Peter's head down in the snow, then buried his face in his hands. She reached out a hand of comfort, but James seemed to regain mastery of his emotions before she could touch him, and he lifted his face from his hands.

"I don't even know if his mother is still alive," he said. "I know nothing of his family, of his tribe."

"You never spoke of such things?"

"He told me very little," James said. "I know little of his life before he came to England."

James got up to inspect their attackers, and she followed. She felt weak, the blood drained from her face, but refused to hide in the carriage while he sorted things out.

Of the four injured enemies, the first—the man with the face half-destroyed from James's initial shot—was also near death and wouldn't last more than another minute or two. The other three were in some stage of dying.

"We should try to get them help," she said. "These three, at least."

"Two of them won't live out the hour. This wretch," James said, pointing to the man Prudence had shot in the back, who was groaning piteously, "might survive, but you hit him right on the spine. If he does, he'll never walk again."

"We have to try."

"And this is the man who murdered Peter Church," he said. "I should put a ball in his head and count the world rid of another filthy vermin."

"And a court of law will see him hanged." She was surprised at the edge in her own voice. "Meanwhile, we'll do our Christian duty."

"All right. I suppose it would be better if he survived, anyway. Then I can question him."

James collected the horses of the fallen and roped them to the team before tying the bodies of the injured men onto the animals' backs. One man groaned, the other cried out in pain. The final man James wrapped in Peter's blankets and carried back to the coach. He put Peter's body in next to him.

James looked at Prudence and frowned. "I need to drive the team. I can't be back here with you."

"I want to sit up front, not back there."

"It's bitter cold."

"Better than sitting alone with a murderer." *And a dead man,* she thought, though this uncharitable thought filled her with shame. Poor Peter. To travel all the way across the ocean only to die almost the moment he reached his native soil.

While James checked the team of horses, Prudence climbed to the perch and drew her cloak against the cold. One of the men tied to the horses groaned. She pulled her hood closer around her face so she couldn't see him out of the corner of her eye.

Panic still swam below the surface like a monster of the deep, all teeth and grasping tentacles. Memories.

For a moment she was not here, she was *there.*

A woman screams while men cut her throat. An old man holds his granddaughter in his arms and runs. A gunshot puts him down, then men bash the infant with the butts of their muskets.

Prudence is running with her daughter in her arms. They see her, they are coming.

"Hold still, you," James said.

The words jolted Prudence from the horror of her memories. She drew back her hood to look. James stood over a groaning man tied to a horse. He pulled back the man's head.

"Leave him be!" she cried. "He's dying already."

James came up holding an empty vial, which he tucked back into a pocket in his cloak. The man was no longer struggling.

"I gave him a taste of soporific dwale."

"What is that?" she asked.

"Meant to render a man unconscious—a prisoner, or an enemy. In this case, 'twill ease the man's suffering. He'll die shortly, but I'd as soon not seem him die in agony."

"Pray, pardon me. For a moment I thought . . ."

When he climbed next to her on the perch, James brought a cloak bundled with goods pilfered from their attackers. It took some coaxing of the horses before they were traveling back down the highway and leaving behind the scene of the violence.

"The second gun was unloaded," James said. "You were bluffing."

"Aye. I'd not time to load it, but thought it might still serve a purpose."

"When did you reload the first pistol?"

"The attackers paid me no mind—their attention was fixed elsewhere. I saw the spilled powder horn and it gave me the idea. I searched the man you'd killed and found a pouch with lead balls."

"Resourceful."

"It isn't the first time I've handled arms."

"Reload the guns." He gestured to the bundle at his feet. "Do it now, before your hands get too numb."

She opened up the bundle, but found only a little canister with powder for priming the pan, not a full powder horn. No balls, either. Only small paper-wrapped packages.

"What's this?" she asked, picking up one of the packages. "Cartridges? How do I—"

"Ah, yes. It's so I can measure precisely. Thirty-five grains of powder. Bite off the end, pour the powder and ball down, then use the paper as a wad at the end when you ram it. Then prime the pan like you would otherwise. Understand?"

"I see, yes."

He watched as she bit off the end of the paper. A bit of the powder got in her mouth, bitter and peppery, and she couldn't help but turn and spit it out at once.

"Pardon!" Prudence said, aghast that he'd seen her spit.

"How dainty." He grinned. "Good, now the other one. Tap the cartridge this time to get the powder to the bottom before you bite."

When she finished, he reached back to the roof of the carriage and scraped off a bit of snow, which he used to wipe at the corner of her mouth where she'd stained it with black powder. She returned the favor, using a handful of snow to scrub at the dried blood from when he'd buried his face in his hands after Peter's death.

"Do you know any of the dead men?" James asked as they continued down the road.

"The one I shot in the back is William Webb, from Andover. He has a wife and children. I don't know how he fell in with such bad characters."

"And the other three?"

"I don't know any of them," she said. "One of them might be from Springfield—he looks familiar. I'm not certain, though."

"Woory started to identify another man. I think that's why they shot him. Goodman Wal—something or other."

Prudence thought about it. "I know a man named Waltham. Another named Walker. They're both from Boston, and Woory might have known them."

"A man whose business is coach and transport knows men from all over," James said. "Even murderers posing as thieves."

"Then you don't think they're highwaymen?"

"No. Do you?"

"I don't know. I have never heard of such an attack. Maybe in New York, but this is New England. But they did command Woory to stand and deliver. He didn't obey—he recognized them. So they killed him."

"Except Peter didn't recognize them, wasn't in any way a threat, and they killed him too," James said. "They would have killed me too. Perhaps even you."

"Once men start killing they don't know when to stop."

He studied her face, and she turned away, uncomfortable under his sharp gaze. "If there's one thing I know," she said, "it's that my sister's husband didn't send them."

"You might know that, but I don't."

"He's not a murderer, James. You must believe me."

"Perhaps." He looked thoughtful. "Here's what I do know. They came for killing, not robbery. I've faced robbers before. They are almost always in ones and twos. Nervous young men with shaking hands, as often as not. They aren't older, well fed, with families. And they don't typically come six at a time.

"And here's another thing," he added. "That last swordsman could have bested me. He didn't. Why?"

Prudence finished loading the last gun, drew her cloak tighter, and put her hands between her thighs to thaw them.

"Maybe he couldn't," she said. "You looked to be holding your own to me."

"When you saw me, yes. He was older than me, and tiring. But that man was a better swordsman than I. Early in the fight, he could have killed me. I'm sure of it."

"I thought you said they would have killed us all. Anyway," she added, "they killed poor Peter without a second thought."

"That might be it exactly."

"I don't understand."

"Their stratagem might have been to lure us out, meaning only to kill Peter," James said. "Then Woory recognized one man, so they killed him too. I fought back. Some of the men tried to kill me, others kept their heads. Dangerous to kill an agent of the king. But an Indian . . ." James raised an eyebrow.

She understood. "If an Indian dies on the road, it draws scarcely more attention than when he dies of disease."

"Or dies from poison made to look like disease." He turned this over. "Yes, you're right. Indians die in New England all the time. Nobody cares except other Indians."

"I care," Prudence protested.

"And so do I. Peter was an odd fellow, a honking goose in the chicken coop, if you will. I can't say we were ever friends—except maybe in the Quaker use of the word—but I'd developed a soft spot for him. And he may not have been an agent of the Crown, but he was *my* agent. Attack my man and I get very angry."

They weren't just words; James looked truly upset. And she had seen real pain in his eyes during Peter's last struggles for breath. She was beginning to rethink her assessment of this man as nothing more than a cunning spy for King Charles. That gave her hope for finding her daughter.

"You can kill an Indian on the road and nobody notices," she said. "And maybe a driver can fall and nothing much happens." Prudence chose her next words carefully. How to make James see what she needed him to see? "But after what happened to my husband, anyone can see what happens when an agent of the Crown dies in New England."

He gave her a sidelong glance. "And what is that?"

"Another agent arrives. And he wants to know what happened to the first. At least that's what happens the first time. Maybe you can tell me what happens when *two* different agents die in suspicious circumstances."

"Prudence Cotton, you are much smarter than I gave you credit for."

"Why do I think that by 'smart,' you really mean 'devious'?"

James laughed, and she smiled back.

The coach entered a clearing of several hundred acres where slumping walls of fieldstone divided a pair of farms. Both houses had been reduced to piles of rubble almost entirely covered in snow. A double hill rose behind them.

"That's what they call Camel Hill," she said. "A few more miles and we'll reach the town of Sudbury."

"Where we may very well find those men waiting for us. They might have fetched reinforcements."

"There's a fork in another mile or two, where the Connecticut Path cuts southwest. It's an old Indian trail that Thomas Hooker expanded when he led the settlers to Hartford. If we take it, we can go through Natick."

"That sounds like an Indian village," James said.

"Praying Indians, yes. But abandoned. The General Court shipped them to Deer Island last winter." She frowned. "Most of them died of hunger and disease, from what I understand. The rest haven't returned."

"And if we go that way, what do we find after Natick?"

"Next is Danforth's Farms—it's a small settlement next to the Connecticut Path." She hesitated. "You don't suppose they'd search for us in that direction, do you?"

"They might," he said. "But I'll still take my chances off the main highway."

When they reached the fork in the road and found it deserted, she put a hand on his wrist. "Now stop the coach and let me drive." When he seemed reluctant, she added, "That way you can be ready with the guns."

Minutes later, when they'd swapped positions and he had his pistols across his lap, she turned to him with a sweet smile. "Oh, and this will give you plenty of time to read my story while I watch the road."

To his credit, this time he did not look nearly so skeptical when he took out the pages and began to read.

Chapter Twelve

They traveled in silence while Prudence drove the team and James read. He finished quickly, then hushed her questions and reread it, this time more slowly. She could barely stand the wait.

A frozen brook lay to their right, marked with solitary boulders that broke the surface. The land on that side of the coach had been cleared for pastures and farms all the way to the opposite hills, while the forest still crowded the road to their left.

Here and there stood farmhouses, some burned, but others intact, smoke curling from their chimneys. A woman stepped out of a house set a hundred yards or so from the road. She shielded her eyes against the sun to study them as they passed.

They were only around the next bend when a woodcutter emerged from the forest leading a mule. The mule pulled a sleigh loaded with lumber. The man waved for their attention, no doubt hoping for news, but they didn't want to get close enough for him to see the extra horses and the bodies draped across their backs.

James put away Prudence's narrative and scanned their surroundings.

"Well?" she asked.

"We're close, aren't we?"

"Yes, about two miles to Danforth's Farms. Maybe three. But what about my story? Do you understand now?"

He continued to ignore her questions and instead pointed. "See that burned house? If we pulled the coach around the back, do you think it would be hidden from the road?"

"I suppose, but—"

"Do that, first. I need time to think."

Fighting her impatience, Prudence took the coach across the hard, flat surface and around the house in question. The front wall had collapsed, but the back stood, held up in part by a brick chimney and its stone hearth. It must have been a year since it was burned, but nobody had touched the farmhouse since—not even, it would seem, to pick through the rubble. There were clothing, old chests, even iron kettles and ladles hanging from hooks on the mantle above the hearth.

When they were hidden around the back, they climbed down from the perch to check the injured men. Perhaps two hours had passed since the brutal encounter on the road. Prudence's nerves could stay jangled only so long, and she now felt more exhausted than anything. The poor night of sleep hadn't helped any. Also, it must be noon, and she hadn't eaten for twenty-four hours.

The first of the two injured men was dead, as they'd expected. They couldn't tell with the second. He hadn't stiffened, and he still felt warm to the touch beneath the blanket, but he wasn't moving, and they couldn't feel any breath with their numb fingers.

"Nothing to be done for it," James said. "If he's not gone already, he will be soon, and it makes matters simpler for us."

He didn't sound smug about it, but it was calculating enough that Prudence winced at the implications. "We should carry him with us, just in case."

"We'll never save his life."

"That's in God's hands, not ours."

"He stays." His voice hardened. "No surgeon in the world could close up that wound. He's lost too much blood already."

She clenched her hands. "Very well."

James's expression softened, and he turned to untying the man's body. "We'll put them both in the coach with the others to keep the wolves off them until something can be done."

She helped him carry the bodies to the coach, where they draped them across Peter and the final dead highwayman. It was a horrible mess, and again it brought her back to the war, to stacking bodies. First at Winton, then among the Nipmuk in her captivity, when children, the elderly, and the ill would fall by the roadside during the long forced marches.

The effort got her sluggish blood flowing again. The sun helped too. It was low in the sky, its light lacking the heat of gentler months, but it warmed her dark cloak and her body with it. When they'd finished unharnessing the horses from the team, her appetite was roaring. The perch box carried Woory's breakfast: a hard block of cheese, a flask of buttermilk, and two boiled eggs still in their shells. James and Prudence shared the food.

James stepped into the ruins and kicked aside snow. He found a fallen wardrobe and tossed open the doors.

"Don't do that," she said sharply.

"Why not? They won't be missing it." He came up with a pair of gloves, a couple of linen shirts, and several pairs of socks. "Most of my possessions are back at your house. I couldn't very well haul out my sea chests without arousing suspicion. Why don't you see what you can find? There must have been a woman of the house as well."

"I couldn't possibly."

"'Twill be less suspicious than riding into Danforth's Farms without any possessions. You do want to find your daughter, don't you?"

"Does that mean—?"

"Will you hurry?"

"But James, it's stealing."

"It's not theft—these people are dead. And we're exposed out here. We don't have time. So quit gnawing at it."

Reluctantly, she searched the ruins. She found a smock, two petticoats, a stay reinforced with rows of stitching that had been made for a woman with a figure similar to her own, and a green linen apron to wear over her petticoats. These she bundled and tied to the back of one of the horses. There was a pair of women's boots of close to the right size, and she happily shed her wooden clogs and put them on. Searching through a broken chest, she found blank papers, ink, a pen, and blotter that had been protected from the elements wrapped in an oiled cloth. This cheered her.

"What do you need with that?" James asked.

"If there's one thing I wished I'd had in captivity, it was pen and paper. I never knew if I'd be able to write my narrative or if my story would die with me."

"Thankfully, it didn't."

"Now I'm in another fight for my life. I don't want to die without telling people what happened."

"Put that out of your head," James said firmly. "You're not going to die."

⚸

Later, sitting on the perch of the carriage, out of sight of the road, Prudence tried again. "You read the missing chapter. Tell me what you think."

"I think it reads like the imagination of a terrified woman who has lost her child, was kidnapped by savages, and misremembers key details. It doesn't make sense."

"You sound like my sister and the reverend," Prudence said bitterly. "And the printer in Boston too. He said the same thing."

James reached for her wrist as she turned. "Steady. I said that's what it reads like. Taken in isolation."

"What do you mean, isolation?"

"I read the rest of the book too. You have a clear eye for details, a sober way of reflecting. You were even sympathetic toward the men who had taken you captive."

"Some say I was *too* sympathetic."

"I've spent the last two months in close company with a Quaker Indian. In many ways he was a fool, hopelessly swept away in his religion. It got him killed in the end. Begging murderers to set down their arms instead of defending himself." James shook his head. "But he was a fool in the same manner as any other man. Not a barbarian or a savage. So when I read an account that paints both sides as saints and sinners, clever one moment and stupid the next, kind to this person and brutal to that one, it makes the account *more* credible, not less."

"Then you *do* believe me."

"I don't disbelieve you—we'll leave it there." He blew into his palms, then opened his overcoat and tucked his hands under his armpits. "You left your daughter with the Nipmuk. They promised to kill her if you didn't return. You didn't. So why isn't the child dead?"

"Squa Laka wanted me to believe it. She tied a cord around Mary's neck and drew it tight." Prudence dug her nails into her palms to block the images. "She tightened the cord until the babe could scarcely manage a whimper. 'If you don't return,' she said, 'I'll draw it tight like this, until she dies.' Laka was angry, frightened, it is true. But I do not think she had it in her to murder a child."

James considered this. "It does sound like Laka saved you from the Nipmuk men."

"She certainly did, yes. Some of them wanted to kill me. They were young and hot, and they believed they were going to die anyway. Why not kill as many English as they could before they fell? In a way they were right, in the end. The English put them all to death."

"You don't name the young English officer. It was Samuel Knapp, wasn't it?"

"Why would you say that?" she asked, surprised.

James took out the pages. "In the meeting where you translated, the sachem's wife looked down on him, so he must have been short. If I remember right, you said earlier that Laka was about your height. You are five feet six, more or less."

"Yes, more or less."

He nodded. "So if you were looking down on a man, he would have to be at least two inches shorter than you. That would put him at five feet four, which is roughly Knapp's height."

She marveled. "That's right."

"Why didn't you name him?"

"I knew there would be no point. Reverend Stone would neither believe it nor let it see print. He holds Knapp in great esteem. He's even hinted that I should marry him, if Knapp would have me. Not that I'd be such a fool."

"No, I would say not. He sounds like a brute, and all too bloodthirsty."

"Those traits stood Knapp in good stead during the recent troubles. 'Tis not so easy to condemn a man for killing Indians in wartime. Such a man is hailed as a hero."

James thumbed through the pages. "How confident are you of your translation of the Nipmuk parley?"

"Very. I spoke the language well by that time."

"So the sachem asks if the English have had enough killing, and Knapp says God will decide. Then the sachem asks if they will kill women and children. Knapp says yes, they will kill every man, woman, and child if the Indians don't surrender. But of course surrender means enslavement in the Indies. The Nipmuk know this by now."

"That's when I should have changed the translation from Nipmuk to English," she said. "I wasn't thinking quickly enough." She shook her head slowly, darkening. "That failure haunts me."

"How do you mean?"

"The very words of the sachem were, 'We killed Sir Benjamin. He begged us for mercy, but we showed him none. We shall kill you too, and all your men and horses. And this woman, and this woman's child. Then we shall kill every English in the land, drive them into the sea.'"

"I don't understand that part," James said. "The war was lost for them. Once they could no longer flee, they had no hope but surrender, slavery or no. So how would it help to taunt Knapp?"

"That's what I mean. The sachem wasn't taunting, he was negotiating. That's their manner—it was a figure of speech. Knapp didn't seem to know—or pretended not to know—what the sachem meant."

James looked confused. "I am uncertain myself."

She turned it over, struggling to take the meaning in Nipmuk and translate it into English. Not only the meaning of the words themselves, but the very Nipmuk way of thinking. It was like taking water and explaining ice to one who has never been cold.

"The sachem was asking the limits of the English warfare. 'Haven't you had enough killing? Has not the time come to make peace?' But Knapp said no, we'll keep killing until God tells us to stop. Then the sachem asked that if the fight continues, will the English at least spare the women and children? Knapp said no, we'll kill everyone. Then the Nipmuk said, if you do that, we'll kill this woman and her child, because they are in our power already. Then we'll try to kill you and your men, and if that continues, we'll fight until we've exterminated you or you have exterminated us. If you insist on a war of extermination, then we will make your cost very high."

"A shame that Knapp did not understand," James said.

"Or perhaps he did. He was not ignorant of the Nipmuk ways. Perhaps he refused a negotiated peace because he was well inclined to slaughter them all."

She hadn't thought it so at the time. She had thought Knapp confused and afraid. But in the months that had passed since Crow Hollow, she had considered Knapp's bloodthirsty nature at great length.

James frowned and chewed on his lip. He glanced down at the pages. "You say there was a massacre, that the English behaved treacherously. Yet details are scant."

Prudence's stomach tightened. "Yes."

"Tell me."

She closed her eyes, fought down the panic.

A crow. An eyeball in its beak.

The flocks of crows had been gathering all afternoon as the Nipmuk waited for the English to arrive. She took this as an evil omen, but the Nipmuk, who wore crow feathers in their hair, were not disturbed. Laka said the birds flocked to this hollow in the evenings so they could huddle together against their ancient enemy: the great horned owls who hunted them on the darkest nights. But later, when the crows fell cawing from the trees to feast upon the dead and the dying, Prudence thought that Laka had been wrong. The crows must have known, must have sensed the evil that would befall the Nipmuk, as if the devil himself had whispered it in their ears.

"Prudence?" James said, his tone concerned.

She opened her eyes. "I don't think I can continue. Pray, forgive me, James."

He placed a hand on her wrist. "Faith, I know you can."

Prudence swallowed hard. "May God grant me strength."

She imagined that she was relaying a tale told her by another, not something she had endured herself. After a moment, her heart slowed its anxious pounding.

"We were unarmed. The Nipmuk, I mean. They had no weapons. The sachem didn't know that the English wouldn't follow the rules of parley that both sides had kept throughout the war. The war was won for the English. They no longer needed to.

"Knapp was furious the sachem wouldn't submit," she continued. "Both sides had put down their weapons for the parley, but Knapp lifted his hand and a dozen men with swords came rushing out of the woods. The Indians had watchers to guard against treachery, but they were fewer in number, plus thin and weak from weeks of forced march."

Again, she had to stop as the memories came boiling to the surface. This time James remained quiet until she had recovered.

"Crow Hollow has no outlet, and soon Knapp had the Nipmuk backed against the hill. There were eleven Indian warriors, including the sachem and two of his sons. A few tried to fight, but most threw themselves to the ground and begged for mercy." Prudence swallowed hard. She could taste bile. "Knapp showed none."

"The sachem's wife must have escaped." James thumbed through the pages. "You mention her again when you lied to Knapp at the village."

"Aye, Laka slipped away while the English were giving battle to the warriors. Knapp raged when he discovered she had escaped. They tracked her to the village. That was no battle, either.

"The sachem was dead, and most of his warriors as well. I screamed at the English to stop, cried for the Nipmuk to run, to save themselves. There was little resistance. Old women were shot in the back. Young children had their heads bashed in. Before that, I'd never seen anything as cruel and brutal as the Indian attack on Winton, or the way they'd tortured the surviving men. But this was worse."

"Yet they call themselves Christians," James said.

"There are no Christians in war." Prudence blurted the words before she could reconsider. Horrified, she put her hand over her mouth. "Pray, pardon me. I shouldn't have said that."

"Go on."

"I was so weak and sick that I could scarcely stand as they laid out the bodies of the dead and made me look at them. Knapp was looking for Laka—he had stood beside her in Crow Hollow, but could not identify her now. That's because she wasn't there."

"And that's when you spoke false?" James asked.

Prudence felt the memories pressing in again. The horror of staring at those bodies, looking through them, terrified that she would see her daughter among the dead. She had swooned, and Knapp ordered her dragged to her feet. Then someone cried they had found Laka.

One of the Indian traitors, a Praying Indian, had identified a woman as the sachem's wife, but it wasn't Squa Laka, it was her sister. Prudence didn't correct his mistake.

"There had been ninety-seven of us in the band. There were only eighty-four bodies here and in the hollow. Thirteen had escaped. One was Squa Laka and one was my daughter."

"But it says here that you told Knapp they'd killed every Indian. And you also told him your daughter had died three weeks earlier and the Indians had let you bury her."

"I spoke false. I couldn't bear any more killing."

"But your daughter, wouldn't you want the English to search for her?"

Prudence shook her head, anguished, unsure how to explain. Her thoughts had been so fevered. She had been so afraid.

"Please, I'm trying to understand."

"Can't you see? The only hope for my daughter was that the remaining Nipmuk escape—if not, I was convinced the Indians would kill her before they fell. It is their way with prisoners. So

I lied. How I wrote it here is how it really happened. You must believe me."

He studied her face. "Are you all right? You look ill."

"I can't let it go. I feel as though I'm still there. A sound, a smell will spark my memories, like fire on dry tinder. Then suddenly I'm back in Winton. People burning in their homes. Women, children, screaming. The Indians have tied my husband up and are cutting off his fingers, his nose, his ears, while he screams for help—"

"Good Lord," James said.

"And the massacre . . . the crows."

"The crows?"

"They came down from the trees . . ." She couldn't finish, could scarcely breathe, could only bury her face in her hands.

"Prudie," he said, gently taking her hands down from her face. "You are strong enough to finish it."

He'd called her Prudie. That was more intimate even than her Christian name. She was so shaken that she almost fell against his shoulder and asked him to hold her. She struggled to regain her composure.

"The crows were eating the dead," she said. "I can see them, hear their calls, the tearing sound of beaks ripping at flesh. It seems so real, it's as if I'm still there. Even the smell of blood. I can scarcely explain, but it is real."

"I've heard of this before," James said. "Men who have survived bombardment in a castle, or lived through a horrific battle. Sometimes they can't escape their memories. It's a living nightmare."

"Early on, I'd wake at night, screaming, drenched in sweat. My sister thought I was possessed of an evil spirit, or under the spell of a witch. Only I wasn't, it was the war. Later, when I wrote my account, Anne wouldn't believe me when I said my daughter was still alive. She thought it was my fevered imagination. She spoke to the reverend, the printer. They stripped it from my account before publication."

James looked thoughtfully at the pages in his hand. "Who else has read this?"

"Only my sister and her husband, plus the printer when I tried to get him to include it anyway. And now you."

"You didn't show it to Knapp?"

"Bless me, no! I detest the man—I'd as soon never speak to him again in my life. Why?"

"I have an idea. Or the beginnings of one."

"Tell me," she urged.

"Let's get these horses back on the road. I don't want to stop in Danforth's Farms. It's too close. What's the next town?"

"If we cut back toward the highway, Marlborough. It's another five miles, more or less. There's an inn."

"Good. We'll stay there."

They left the coach itself hidden behind the ruins of the farmhouse. James and Prudence rode two of the highwaymen's horses and led the last, together with Robert Woory's team, who seemed relieved to be free of the burden they'd dragged all night and half the morning.

Prudence didn't have a pair of stirrup stockings to cover her to her waist, as proper women wore when they rode. The pistol tucked into her apron made her feel even less ladylike.

She rode next to James, wondering how long she could wait before pushing him about her daughter. He seemed lost in his own thoughts, his brow furrowed, his gaze distant.

His suspicions had fallen on Samuel Knapp, that much was certain.

CHAPTER THIRTEEN

Not long after they had set out again, James cast a glance at Prudence. She met his gaze eagerly, clearly bursting with questions. Within five minutes of regaining the highway, he was ready to share his conclusions, but instead he made her wait. He was enjoying watching her squirm with curiosity, and he wanted to think about *her* for a moment, if for no other reason than to get his mind off the murder of Peter Church.

Prudence Cotton was becoming one of the most interesting women he'd ever known. She had a sharp mind and a flare of independence. And determined as the devil himself. She'd forced her way into the coach, helped him bluff his way past the gates in Boston, and then calmly shot a man in the back.

Yet at the same time she was sensitive and vulnerable. When telling about Crow Hollow, she'd been on the verge of tears most of the way through.

Be easy on her. You only know the half of what she's suffered.

That wasn't the point. The point was that the pain and need in her eyes made him want to take her in his arms. Comfort her. And yes, if he were to admit to his less-than-noble desires—call them lusts, to be absolutely clear—he wanted to do more than comfort.

He wanted to release her raven hair from that silly head rail, wanted to free her breasts from her waistcoat and stay, wanted to get her out of her apron and petticoats. Well, maybe when they got somewhere warm.

"I can't stand it anymore," Prudence blurted. "What are you thinking about? You have to tell me."

"I'm thinking about what you said," he lied. "About speaking Nipmuk. Who else knows?"

She looked confused. "Everybody. It's in the book."

"Aye, but in a subtle way. I'd been under the impression you spoke a few words, maybe a phrase or two. It's only clear in the missing chapter that you can understand actual conversations."

"I don't talk much about the language. Every town, every congregation, has people who lost family. When people question me, it's only to confirm their own beliefs about the war."

"What does that have to do with speaking Nipmuk?"

"You don't learn a foreign tongue from a jailer," she said. "You learn it through long, struggled conversations. A mutual attempt to understand. You learn it from a friend."

"I see. And that proves your sympathy with the savages."

"I should not have prevaricated, I should have stated the matter baldly. Indicted Captain Knapp for his brutality, whether the charge be believed or no. He was offered peace, but chose cold-blooded murder instead. The world needs to see that."

"So how many know the extent of your Nipmuk?" James asked. "Only the ones who've read this chapter?"

"The same. Anne, her husband, the printer. So what is it, what are you thinking? Tell me."

"I start with the assumption that the highwaymen intended to murder Peter Church all along. Maybe they'd have killed the two of us too—they shot Woory casually enough—but Peter was their real target. Maybe it was revenge for disrupting services yesterday, or maybe the conspirators hate all Indians and wanted to kill him for that."

"Except if you were right about the other thing—that they were already poisoning him from the first night you arrived—it couldn't have been about Sunday services."

"Exactly," he said, pleased at how her mind worked. "And they continued poisoning him up to the moment we left. To make it look like actual disease. It was planned all along."

"Only he left before they could finish him," Prudence said. "That's why they sent men to attack us on the road."

"Keep going," he urged. "Why am I asking about the language?"

Her face lit up. "Because Peter spoke Nipmuk. Maybe that's why they wanted to kill him in the first place." She grew even more animated. "There must be something they don't want you to find out from the Nipmuk. Something about what happened to my husband or my daughter. But *I* speak it. I can go with you and translate!"

He smiled at her enthusiasm. "All we have to do is track the Indians into the wilderness and hope they don't kill us."

"I can do that. I can help."

James scanned the road ahead. The farms were growing thicker, and people were out in some of them, feeding livestock or carrying milk from barns. People eyed them, but as of yet nobody came running to the road to question them or ask them for news or mail.

"We must be close to Danforth's Farms," he said. "Time to concoct a story."

"Oh, yes. What should we say?"

"I'll be fine, it's you I'm worried about. Keep your face bundled against the cold. That will keep anyone from recognizing you. If we're challenged, you're my wife."

"Your wife! I could never say that."

"Fine, then you're my lover from the city. You've run away from your husband with a handsome young stranger."

"James!" She sighed. "All right, I'll be your wife."

"Thank you, my dear, I'd be honored. Where is your father? I should ask his permission. Then the church should publish the banns. That way you can be assured I'm not already married."

"You're not, are you?" she asked.

"What does it matter, if it's only playacting?" He smiled at the worried look on her face. "I'm not married. Yet."

"Oh, you're terrible." She looked like she was trying, but not quite succeeding, to look offended. "Anyway, magistrates marry us in New England, not the church. Marriage rites are not biblical."

"Is that what they claim around here? You people have some odd customs."

"How do we explain the horses?" she asked.

"We'll say we're from Winton—we're trying to rebuild. We bought goods in Boston, including these animals to help on the farm."

"These aren't draft horses," she said.

"Did I say farm? I meant for the coach service I'm hoping to establish."

"Better."

Their discussion was fortuitously timed. They came over the next rise and into Danforth's Farms a few minutes later. A wooden palisade cut across fields and cleared forest to enclose an area that was roughly half a mile square. The gates were open and nobody manned the watchtower.

Inside the gates they found a tidy village of thirty or forty houses wrapped around a commons. The snow had grown thicker the farther inland they traveled, and here it was a fluffy blanket two or three feet thick across the commons and atop the roofs.

A box-like meetinghouse with a squat steeple marked the near side of the commons, its outer wall abutting the road. Snarling, grimacing wolf heads had been nailed to the meetinghouse above the reach of dogs, with names scrawled right on the building to indicate the men who'd claimed the bounties.

A cold, miserable-looking fellow sat at the stocks in front of the meetinghouse, his hands, head, and feet sticking out the holes. He strained to turn his head as James and Prudence rode past.

"What cheer, good folk," he offered in greeting. "Any news from Boston?"

"Governor Leverett traveled to Hartford to negotiate the border with Connecticut," Prudence said.

"I heard that already. Anything else? Pray, slow down."

They slowed the horses. "A French fleet was spotted off Nantucket," Prudence said. "Five ships of the line."

"Oh, that's something new. Thank you, Goodwife. And a good day to you, sir."

There were others about, watching curiously from their stoops, and James didn't want to appear unsociable and thereby make himself look suspicious. He turned in the saddle as they passed the man.

"What of the weather?" James asked. "Think these clouds will bring snow?"

The man turned his eyes skyward. "Could be. Hard to tell from not knowing."

"What was that supposed to mean?" James asked Prudence when they'd left the man behind and trotted alongside the commons.

"That's what passes for Puritan wisdom in these parts. You know, like 'a hot iron pierces sooner than a cold one.'"

"That sounds painful," he said. "Anyway, I suppose it's best not to predict the weather in these parts. If you guess wrong, they throw you in the pillories."

"And guessing *right* gets you accused of witchcraft. Only the devil knows the weather."

If she hadn't raised an eyebrow, he'd have thought her serious. Others hailed them as the Connecticut Path left the commons and divided two rows of houses on its way out of town. Prudence did most of the talking, greeting people and asking if the road ahead had been cleared of snow. It had until Marlborough. After that, no. Not until it connected with the highway outside Springfield.

She stopped to chat with one woman for a few minutes, even asked if any riders had come through earlier that day, because they'd found a hat someone had dropped on the road. No, nobody had entered or left the village all day. They were the first outsiders since before the Sabbath.

"I didn't recognize any of those people," Prudence said when they'd regained the open country. "So I figured there was no harm in asking."

"You'd make a good spy."

"Is that your way of telling me again what a good liar I am?"

"There's a difference between lying for gain or to cause harm, and lying for duty or honest purpose."

"Lying for honest purpose. Clever wording."

"But it's not just that," he said. "You carry yourself well, you keep your wits in a scrape. A clever woman makes a good spy if for no other reason than men discount her. Men like to impress a woman, so they'll blather and boast."

"Are there many female spies?"

He thought about the few he'd known. "Not nearly as many as you'd expect."

"Women have more scruples," she said. "We are reluctant to give them up."

James chuckled at this. "No, I wouldn't say that."

"Well, I happen to like mine," she said firmly, "and have no intention of surrendering them."

"You'd better get over some of them in a hurry. As soon as we arrive in Marlborough, I'm going to find us a room in the inn. That means more lying about being my wife."

She fixed him with a horrified look. "The roads are quiet—there will be more than one room at the inn, surely."

"For a husband and wife traveling together? 'Twould raise less suspicion to ask separate quarters for one's dog."

"But I . . . we can't . . ."

"I'm not going to attack your virtue," he said. "So put that out of your mind. Or are you worried about what people will think?"

"As a matter of fact, I am. People may not know me by appearance out here, but everyone has heard of me. When this all gets out—and it will, you know it will—every detail of our journey together will be known. Including the part where I spent a night at an inn with a strange man from England. Meanwhile, you'll skip your way back to London to give your report, and if any of your friends hear what happened, they'll grin, you'll wink, and they'll slap you on the back."

"You must take me for a complete scoundrel."

"I haven't decided yet."

"I'm not the winking sort."

"I hope not, James. But I reserve judgment."

He grunted at this. Nevertheless, she was probably right about what people would say. "I'm sorry, there's no way around it. You might face some humiliation."

"Humiliation is only one of my worries. They hang adulterers in New England."

"Then I'll take you back to England if that's what it takes to keep you safe. Good Lord, woman, do you want to help your daughter or not?"

"Of course I'll do it for my daughter. Is that what you're promising?"

He stopped and turned in the saddle. "Ah, you're clever."

"Clever enough. Peter is dead because of you. Goodman Woory too. I don't mean to join them."

"I didn't kill those men."

"But they're dead because of . . . whatever it is you're doing out here. Which is what, exactly?"

"To find out what happened to Sir Benjamin."

"So you say."

She was getting uncomfortably close to the truth. "I won't sacrifice you to my cause, if that's what you're driving at. Whatever kind of scoundrel I am, it's not that."

"Do you swear it?"

"Did I play the coward when those men attacked us on the road?"

"Nay, you fought like a lion." She nodded. "So you'll swear it?"

"I swear I will do everything in my power to keep you from harm."

"Everything?"

"Everything reasonable—there are murderers after us, after all." She still didn't look satisfied, so he added, "I swear that I will not lay hands on you, so help me God, even if we have to spend the night in the same bed."

"Heaven forbid." She nodded. "And my daughter. You will help her. Swear it."

"Now that's going too far. What are you giving me in return?"

"What do you want?"

"I want you to translate. I want you to lie when necessary. When the time comes, you will testify against Knapp, Fitz-Simmons, Reverend Stone—anyone who might be implicated in the murder of Peter Church and Robert Woory and any other crimes we uncover."

"I would testify against my own sister if she were guilty of murder."

"Then I'll swear to help you find your daughter."

James met Prudence's gaze. For a long moment they stared into each other's eyes. At last he looked away to keep an eye on the road, but still he felt her watching him. Probing, testing. Looking for some sign that he was lying or trying to deceive her in some way.

He wasn't, he was absolutely sincere, and it was a good thing too. Something inside his head was ringing, warning him. Every bit of experience James had ever had in life told him that crossing this woman would be dangerous.

Whatever had kept her docile and compliant while living under the roof of her sister and the reverend was gone now.

Chapter Fourteen

Prudence started to grow nervous by the time they rode into Marlborough in the early afternoon. Now that her bravado was fading, she found herself thinking of spending the night in the same room as this restless, aggressive man. And most likely the same bed too. Heaven help her.

It would have been much easier to share a bed with Peter Church. A Quaker and well into middle age, she wouldn't have worried about him groping her with lusty hands in the middle of the night. Not that she truly thought James would try anything, but she doubted she'd be able to sleep for the worry of it.

At first glance, Marlborough didn't seem much different from Danforth's Farms, maybe slightly larger and more compact. There was an inn and tavern, together with a blacksmith shop in the middle of town. A mill sat by the brook, with the millrace clogged with ice and a waterfall of icicles flowing from the spokes of the mill wheel.

The palisade that shielded the town was charred here and there, and the houses inside the gates had also burned to the ground. The Indians must have forced their way in during one of their raids.

The inn was a tidy place called The Golden Lion, with a red sign and a yellow lion rampant. James asked for a room under the name of James Smith. There was one available. It had a single, not-very-large bed. But when James glanced at Prudence with a question in his eyes, she nodded and said it would do. James told the innkeeper it would be acceptable.

The price seemed outlandish, but James paid without haggling. Then, when the innkeeper asked for an extra shilling to pay for the feeding and care of so many horses, he paid that too, and without complaint. Maybe he was as relieved as she that the keeper addressed her as Goodwife Smith.

Then again, money didn't seem to be an issue. At supper, James paid ten pence to be served wine instead of the ale that came with the meal. She was unused to its sharp taste and drank it in little sips. The food was surprisingly good, cuts from a suckling pig cooked with tart apples. Wheat bread from finely milled flour, and not a corn pudding in sight, which was a relief. Instead, an apple pastry for dessert, hot and sweet.

"What is that flavor?" James asked after the first bite. "That's not molasses."

"Maple sugar."

"Maple, like from a tree? How strange."

"You don't like it?"

"It's delicious, so long as I don't think too hard about its origins."

"Isn't that true of most foods?"

He smiled at this.

There was something she'd been curious about, and now she found the courage to ask. "How is it that you began to work for the king? Is it a family . . . I don't know, a *trade*?"

He smiled at this too, and she felt foolish.

"I mean, was your father a spy?"

"My father was a Roundhead. Hung as a traitor after the Restoration."

Her face flushed. "Pray, pardon me."

"You don't need to apologize."

He reached across and put his hand over hers in a comforting gesture. It was somewhat improper, even though he was likely acting a role for the benefit of the maid who was still coming and going from the room. After a few seconds, she withdrew her hand from the table to put it on her lap with the other.

"I don't like the word 'spy,' it's so coarse," he said. "Not to mention that they hang spies, and that's true almost anywhere you go. An agent of the king, on the other hand, may be about any sort of business at all."

"And what are *you* about, James? What truly brought you to Boston? Not the murder, I know that's a story for my benefit."

"Ah, no you don't," he said with a half smile and a raised eyebrow. "You'll have to be a good sight more subtle than that." He finished his wine and waved for the maid to come pour him more.

"Let me attempt subtlety, then," she said when the maid had gone. "Why Boston? You seem to think that New England is filled with rustics and governed by bumpkins, so why not do the king's duty in France instead? Is this punishment for some indiscretion, some failure?"

"The contrary. This is a thorny problem to resolve. If I manage, if I return in triumph, there's a great opportunity waiting for me in London."

"What kind of opportunity?"

He studied her carefully. "I don't suppose there is harm in the telling. I haven't kept my ambitions secret in London, so why do so here?" He took a drink of wine, then set down the goblet. "King Charles has opened a position as chancellor of his agents for foreign affairs and internal dissent."

"Lord Spy, you mean."

He shrugged. "In a manner of speaking. And if I return in triumph, I intend to ask His Majesty for the position. If it's given me, I'll be knighted, awarded lands."

"Can you tell me how you ended up working for the king? Did you volunteer?"

"I was recruited. It was your own husband, Sir Benjamin, who approached me."

"That must have come as a surprise."

"How so?"

"Given that your father was a . . . was, you know . . ."

"Hanged as a traitor for the other side? Well, yes, it would have been, but Sir Benjamin was rather more careful than to simply blurt out what he was about. By the time I realized who and what I was, I had been in the king's service for two years already. There was little room for surprise."

"I don't understand."

"This would have been 1670. I was twenty, studying law at Oxford. Sir Benjamin was a young professor of literature. We were reading the works of William Shakespeare—perchance you've heard of him. He was a great playwright early in the century."

"I've read him! Of course," she added hurriedly, "you cannot playact in New England. It is a sin to deceive."

"And I see you believe that with all your soul."

She ignored his sarcasm. "Go on."

"It was a great controversy. The Puritans at home had also banned the theater during Cromwell's reign, and there were plenty in Oxford still who saw Shakespeare as unseemly and vulgar, at the very least."

"Shakespeare's language is not always temperate," she conceded, though she couldn't see any harm in reading the stories. It was no worse than reading Dante or Petrarch, and certainly better than Chaucer.

"When the Puritans were burning the folios," he continued, "some rare earlier quartos had found their way to Holland. Sir Benjamin hired me to travel to Amsterdam to acquire one of them and carry it secretly to his library in All Souls College, Oxford. Later, I took trips to Paris and Rome, even Constantinople, to deliver and secure rare manuscripts. Not only for Sir Benjamin, but for Lord North as well. Once, I met King Charles himself as I passed him some bundle of papers or other. When I asked Sir Benjamin about it later—this was as he was leaving for Boston, which I didn't yet understand—he told me the truth."

"And what was that?"

"That I'd been in the service of the king for some time now. Most of those missions had been to pass secret missives to spies and diplomats, not to transfer manuscripts at all. So I was already fully implicated."

"You still had a choice in the matter. There is always a choice."

"Of course, but why would I have chosen otherwise? I was offered the chance to travel throughout Europe, paid a handsome sum for my services, given every opportunity to advance with loyal service."

"But your father fought for the other side."

His voice hardened. "He was a traitor and a fool."

"Is that why you want the position as the king's chancellor?"

"I don't follow."

"To show the world that you're the king's man. Surely, people whisper about you, gossip. Speculate about your loyalties and call you a Roundhead behind your back. But if you're the chancellor of spies, one of the king's most trusted men, then maybe they'll stop."

James looked thoughtful at this. "I had never considered that. I'm an ambitious man, and His Majesty rewards loyal ambition. That's why I'm reaching for the position of chancellor. Not because of my father. I don't think, anyway."

"It doesn't have to be one reason or the other," Prudence said. "Add two weights instead of one if you want to tip the scales."

"I later worked for two years in France," he continued, "fighting against those treacherous snakes. It was exciting and dangerous. But we had plenty of silver and to spare, every food and pleasure at our hands."

"This explains why you're so free with your money." *And women*, she thought. He was handsome, and the French women notorious. What temptations he must have faced.

"In France, this would have been considered frugality," he said. "I once spent one hundred fifty pounds in six days in Paris."

She didn't know what to say to this. That staggering sum could buy a house in Boston.

"Pardon," he said. "That sounds like a boast. I don't mean it that way. But His Majesty has more money than he has loyal men. Sometimes with the former he seeks to buy the latter."

"I see. And did he buy yours?"

"No. I serve out of duty."

"To what?"

"To king and country." He sounded surprised by the question. "Even you should understand that."

"I understand loyalty." It was hard for Prudence to articulate, even to herself, why James's answer was disappointing. "We're English too, you know."

Another couple came into the room for supper, and Prudence and James fell silent as the others sized them up. The woman was young, maybe twenty, and looked vaguely familiar, but Prudence couldn't place how or where.

A few minutes later, James yawned and stretched his legs. He twisted his neck, which popped. He gestured at the inn girl, who was feeding wood into the fire, and made a little gesture as if using a bed warmer, then pointed to the stairs. She nodded and filled the pan with coals, then went upstairs.

"Are you going to bed already?" Prudence asked.

"I'm exhausted. Aren't you?"

"A little. But I think I'll sit up for a bit. That wine went to my head."

"You barely had any. But very well. I'll leave you some space in the bed."

"Thank you." The other couple was watching, the man smoking a long pipe, so Prudence added, "Good night, dear."

James winked at her. When the girl came back down, he disappeared up the stairs. The floor overhead creaked for a few minutes, then was still. Prudence would wait an hour or so to make sure he was asleep before going up. She had brought her pen, ink, and paper with her, and she spent a few minutes writing what had come to pass since she'd left poor Old John Porter at the woodshed.

"Goodwife Cotton?" the young woman said from the other table.

Prudence turned, startled. She only just kept her wits. "It's Goodwife Smith now."

"Oh, yes. Of course. I hadn't realized you'd remarried. My sister didn't say anything about it."

"I only married recently. Pray, pardon me, Goodwife—"

"It's me, Hannah Platt. I'm Goody Stevenson now."

"Of course, I'm so sorry. Hannah! Rebecca's sister. You're so grown up. Goodness, are you expecting?"

Hannah's hands had been resting on her belly, and now she smiled at her husband, who gave a contented nod between puffs. He was a handsome fellow with a prosperous look about him, maybe in his midtwenties, though Hannah couldn't be older than nineteen.

"I'm sorry I didn't recognize you early enough to meet your husband," Hannah said. "What are you doing in Marlborough?"

"We're moving back to Winton."

"Of course. That's right. I've read your narrative. It was so enthralling."

Prudence was squirming. Suddenly, going upstairs while James was awake didn't seem so risky. She forced herself to remain calm.

"Why are you on the road?" she asked.

"We were visiting my grannie in Springfield," Hannah said. "She's not well. We're on our way back to Boston, though. Wait until I tell Rebecca I saw you. I can't believe she didn't tell me you'd remarried." Hannah smiled. "I'm giving her a good scolding."

"I don't think she knows. I've been keeping my own company—too much notoriety after my account was published. It's not good for one's vanity." Prudence yawned, then rose to her feet. "Pray, pardon me, but it was a long day and I promised my husband I'd retire early."

A flicker of disappointment washed over Hannah's face. "Yes, of course. I'm sorry."

Prudence touched the young woman's hand. "I'll look for you and Rebecca next time I'm in Boston. It has been too long since we've talked."

The young woman looked happier at this.

"Goodnight, Hannah. And you, Goodman Stevenson. May God be with you both."

Prudence braved the frigid outhouse out back instead of using the chamber pot upstairs. When she reached the room, she eased the door open as carefully as possible and slipped inside. With any luck, he'd be asleep already.

"That was quicker than I was expecting," his voice said from the bed. "I thought you'd be down there half the night."

She shut the door and latched it. "I was recognized."

He shifted abruptly in the darkness, as if sitting up. "Really? What happened?" He started moving around.

"No, it's all right. Lie down. Pray face the wall while I change clothing."

She undressed quickly in the dark, then groped for the clothing they'd salvaged from the burned farmhouse. She pulled on a nightgown and nightcap and changed her socks for dry ones while telling him about her encounter with Hannah.

"Not good," he said when she finished.

"It all depends on how quickly Hannah sees Rebecca. Her sister is something of a gossip—once she knows, the news will cross Boston in a few hours. Then it will get to Reverend Stone and he'll know how to find us."

"We'll be far ahead by then, probably in Indian country already. I'm more worried about those riders catching us in an ambush."

"You fought them off once. Would they really try again?"

James lay back down. "They were careless that time. They didn't expect what we gave them."

No, they wouldn't have expected it. The way James had thrown himself into violence, shooting and hacking, would have taken anyone aback. Three of their number dead. They would remember that next time.

You killed one of those men yourself. They weren't expecting that, either.

"They have to know we're on our way to Winton," James said. "If they catch me alone, I'm a dead man."

"You're not alone." She shifted on her feet. The cold of the floorboards seeped up through her socks.

"I appreciate that, but they'll be ready for you next time too. I need to reach Springfield. I'll have help then."

"What kind of help?"

He shifted in the bed. "Are you climbing in where it's warm or standing there all night?"

"Is standing here all night a possibility?"

"Come on, I'm all the way over by the wall. I won't touch you."

At last she ventured over and pulled back the covers. There she stood for a long moment until he grumbled that he was getting cold. Finally, she climbed in quickly and pulled the covers up. She felt his body next to hers, but thankfully, his back was turned.

"You can trust me," he said. "I am capable of mastering my urges."

"Let's not talk about your urges."

"This might surprise you," he said, "but women have urges too. They're not all as cold as Newfoundland."

"I know that." Prudence felt prickly at this. "I'm a human of flesh and blood. I have desires too."

"You do?" He sounded shocked.

"I was married nigh three years, Master Bailey. I am a woman of flesh and blood."

"So now it's Master Bailey, is it? Generally, women get *more* familiar when they climb into my bed, not less."

"I shall pretend I don't know what that implies."

He chuckled. "A jest, that's all."

"Of course," she said, drily. "I understand both lovemaking and jests. You think girls—even unmarried girls—don't talk about men?"

"I hadn't thought about it much, to be honest. But yes, I can imagine that easily enough."

"You should see the way the Branch girls coo over handsome men. I heard them talking about you, in fact."

"Really?" He rolled over to face her. "Tell me more."

"Lucy thought you'd make a fine husband. It's a good thing you left when you did or she might have come to your bed the first time Peter was out."

"Who said she didn't?" This time he didn't sound like he was joking.

"What?" She shot out of bed. "You didn't!"

"No, I didn't. I could have, though. She made her interest clear enough. And I'm plenty man enough that I wanted to, that's for sure."

Prudence climbed back into bed. "You can turn back to the wall again."

He obeyed with a sigh. "There is nothing about this situation that suggests that a good night of sleep is in store."

No, there wasn't. All this talk had left her flushed, and a new worry niggled at her. Supposing James *didn't* behave himself. Could she guarantee that her own response would be virtuous?

Chapter Fifteen

They were back on the road the next morning after a quick breakfast of cold bread, milk, and hard cheese. Prudence ached all over,
and she was exhausted from a poor night of sleep. The inn had
been cold and the bed hard.

To keep up their story, they rode two horses out of town and
led the rest. The inn's stable boy had cared for the animals well, and
they weren't as surly to be on the road as Prudence had expected.
They made good time for the first two hours.

The day wasn't as frigid as the past two, but the easing tem-
peratures were accompanied by snow. At first it fell as light and
fine as flour through a sifter, but gradually the sky turned from a
slate gray to the shade of twilight, though it was midday. Soon, the
snow fell in fat, lazy flakes, gradually growing in intensity.

James had been riding in silence, his brow furrowed and his
gaze distant, but now he looked skyward. "Was that thunder?"

"Aye, thunder snow."

"I've never heard of such a thing."

"They say that when there is thunder during a snowstorm,
someone important has died."

His face darkened and he drew his lips into a narrow, hard line. Prudence studied him, worried. "What troubles you?"

"I have been thinking about Peter Church. He may not count as important in the celestial mathematics of such things, but he was important to me. I will bring the king's justice upon those villains, Prudence, as God is my witness."

She knew what it was like to fall into dark, brooding memories, so to distract him she asked him about France, and he was soon telling her about Versailles, where the Sun King was building a palace of such magnificent size and opulence that she could scarcely imagine it. The grounds alone were the size of Boston, he claimed. He seemed to cheer in the telling.

Within an hour, a good two inches had fallen, and every stone wall, house, and barn carried a fresh white cap. Where the ground was flat they found it difficult to pick out the road from the surrounding fields.

About an hour later, they passed a horse-drawn sled carrying hogsheads of grain. The driver hailed them, demanded where they were going and from where they'd come, then asked for word from Boston. The news about the French off Nantucket agitated him greatly. He was still rumbling something about a war with the French in Quebec when they finally pulled out of earshot.

"Haven't we had enough war?" she asked James.

"You'll never get rid of it. War is the natural condition of man."

"It shouldn't be. Not here, anyway. New England is consecrated for the Lord."

"Don't deceive yourself. The devil is about his mischief here, just as he is anywhere."

"But he shouldn't be," she insisted, more out of stubbornness than because she was convinced he was wrong. "He should have no place here. When every Godly soul bends his knee, Satan shall be dead in this land."

"Dead?" James said. "What a shame to leave so many fatherless children in Boston."

Prudence turned away with a snort and urged the horse ahead. But she couldn't get the image of the devil's fatherless children out of her mind, and an inadvertent laugh burst from her mouth. James came up beside her, grinning mischievously.

They'd hoped to make it to Springfield by nightfall, but they were still twenty miles outside the town and struggling through a foot of snow when James called a surrender and they started looking for lodging. The storm was easing, but in its wake came a biting wind that drove snow across the road. It stung at Prudence's face and dug deep into her lungs.

They passed through a sleepy hamlet locked in by snow. There was no inn. James stopped his horse and eyed the houses.

"Don't you think we're better off trying one of the farmhouses outside of the village?" she asked. "Less gossip to pass around."

"Probably, yes. I was just looking. It's so beautiful."

Was it? It wasn't much different from fifty other New England villages, except that it did look white and clean with all the snow and icicles. The village meetinghouse boasted a steeple that was too tall to merely serve as a bell tower and seemed almost vain, except she did admit it looked striking against the snow-covered pine hills behind the town.

"'Twould be even more handsome with candles in the windows and Advent wreaths above the lintels," James said. "It's December nineteenth already. Why aren't they decorated for Christmas?"

"We don't celebrate Christmas," she said. "That's a Papist, pagan celebration."

"Nonsense."

"They still celebrate it in England?"

"We do have dissenting sects who eschew the holiday, but it's hard to imagine a whole country of Christians casting it aside. I suppose you don't have plum puddings, yule logs, fruitcakes, or gift giving, either."

"No, those are all pagan rituals."

"Drains the pleasure from life, that's what it does."

He seemed more disgusted by this than anything he'd seen so far in New England, and as they rode out of town she felt a twinge of shame. Her husband had often raised an eyebrow at the quirks of local customs, but somehow he'd never made her feel embarrassed about her home.

James began searching for a farmhouse to beg lodging as soon as they got out of the village, but they'd entered another stretch of ruined homes from the war. It was growing dark, the horses were shivering, and Prudence was about to suggest they turn around, when a light flickered from behind windows ahead of them just before the road plunged back into the forest.

It took some pounding to bring the startled owners of the house to the door. James exchanged introductions with the couple, who were named Meyer, then asked about spending the night. While he spoke, Prudence looked over his shoulder into the front room and was dismayed by what she saw. The simple, two-room house held half a dozen young children already, plus the couple. The place was tidy but hardly prosperous.

Goodwife Meyer was a stout, kindly faced woman with ruddy cheeks, who seemed more intrigued by the unexpected visitors than suspicious. But when James asked about a bed, she cast a doubtful glance at her already-crowded living quarters.

James got out his purse. "I'll pay you, of course. Six shillings for a bed and supper, plus stabling the horses in your barn. Is that sufficient?"

That was overly generous, and the woman's eyes widened as she glanced quickly at her husband.

"We could put the boys in the barn," Goodman Meyer said quickly.

"Pray, don't trouble yourself," James said. "We'll take the barn. Do you have fresh hay and extra blankets?"

"Of course, but I could never ask guests to sleep with the animals."

"We have to rub down the horses anyway. We may as well sleep out there too. No, no, I insist. Here, take the money."

It went back and forth a couple of times before the couple relented, obviously torn between the money and the desire not to cheat their overly generous guests. A few minutes later James and Prudence were leading the horses back to the barn, laden with blankets and a clay pot holding succotash—corn and beans cooked in lard—together with a bit of salted pork and corn bread wrapped in a cloth.

"Whatever else you can say about New Englanders," James said, "they are dignified people. And even the poor have plenty of food."

"So long as you like Indian corn," she said.

Prudence wanted to ask him why he'd given them so much money. It was more than he'd paid Reverend Stone, only in this case for a cold night in a barn and little meat with supper.

She was initially pleased that the barn smelled more of straw than manure, but she soon discovered this was because the wind driving through the chinks in the wood planks kept it well ventilated. The family's sheep huddled in one corner, which they shared with a milk cow, leaving plenty of room for the horses. It was so cold that Prudence and James soon moved their own hay beds back by the animals. They slept in all their clothes.

Sometime in the night, she woke to find herself snuggled next to James. Worse, as she came to, she realized that she had her arms around him, and not the other way around. He was nice and warm. If not for her feet, which felt like blocks of ice, she'd have been quite comfortable in spite of the wind groaning against the barn planks.

Still, she pulled gently away until there was distance between their two bodies.

It was only proper.

Prudence woke in the morning to men's voices outside. She sat up in the straw. Light streamed through a gap in the roof, and the animals were stirring, growing restless for their breakfast.

James stood near the barn door, his boots on, pistols in hand, and sword tucked into his belt. The way he carried himself, tense and coiled, reminded her of that moment in the coach before he'd knocked open the door and sprung out shooting. He spotted her rising and lifted a warning finger to his lips.

One of the voices rose outside, calling to someone else. A horse snorted, and she heard shuffling that sounded like more horses. A group of riders, then.

The voices trailed away. James didn't take his eyes off the door, but he lowered the pistols.

She made her way quietly over. "What is it?" she whispered.

"I couldn't pick out much. They're looking for someone. No doubt us."

"The highwaymen again?"

He didn't answer. For a long minute they stood in silence. Then footsteps sounded outside. James tensed again and pushed her behind him.

But when the door creaked open, it was only Goodman Meyer. The snow lay all trampled outside and up to the house, but there was no sign of riders.

James hastily put away the guns, but not before Meyer noted them with a frown. His eyes flickered to Prudence, and there was deep suspicion there.

"This is your lawful wife, Goodman Smith?" he asked. "You haven't run off with some man's daughter, have you?"

"Of course she is my wife. What do you take me for?"

Meyer lowered his eyes. "Pray forgive me, good sir."

"No need to apologize, I understand. A man's hospitality doesn't extend to protecting criminals and adulterers. But we are neither of those things."

Meyer glanced at Prudence and blushed hard. "I beg your pardon."

She nodded demurely, as if accepting his apology for the slight. Inside, her heart was pounding.

"I was certain you were innocent," Meyer continued. "They claimed you robbed a coach and stole the horses. That seemed impossible."

"Then you didn't tell them we were here?" James asked.

"There were four men, demanding and rude. And there was something . . . *untrustworthy* about them." Meyer shook his head. "Nay, I said nothing. You were fortunate the wind swept away your prints, and they thought you were most likely further east, anyway."

"Thank you for that," Prudence said.

The man hesitated and looked them over again. "I was sure they were up to no good. But then I saw your pistols, Goodman Smith, and I wondered . . ."

"That is only natural," James said. "Any other man would have wondered the same."

Yet he seemed at a loss to explain why he'd been standing at the door with a sword at his belt and two pistols in his hands if he weren't up to something suspicious, and the suspicion hadn't entirely faded from Goodman Meyer's face.

Prudence took James's hand and gave him a sympathetic look. "You had better show him the king's commission. We can trust this good man."

The hesitation vanished from James's eyes. "Of course we can."

He pulled out the king's commission from his cloak and showed the seal to Meyer, but not, she noted, the actual contents.

Meyer stared, mouth agape. "An agent of the king? Are you moving against our rights and privileges?"

"Of course not. His Majesty respects the colony's charter. I'm only here to settle some matters stirred up in the war. I brought my wife, as we are considering settling in this Godly country. I didn't expect to be attacked on the road."

"Nay, I would think not. Not here. The devil must truly be abroad in the land."

"Indeed, he must."

Prudence pretended not to notice James's significant look.

James seemed glum when they were back on the road, leading the horses west toward Springfield. The wind was finally easing.

"To tell the truth, I feel like the devil myself," he said. "Introducing the forbidden fruit into the garden."

"How do you mean?" Prudence asked.

"Goodman Meyer won't be so quick to take in strangers in the future when he finds out that you were not, in fact, my wife. Perhaps that shouldn't bother me, but it does."

She had her own worries on that score. "Once this gets out, the scandal will sink me."

"All you have to do is convince your brother-in-law of your virtue. The reverend will shield you."

"Nothing shields a woman from malicious gossip. The likes of Goody Brockett will be whispering about me to their deathbeds." She shook her head. "I'll have to move to Providence."

"How will that help?"

"There's a reason they call it Rogue's Island. Rhode Island is the chamber pot of New England. They even tolerate Quakers and Baptists."

"Even that? No, never." He smiled.

"Don't mock. This is serious."

"I can tell. But why settle for Providence? Come back to England. There's a place for the likes of you in the service of the king. You've got a quick mind and steady nerves."

"I could never do that," she said, firmly. "My people are here. I belong in New England."

He shrugged and they rode on for a stretch. The other riders had continued east, back toward Boston, and their tracks seemed to be the only ones across the fresh snow from Springfield to the west. They came to the junction with the main highway again. Two men led a team of mules in drawing a flat plow to clear snow from the road, and they followed the plow toward town.

"How about you?" she asked James. "When you see all this empty land waiting to be manured, doesn't it make you want to settle?"

"You mean what I told Goodman Meyer? No, that was another lie. My allegiance is to the king."

"And he has no need of men like you in the colonies? You're not alone in the New World—you already admitted as much."

"Of course there are others. It's the only way to counter the French and the Dutch. But, well . . ."

"What?" she pressed.

"There's the position of chancellor of royal agents to consider."

"Perchance you could take the position and stay in New England."

"No, I could not."

"I see." She felt disappointed in a way that was hard to identify.

He cleared his throat, turned away from her gaze. "If they're plowing the road, we must be near Springfield," he said. "Keep an eye out for a place to get the horses off the road. I'll be going into town alone."

Chapter Sixteen

James entered Springfield on foot, dressed like a Puritan. He wore a felted hat and long stockings gartered to his breeches—all items taken from the burned-out house where they'd left Woory's carriage and the bodies. He strolled down the middle of the main street as if he had lived there all his life. He kept his head low, his face bundled behind a scarf, touching his hat and greeting people when they looked at him.

Springfield wasn't a large, bustling city like Boston, but it wasn't a provincial village, either. A respectable cloud of wood smoke capped the town. Several streets crisscrossed a flat stretch of land on the bluffs overlooking the Connecticut River, packed with houses and shops all shoulder-to-shoulder. There had to be a thousand inhabitants, and that gave James some small measure of anonymity as he scouted the town.

Before entering Springfield, he'd studied and deciphered the coded instructions for how to find his associate, Richard Cooper, but the man's shop and home were not where his information claimed they would be. Prudence had warned him that Indians had sacked Springfield, but he was unprepared for the din of hammers and saws. Every other lot was a building site, with men raising roofs, masons rebuilding brick chimneys, carts unloading boards. When James got to Cooper's house, he found it replaced by a lumberyard.

But there were only so many places the man could have relocated, and after about a half hour, he found what must surely be the man's home. It was two stories, with a high, pitched roof and dormers in the attic. The lower level was a shop, with a flat wooden sign carved in the shape of a barrel and encircled with iron bands, simulating hoops. Two boys came out of the shop rolling oversize barrels, which they then helped their father load into the back of a cart.

As attested by his name, Cooper had come from a long family of artisans before joining the king's service, and he had settled back into the family trade while he awaited the king's pleasure. That would come today, whether or not Cooper was ready for it. James entered the shop.

The inside was warm, with a roaring fire in one corner, and smelled of hickory and ash. Piles of staves lay in every corner. Shavings and wood chips covered the floor a quarter inch deep, except near the fire, where they'd been carefully swept clear. Workbenches held barrels, buckets, and piggins in every stage of construction. Metal must be scarce, James noticed, because the hoops were all wood as well. Apparently the only iron hoops to be found were the ones on the sign outside.

A man without a cap, forearms bare, his hands huge and rough, was taking payment from a woman in return for a butter churn. James had worked with the man in France several years earlier, but he might not have recognized his old friend on first glance if he hadn't been expecting the man. Cooper was older, sturdier, his hair thinner and his nose and ears lumpier. He wore a settled look.

James untied his scarf and removed his hat as the woman passed him with a nod and a look that turned to curiosity as she perhaps realized that he was a stranger.

"What cheer," Cooper said.

"What cheer indeed," James said.

Cooper's eyes held a question about business, a hint of impatience. "Well?"

"Do you have a barrel sturdy enough to ship a man back to London?"

Cooper's eyebrows lifted. "You! Why, you devil. I had no idea it would be you."

"You didn't get the letter? Who were you expecting?"

"What letter? No, I wasn't expecting anyone. But I heard." He whistled. "Oh, have I ever." Cooper turned. "Sarah!"

A pretty woman appeared, about Prudence's age, perhaps in her midtwenties. A good ten years younger than Cooper, but it was clear from the first glance between the two that she was his wife.

"It's the man from Boston about the iron," Cooper said. "Mind the shop, will you? Lang will be in for those pails. Make sure he doesn't try to short you or take them on credit. That scoundrel still owes me ten shillings."

Once she was behind the counter and Cooper had led James into the front room of his house, the man turned. "What a heap load of trouble you've got yourself in already. I'm surprised you're even alive."

"No more trouble than that time you stole that French priest's sheep and dressed it in a woman's bodice."

Cooper grinned, revealing a mouth still full of straight, white teeth. Then he turned suddenly sober and glanced back over his shoulder toward the shop where he'd left his wife. "Different times, my friend. Different times."

Two young boys, no older than three or four, sat in front of the fire, whittling on the end of broken barrel staves. Cooper scooted them out of the way, insisting that James take off his boots and prop his feet in front of the fire. He fetched a flask of beer and pressed a pipe into James's hand. With the fire warming his feet, the beer his belly, and the pipe his lungs, James started to thaw for the first time in days.

"So you're in trouble," Cooper said, this time more insistently.

"Some trouble," James admitted. "What have you heard?"

"Riders came through yesterday looking for you. They claim you ran off with some woman in Boston. That her family tried to get her back and you killed a couple of men. Someone said you'd taken up with an Indian and turned highwayman, but I had doubts about that much."

"Oh, it's all nonsense. Well, mostly."

"How about the part about the woman? Not that it matters to me, but you know how these Puritans get."

"That part is true enough," James admitted. "Did they say who the woman was?"

"No. Some young widow."

"Prudence Cotton," James said.

Cooper's eyes widened. "The one who lived with the Indians? Reverend Stone's sister-in-law? That Prudence Cotton?"

"Is there another one?"

"You *are* in trouble, Bailey. Where is she now?"

"Freezing in a barn outside of town," James said with a twinge of guilty conscience as he compared her circumstances to his own comfort. "I needed to see you alone, first."

"Make sure I wouldn't string you up for fornicating, eh?"

"Word had it you'd taken up with the natives. Had to verify your loyalty."

"I've done some taking up, that I admit." Cooper glanced at his boys with a shrug. "Met a good woman, married her, fathered a couple of children. But don't worry, I can hold my tongue."

"And you're still loyal to the king?"

"Aye, that I am." Cooper took the pitcher and refilled James's mug. "But I'm about the only one in these parts who is. These New Englanders consider themselves to be under the laws of God, not king and Parliament. If not for the French up north and those conniving Dutch in New York, they'd be even more restless."

"That's the worry of the Crown, and why I'm here."

"How do you mean?"

"It's time to rein in certain privileges."

Cooper's tone turned cautious. "What do you mean, rein them in? You're not talking about the charters, are you?"

James didn't speak but raised his eyebrows slightly.

"You don't say. That's bound to get ugly." Cooper sat down and lit his own pipe. "Although it sounds like it's ugly enough already. This thing with Prudence Cotton will see your neck in a noose if you're not careful."

"Forget about Prudence—I haven't laid a finger on her, and I won't. She's desperate for answers about her husband, and what happened at Crow Hollow at the end of the war."

He didn't mention the part about her daughter, Mary, still being alive. That would sound outlandish.

"Aye, Sir Benjamin. Another king's man who took up with the local folk. It's an easy trap to fall into."

"Are you suggesting that Sir Benjamin betrayed his loyalty to the Crown?" James asked.

"Not at all. But his eye was on the Dutch and French, not good English folk. He operated openly as the king's representative, but there was no talk of challenging New England's privileges. They'd have turned on him if he had."

"And if the king had called on his services to do just that?"

Cooper shrugged. "He would have answered the summons, I suppose. 'Twouldn't have been easy. You live here a spell and you find your sympathies shifting. Especially if you fall into the company of a good woman."

"I can well imagine."

Cooper fixed James with a sharp look. "You're sure there's nothing going on with the widow? Sir Benjamin found her enticing enough."

"Certain," he said firmly. "I'm going back to London as soon as this is settled."

Cooper raised an eyebrow and took a puff from his pipe. "So you say."

"There's a position open as the king's chancellor, and I mean to take it. That means no entanglements."

"Ah, yes. Ambition. Well, then. I will believe that." Another puff. "Tell me how you find yourself in this predicament."

James explained most of what had befallen him since he'd arrived in Boston, from his rude reception by Samuel Knapp, to the way Peter had disrupted services and his trial, as it were, at the hands of Stone, Fitz-Simmons, and Knapp. Then, Peter's ugly death on the highway, followed by James and Prudence's flight across Massachusetts.

He did leave out a few things. How he'd nearly bedded Lucy Branch. The name of the family who'd hidden James and Prudence in their barn, then lied to the riders. That Prudence thought her daughter was still alive. This last bit not so much because he didn't trust his old companion, but because he didn't want to raise more suspicions about his involvement. It was not, James told himself, personal.

"Are you sure someone was poisoning the Indian?" Cooper asked. "And under the reverend's roof too? That's a devil of an accusation."

"Peter Church recovered as soon as he stopped eating their food. Then the highwaymen murdered him on the road anyway. Peter was unarmed and no kind of physical threat."

"Hmm."

"Any speculation about motives?" James asked.

"My first thought was revenge. Quakers are banished from Massachusetts, and this one provoked a violent outburst. But that's no motive for murder. No, I suspect they're hiding something from you in Winton, something that only the natives know. And this Church fellow spoke Nipmuk, right?"

"Very good," James said, impressed. "It took me two days to puzzle that out."

Cooper gave a shrug, as if it were nothing, but didn't quite scrub the satisfaction from his face. "Easy enough to do here in front of the fire with a good pipe in my hand. I wasn't facing murderers on the highway."

"That touches on the central mystery of this matter," James said. "Why did the Indians attack Winton, when they had pledged eternal amity?"

"The devil put it to them, I should say."

"I do not believe that, and neither do you." James considered further. "Who might have administered the poison to Peter Church?"

"I can't see any of them doing it. Reverend Stone is a good fellow—at least by reputation—and Widow Cotton's sister . . ." He shook his head. "You and I both know a woman can be as ruthless as a man, but her own sister?"

"Prudence says no. She's adamant." James shrugged. "What about the attackers on the road? The deputy governor, perchance? He has the means—he could raise the men."

"I don't know much about William Fitz-Simmons, but I can't see a motive."

"New England sovereignty. I'm a threat."

"How is murdering government agents going to help him with that?" Cooper asked. "No, I would expect him to cooperate, to confuse and lie if there's something to be hidden about Sir Benjamin's death. But he's a political sort, and this is a political matter. Murder is too blunt an instrument."

"I'm not convinced," James said. "Anyway, what about Captain Knapp?"

"Knapp, yes. He's a brutal sort—proved it in the war. If he were implicated in Sir Benjamin's death, he might kill for that. That might explain the attack on the highway, but what about the poison?"

James shook his head. "Knapp had no access to the Stone kitchen that I can see. No way to poison Peter Church. What's more, how did he catch us so quickly on the highway? Someone must have told him. Someone living with the Stones."

"So we're back to the reverend and his wife," Cooper said. "Only that's impossible."

Two girls came down the stairs holding their primers and slate boards, which they carried to the table on the opposite side of the room. The girls were older than the two whittling boys, maybe eight and ten years old. And yet Cooper had only been in the country six years.

When he turned, Cooper was studying him. "Prudence Cotton wasn't the only war widow," he said. "My own Sarah was among them."

The girls stared at James with naked curiosity before their father urged them to take up their books instead of gawking. One of the girls, James was surprised to see, had dark, shiny hair, thick and straight. Skin the color of hickory. A sharp nose and prominent cheekbones. The only other person James had seen who looked like that was Peter Church. This girl looked similar enough to have been his daughter.

Cooper lowered his voice. "There were plenty of orphans too, and not all of them our own."

"I don't understand."

The man's tone turned defensive, even as he lowered his voice further, to a near whisper. "She is a Christian soul. I won't have you speaking ill."

"I mean no ill," James said quickly. "But her people . . . what of them? Was there no relative to take her in?"

"Ah. So far as we can tell, she had none. Living, that is. We're Abigail's people now."

"Abigail? That's her name?"

"Her name was Quipamian . . . something or other. We couldn't very well call her that. What is that expression on your face? What are you thinking?"

"There is no expression," James said, not entirely truthfully.

"Abigail even speaks English—she picked it up quickly. Not even an accent. You know how children learn. She'll be one of us, and I'll love her like any of my other children."

"Of course you will."

A week ago James might have accepted all of this without a second thought. But almost at once he thought of little Mary Cotton. If Prudence was right, and her daughter was still alive, Mary would be speaking Nipmuk fluently by now, being raised to think of herself as one of them. Maybe they'd even given her a Nipmuk name. The thought was confusing, unsettling in a way that was hard to define.

The two men took their chairs closer to the fire, where they could converse without the children overhearing.

"I need to fetch Prudence from the barn and bring her somewhere warm," James said. "Can your wife be trusted?"

"No," Cooper said. "I mean, yes, she's very trustworthy. But she's also devout and loyal to the colony. If she finds out that you're the instigator of this trouble, and that you're traveling with an unmarried woman . . ." His voice trailed off.

"Understood."

"If you're right about Samuel Knapp, Springfield isn't safe. Two of Knapp's brothers live here. One is a selectman, and the other postmaster. Plus at least forty men who served with him in the militia."

"Postmaster, you say?" James asked. That gave him an idea. "Have you ink and paper? I have a letter I'd like to post to the colonial government of Virginia."

Cooper raised an eyebrow but fetched the paper. When James had written and sealed the letter, he handed it over. "It's time to get back on the road, but first I want you to get this letter to the postmaster."

Cooper nodded. "Before you leave, let me fetch you provisions. It's the least I can do."

"You'll do a lot more than that," James said. "You're coming with me to Winton."

Cooper blinked. "I can't do that. I've got a shop to run, a family."

"And an oath to serve King Charles. Your business and family are what you do while awaiting the king's pleasure. I am calling on you now to fulfill your duties."

"Lower your voice. My children—"

"Will you do your duty? Or have your sympathies shifted, as you put it?"

"Bailey, please. I'm old now, soft. What would it help you?"

"Oh, I don't know," James said with a touch of sarcasm. "An extra hand to wield a musket or a sword. A witness if they try to kill me. Complications if they try to kill you too. Who could possibly see any aid in that?"

"If they kill me I'll leave a widow twice over, and four orphans."

James was growing irritated. "We're not sending you twenty pounds a year to make barrels and sire a bushel of squalling whelps."

"Damn you, Bailey. That was low."

"Do your duty, man."

Cooper looked like he would keep arguing, but gradually a look of resignation passed over his face. "Very well," he said. "Where is this barn where you've got the woman and the horses?"

James told him.

Cooper nodded. "Go back and wait while I post the letter. Then I'll pack a few things for our journey. Tell my wife a quick lie, heaven forgive me, and meet you on the road."

"I'm not leaving yet. Not until I'm sure."

"You don't trust me?"

"In all good faith? No, I do not."

Cooper stared at him, his jaw clenching. "Very well. Come with me."

They passed the girls as they left the house to enter the shop. Cooper bent and kissed them each on their foreheads. The girls squirmed and grimaced, but they clearly loved the attention.

"Papa will be taking a short trip to Boston. Be of good cheer and lend a hand to your mother in the shop while I'm away. And make sure your brothers don't get into mischief."

When the men entered, there were no customers in the shop and Sarah Cooper was sweeping the floor with a birch broom, its ends slivered and lashed down. She hummed to herself as she worked, bending to brush shavings into a pan and then feed them to the fire. The fire blazed and crackled.

When she spotted her husband, she brightened and gave him a playful smile. "Bless me, but this is a fire risk. One stray spark, dear husband. One stray spark."

"Pray, pardon me, Goody Cooper," her husband said. "If I cleaned up, you would have no reason to bend over and collect the sweepings. And then I should have no excuse to admire your bottom."

Sarah blushed furiously but looked delighted as Cooper took her in his arms. He nibbled at her neck, and she giggled and play-fully pushed him away.

"What will your guest say? Bless me!"

"Why do you think I'm doing it? Goodman Bailey needs to see the benefits of marriage so he will do his duty and help settle this country."

It was the sort of playful banter that James normally enjoyed, but there was something about the tableau that made him twinge. The girls in the next room with their slates and primers, the wife with a healthy color and good cheer. They held obvious affection for their father and husband. James was about to snatch the man away and put his life in danger.

Cooper made up a story about needing to secure a shipment of iron goods waiting on the docks at Boston Harbor. He didn't have the ready money, but the shipment was worth a sizable sum and the Dutch merchant would only take silver and not credit. Cooper needed to collect some debts, and that meant traveling to Boston himself.

James's sorrow grew as Cooper told his tale with convincing detail, and his wife accepted his coming absence without complaint. At first James thought his melancholy was because of the great risk he was putting the family in. Who was to say that Cooper wouldn't end up like Peter Church, only leaving a widow and orphans behind?

But it was more than that. It was a wistfulness for the love this good, simple woman had for her husband. And he for her. James could see it; this was no trifle for Richard Cooper. He kissed her gently on the cheek and held her a moment too long with his eyes closed.

At that moment James felt as though he had never truly loved anyone the way these two loved each other, had never been loved. *You chose your life*, he told himself. *It wasn't pressed upon you.*

Outside in the street, Cooper shut the door behind them. "Go on, then. I'll need time to gather some things for the road. Keep two of the horses saddled. I'll bring my own and dispose of the rest."

It took effort for James to harden his heart. The temptation was too great, and the stakes too dear, for him to be soft on the man and let him return to his family and trade. And he needed Cooper to know the deadly seriousness of his intentions.

"I'll wait, but so help me, if you don't show up, my last act on these shores will be to tell every gossip in New England that you're a no-good spy."

CHAPTER SEVENTEEN

James expected Richard Cooper to be a grudging companion if he showed up at all, but the man had regained some of his earlier cheer by the time he arrived at the barn outside of town. He climbed down from his horse, handed James a coin purse, and bowed extravagantly.

"Your treasure, m'lord," he said with an ironic flourish.

"What's this?"

"I sold Woory's horses to a shifty fellow I know. At a steep discount, since the beasts were sight unseen, but he didn't ask questions."

"That's the point of shifty fellows," James said and tucked the money into a pocket in his cape. He felt guilty that he'd mistrusted his old friend. "Every man should have one at hand."

"And I suppose now I'm yours." Cooper raised his eyebrows. "That's a reversal from France, isn't it? I truly have gone soft."

Prudence had looked worried since the mention of selling Woory's horses, so James assured her that when they returned to Boston he'd dispose of the money properly. But their new companion was right, there was no sense in abandoning the horses—not to mention the suspicion that would have aroused when someone discovered them in the barn.

Cooper told them of a road leading out by the ice pond that would get them around Springfield and onto the road to Winton, so they set off in that direction.

Prudence and Cooper had apparently never met before, and she seemed disconcerted by his friendly familiarity as he asked her about Boston, about the Nipmuk, even about Crow Hollow.

After the fifth or so probing remark, James said, "Let be with the interrogation. You sound like the Papist inquisition."

He blinked. "Pray, pardon me, Widow Cotton."

"It's no bother, Master Cooper," Prudence said. "It's my narrative, I understand." She turned to James. "When I meet people, they seem to feel as if they know me already. They know me from my narrative, you see."

James understood well enough. There was an intimacy in her account, and he'd felt the same way when he first met her. "Be that as it may, it must be a bother."

"Aye, that it is. And also a sound lesson in the pitfalls of vanity, and a reminder to be humble before God and man."

They passed the pond, where men were at work on the ice. They sawed out great blocks, hooked them with enormous tongs to lift them clear, then loaded them onto sleds to be carted back into town. The ice would be covered in sawdust and stored in ice houses to be used through the warmer months of the year.

The three riders swung back around to the highway shortly thereafter, having bypassed Springfield. The road traveled next to the Connecticut River, which cut a wild, vigorous passage through the forests and hills. Later, rocks forced the road away from its banks.

Here the fields thinned before disappearing entirely. James had thought the landscape west of Boston savage enough, but this forest was deeper, more intimidating still. No ax had ever touched these woods. The trunks of the largest oak and maple were so great that two men could not have encircled them with their arms outstretched. The road narrowed at places until a heavily laden cart would have struggled to pass.

And James spotted animals too: several deer, a fox, some sort of weaselly creature that blended into the snow except for its black nose, and a pair of curious furry animals who looked like they were wearing masks and walked with a distinctive waddle. Prudence called them raccoons.

Later, they entered hills where stands of towering pines reached into the leaden sky. Each tree would have made a fine mainmast for the flagship in His Majesty's fleet. Cooper warned James not to leave the road. The snow wells that had formed around the bases of the pines were six feet deep and could swallow a horse to its withers.

"My husband bought land near here," Prudence said when they came down into a valley again. "Two hundred acres. He wanted to settle with some other families. See that stream going down to the river? That's where he intended to build a mill. That cascade was going to become the millrace."

"Seems like a fine bit of land," Cooper said.

"Then the war broke out."

"Do you still own the land?" James asked.

"I couldn't say," she replied with a frown. "My brother-in-law settled Benjamin's estate. He holds the proceeds for me in trust."

Given more time, James would have liked to see those documents of trust and find out exactly what the reverend was doing with Prudence's money.

Stone was quite prosperous, and Puritans paid their ministers well. Still, even a man of God could be tempted by the unguarded wealth of a young widow. Perhaps he was helping himself to funds, justifying it as the price for Prudence's upkeep.

Perhaps. But proving it would be hard, and in any event, was that sufficient motive for murder? And if Stone were a murderer, why not kill Prudence herself and let the money fall into his wife's hands as Prudence's sister and heir?

The shadows were growing long when Cooper told them to wait while he rode ahead with some of James's money to secure lodging.

James jumped down to stretch his legs. He tried to help Prudence down, but she declined.

"My feet ache. I'd rather not."

"How so? We've been riding all day."

"From the cold, James, not walking."

He didn't like this, and he remembered how he'd left her in the cold barn while he'd toasted his feet by Cooper's fire.

"Let me take a look," he said and pulled at one of her boots.

"I can feel them, they're not frostbit. They hurt is all."

Still, he persisted. She winced when he got the boot off and then gasped as he peeled back the sock to look. Her toes were a rosy red, with an almost blistered appearance. His hands were hardly warm, but her feet still felt chill when he took hold of them.

"You've got chilblains. We need to get you inside and soaking these feet."

She peered down with a worried look, but he was already putting her sock back on. It didn't help that her socks were damp, either. He couldn't decide if rubbing her feet would help, or simply cause her more pain, so he laced up her boot without doing anything.

James looked down the road. "Where is that devil, anyway?"

"Why didn't we all go together? Doesn't Goodman Cooper trust this man already?"

"He's undoubtedly another of Cooper's shifty fellows. And no, you never trust a shifty fellow."

"I don't know many shifty fellows," she said. "Only you, James." Her voice was perfectly innocent.

"Hah. Well, I'm sure it will be fine. These men have their loyalties, if you know what I mean."

"The god of mammon."

"Exactly."

Cooper was grinning when he came back. "We have the house, and we have it to ourselves. I paid the man to ride back to Springfield and stay with his brother for the night."

"Will he be passing this way?" James asked.

"Aye, as soon as he can saddle up a horse. Best keep your heads down, the both of you."

James pulled his cap low and his hood up as the horses continued up the road. Prudence did the same. It seemed a bigger risk for her, given how well she was known in these parts, but he wasn't sure it mattered anyway. It all came down to how trustworthy Cooper's man was. Almost by definition, not very.

A chestnut horse came trotting down the snowy road minutes later. Neither side offered a greeting as they approached, but James couldn't help but glance over as the man passed. The man met his gaze. He looked like the sort of weasel James had expected, with too-narrow eyes, a large forehead, and hair pulled back and greasy. Dirty hands, an underfed horse. Breeches threadbare at the knees and worn boots in the stirrups. He disappeared to their rear.

"I hope the bedding is free of vermin," James said, imagining what sort of house a man like that would live in. Filled with fleas and lice, no doubt.

"I wouldn't count on it," Cooper said. "And I'd check the meat for maggots too."

"I knew that man in Winton," Prudence said with a glance over her shoulder. "Goodman Burrows, though there's nothing good about him."

"You were supposed to be keeping your head down," James said.

"As were you."

He grinned at this.

"Burrows was accused of witchcraft," Prudence continued. "A child saw him dancing naked in the forest with three imps, holding a black mass. His defense was that he'd been in Boston at the time. Three men signed an affidavit testifying they'd had supper with him on the night in question."

"You'll have to admit that sounds like compelling evidence," James said.

"Except that the morning following the night in question, two other people had spotted cloven hoofprints in the snow," she said.

"A stray goat."

"Walking across the roofs of town?" She shook her head. "That could have only been the devil or one of his imps."

What nonsense. James grunted his disbelief.

"The only thing in New England more dangerous than practicing witchcraft," Cooper offered drily, "is disbelieving in witchcraft."

"I don't disbelieve in witchcraft," James said. "Of course the devil is abroad in the land, and he's looking for recruits. No right thinking man would claim otherwise."

The others seemed satisfied with this answer.

Nevertheless, it did seem curious that witchcraft accusations would sweep through an area, leading to mass denunciations, a trail of beatings, censure, and sometimes even hanging of the accused, only to have people retract some weeks or years later. Anyway, James had learned through hard lessons in His Majesty's service that most explanations were natural, not spiritual. But there would be no convincing these two.

They rounded the corner. A rude log cabin sat against the highway, surrounded by a small clearing of several acres on flat, rocky ground. The barn wasn't much bigger than the outdoor privy. A sluggish, desultory trickle of smoke leaked from the chimney of the house itself.

"There it is," Cooper said. "Word has it that Burrows lived here through the war. Yet look at the house. Right on the road, but never burned, never looted. And not one greasy hair harmed on the man's head. It's hard to imagine how that would happen unless Burrows was in league with those devils."

"The Indians may be heathens," Prudence said. "But I never did see them consorting with Satan."

Cooper offered a shrug. "The good news for us is that no other Godly company will have anything to do with the man. That makes him easily bribed."

Perhaps too easily, James thought, as they dismounted to check out the house. Even now this Burrows was hurrying to Springfield, where there were men who would pay handsomely for word of three strangers on the road.

Chapter Eighteen

"Is she asleep?" Cooper asked in a low voice. The two men were smoking pipes by the fire, while Prudence lay in one of the two beds, her eyes closed, but not asleep.

It wasn't hard to stay awake, the way her toes were itching from chilblains, and the other itching all over her body—perhaps imagined—of the no-doubt lice-infested blankets in which she slept. It smelled strongly of a man, and not the good kind of masculine smell, but stale sweat.

There was a second bed, and the men would be sharing that one. Why there was a second bed, she couldn't tell, since Burrows apparently lived alone.

As shameful as it was to admit it, she'd rather be in the clean, comfortable inn, sharing a bed with James, than in Burrows's disgusting bed alone.

Or maybe you'd like to be sharing a bed with James, regardless of the circumstances.

She quickly put this unholy thought out of her mind.

"Prudie?" James said.

She didn't answer. It may have been deceptive, but she desperately wanted to overhear their conversation. They were hiding things from her, and she wanted to know what.

"She's asleep," James said after several seconds.

"Did you call her Prudie?" Cooper asked with a chuckle. "Bless me, but that's familiar."

"A friendship, nothing more. We've already suffered a good deal together. Anyway, I believe her trustworthy."

"Does she know the real reason you came to New England?"

"She's a clever woman. I'm sure she has guessed."

It was flattering that he thought so, but in truth, she hadn't. James had arrived in Boston ostensibly to investigate Sir Benjamin's death at the hands of the Indians, and she supposed the Crown had legitimate reasons to question the death of its agent. And yet his actions seemed entirely too disrupting, too determined to cause an uproar, to be explained with such a direct motive. But she couldn't puzzle out what his real intent might be.

"If she's as clever as you think, she's dangerous."

"How so?" James asked.

"A woman like that offers her first loyalty to God, as she should. Next comes her country. These Puritans are fanatical about that."

"Her country is England."

"Her country is *New* England. Never forget that. Some day they will press the issue, you'll see."

"It's my duty to make sure that doesn't happen," James said. "Besides, even the most devout woman has higher loyalties than God and country."

"You mean her husband and child? They're both dead."

"Then justice for their murders."

So he hadn't told Cooper about her daughter. Was that because James didn't believe Mary was still alive? Or because he didn't trust the man?

And what was this about her loyalties to New England? It had never occurred to her that New England might declare open treason. Perish the thought. They were English through and through, and without the protection of the mother country, they would quickly fall prey to ravenous wolves like France or Spain, or even the Dutch. To say nothing of the powerful tribes of the wilderness like the Iroquois.

"What more justice do you want?" Cooper said. "Knapp and his sort put an end to the Indian trouble. Those beasts are utterly destroyed or sold into bondage. They are nothing but ghosts in this land. Someday they will be only a memory."

"You assume the Indians are responsible."

"You've read Widow Cotton's story, haven't you? She saw them cutting off Benjamin's fingers. She heard his screams as he begged for death."

"Yes, I know."

"They pulled out his intestines like he was a wretched pig at the slaughter," Cooper continued.

Prudence squeezed her eyes shut. A tremble worked down her back. Please, let them stop.

"Aye, and told her later that they'd eaten his liver, the brutes," Cooper said.

Prudence shoved a corner of the filthy blanket into her mouth and bit down to keep from screaming.

"Shh," James urged. "Keep your voice down. Even asleep she can hear you. You'll surely give her nightmares. Prudie," he said softly after a few seconds. "Are you awake?"

Again, she didn't answer, but his soothing tone eased her pounding heart. She pulled the blanket corner from her mouth and wiped her mouth quietly on the back of her hand.

"You fancy her, don't you?" Cooper said.

"Whether I do or not is beside the point."

"I'm telling you, there's something seductive about these women, about this place."

"And I tell you, I'm leaving. The moment my business is done, the *Vigilant* will carry me back to England where I will claim my prize."

"And the widow wouldn't dream of leaving New England, so there you have it. Ah, well."

"She's only a woman," James said. "Anywhere you go, you'll find them just as beautiful."

His words cut. How could he be so kind and gentle one moment, so cruel the next? When they'd come into the house, the first thing he'd done had been to heat water on the hearth to soak her poor, chilled feet. He'd then washed her socks and set them out to dry and made sure she had warm ones to put on. He'd given her bed the cleanest blankets he could find (such as that was possible), and used the bed warmer, as if he were the woman and she the man. All because he was worried about her feet.

He only needs you able to walk and ride, that's what matters to him.

"If all of that is true, why did you bring the widow?" Cooper asked.

"She got me out of Boston. After that, I fully intended to leave her in Springfield and continue on alone. Prudence is safe enough on her own—she enjoys a certain repute, after all."

"To be easily recognized is not always a good thing in New England. Most people love her, but there is some jealousy, some of the usual gossip. Still," Cooper added, "you're right. All she has to do is announce her presence and she's untouchable. So why didn't you leave her?"

"She's useful. She killed a man on the road, might have saved my life. And she's clever too. Has helped me figure out several things that I otherwise might not have seen."

Listening, Prudence felt a swelling of pride that James would consider her an asset, almost an equal. Not only was he a man, but a worldly sort too, out on grand adventures. And she was only a simple girl from New England, born of a simple people.

Even her husband, who had seemed to love her, couldn't help but laugh at some of the silly, naïve things that would come out of her mouth. Once, after she had pontificated at some length how playacting was the devil's work (the memory made her cringe in embarrassment now), Benjamin had gone to the bookshelf without a word, then pressed a folio of Shakespeare's plays into her hands. "Start with *Macbeth*. It has witchcraft, murder—every diabolical thing you can imagine. But read it and tell me that Shakespeare's work is of the devil."

Of course she had read it, and everything else in the book, and many times too. Next to some of the more beautiful psalms, it was the most wonderful thing she had ever read.

"Prudence Cotton is a handsome woman," Cooper said. "Are you sure there's not another motive?"

"How many ways must I say it? Leave it alone—I am not enamored of the widow."

Just as quickly, Prudence's pride deflated. Here came a whisper of disappointment in its wake. In spite of his earlier protests, she'd noticed the way James looked at her when they rode, so she hadn't fully believed them. What's more, she now realized that she'd been hoping, somewhere inside, that he was beginning to have feelings. And if she were honest with herself, her own feelings for him were growing.

This, however, was a definitive statement.

Don't be a fool. That would be impossible anyway. He's not Benjamin—he won't stay in Massachusetts. He's on his way back to London.

"There's one other thing," James continued. "She speaks Nipmuk."

That's right. You're a tool in his hands.

"And you no longer have the Indian," Cooper said. "Ah, yes, I remember. You wish to speak to the Indians. Do you think the widow unreliable in her account?"

"Nay, she is not unreliable. She has a fine memory and is a keen witness. But I have questions. Why did Winton's neighbors attack, when they had pledged eternal friendship? The treachery must have come as a surprise, or Sir Benjamin would not have been in Winton with his family when it came. Perchance another survivor in Winton will have more substance on the matter. If not, I will look for the Indians to hear their account."

"A shame your Praying Indian died. The better to preserve your scalp when you meet the savages. Yet, 'twould seem the old fool came all the way from England for naught."

"Bite your tongue," James said in a sharp voice. "Peter Church is dead. He gave his life in service of the Crown."

"Forgive me, I misspoke." Cooper sounded genuinely contrite. "It occurs to me, however," he added after a moment, "that if you truly hoped to disrupt these Puritans, to rile them, there's no better way to kick at the wasp nest than bringing in a Quaker to blather on like an idiot, as they do. Except, maybe, a Quaker who was also a Nipmuk. Seems that it worked a little too well."

"Admittedly, yes. I didn't think his life would be in danger or I wouldn't have done it. And Indian or no, I swear I will find his murderers and see them hanged."

"At the end of the day, the Indian's death only provides more powder for your musket. A better excuse to do what you came to do."

"Right. I have plenty of reason, now. No matter what happened at Winton and Crow Hollow, Peter's murder is more than sufficient cause. Even those stubborn oafs in Parliament will concede."

Cause for what? Concede what?

Suddenly, Prudence knew. The charters. Her mouth went dry.

He'd come for the charters of the New England colonies: Massachusetts, Connecticut, New Hampshire, Plymouth. Even feisty little Rhode Island.

There was no need to sever their connection to England, because they were already, de facto, independent of both king and Parliament. They could appoint their own governors, make their own laws, keep their own courts. They were, and always had been, free of the tyrants in England, both Oliver Cromwell and the kings alike.

But if King Charles—or rather, his agent—seized the charters, what would New England become? Why, no better than Virginia or New York. A Crown colony, under the complete domination of the whims of English politics.

She couldn't let that happen. Somehow, she had to get warning back to Boston. Reverend Stone would know what to do. But how to do it?

And then the answer came to her.

CHAPTER NINETEEN

Prudence was acting strange the next morning. First, she spent so long in the privy that James went out and knocked, jokingly asked if she'd frozen to the seat. In reality, he was afraid that she'd taken ill. She'd eaten little of the hot oatmeal they'd boiled for breakfast, and spoken less.

She insisted she was fine, and she came out a few minutes later with her cloak drawn tight against the cold. But twenty minutes later, when they were back in the saddle and traveling north, they hadn't ridden more than ten minutes up the road when she cried out that she'd left something at the house. What, she wouldn't say, but she had to go back and get it.

James said he'd go back with her, but she insisted on going alone.

"Well then, what is it?" he demanded, a little irritated by the delay.

She looked hurt, which made him feel guilty. "You're a man. You wouldn't understand."

And with that, she turned the horse and trotted back.

"The devil take us," Cooper said. "Not now."

"Not now, what?" James asked, confused. "What the devil is she doing?"

"You've never been married," Cooper said, "or you wouldn't need to ask that."

"What do you mean? Oh!" James added, his face flushing. "She's having her monthly courses."

"Every day I thank the good Lord that I'm not a woman," Cooper said. "Imagine being on the road and facing that?"

"Yes. Well. We don't know for sure, so keep your mouth shut when she gets back."

"What else could it be? Either that, or she's a spy, and she's gone back to meet Samuel Knapp on the road, to tell him our plans."

They both laughed at that, but later, James found himself looking over at Prudence to see if she were giving any guilty signs. For that matter, could he even trust Cooper? Six years with the natives, after all.

Just in case, it wouldn't hurt to be more guarded with his information.

※

The weather warmed throughout the day, and by late afternoon the three companions were able to shuck off their cloaks whenever the road came into open meadows next to the river. They overtook a man with a cart, and then two boys crossed their path riding a pony, dragging an empty sledge toward Springfield.

An hour later the highway forked, with the main road continuing along the river, while the other was almost completely covered in snow as it returned to the forest. Both roads led to Winton, Cooper claimed, but the second, forested road would be safer. Slower, but empty of traffic. So they entered the woods.

It was soon clear why the second road was little used. After about a mile they emerged from the woods and into fields that surrounded a desolate village. Nearly every house had burned to the ground, and there wasn't a soul to be seen. They dismounted to clear broken carts that had barricaded a small stone bridge over the creek, then passed the skeletal remains of the flour mill before passing out of town.

A few miles farther, they approached another desolate village, only this one was Indian. Wigwams lay in charred ruins, partially overgrown by leafless vines, and here and there were overturned reed baskets or corncobs sticking out of the snow, their kernels long-since gnawed away by mice or voles. A human skull, buried in frozen mud almost up to the eye sockets, stared at them dolefully as they rode by.

James wanted to dismount and look about, but Cooper and Prudence both begged him not to, so they continued. After that, Cooper grew quiet, refusing to engage in conversation, and later he said that he'd fought a battle in that very spot against a group of Wampanoag, with King Philip himself at the head of the enemy forces. Three English fell, "knocked on the head," as he put it, and two more were taken captive. Their disemboweled bodies had come floating down the river a few days later. But when James asked if Cooper had been present at the destruction of the Indian village, he refused to answer.

Prudence kept looking over her shoulder as they left the Indian village. At first, it seemed a nervous reflex, as if she expected the skeletons of the dead to come shambling up the road after them. But as they continued, her interest in the road behind only grew. James watched surreptitiously, growing more suspicious by the minute. Once, she caught him watching and looked quickly, guiltily away. Now he was convinced.

He came up beside her and grabbed the reins to pull her horse to a stop. "That's far enough."

"What? Why are we stopping?"

Cooper turned his horse, a scowl playing across his face. "What's going on here?"

"That's what I'm wondering," James said. "Prudence? What's on the road?"

"I don't know what you're talking about."

She sounded legitimately confused. For a moment he was almost convinced.

"You've been studying the road behind us since we left the Indian village. Maybe before, but I wasn't paying attention."

"James, please. We're almost to Winton. I'm only nervous, is all. Aren't you worried about an ambush?"

"I wasn't before. Now I am. And I certainly wasn't expecting an attack from our rear. Who would come that way? We haven't seen a soul. Unless someone knew."

"The Indians," she began. "They might still—"

Without waiting to see what additional lies she'd try to wedge into place, he jumped from his horse, grabbed her by the waist, and dragged her from her horse. She let out a little cry and suddenly looked terrified. He drew his dagger.

"You've turned into some kind of liar. But you're not good enough to fool me."

Cooper's initial confusion faded, and he wore his own hard look as he joined the other two in the road. He swept aside his cloak and drew his pistol. He deliberately checked the powder in the pan and rested his thumb on the cock, ready to draw it back from half to full cock.

Prudence's eyes darted from side to side, and her bosom heaved as she seemed to struggle for breath. James felt like a wretch for putting her to such terror, but he was more certain than ever that she was up to something, and this was not the time or place to be playing games.

"Something happened today," he said, "because you were fine yesterday, and now you behave as if something were amiss. Did you see something or someone at the villages we passed?"

"No, nothing. I swear it."

"Those boys on the road? The man with the cart? Did you pass them a message?"

"I've never seen them before in my life."

"Wait. Last night." He thought about his conversation with Cooper. "You weren't asleep, were you?"

She hesitated a fraction of a second. "I slept all night."

"Stop lying," he said in a cold voice. "It is insulting to me. I'm trying to help you and this is the credit you give. Don't you love your daughter?"

"James, please." Her lip quivered.

"How are you so quick with the lies? What happened to the honest, Godly woman I met in Boston?"

This was apparently too much for her, because her eyes filled with tears and a little sob came out of her mouth. James felt low and miserable, wanting suddenly nothing more than to wrap his arms around her and offer comfort. Instead, he kept his jaw clenched, his eyes narrowed.

But he couldn't maintain his anger. After a moment, he sighed and softened his expression and voice. "Prudie, whatever you did, tell me."

"I heard what you said about the charters."

"Ah. And you did something, didn't you? It must have been when you went back to the house. You led us to believe it was your monthly courses, but that was a lie, wasn't it?"

She wiped her eyes with the back of her hand and looked at her feet. "Aye. It was a lie."

"What did you do?"

"This morning when I went to the privy, I took my pen and papers. I wrote a letter. I wanted to leave it in the house, but you and Master Cooper were always there. So I contrived to return."

A cold fear settled into his gut. "What kind of letter?"

"A letter for Reverend Stone and Goodman Fitz-Simmons in Boston. I needed to warn them you were after the charter. I promised to pay Burrows if he would deliver it."

"Was it sealed?"

"No, it was open. I didn't have wax."

Cooper put away his pistol, groaning. "Damn you, woman."

"Wasn't it clear?" James said. "We told you, he's a *shifty fellow.* Do you know what 'shifty fellow' means?"

Cooper threw up his hands. "It means he's shifty!"

"Which you suspected already," James said. "Or you wouldn't keep checking the road behind us. You know full well he might have sold us out in Springfield."

James cast a glance at the road behind them, but the twisting, snowy trail was empty as it passed through the bare trees.

"There are people looking for you in Springfield," Cooper said. "Now Burrows knows who you are. He's going to sell that information. He probably already has."

Prudence looked up, chin jutting out defiantly. "There's nothing they don't already know. We're on our way to Winton. Samuel Knapp is probably waiting for us already. I don't see what's such a secret."

James stared at her, exasperated almost beyond words. "I'm not a fool, Prudence. Why do you think we were so careful in Springfield?"

"So they wouldn't catch us on the road?"

"No, so they wouldn't see that we were going to Winton and not south to Hartford like they believed."

"To Connecticut? Why would they think that?"

He forced patience into his voice. "What's the first thing they did when they discovered we'd fled Boston?"

"They attacked us on the highway."

"First they had to determine that we'd left Boston in the first place. The men at the gates confirmed that, together with the missing carriage and Robert Woory. And I told Woory we were going to Hartford. He marked the transaction in his ledger. So when they checked Woory's records . . ."

She scoffed at this. "They'd never believe that. Not when your business was in Winton and Crow Hollow. Even I could recognize such an obvious lie."

"She has a point," Cooper said. He had lowered his pistol and now put it away. "Nobody would expect you to tell Woory your true destination."

"I left my sea chest in the guest bedroom at the reverend's house. There is a hidden panel at the bottom, quite easily and intentionally discoverable. I left a letter purportedly written to the Crown."

"How does that alter the situation?" Prudence asked.

"I said that Peter had disrupted services, enraged Fitz-Simmons, and so we could no longer trust the deputy governor to carry out the king's wishes. Instead, I was going to Hartford to meet with Governor Leverett directly."

Prudence's defiance evaporated from her face, replaced once again by uncertainty.

"Finally, when we were in Springfield, I had Master Cooper post a letter with my seal to the royal governor of Virginia, telling him I'd be in Hartford but would come down to settle some matters in Jamestown when I finished. Do you know who the postmaster is in Springfield?" James put away his dagger. "Francis Knapp, Captain Samuel Knapp's brother."

"I see," she said. "And the road goes south from Springfield to Hartford, so we might really have been traveling that direction."

"Exactly."

"What if they sent men in both directions to look for us?" she asked.

Cooper grunted at this as he remounted his horse.

"How many men do you think these traitors have?" James asked. "Come on. We'd better hope we reach Winton first."

"Not likely," Cooper grumbled. "We're on the slow road, remember?"

"It all depends on how quickly Burrows sells us out," James said. "Exactly how shifty is this fellow, anyway?"

"He'd sell his mother to the devil himself for the right price. Believe me, they know. They'll be after us."

They picked up the pace, but it was slow travel along the snowy, rutted road.

"James," Prudence said a few minutes later.

He turned and looked at her.

She licked her lips. "I'm sorry, really. But you must understand. It's our charter, our liberties. You must understand its importance."

"Is it more important than your daughter?"

She didn't hesitate. "No."

"You should have trusted me."

"Will you still help me find her?"

This, he didn't answer.

CHAPTER TWENTY

James led the others cautiously into Winton. Women were out sweeping snow from in front of their houses, while men chopped wood or tended to stock. The sound of a hammer rang through the air. He saw nothing to raise his suspicions, but he stayed wary all the same.

"Do you see that trail?" Prudence said when they'd passed the first few houses.

She pointed to what looked like a sheep path, nothing but a slight indentation in the snow. It traversed a field, bisected a stone wall, and disappeared into the woods beyond.

"That leads you to Sachusett," she said. "The old Nipmuk village. It's no more than a mile away. The two villages lived side by side, peacefully—a full twenty years with no trouble."

"A shame," James said.

"They always said in Springfield that if trouble came, the Winton militia wouldn't fight," Cooper said. "They were too cozy with the Indians."

"Why would we?" she said. "Captain Knapp came through, trying to rile us up. We'd go fight against the Narragansett, yes.

Or even against the Nipmuk besieging Springfield. But we had no quarrel with our neighbors. The sachem of Sachusett had pledged peace and eternal brotherhood."

"Eternal up until the bloody attack, that is," Cooper said. He sounded more bitter than angry.

Prudence looked away with a sorrowful expression.

"I assume the Indian village is destroyed now," James said.

"I'm not sure," she said. "Must have been. But the Indians carried me away before it happened."

"Aye, it's gone," Cooper said. His voice was hollow. "I was there. After the Battle of Winton, we sent a revenge party to Sachusett. It was ugly business."

"War is never pretty," James said.

"You know that Indian village we passed through earlier?" Cooper asked. "That's what Sachusett looked like when we were finished."

James turned in the saddle to study the Indian road as they passed. Such a modest trail, it was hard to believe that it had led to so much violence in both directions.

"Anyway," Cooper continued after a moment, "if you continue that way, ford the creek and follow the Connecticut River, you'll be in Indian territory by nightfall."

"So the Nipmuk *aren't* exterminated," James said. "They have more villages?"

"Oh, they're gone, so far as we know," Cooper said. "But there won't be any English settlement north of the creek any time soon. Because there's always another tribe, isn't there? No matter how far you go, you'll always find another enemy. And to the north you also find the French trappers and missionaries."

"No doubt whispering lies about us," James said.

Cooper nodded. "Always."

"There's something else on the end of that trail," Prudence said. "Crow Hollow."

James was of half a mind to take a detour through the site of Knapp's massacre of the unarmed Indians, but they were coming into Winton proper. Now that they were closer he could see signs of past violence. Empty, rubble-filled lots left gaping holes between the standing houses, many of which had been rebuilt. Of the two meetinghouses sitting across from each other on the commons, the first, larger building was missing its roof and the rear wall. Snow covered the floor inside and clung to the charred beams. The pews had burned.

"Looks safe enough," Cooper said, glancing around. "A few nosy Puritans staring at us, that's all. Maybe I was wrong about Burrows. Most likely he took the money and bought strong drink when he was in Springfield, came home roaring drunk, and never noticed Widow Cotton's letter."

"Sooner or later Burrows will sober up," James said. "And then we'll have trouble."

Prudence winced.

He should let her twitch for a bit—this was a snare of her own making—but mostly he felt sorry for her. And maybe he should have trusted her more, told her his plans for throwing Knapp's men off their trail. She might have been more circumspect in her actions.

James turned to Prudence. "Your old servant—Goody Hull, was it?"

"Aye."

"And is she trustworthy?"

"She is. You wish to speak with her?"

"She survived the attack, remained in Winton after you were carried away. Mayhap she possesses information that yet eludes us. Where does she live?"

Prudence gestured with her chin. "Go past the new meeting-house. See that lane? Follow it to the end. It's the last house before the forest."

They rode down the commons, which wasn't flat but swelled to a small hillock in the middle, maybe a dozen feet high. Several paths had been carved in the snow to its top, and two girls went sliding down on a sled made of planks atop two wooden runners. On the opposite side, three boys were building a snow castle.

"I never thought I would see children playing here again," Prudence said. "Not after what happened on this very spot."

"People carry on," James said. "Memory fades."

A young girl hurried past dragging a sled, and Prudence watched her go with big, sorrowful eyes. "I only hope that some-day my Mary . . ." Her voice trailed off.

"I'm sure that she will," he said. "Have faith."

"Thank you, James. That is kind of you to say."

The last, fading remnants of his anger vanished. There was no use carrying it any further. She'd made a terrible blunder, make no mistake, but it had apparently cost them nothing.

One of the boys looked up and pointed. "Look, it's Widow Cotton!"

"Hurry," Cooper urged, "or there's bound to be a disturbance."

They urged the horses to pick up the pace. When they reached the end of the commons, Prudence drew short. She stared forward. It took James a moment to figure out what had alarmed her.

They were in front of the new meetinghouse. It was smaller, the wood still pale and unaged, the icicles on the roof draping from fresh cedar shingles. The doors were painted a somber brown. But surrounding the building was grisly evidence that Winton was fighting back against the wilderness.

At least twenty wolf heads leered from where they'd been nailed to the building, with fresh blood in several cases running from the severed heads to congeal against the boards. Even more gruesome was the pair of human heads resting on poles. These had been there some time. The lips and noses had rotted away, the eyeballs had been plucked out by crows, and the straight black hair had half fallen out.

The poles stood right next to the road. The hollow eye sockets seemed to gape at them as they approached.

Prudence looked away, her face turning pale. "I don't want to go past."

"They're dead," Cooper said. "The vermin can't hurt you now."

"They're not vermin, they're human beings."

"They proved themselves nothing but savages. And if the heathens return, they'll take one look and know what happens to savages in these parts."

Cooper's voice was so hard that James almost forgot that his former companion had himself adopted an orphan girl from these same savages. It was a strange contradiction.

Prudence looked up. "I knew these men. That is Mikmonto, the sachem. That's his half brother, Nimposet. During the battle he killed an English woman by crushing her head with the blacksmith's hammer. He kept hitting and hitting."

"He has his reward, the brute," Cooper said. "I hope they made him suffer."

"Hold your tongue," James told him. "Look away, Prudie."

A shudder worked through her, and she gripped the reins so tightly her knuckles were white. But she nodded and obeyed.

Perhaps smelling the wolf heads, the horses grew jittery as they rode around the meetinghouse to the lane Prudence had identified earlier. They didn't calm until the wind had shifted and they no longer faced the grisly scene. The three companions rode down the lane to the very end, where they came upon a small brick house with a clumsily patched roof and a yard overgrown with the bare, thorny branches of brambles jutting from the snow.

James glanced back up the lane. Two women stood at its head, staring after them. One whispered in the other's ear.

"Take the horses around back to the barn," he told Cooper as the three of them dismounted. "Find them water and something to eat, if you can. But keep them ready to go. And check your powder, make sure it's dry."

Cooper did as he was told. James took Prudence's elbow and led her up to the door. She still seemed to be suffering under the spell of whatever memories had come clawing up when she'd spotted the Indian heads.

"Are you ready?" he asked.

"I don't know. Honestly, I'm not sure I can face the widow. I saw her husband die and did nothing to stop it."

"She was there, she knows you were helpless to stop it."

"I never saw her that day. The Hulls lived on the other side of the village. I don't know how she escaped—I only saw what happened to Goodman Hull."

He nodded, attempting sympathy, but there was no time to patiently work her through this.

"We're rather pressed," he said. "I can only assume that Burrows saw your note, hurried back to Springfield, and found Knapp looking for us. The brute might be riding hard up the road as we speak. The moment Knapp reaches Winton, someone is going to point helpfully down this lane."

She took a deep breath and nodded. "I understand."

"I'm a stranger here. Goody Hull knows you and trusts you. You must keep your wits about you. Ask her the right questions, find out exactly what happened that day. Can you do that?"

"If I must."

He knocked.

An old woman with an eye patch opened the door. She held the end of her shawl over her face, like the old women James sometimes saw in London who ventured from their houses rarely, and with great fear of breathing diseased air. He couldn't see why that was necessary here.

Prudence hesitated only a moment before seeming to recover her wits. "Goody Hull, what cheer. It's me, Widow Cotton. May I come in?"

"It's Widow Hull now, my husband—Prudie?" the woman said from behind her shawl. Her good eye teared up. "Bless you child, you've returned. Oh, praise be!"

There was something strange about her voice, as if she had a defect in her speech.

The woman dropped the shawl so she could put a veiny, gnarled hand against Prudence's cheek. It was then that James saw what she'd been hiding.

Half of the woman's face was missing.

Chapter Twenty-One

As Goody Hull led them inside to the single room that was her keeping room, her kitchen, and her bedroom alike, Prudence fought to get over her shock. She'd been battling her memories ever since they'd entered Winton. The houses where people had died, the commons where the Nipmuk had scalped, tortured, and murdered captives. The dead Nipmuk warriors outside, with their hollow, rotted stares.

And now, poor Goody Hull. Half her nose was gone, and her cheek had been crudely stitched together and then had healed in a mass of pink scar tissue that ran from her jawline to her neck. To turn her head required moving her entire body. It was all Prudence could do not to scream, or at least slap her hand over her mouth.

Take hold, woman. Goody Hull has suffered all you have, and threefold.

The old woman seated them on a rough bench next to a small, nearly extinct fire, then moved slowly to take a seat opposite. Prudence glanced at James. If he was horrified, he didn't show it.

Goody Hull frowned. "I am poor, and I don't have much to offer. And I can see you must be famished from the road." She started to rise. "I could heat a little cider from the jug. That will warm your bones."

"Please, good woman," James said. He rose to his feet and eased her back down. "Don't trouble yourself. We can see to that."

Prudence was already up and pouring cider from the jug into a kettle, then shifting it to a hook over the fire. She tossed in two split pieces of firewood before she noticed that the wood basket was practically empty. The widow was watching her feed the fire with a miser's careful stare.

"I'm so happy to see that you've remarried," Goody Hull said, turning her gaze from the wood basket. "And to such a handsome young man too. You must be a fine man to win Prudie's hand, Master—?"

"James Bailey," he said quickly. He and Prudence exchanged glances.

"A good, strong name. What brings you to Winton? Are you settling here with my dear Prudie?"

"No, not just yet," Prudence said.

The woman's face fell. "I see."

She had likely been hoping to serve Prudence and her new husband. The crippled widow would be even less use as a servant than Old John Porter, but Prudence found herself aching to offer the woman something, anything, to ease her poverty.

"Before I forget, let me settle your accounts," James said. He reached into his cloak and removed from his purse three guineas, which Goody Hull stared at without taking from his outstretched hand.

"Accounts?" She began to reach for the money, then withdrew with a flinch, as if he were Satan offering forbidden fruit from the garden.

He took her wrist and pressed the coins into her palm. "Nay, it is yours," he said smoothly. "There was a small bequest in Sir Benjamin's will."

CROW HOLLOW

"But Reverend Stone already gave me fifteen shillings."

Fifteen shillings? Was that all Prudence's brother-in-law had given the widow? Why hadn't Prudence paid closer attention to the settling of the estate?

James's expression darkened for a moment, before smoothing again. "Fifteen? Pray, pardon me. I thought you'd already been paid thirty." He fetched another half crown and five silver pennies, which he added to the gold coins already in the widow's hand. "There, now you have the full bequest."

Goody Hull stared at the money through her good eye, her ruined mouth slack. Her voice trembled. "I don't understand."

"There was apparently some mistake," Prudence said. "This is the rest of the money."

"But it's so much."

"Nevertheless, it's yours," James said. "In gratitude for years of service to Sir Benjamin and his family. He wanted to leave you something."

"Oh! 'Twill make such a difference. A tremendous difference indeed."

The widow rose shakily to her feet. She opened a small cedar box sitting in a brick niche next to the hearth and dropped the coins in one by one. Prudence gave James a grateful smile. He shrugged, but looked pleased.

"It has been so long," Goody Hull told Prudence when she returned. "I never saw you after that day in Winton, when my Peter was killed by the savages. He was a good man. A fine man."

"Is that when you were injured?" Prudence asked.

Goody Hull lifted her shawl and held it up to her face. Her good eye stared into the fire.

"Many people suffered," James said in a gentle voice. "Don't be ashamed for what happened to you. Be grateful that the good Lord spared your life."

It was the perfect thing to say, because Goody Hull lowered the shawl slowly. "Pray forgive an old woman her vanities, Master Bailey."

He reached across and squeezed her hand.

James gave Prudence a significant look. *Now.*

She swallowed hard. She had to do this, she had to revisit those days, even if it meant tearing off scabs and opening wounds only partly healed.

"Do you remember who told us to return to Winton?" Prudence asked the old woman.

"Of course. It was those treacherous beasts in Sachusett. They said we'd be safe."

"No, it wasn't the Indians. We were on the road to Springfield and some English riders came up. *They* told us to return. They said King Philip was attacking Springfield and we'd be safer at home."

"That's right, I'd forgotten that," the old woman said. "It was the militia. And only a few riders. The rest had gone on ahead to Springfield."

"I was in a carriage, feeding my child, and I didn't see who it was. Do you remember who told us?"

Goody Hull frowned. "I can't remember. Sir Benjamin was arguing with them, I remember that. It was someone from Boston."

"Captain Knapp?"

"I—I'm not sure. Perhaps. I didn't know the man at the time. I only met him later, when he came to Winton after the attack. A brave man. He charged into the meetinghouse and rescued us."

Yes, but only after an awful siege that had lasted a day, a night, and a day. By then, Prudence was already in captivity and miles away, had already seen such horrors. The memory of that day was like a hand squeezing her heart, and suddenly she had a hard time breathing.

Prudence had awakened at dawn to the sound of a hollow thump. Still half-asleep, at first she thought it was distant thunder.

It was September, and the weather was unusually hot and humid for the lateness of the season. But then a scream cut through the air, and she was instantly awake, reaching for her husband with one hand and her daughter's cradle with the other. Benjamin was already sitting upright and grabbing his boots.

Two more thumps. This time it was unmistakable. Musket fire.

Benjamin raced downstairs to grab his guns, while Prudence pounded on doors to wake the servants. Young Ellen came staggering into the hallway, hand over her mouth, eyes wide. She was only twelve, a local girl who had been hired to help with Mary. From the room down the hall emerged Benjamin's manservant from London, a young fellow named Jonathan Brown. He went downstairs to help Benjamin with the guns, while Ellen stayed terrified and trembling with Prudence and the baby.

"They're going to kill us!" Ellen kept screaming.

Prudence propped Mary on her hip with one hand and used the other to give the girl a good shake. "Keep your wits. You must be calm."

As soon as Prudence had the servants up and dressed, she hurried to the window. Benjamin and Jonathan stood on the front porch below her, shouting at people to take refuge in the house. English men and women were racing back and forth across the commons, pursued by Indians.

There were at least fifty young men in the Nipmuk raiding party, armed with muskets, hatchets, stone clubs, bows and arrows, and even rusty swords. Most wore nothing but loincloths. Several had surrounded Goodman Halpern, who was dressed in his nightclothes, and they smashed at him with their musket butts, jeering.

The Nipmuk had already set fire to three houses on the opposite side of the green, and this was presumably where the people fleeing across the commons had come from. A pair of Indians were pushing a wagon filled with burning hay up against the wall of another house. Two women had opened the upstairs window of the house in question and hurled down bedpans, pots, wooden ladles—anything they could get their hands on to drive away the enemy and their wagon of burning hay.

Meanwhile, in the commons, Goodman Halpern struggled to break free from his tormentors. Blood streamed from a cut above his eye, but he was still on his feet.

"Over here!" Benjamin shouted. He and Jonathan strode toward him with muskets leveled at the Indians.

Halpern spotted them and tried to get loose. He had taken two steps toward the Cotton house when an Indian stepped behind him with a blacksmith's hammer and landed a crushing blow on the back of his skull. Halpern fell. The Indian stood over him, smashing at the man's head again and again while his companions screamed in delight.

Prudence had gaped in horror. She recognized the killer. His name was Nimposet, one of the sachem's half brothers, and she'd spoken to him many times. He would come to her house to trade honeycomb or a basket of wild leeks for a pair of wool socks or a few nails. Once, when her horse had come up lame in the middle of a rainstorm, he and another Indian had appeared wearing friendly grins and offered to carry her into Winton so she wouldn't have to walk on the muddy road.

What, in the name of all that was holy, had turned Nimposet into a murderer?

Benjamin and Jonathan hurried across the green, too late now for Halpern, but maybe in time to rescue a few of the others. They lifted their muskets and fired. Neither shot hit. Several Nipmuk, led by Nimposet, made as if to charge.

Ellen was screaming again. Prudence handed Mary to the girl, who almost dropped the child, and ran downstairs after her husband and the boy, determined to stand by their side rather than cower indoors in fear.

At that moment, a disturbance sounded near the meeting-house. Half the Englishmen in town were in Springfield, trying to relieve the siege, but several of the remaining men were gathering with swords and muskets, while others fled the burning houses to take refuge in the meetinghouse. Nimposet and his fellows turned to face this new threat.

At first Benjamin wanted to set off to help, but they were completely cut off by the main body of the enemy. And several villagers had spotted the armed men in front of the Cotton house and were now racing in their direction, screaming for help.

The next hour was a horror. The Nipmuk lit one house after another on fire. The English inside fled their burning homes and tried to reach the safety of those buildings being held against the savage assault. Several made it safely to the Cotton house. Others fell, heads split open, throats slit, musket fire cutting them down. One boy reached the house after surviving the gauntlet, only to die a few minutes later as his life's blood emptied on Prudence's floor.

Inside the Cotton house, fear and bewilderment raged as hot as the fires around the commons. Women screamed for their dead children, and children for their parents. Men and boys fired from windows or out the door and drove away Indians trying to set fire to the house. Prudence tended to wounds. Some women helped her, while others sat with dazed expressions on their blood-spattered faces.

Sweet heavens. Why now? There hadn't been so much as a single shot fired between Winton and Sachusett during the first several months of the war, and regular meetings had taken place between the two sides to reassure each other of peaceful intent. Why would Mikmonto send his warriors to attack now?

She found her husband. "Should we fight our way to the meetinghouse?"

Benjamin gave a grim shake of the head. "We have four men, counting Jonathan. We'll never make it."

"The women can fight too." Prudence glanced to the center of the room, where more than a dozen people huddled. "Some of them, at least. Goody Wentworth and Goody Jones, plus myself. That makes seven, counting the men."

"We only have three muskets—we're a gun short already."

"A sword, then. A poker from the fire." Prudence's mind cast about desperately for ideas. "Perchance we could overwhelm some Indians next time they attack and take their weapons."

"No. We wait here." His voice was firm, with no room for argument. "If the powder holds up, we can fight them off until either they exhaust themselves, or we're relieved from Springfield."

What relief would that be, she wondered bitterly. Springfield was fighting its own battle, and she could scarcely believe that anyone had escaped Winton in order to warn them, anyway.

The assault continued on and off all day. More houses went up in flames, one by one, until thick black smoke smothered the sky. The air inside was thick with the smell of blood and sweat and the stench of the dead boy, who had lost control of his bowels as he died. But nobody wanted to put him outside. During lulls in the fighting, the Indians were torturing captives and abusing corpses.

At night, the Nipmuk made several more attempts to burn the house. Once, a ball of flaming rags caught the roof on fire, but Prudence had earlier led a silent expedition after dark into the backyard, and they'd filled every vessel in the house with water. They punched a hole in the roof, climbed out, and doused the flames.

When dawn returned, they woke to see the meetinghouse on fire and people fleeing ahead of the inferno. As they watched in horror, villagers came streaming out only to be clubbed or hacked to death. For a long time, the survivors inside the Cotton house could only watch, weeping and unable to help.

Prudence could barely stand. Mary had been wailing for two hours, and nothing she could do would comfort the child. Not even nursing would calm her.

Suddenly, someone screamed that the back of the house was on fire. While they'd been watching the meetinghouse, several Indians had somehow come up behind and pushed another burning cart against the walls. Benjamin and Jonathan rushed out, but a hail of bullets drove them back.

Soon the house was on fire all around them. Smoke choked the air. They tried to go out the front, but more Indians had gathered and were dancing around, whooping and taunting. One by one the villagers were murdered as they fled the burning building: women, children, and the elderly. A few they dragged away, and for no apparent reason. These they kicked and jabbed but didn't kill.

A man stood alone in the middle of the commons, standing tall and erect. He stared at the house through narrowed eyes.

It was the sachem himself. Mikmonto. So proud. So haughty.

The strange thing, Prudence thought, was that his expression had never changed. Not when she fell into captivity. Not even when she'd entered Winton again with Cooper and James and spotted his head sticking on a pike. Even dead, even half-rotted with his eyes missing, somehow he still carried that same look. It seemed to carry a message.

I have won.

CHAPTER TWENTY-TWO

"And then what happened?" James asked. He was studying Prudence with an intense expression.

She blinked and looked around Goody Hull's humble front room. The fire had died to throbbing coals. The widow had closed her remaining eye and looked pale and on the verge of fainting.

Only gradually did Prudence realize she had been sharing all of her memories of that awful day aloud. She'd begun with the intention of drawing out Goody Hull, but had instead told her own story.

"You know it already. It's in my narrative."

"The Battle of Winton is half of one page," he said. "There's no detail to that part."

"That's enough detail for anyone."

"Prudie, you must. If I'm to—" He stopped and glanced at Goody Hull. "We must chronicle what happened. It's the only path to the truth."

Prudence swallowed hard and nodded.

"When the fire was too much to bear, we fled the house. Jonathan came out first, and they knocked him over the head.

Then came a woman and her two daughters. They knocked them over the head too. Finally, Benjamin got control of the survivors and led the rest of us out together. Someone got shot and my husband tripped over him. I went to his side screaming, thinking he'd been killed. Someone grabbed me and dragged me off. Benjamin got up. Later, they put the prisoners in the middle of the commons. Some they abused."

Goody Hull groaned. "My husband. He was there. I saw what they did to him. They tortured him, mutilated him."

Prudence reached over and put a hand on the woman's hand. "My Benjamin too."

"How did you survive?" James asked the old woman.

Goody Hull touched a hand to the twisted scar on her face. "One of the Indians hit me in the face with his hatchet and left me for dead. Goody Harris and Goody Tilman dragged me away. Some of us hid in a barn, behind bales of hay. They came for hay to set their fires, but they never did find us."

Prudence turned to see James studying her. "But you saw them kill Goodman Hull, your husband, and the others?" he asked.

Prudence nodded. "Aye. They took the survivors to the commons while they tortured and murdered. That's when they finally killed my husband. When they'd had their fill, they marched us into the wilderness."

James had a curious look on his face, like he was trying to figure something out. "Back to Sachusett?"

"No, we never went to their village. They must have known 'twould be the first place the militia would go when they saw what had happened to Winton."

"And then?"

Her mouth felt dry. If she closed her eyes, she knew she would see the crows. The eye in the beak.

"They took us north. You've read the rest of it."

"Why did they do it?" Goody Hull asked, her voice plaintive. "We never did them no harm. Why would they hurt us?"

Prudence had asked herself that many, many times. She'd asked her captors, but they'd never given a good answer. Perhaps Mikmonto had heard about the slaughter of the Narragansett, or maybe it was nothing more than suddenly believing that King Philip and his allies stood a chance of wiping out the English.

"Wait a moment," James said to Goody Hull. "I thought you said Knapp rescued you in the meetinghouse. But you said you hid in a barn. Which is it?"

"The meetinghouse," the old woman said. "Five of us had been hiding in the barn. After all the screaming, it grew quiet, but we didn't dare leave. It was so hot. I was so thirsty. And faint from my wounds. The barn stank. They'd killed all the animals, and in the heat they were squirming with maggots and flies. We waited for three days without daring to leave. Then we heard voices. English voices, so we came out."

"The militia?" James asked.

"First it was other survivors," Goody Hull said. "They'd hid in the woods or behind stone walls. We went to the meetinghouse, or what was left of it. We were trying to fortify it when the militia returned."

"Of course it would be Captain Knapp at the head," James said.

"I wouldn't have expected it," Prudence said. "Knapp was from the coast, and his forces mostly Plymouth and Boston men. I'd have expected Captain Pearson—he was the head of the Springfield militia, and his sister's family lived in Winton."

"We were glad to see him, though," Goody Hull said. "He was our savior, Captain Knapp. After he finished off the brutes, we were happy to see him settle in Winton."

Prudence sat up straighter. "What do you mean? He lives in Boston."

"Only until spring, that's what they say." Goody Hull turned her head, almost birdlike, to fix Prudence with her good eye. "Why, Goody Cotton, you were the one who sold him your land."

"No, I didn't."

"*Someone* did, and in your name too. Six hundred acres right here in Winton that he'll be farming with his brothers, and another two hundred where Sir Benjamin wanted to build the mill."

Any doubts Prudence might have cherished now vanished. Her face grew hot with anger thinking how Knapp had profited from this ungodly business. She exchanged glances with James, whose mouth settled into a tight line.

"How else would we resettle Winton?" Goody Hull continued. "Half the town died that day. If it weren't for good folk like Knapp and his men bringing their families, the wilderness would soon reclaim this land. Why, even the deputy governor is coming. Goodman Fitz-Simmons owns most of old Sachusett now."

"Oh he does, does he?" James said. "Well, now we know."

⚘

James was still digesting this new piece of information when the door to Goody Hull's cottage flung open. James and Prudence were both on their feet before they saw that it was Cooper. The man glanced at the widow and recoiled from her ruined features. His horrified expression vanished in a second, but the old woman looked aghast. She whipped the shawl in front of her face to hide it.

James had reached for his pistol, but now he removed his hand from his cloak. "What is it?"

"A man is standing at the head of the alley. He's holding a musket."

James rushed to the door. Sure enough, a solitary figure stood next to the meetinghouse, staring hard down the lane in their direction. He glanced back over his shoulder toward the commons, as if expecting someone.

James ducked back in. "Prudie, we have to go. Now."

"Already?" Goody Hull said as Prudence sprang to her feet. "Oh, couldn't you stay a spell?"

James turned on his heel without offering additional explanation and raced after Cooper as he ran around the side of the house toward the horses. Prudence joined them, with the widow's thin voice still calling after them, begging them to tarry. Moments later, the three companions were back in the saddle.

When they rode into the lane, James fully intended to charge the single man guarding the end of the lane. If the villain tried to stop them, James would blow out his brains. But in the few short seconds since Cooper had raised the alarm, two more men had arrived, one of them on horse.

The rider was Samuel Knapp. No covered face this time—if indeed that had been he on the road. This time he sat proudly in the saddle, his lips pulled into a sneer.

The first man was still glancing over his shoulder. No question what that meant. More men were on the way.

To James's rear, the lane ended shortly beyond the widow's cottage, where it gave way to pasture. At the moment, the open land was a solid field of white, stretching perhaps a half mile until it reached the forest. Not a single track or trail broke the expanse. There might be rocks to break the ankles of horses or other hidden obstacles to send riders flying from their saddles. But he didn't see as he had a choice.

"This way!"

He turned his horse toward the pasture. Prudence and Cooper followed on their mounts. The animals plunged into the snow. Shouts sounded at their backs.

James led the horses as fast as he dared across the field. He glanced over his shoulder to see Knapp giving chase, with the men on foot following. The latter struggled when they reached the knee-deep snow. James led his companions a good two hundred yards into the pasture, before ordering Cooper to follow him about. The two men wheeled around.

Knapp drew short when the two sides were roughly a hundred yards apart. He held a musket, against James and Cooper's pistols, which would be useless at this range. But Knapp's companions on foot had fallen well behind, and he must know that if he fired, he'd have only one shot. Then James and Cooper would charge him.

"Prudence Cotton!" Knapp roared. "Come away from those villains at once."

"The devil take you, Samuel Knapp!" she answered. Though she wasn't armed, she'd come up beside James and Cooper.

"This is your last chance, *woman*." He spat this last word as if it were a curse. "Leave these men or suffer the consequences."

"You will burn in hellfire," she snapped. "But first you'll swing from a rope, I swear before God, you miserable cur."

Knapp let out an incoherent bellow of rage. He lifted his musket to snap off an ill-advised shot. The range was too great, and the musket was the only advantage he had until the rest of his men could catch up. The fool.

But Knapp was aiming not at the men, James saw to his horror, but at Prudence. She must have seen the same thing, because she flinched. The cock fell, the flint struck. Fire and smoke belched from the end of Knapp's musket, followed a split second later by the audible thump of ignited gunpowder.

Fear sucked at James's intestines. He had time to see Prudence's eyes widen slightly.

No, please. God, no.

But a hundred yards was a long shot to take from the back of a horse. The ball whizzed past with an audible whoosh of air. Knapp had missed. Prudence was unharmed. James let out his breath in a gasp. He hadn't even realized he'd been holding it.

Triumph rose in his breast. "Now we have him!"

"Look!" Cooper cried, before James could order a charge.

Two more riders burst from the edge of the lane and came charging across the field. Behind them, two more men on foot slogged into the snow with muskets in hand. And the first two footmen continued to doggedly wade toward them. There were now seven enemies in all.

James had no choice. It was flee or be killed. He shouted for Prudence and Cooper to follow, and they galloped recklessly across the snowy pasture toward the woods on the far side.

CHAPTER TWENTY-THREE

They were still a hundred yards from the trees when Cooper's horse stumbled and fell. The man flew over the horse's head with a cry. He almost disappeared into the snow before he came up, covered in white. His horse screamed in pain as it tried to regain its feet and failed.

James grabbed Cooper's arm and helped him onto the back of his own horse. It took precious time. By the time he was ready to go again, Prudence had reached the woods. James turned in the saddle, expecting to find the enemy almost on top of them.

But to his relief, the distance between the two groups had grown. Knapp had waited for the other two riders, and the three men now forged slowly across the snow, directly behind them. The three footmen, on the other hand, cut northeast at an angle.

The reason revealed itself as James studied their approach. If James had hoped to simply disappear into the woods, it was apparent this would never work. The ground had begun to slope up already; by the time he reached the trees, he'd be on the side of a hill and climbing steeply. The snow was heavier there, caught in great drifts, and various snags, rocky outcrops, and other obstacles would make foot travel difficult enough. On horseback it would be impossible. The steepest ground was to the north and west. The enemy expected their quarry to lose the horses at the woods, then cut east on foot, where they'd be intercepted.

James saw no other choice. Here in the open, two men with pistols against a half-dozen enemies with muskets, he wouldn't stand a chance. And they were now so far outside Winton that there would be no witnesses to see how they'd been gunned down in cold blood.

Cooper had apparently come to the same conclusion. "Maybe we should surrender."

"I won't surrender to those murderers."

They reached Prudence, who had already dismounted. "Hurry. This way. Into the woods."

"We'll never make it," Cooper insisted. "They'll follow our tracks."

James wasn't going to argue the point. "Over there," he said, pointing to a fallen tree, its broad roots torn up and presenting a shelter of sorts. "If we hide there—"

"That won't work," Cooper insisted. "Listen, they won't hurt a woman."

"I wouldn't count on it," James said.

"So they can hardly murder us if we surrender, not with her as a witness."

"For the love of God," Prudence cried. "Will you trust me? *Please.*"

She'd already waded a good twenty feet into the woods and was gesturing violently for them to follow. The two men glanced at each other, and James saw Cooper come to the same conclusion at the same time. Without another word of complaint, they abandoned the horses and charged after her. In a moment they'd reached her side, and the three continued together.

James was the younger and stronger of the two men, so he got in front to forge a trail for the others to follow. It left a fine trail for their enemies to follow. Already, he heard shouts from behind and knew that Knapp and his men had gained the trees.

The forest closed around them. It was a mixed woods of pine and hardwood, with the thick branches of the former shielding them from the men below. It sounded like they were perhaps a hundred yards back. And, James reminded himself, there were more men who would be cutting into the forest to the east.

The largest drifts reached almost to James's thighs, and he was soon tiring. Every time he bumped a pine tree, it sent a shower of snow cascading onto his head and shoulders. The hill grew steeper and steeper, their progress slowing by the minute.

"Let me up front," Prudence urged a few minutes later.

"I'm stronger. If I go first"—he stopped to catch his breath—"we'll all move faster."

"It's not a question of speed." She drew in a ragged gasp. "James, please."

He was nigh exhausted from the climb and the slog, so he slowed while she pushed first past Cooper, then James. She struggled another twenty feet or so, so slow that he wanted to shout at her to move aside. She reached another fallen log, jumped over the top, took several steps forward, then backed up slowly. She climbed on top of the log.

"Up here, quick."

They joined her on top of the log. It had fallen over a rocky ledge and was now propped against the rock like a ladder at an angle. The ledge was covered with huge, icicle-like protrusions, each one stacked on top of the next from cycles of freezing and thawing, and yellowish brown from the minerals leached from the soil.

To James's astonishment, she started to scale the ledge instead of going around it and looking for a gentler way up. The two men followed. The rock and ice numbed James's hands, and climbing the seven or eight feet up took so long he was afraid the enemy would catch them before they made it.

Once they were all up top, Prudence snapped off a pine branch and used it to sweep snow over the edge.

"Go deeper in," she urged. "Quickly, out of sight."

James glanced down before obeying and was shocked to see that it appeared that they'd climbed over the log and then disappeared. Yes, you could see that someone had shoved a bunch of new snow over the top of the log, but it looked like it must have fallen from the top of the surrounding pine trees. So unless someone had climbed into those trees . . .

Voices sounded below. So very close now. He shrank away from the edge.

"Now where have they gone?" Knapp said, his voice ripe with irritation.

"The devil take me!" a worried voice said. "They've disappeared. It's witchcraft."

"Don't be a fool," Knapp snarled back. "Spread out. They must be near."

Meanwhile, the three companions kept going in, deeper and deeper. Prudence waved to get James's attention, then clarified with hand gestures. He picked up her meaning: *You take the lead, cut this way.*

Her gestures were smooth and practiced. It must be a sort of hand language she'd learned from the Nipmuk. And that clever bit with the log and the ledge and the pine branch—that must have been a trick picked up from her captors as well.

He shouldn't have been surprised. It was known even in London that the only way to track natives through the woods was by using other natives. The English were helpless in the wilderness.

James felt some of that helplessness now as he kept going, always steeper and deeper. The cold and wet crawled up his legs, and exhaustion settled into his bones. Prudence insisted they keep going. He began to shiver, and not just with cold.

The woods themselves were almost more frightening than the enemies they'd left behind. The nearest to these woods he'd experienced had been the estates at Fontainebleau, south of Paris, where King Louis had hunted stag and wild boar. But that was a forest where old stone walls and ruined cottages marked human habitation, where if you kept going for a few minutes you'd soon enough come across a trail used by gamekeepers or illegal woodcutters.

This was the edge of the great North American wilderness, scarcely a mile or two beyond the last town on the frontier, but already vast and wild and dangerous. Here he saw bear tracks, later a pile of droppings from some deer-like creature, except the pellets were much larger.

Cooper had been taking a turn at cutting a trail and suddenly drew short. "Sweet heavens."

An enormous creature stood watching them from a dozen feet away. It was shaped like a deer, only six feet high at the shoulder, with an enormous, horse-like head. Its antlers spread wider than a man's reach, with vast, paddle-like ends that looked like they could pick up a man and toss him twenty feet. It must weigh a hundred stone. Maybe more.

He'd heard of these monsters. A moose.

"Stand still," Prudence said. "Make no movements."

The moose stared at them for several tense seconds before turning and strolling casually away. Its legs lifted so high with each step that the deep snow presented it no trouble. It crashed through the pines and was gone. James's heart was thumping in his ears.

They continued another twenty minutes until they reached a meadow that stretched along the top of the hill. An animal path cut over the ridgeline to the opposite side. From the clearing they could see back toward Winton and the surrounding countryside. At this distance, the village was a tiny, huddled mass of houses in the midst of a vast wilderness. To the north and west, hills and valleys and more hills, all the way to the horizon. Unbroken by any settlement or clearing.

It would take the English a thousand years to settle this continent, James thought, if they ever managed.

To get his mind off his cold, wet feet, he examined the contents of his cloak. He still had his pistols, his coin purse, and his other effects, so far as they would help. What he needed was a satchel of food or some dry socks.

"So we've escaped," James said. "Now what?"

"Let's say two hours to dusk," Cooper said glumly. "After that, we freeze and die. My poor wife and kids."

"Such gloom," Prudence said. "Keep faith, the both of you."

"I see no way out of this predicament," Cooper said. "I only pray that death comes quick."

Prudence wore a curious sort of smile that James found comforting. After that little trick escaping Knapp and his brutes, he was more than happy to trust that she had a plan.

"Only Englishmen freeze in the woods," Prudence said.

"That is hardly a comfort," Cooper said. "Being English, and not Indian."

But James understood. "So perhaps we should follow the ways of the Indian. Prudie?"

She gave the two men a smile and a bold wink, before setting off again without another word. The two men gaped at each other for a long moment, then rushed to catch up.

James was relieved when Prudence took charge and cut down any objections Cooper voiced.

Since entering the woods, James had felt jangled, helpless. For the first time since entering New England, he had no plan. The cold, the loss of their horses, and above all, the wilderness itself left him feeling not unlike how he'd felt in those terrible days at sea, when the storms hit and immense waves smashed brutally over the deck.

The forest was alive. Noises in the trees and brush, the way the upper branches shook from some unseen, unfelt breeze. It was as if the trees were moving of their own accord, passing whispers about interlopers. Every twig snap or bird song sounded like an Indian, Nipmuks watching, waiting to take their revenge.

He thought of all the times he'd scoffed at tales of faeries in the woods, or witches holding their black masses deep in some hidden cove. Those stories didn't seem so implausible now.

Prudence found a hollow between a pair of giant, knobby boulders that appeared to have been dragged from some great distance and then dropped. She told the two men to break off the dead lower branches of pine trees and set them on one of the rocks where they'd stay dry. She asked for James to lend her his dagger. When she had it, she set off back the way they'd come.

"Where has she gone?" Cooper asked, his voice tight, nervous. "'Twill be dark soon."

There was some comfort in knowing that James wasn't alone in his fears. "Lucifer only knows."

"Shh, don't speak that name." Cooper glanced around, frightened.

Aloud, the man's fears sounded ridiculous. And that made James feel better. "What, are you afraid you'll draw Old Scratch?"

"I don't know," Cooper said, defensively. "Maybe."

Prudence returned, James's dagger in one hand and a small bundle of what looked like broken thatch in the other.

"One day the Sachusett warriors got hold of a cask of spirits in one of their raids," she said. "They got roaring drunk that night. Strange Indians came into camp, and they started drinking too. One of these strangers pulled me aside. He stank of alcohol. I thought he was going to—well, you understand."

As she spoke, she handed Cooper the bundle, which turned out to be shredded bark, and returned the dagger to James. Then she took out his pistol and slapped the barrel against her palm to dislodge the wad of powder and ball inside. She gave James the ball and collected the powder into the palm of her hand. At last he understood what she was about.

"He spoke excellent English," she continued. "Claimed he was a Wampanoag. 'When you English came here, you were babes,' he told me. 'Sick and starving. We showed you how to gather clams and oysters, how to plant corn, how to net alewives from the streams. Now that you are settled, your cattle multiply across the land. Your settlers kill the game and clear the forests. You are like a child who has grown up and throws his father out of his house.'"

"That's hardly true," Cooper grumbled. "The settlers at Plymouth had scarcely landed when they came under attack by those brutes."

Now that he could see what Prudence intended, James helped her use the broken sticks to make a good nesting spot for a flame. There, they placed most of the shredded bark. James kept the rest aside. Prudence added a pinch of black powder to what was already primed in the pan, drew back the cock, and struck it with the flint. At the flare, James held a bit of bark to the pan. When it caught, he shielded it from the wind with his other hand, blowing on it gently as he tucked the flaming end into the nest of sticks and bark.

Prudence protected the small fire with her body while she fed it sticks. "A few weeks later," she continued, "they said that the Wampanoag warrior had been killed."

"Who was he?" James asked.

"He said his name was Metacomet."

Cooper drew in his breath. "King Philip. The villain himself."

"That wasn't in your narrative," James said.

"The Indians destroyed Winton, slaughtering men, women, children. They tortured my husband to death. They took me and my daughter into captivity. At the end, they tore Mary from my arms. How does it sound if I report the enemy's perspective with such obvious sympathy?"

James saw her point. And yet. "If neutrally told . . ."

"There is no neutrality in the telling," Prudence said firmly. "The words themselves shape the truth of the matter."

That was the end of the discussion.

Chapter Twenty-Four

It wasn't long before the three companions were sitting with their backs against the adjacent boulder, which absorbed and reflected heat. The yellowed ice encrusting the edges had first dripped and now trailed a steady stream of water, but they'd channeled it to run away from their makeshift camp. Broken pine boughs enclosed the two boulders, sheltering them against both the wind and prying eyes who might spot the campfire from a distance.

As he warmed back to near alertness in front of Prudence's fire, James's wits began to thaw as well. A plan coalesced in his mind. He found a flat stone and took out Prudence's diary pages and his quill. The plume was bent after the adventures of the past few days, but not broken. He removed a vial of amber liquid from a cloak pocket, unscrewed the top, then blew in his fist to warm it before beginning to write between the lines of Prudence's fine, even script. He scrawled by feel, rather than by sight, since he couldn't see the words.

Prudence saw what he was doing and tried to snatch away her pages. "Don't deface that!"

He held them out of reach. "Don't worry, I'm not harming it." When she'd calmed, he showed her.

"There's nothing there. I don't understand."

"He's writing an invisible message," Cooper explained. "The ink is a tincture of onion juices, which gives its message only when heated over a candle. If James is intercepted, it will only appear that he's carrying the missing chapter from your narrative. He won't be hanged as a spy."

That was mostly true, except that James wasn't going to be the one carrying the papers. But he wouldn't explain this until later, as he still had a few details to consider.

When he finished, they used the failing light to construct a few snares of bent saplings and twisted loops of birch bark to catch a hare or squirrel while they slept. Prudence searched the hillside for likely places to set them. Meanwhile, it would be a hungry night— nobody had grabbed food from the saddlebags before Knapp and his men drove them into the woods.

By the time they returned to the fire, James had put the final pieces of his plan together. He sketched out the bones of it for Cooper, who listened with a deepening scowl when he heard how James would send him off alone to summon help from New York.

"They'll kill me," Cooper said when James had finished.

"Only if you're caught." James slapped his old friend on the shoulder to give him courage. "This is no worse than that time at Versailles, when the pope's assassin tried to knife you in the spleen. You took that for an adventure, remember?"

"I didn't have a wife and children then," he said gloomily.

"You'd rather forge into the wilderness with Prudence?"

Cooper grunted. "I'll need supplies. I can't set off for Hartford like this. I'd better return to Springfield, first."

"They'll be watching your house," James said. "And you obviously cannot trust your shifty fellow."

"Nay, I won't trust Burrows," Cooper said. "But I know Springfield, the back roads and country lanes. I know unguarded homes where I might pilfer a meal or two." He glanced at Prudence. "A shame that it's necessary."

"I made an unforgivable error," Prudence said. "Why did I write that letter? What madness took hold of me?"

"Set it aside," James said. "Anyway, we can't be certain that is what caused our troubles. Knapp may have discovered our ruse in Hartford, then doubled back, guessing correctly we'd be riding to Winton."

"The biggest difficulty isn't Springfield," Cooper said. "It's what happens when I ride south into Connecticut. I'll have to pass through the breadth of the colony to reach New York."

"There's a man in Hartford. Another fellow taking the king's money. Ten pounds, six, these seven years. He won't accompany you to New York, but he'll hire the men who will."

James took out his purse and removed three gold guineas, which he placed in Cooper's palm. "This should be sufficient to pay your expenses."

"Knapp will have spread word," Cooper said. "No doubt offered a reward. Do you suppose ten pounds, six is enough to compel this man of yours?"

"Ten pounds, six, and an oath of loyalty. The same oath you and I took in all good faith."

"I see. And do you intend to share his name or will you have me knocking on every door in Hartford until I find the man?"

"I wrote his name and street on the last page of Prudence's chapter. Candle flame will give up the secret."

Cooper stared at the coins, still sitting in his palm. They glowed a ruddy yellow in the light of the fire.

With every moment of hesitation, James's concern deepened. Cooper had lived six years in New England, married a handsome Puritan woman, and fathered her children. He'd survived the war, had voiced strong opinions during the previous two days about the natives, had even let slip once or twice criticism of the mother country.

Only one thing kept Richard Cooper from being a New Englander in every sense of the word: twenty pounds a year from the treasury of King Charles. Those were meager wages to buy a man's loyalty, oath or no.

But swear the oath, he had. Take the money, he did. He'd have known, even as he sired children by Sarah Cooper, prospered his business, and cut new notches in his belt to match his swelling affluence, that someday the Crown would come knocking, demanding that he do his duty.

Prudence must have been chewing over the same worries. "James," she said. "Are you certain?"

"Have faith. Master Cooper will do the honorable thing."

Cooper let out a long sigh. At last he tucked away the gold coins. "Aye, I'll do it." He looked up. "It may well be safer than your path. Are you still set on entering Indian territory?"

"That I am," James said. "If there are survivors from Sachusett and Crow Hollow, I intend to question them."

"Tell me your suspicions."

"We know there is a deep conspiracy. We struck down three men on the highway, yet Knapp was able to raise several more to beset us in Winton."

"Motivation?" Cooper asked.

"At first I suspected hostility toward the Crown. I'd hoped it, in fact. No greater justification would I need for seizing the charter of the colony than open sedition."

Prudence's face fell at his bald declaration of intent, but she didn't say anything.

"But no longer?" Cooper asked.

"No longer," James confirmed. "According to Widow Hull, Samuel Knapp and William Fitz-Simmons now own vast tracts of land on the frontier. Some belonged to Sir Benjamin, the rest to the unfortunate Indians whose bones lie moldering amongst the desolation of their villages."

"The Indians brought that vengeance down upon their own heads," Cooper said. "They made the first attack."

"Perhaps." James was still unsettled on that score. "But as for the conspirators, I suspect each and every one of the men we have faced would be found in possession of land that had once belonged to another."

"The beneficiaries of the war," Cooper said. "I suppose someone must profit thereby."

"If it were only that, then why so anxious to stop us? Why attack us on the road and risk massacring us not a hundred paces from the Winton commons? Why murder Peter Church, if not because he spoke Nipmuk and Abenaki?"

"And the reverend?" Cooper asked. "Where does he figure in this scheme?"

"He figures nowhere," Prudence said, firmly. "That much I know for certain."

"He was quick to offer lodging to two strangers," James said.

"That was simple hospitality!"

"And he held court with the others when they seized us in Boston. Knapp and Fitz-Simmons trusted his counsel. Why, if they are thieves and murderers and he is not?"

"They trusted him because he's our minister, and it was his congregation Peter disrupted. Please, James. I assure you he is innocent."

James admired her loyalty toward her sister's husband, but with every passing day he was more convinced she was wrong. Stone had sold Sir Benjamin's land to these men, had no doubt pocketed most of the wealth instead of keeping it in trust for the widow.

There were no other suspects in the Stone house. He could rule out Prudence and the children, and he couldn't see a way to implicate Prudence's sister, either. Of the servants, Old John Porter had proven himself with decades of service and was deaf as a stump. Lucy and Alice Branch, buxom and delicious as they were in appearance, seemed mentally incapable of concocting such a scheme, no matter how one looked at it. That left only the reverend.

"If he is innocent," James said, "I'll testify on his behalf, I assure you. If not, he must pay for his crimes."

"If you are so certain," Cooper said, "then why set into the wilderness to look for the Indians?"

"They have valuable information. Why did the Nipmuk attack when they did? Why did Knapp slaughter them at Crow Hollow?"

"You won't get answers. You may as well trust the devil himself as those savages."

"If the devil held the truth of the matter," James said, "then I would question him, too, and without hesitation."

Cooper smiled at this. "Very well, I see you're determined. But promise me one thing, Bailey. It's not for love of a woman, is it?"

Prudence stiffened next to James.

"No," James said, perhaps a little too quickly. "But make no mistake. If Prudence's daughter is still alive, I intend to see her returned to her mother's arms."

She reached for his hand in the dark and squeezed it.

"I don't believe it," Cooper said, looking back and forth between the two of them. "I don't believe either of you."

❧

The fire died in the night, and the wind gathered its strength until it shrieked through the branches of their shelter. The three of them slept huddled together, shivering, turning, mumbling in and out of sleep. The awful night seemed endless, and it was with relief that

James finally woke from one of a dozen fitful dozes to see the gray seeping through the bare branches. One by one they groaned and climbed to their feet.

James inspected the feet and toes of all present for frostbite. Prudence's chilblains had returned, but other than that, all seemed to be in order. He was relieved. It was a wretched thing to be caught out on a winter night in the woods. Without Prudence's clever thinking, they'd have suffered much worse.

Only one of the traps had done its duty, catching a gray squirrel with huge eyes. At least he *thought* it was a squirrel. When he held it up it had long membranes between its legs, giving it an almost bat-like appearance. The others called it a sugar squirrel and said that they glided from tree to tree and in the spring lapped the sweet sap from maples. It sounded fanciful, but there was no denying the creature's strange appearance.

"Enjoy your meal," Cooper said as he stomped his boots and slapped his hands together to warm them. "I'm not so hungry I'll eat a furry rat. Anyway, I should have food by afternoon."

By the time Prudence had stoked the fire, and James had the creature gutted, spitted, and cooking over the flames, Cooper was setting off over the hill through the snow. A few moments later, he was out of sight. Moments after that, James could no longer hear him, either.

"Will he be all right?" Prudence asked.

"I hope so. But it's dangerous business, there's no denying."

"And you trust him not to betray us?"

James turned the squirrel, whose skin had begun to sizzle. "As much as I trust anything in New England. Which is to say I'm hopeful, but not certain."

"That's hardly comforting. Anyway, you can trust me, James."

"I know." He gave the squirrel another turn. So little meat. "Cooper was trustworthy enough in France. After Sir Benjamin, he was the man most responsible for teaching me what I know about the craft. At his hand, I learned how to pick locks, how to formulate coded messages, even how to fight with the rapier and saber. But something has changed."

"He's older. That settles a man."

"Older, maybe. And he's a father, with responsibilities that distract from his duty to his king." James considered. "Or maybe it's the wilderness, the frontier. The war with the Indians. New England seems to change a man. The English I meet here are different, somehow, from even the Puritans back home. More earnest, perhaps. Even more devout."

He glanced up from his work cooking the squirrel, expecting her to argue, but instead she looked thoughtful.

"I was born in Boston," she said, "and have never been to England, so I don't know. But it does seem to me that the English arrive in the New World—how shall I voice it?—cynical and hardened. And yet overconfident at the same time. They've never seen a gale howling off the Atlantic, capsizing boats and washing away coastal villages. They've never set off for the next town not knowing if they would be attacked by wolves or murdered by angry natives. They don't live on the edge of an unknown wilderness."

It was imperfectly described, but he felt that she was scratching at the same spot that had been itching at his mind these past few days. Further discussion might better voice what both of them had identified. For now, he only knew that people were changed by the New World in ways he couldn't fully identify.

"What will Master Cooper do when he makes contact with the king's agents in New York?" she asked.

"He means to raise help so our return to Boston won't see us climbing the gallows."

"They wouldn't hang us, would they?"

"No," he said after a moment of thought. "Too public. Rather more likely they'll murder us on the road. Or try, anyway."

"At least then we'd have a chance."

"Without horses or saddlebags? Without ball or powder?" He shook his head. "I'd as soon take my chances with the Indians."

CHAPTER TWENTY-FIVE

The flying squirrel gave no more than a mouthful each. James was almost relieved. It tasted like a gamey piece of venison, only with a distinctly muddy aftertaste. So much for his hope that "sugar squirrel" meant it would taste vaguely of maple-tree sap.

When they finished, Prudence wasted what seemed like valuable time searching for a moose trail. But when she found it, he was soon glad she had. It led over the ridge, picking through the trees, avoiding snags and rocky knolls. The snow up top must have been three feet deep, but the animals had packed it down and saved James and Prudence from wading through the snow. After a couple of hours of tromping, James felt almost warm. All except his feet, which had become blocks of ice.

They continued trudging along the ridge until it came into a little vale, carved by a stream that had frozen into a white ribbon as it cascaded over the rocks. Birch trees glistened in the midday light, with each branch and twig coated with a fine dust of white. The rocky walls on the opposite side of the little valley gleamed with a vast icy sheet several feet thick.

James was lightheaded with hunger. He'd spotted some sort of partridge or quail earlier, but had declined taking a shot with his remaining loaded pistol. Now he was regretting that decision.

He eyed the stream. "You don't suppose if we broke through the ice we could fish for trout, do you?"

"I spent last winter with the Nipmuk. We were on the run and hunger was a constant companion. They never tried it. In a pond, yes, but not a little brook like this."

"Meaning it can't be done?"

"Not likely, or they would have tried."

Prudence didn't sound worried, and he looked her over, surprised. She seemed vigorous and full of energy.

"Aren't you faint with hunger?" he asked.

"I'm famished. And my legs are ready to collapse."

"You sound pleased with that. I'd half expected to be carrying you by now."

She'd been studying the little valley, as if trying to orient herself, and now looked at him with a smile. "Aye, but I entered the woods fat and content. Last time I stood in this spot I'd gone two weeks eating nothing but insects and tree bark."

"That doesn't account for the smile. Come now, you're hiding a secret."

"Perhaps I am, James. Follow me."

She led him alongside the bank of the frozen stream. They trudged through the snow until they reached the end of the valley. It was a little meadow marked here and there with mounds of drifted snow and ringed by a steep, rocky slope that blocked their passage. It was a discouraging sight. What now but turn around?

Prudence bent and pushed snow from one of the mounds. "Lend me a hand."

Together they cleared the snow from what turned out to be an Indian house of sorts, its internal structure of cut poles collapsed and the deerskin roof and walls gathered into a pile. They pried the skins from the frozen ground to reveal a mat of frozen rushes that had once served as the floor. Prudence tromped around for a minute before she stopped and shook her head.

"Not this one," she said. "But keep cheer, it's under one of these."

"What is?"

"There is a basket of corn seed hidden in a hole beneath one of these wigwams."

"Is this Sachusett? I thought it would be bigger."

"This? Bless me, no. This was a refuge. Mikmonto knew Sachusett would come under attack as soon as the militia freed Springfield from the siege. But he first needed permission to travel north—the Verts Monts Abenaki were neutral in the war. Until that happened, he needed somewhere to hide. He led a false trail west and came here to hide. We stayed here until the food ran out."

"Then how can there be corn?"

"No matter how hungry, you cannot eat all the seed. Someday, Mikmonto thought, the English would be driven off, and they'd need something to plant."

As they were talking, they'd knocked the snow from another mound and peeled it back. This one also gave no indication of disturbed soil beneath. At this rate it would be after dark before they got all twenty or so mounds cleared. Prudence trudged through the snow, examining each of the mounds in turn and looking up at the hillside to reorient herself.

"This one!" she cried. "Over here. I remember now."

This mound was no bigger than the others, but the skins had frozen on top of each other and seemed positively cemented to the ground. It took a good deal of digging with numb fingers and yanking back and forth until they finally got it loose. Then a layer of rushes, partly rotted and completely frozen. They had sagged over the top of a hole, as Prudence had said. Excited now, they dug away until they got the rushes out of the way.

And then stared in dismay. There was a hole, all right, neatly scooped from the earth and cleared of roots and stones. But it was empty.

"I don't understand," she said, her voice defeated. "I saw Mikmonto's wife lower the basket in herself. This is right where Laka left it. Could it be animals got here first?"

"Except the floor was undisturbed," he said. "A bear would have torn up the floor. Rodents would have left the basket. One of the hungry Indians must have come back around for it."

"No," she said. "They'd have never done that. And when? We never came within thirty miles of this spot until the return to Crow Hollow."

"Someone must have done it."

"I suppose so."

Prudence, to her credit, didn't moan or complain, though he could tell from the slump of her shoulders that she was discouraged. She walked thoughtfully among the other snow-covered wigwams.

"Let's look for the trail," she said. "It leads up through the woods."

Soon enough they found it. Like the other trail, this one had also been used by animals. Deer droppings marked the ground, together with the prints of their cloven hooves. Other tracks: little five-fingered hands with claws, like a weasel or maybe a raccoon. And then the paw of some giant cat, which Prudence called a cat-amount, which was some kind of lion.

"Only not so big as the ones that live in Mohammedan lands," she said, "nor as dangerous."

"I'll trust your word on it."

They'd crested two more hills, and it was already late afternoon. By his estimate the date was December 23, one of the shortest days of the year. And only two days from Christmas, he thought gloomily. If he were in England, he'd have taken leave of the king's service to visit his parents in Lewes. He would sit in front of a fire drinking mulled wine, smoking a pipe with his brother and father, perhaps eating a generous wedge of his mother's fruited cake, soaked in brandy since the autumn. His nieces would gather around, insisting he tell stories about his time among the wicked French. This he would do with relish, inventing lurid details when necessary.

Instead, he was in this frozen wasteland. To slake his thirst, he ate snow, but this only made him shiver more. They hadn't yet made camp, and if the temperature fell before they were able to light a fire, they could find themselves in serious trouble.

You're already in trouble, friend.

For some reason, the words came to his mind in Peter Church's slow, questioning tone. Why he was thinking of the murdered Indian now, he couldn't say.

Prudence stopped and squatted. "Look."

She brushed snow away lightly with her fingers to reveal the left half of a single, human-shaped print where it touched the edge of the trail. The outlines were indistinct, and the shoe or boot had no heel. Neither was it the mark of a wooden clog like people wore in town.

"Indian?" he asked.

She nodded. When she rose, her face shined eagerly, though the confirmation filled James only with dread. As they continued, Prudence picked up the pace until he could scarcely keep up with her.

Prudence stopped only when he insisted, pointing out that if they waited any longer, they wouldn't be able to light a fire.

This time, Prudence searched out a drift of snow pushed against a rock, then packed it down and used a stick to hollow out an opening while James gathered wood. She showed him which tree to scrape for its bark. After that, he was able to light the fire himself. He didn't like their position on an exposed ridge, worried that the fire would be visible for miles. But it was too late to search for another spot.

When he had the fire going, he found Prudence on her hands and knees, her head and shoulders in the cave. She shoveled out snow, pushing it behind her like a badger digging in the dirt.

"We're spending the night in there?" he asked, doubtfully.

"'Twill keep us warm."

"Sleeping in the snow will keep us warm?"

"It's not the same as climbing beneath four blankets in a freshly warmed bed," she said, "but it will be no colder than the temperature at which water turns to ice."

"That sounds frigid enough to me."

"Trust me, James. It's what animals do, and it's how a Nipmuk will survive in the woods if he's caught out and there's plenty of snow. He makes a snow cave. We'll stay warm enough." She took a stick and punched two holes in the roof of the cave.

"Then why are we lighting a fire?" he asked. "We have nothing to eat and we can't use the warmth if we're sleeping in that hole."

"In case there are any Nipmuk or Abenaki around. It will help them find us."

"About that—"

"It's too late for second thoughts, James. We have no way back, only forward."

"And you're sure they won't take our scalps and torture us to death?"

"It depends on how angry they are."

"I find that less than reassuring."

"We're close. My daughter is near. I must find her, no matter the risk."

There was no arguing. Even if he'd wanted to go back on his word, turning around was impossible at this point. The unsettling thing was how thoroughly their roles had changed over the past day. His confidence was shattered, while Prudence only seemed to grow more sure of herself, more competent, as they plunged deeper into the wilderness.

The wind had picked up, and so they loaded sticks onto the fire and then approached the hole. Prudence dropped to her belly and squirmed forward until she disappeared inside. She called for him to enter. Fighting his fear of tight spaces, he obeyed.

Once inside the snow cave, he was surprised at how comfortable it was. The space was tight, but with room to turn around, so long as one didn't try to rise above one's knees. The snow was soft, and while it wasn't warm, exactly, neither was it frigid.

"As our body warmth fills the cave," Prudence said, "the ceiling will melt, then refreeze into a crust. That will keep it from collapsing on us in the night. Until then, try not to hit your head against the ceiling."

He stretched out and accidentally elbowed her in the dark. "Pardon me, there isn't much room."

"We should sleep together. To conserve heat."

They opened their cloaks and embraced each other, then spent a few moments squirming around until they were fully wrapped in both cloaks.

The snow muffled the wind, and all he could hear was her breathing. Her breath was warm against his neck. Without thinking, he lifted a hand to her face. She gasped.

"Pray, pardon me," he murmured.

She grabbed his wrist and held his hand in place before he could pull away. "Your hand is cold, that is all. But please, I'm frightened. Your touch comforts."

"You don't seem frightened. I thought that was just me."

"I was in good spirits so long as we kept moving. Now that we've stopped, the memory of it all comes rushing back. My mind is galloping."

He held her tightly and cupped her face in his hand while brushing her cheek with his thumb, all in a manner that he hoped was comforting and not aggressive. He wouldn't want her to think he would take advantage.

But as soon as the thought came to his mind, he couldn't cast it aside. In spite of the hunger and the cold, the exhaustion and the fear, he soon could think of only one thing. Every time Prudence shifted against him he could feel every curve of her body: the soft swell of her full breasts against his arm and chest, her thigh pressed between his legs, her lips brushing against his neck.

Don't you think of it, he told himself. *Only a knave would press himself upon a woman at a time like this.*

"Thank you, James," she whispered.

She moved her hands, and to both his pleasure and his horror, he felt her cool fingers beneath his undershirt and against the bare flesh of his side. She moved her hand up to his chest.

"Prudie," James said, licking his lips. He was of half a mind to tell her to stop, while the other half wanted to put his mouth against hers and his hand on her breast.

"Pray pardon me. It—it may seem improper." Yet she didn't move her hand from his skin. "But we are so cold. It is only for warmth."

Was she saying that for his benefit, or her own? Either way, he wasn't fooled. If she'd been huddling here with her sister, she'd hardly rest a hand against Anne's bare breast.

He cupped her head and pulled it toward his. Their lips came together. Prudence let him kiss her lightly, but pulled away after only a moment.

"Did you have her?" she asked.

"What do you mean? Who?"

"Lucy Branch. Did you have her?"

"No, I already told you."

"I know, but—" Prudence hesitated. "I thought perchance you had lied to spare my sensibilities."

"I didn't take advantage of Lucy. I hope you believe that."

She let out a low laugh. "I wasn't worried about *you* taking advantage of *her*. You wouldn't have been the first young man she's pressed herself against."

"No?"

"Lucy is a passionate girl. It gets her into trouble. And you are a man, you are far from home and among strangers. If a comely servant girl were to give you leave . . . but I need to know if you have an understanding with Lucy."

"I kissed her," he confessed. "And I almost succumbed. But it did not seem right. Too dangerous for Lucy, and she made feeble protests about her virtue. What's more, if I had, she'd have expected me to approach your sister to ask permission to marry. She let it be known."

"She said that? Then Lucy must be truly smitten." There was a smile in her voice.

His ardor had begun to cool, yet he felt as though he had scarcely taken control. A moment longer and he'd have attempted to seduce Prudence. In the morning, she'd have thought him a monster, while blaming herself for a moment of weakness.

James was about to suggest that she move her leg so it wasn't pressing into him just so, when Prudence's hand began to move against his chest again. Her fingers brushed over his nipple. In an instant, he had lost whatever restraint he had so recently wrestled under control.

He kissed her. This time she didn't pull away.

She untied his jerkin to loosen it, then ran both hands along his body beneath his undershirt, from his belly to his chest. His body shuddered, half passion, half cold. He kissed the length of her neck and she sighed. His hand lifted her petticoat and trailed along the inside of her thigh. Her sigh turned to a moan. His fingers brushed against her soft mound, but then he pulled away.

"Are you sure?" he managed.

"Am I wrong?" she said. "Have I read you false?"

"No, you have not."

"We are cold, you and I." Her fingers tugged at the lacing of his breeches. "There is nothing wrong with wanting to be warm."

And with that, she got the leather lacing free and one hand reached in to pull him free of his breeches and his small clothes, even while her mouth found his again. Her passion, her confidence, was almost . . . well, almost *French*. To have it emerge so unexpectedly from this beautiful, shy young Puritan woman was the most arousing thing he'd ever experienced in his life.

They didn't undress, except so far as necessary, and they kept wrapped in their cloaks. Once she had her own underclothes out of the way, she pulled him on top of her, grabbed a hold of him between the legs, and guided him in.

She was warm and already quite damp. As he moved on top of her, she dug her fingers into the small of his back. Her back arched. He moved faster.

They could not have come together with greater urgency had they furtively found each other in Reverend Stone's own house. All too soon, they were shuddering together, Prudence moaning, then collapsing in a panting heap.

They lay for several moments in silence. He could feel her heart thumping next to his chest, only gradually slowing. It was comforting, soothing.

"Thank you, James."

"That is the second time you've said that."

"I was thanking you for different things."

He smiled at this.

"I am no longer cold," she said.

"Nor I."

Yet he was still confused. Was this not a sin in Prudence's mind?

James's first experience with a woman had come in Paris, with Richard Cooper distracting the girl's father elsewhere in the house with talk of business. She was a pretty thing named Giselle du Pont, the daughter of a cloth merchant, and he had been working for several weeks to seduce her, convinced he was in love.

Afterward, as the two Englishmen strolled back to their lodgings on the Rue de Glatigny, Cooper said, "You did take a hard piss afterward, didn't you?"

"No, why?"

"These French girls are not always clean. Always take a hard piss. Otherwise, you never know when your cock will rot and fall off."

Cooper had said this with a winking tone, but James was offended. Not Giselle du Pont! She'd been a virgin. Only later did he learn that not only had Cooper slept with her already, but so had the other two English agents in Paris. Since then, James had always got up to take a piss after making love.

Unfortunately, he'd trained his body sufficient that he was now feeling the unmistakable urge to go outside and empty his bladder, even though he was quite certain that it didn't need emptying. It was early in the evening. He'd be waking all night anyway until he finally went. He pulled on his clothes, unclasped his cloak rather than pull it off of Prudie, and made to crawl out of the cave.

"Where are you going?" She sounded nervous, as if he were suffering regrets and needed to get away from her as quickly as possible.

He wanted to reassure her, but he was embarrassed to admit what made him get up. What if Sir Benjamin had told her what the foolish young men of His Majesty's service believed they should do to avoid the pox? She would be hurt and offended.

"I'm going to put the rest of the wood on the fire. It will only take a moment."

His head cleared as he got outside and rose to his feet. The wind cut over the hillside, so sharp and cold that it snatched the breath from his lungs. The fire had almost died, and he used a stick to poke at the coals while he gradually fed it the rest of the firewood.

He'd made love to Prudence Cotton. What had he been thinking?

She was a lonely, frightened widow. A New Englander, with all of the provincial attitudes that implied. Born in Boston, once resident of the tiny village of Winton. He was an agent of the king, worldly, and soon to return to London, Paris, Amsterdam.

James had never played the knave. He would never coerce a woman, and certainly never force her. He didn't use trickery and lies to get her to spread her legs. Nevertheless, he had enjoyed the benefits of his position. He spent freely of the king's money, he profited from the power that came with the king's commission, and he had often used his confidence and handsome appearance to seduce women. Never against their will, no, but neither had he led any of them to believe there was anything more in their love-making than a bit of pleasure, freely shared.

Why had Prudence asked him about Lucy Branch? She hadn't seemed jealous or judging. No, she'd wanted to know if he had an understanding. There was no reason for that unless Prudence meant that making love to her would be accepting an understanding with her, instead. Of course she would. She was a devout woman living under the roof of one of Boston's most prominent ministers. A widow, yes, so not a young maid, and her passions had been quite manifest.

She'd wanted him as badly as he'd wanted her. But only with a certain understanding in mind. Only then did he have permission.

Prudence hadn't tricked him. She'd been quite clear.

Make love to me, James, and we will be betrothed to marriage. Our sin will be minor, soon atoned by a legal and lawful wedding.

James groaned, disgusted with himself. If he'd been anything but a fool, he'd have stopped it before it had gone any further. He'd had the presence of mind to do so with Lucy, why not this time too? Was he a rutting dog that he hadn't been able to control himself? And now what? How would he possibly escape without wrecking her heart?

You don't want to escape. Admit it.

There it was. He didn't. That was the truth of the matter. He wanted to bring Prudence back with him to London. If she wouldn't go, then (heaven help him) he would stay with her in Boston. Could he do that? Surely not. If for no other reason than that the New Englanders would consider him the devil in human form once this matter was settled. And there was the great prize waiting for him in England. Would he cast aside the position of king's chancellor for a woman?

You are doubly a fool.

James stepped away from the fire to piss. The moon had drifted behind the hillside at his rear, revealing a swath of stars in a huge, flickering belt stretching across the vast bowl of the sky. The distant hills were visible only by their deeper black shadows and mounded all along the horizon.

Again, he was struck by the desolation of the land into which they'd entered. And yet he knew it wasn't empty. All manner of animals would be noting their presence, some of which—wolves, bears, lions—would happily devour him. And Indians. Never forget that.

An owl called in the woods: hoot . . . hoot . . . hoot-hoot! From some distance came the faint but emphatic reply: hoot . . . hoot . . . hoot-hoot!

To James's ears it sounded like the call of sentries, warning. Intruders had entered their lands.

CHAPTER TWENTY-SIX

Prudence woke in James's arms. A gray light seeped through the entrance into the snow cave. For a moment she lay there, swimming in and out of a hazy, pleasant state of near sleep, her dreams clinging like cobwebs to her mind.

Then she remembered everything that had passed between them in the night. She felt a twinge of guilt deep in her gut, like the devil's fingers had taken her bowels and given them a sharp twist.

And then, surprisingly, it was gone.

She *should* feel guilty. How many sermons had she heard during her life warning her of such a situation? The devil worked in a moment of weakness. Relax your vigil—especially with a man, a stranger—and you would give yourself to the most heinous sin. Prudence had proven all too frail, all too weak. She shouldn't simply be guilty, she should be disgusted. And yet.

She'd awakened a few times in the night, always nestled in James's strong arms. His breathing came low and even. Once, he'd murmured in his sleep. She put her head against his chest. It felt too right lying here to be a sin.

He shifted as she extracted herself, but he didn't wake. It seemed late, and her bladder was full to bursting. A dull, gnawing hunger was awakening in her belly.

Prudence crawled out of the snow cave. Outside, the sky was brilliant blue, with the sun well above the horizon. The chill was gone from the sky, and the slushy puddle surrounding the ash of the campfire had not yet refrozen.

Looking across the hills, she saw nothing but mile after mile of unbroken forest. This was French and Indian territory, full of trappers and deer hunters, not the villages of the Nipmuk, Narragansett, and Pequot of New England, where they raised squash, beans, and corn in little clearings. One would look at this landscape and think it empty, unpeopled.

There was something about the fresh air, the blue sky, and the good rest that filled her with hope. As she emptied her bladder she searched for and found the Connecticut, cutting north into Verts Monts. Follow it and they could not help but find the surviving members of Mikmonto's tribe. A day, two at most.

When she finished, she lowered her petticoats and turned back toward the hole in the snow. A man was standing there. Prudence cried out in surprise.

He was a tall Indian, about thirty years old, holding a short club with a stone head. He had a sharp nose and piercing, intelligent eyes. The man wore deerskin leggings, a gray wolfskin mantle draped over his shoulders, and deerskin moccasins decorated with porcupine quills.

Leather bands adorned with glass beads encircled his upper arms. His hair was cut to the scalp on the first two inches above his ears, leaving only the uppermost part of his head covered with his fine black hair. A rabbit hung by its feet from a thong that had been laced through the wolf pelt. Blood tinged the fur at its throat.

In addition to the club, the man had a curved English knife entwined in the rope belt at his waist. It was the type of blade an

Indian used for gutting prey, but she'd also seen them used to scalp enemies.

Her cry seemed to have momentarily left the Indian flat footed, but now he sprang at her. She stumbled back with her hands held outstretched. The man swung his club, and she ducked as it came toward her head. It missed her head but struck a glancing blow against her shoulder. She dropped to the ground. The Indian fell on top of her.

"James!" she screamed. "Help me!"

But he would still be asleep in the cave, and the snow would muffle any sound. A gale could be howling outside and he wouldn't hear it.

The Indian slipped in the snow as they grappled. Prudence tried to crawl away, but the man was strong and had murder in his eyes. In an instant he was straddling her, the stone club lifted above his head.

At last she found her wits and her Nipmuk. "No! Listen! I'm a friend."

He stopped, his eyes widening. He said something back. She didn't understand; it was a different dialect.

"Friend," she repeated in Nipmuk. "Don't kill me, please, listen. Listen!"

A familiar snicking sound came from behind him. The Indian whirled.

James stood at the mouth of the cave, his pistol lowered calmly at the man's chest. The snicking sound had been the drawing of the cock. The Indian snarled and sprang to his feet. James's face was a mask of stone, but there was violence in his eyes that mirrored the look Prudence had spotted moments earlier in the Indian's expression.

The instant the Indian was clear of Prudence, James squeezed the trigger and the hammer fell. There was a flash and a puff of smoke, and the Indian flinched as if in anticipation of the ball that would slam into him.

But the gun had misfired. After so much moving around, then the weapon lying uncovered in the cave during the night, perhaps the powder had come loose or become wet. Out came a little smoke, the smell of gunpowder, but the ball didn't fire.

Both men recovered at the same time. James dropped his pistol and reached for his dagger. The Indian threw his stone club. The distance was short, no more than a dozen feet, and the aim was true, but James moved impossibly quickly. He ducked to one side and the club spun past his ear. It buried itself in the side of the snow cave.

James sprang forward with the dagger. But the Indian was already drawing his own knife. As James came by, the other man dropped to one knee and thrust up with his blade. Both men missed. They came around for another go.

"James, no!" Prudence cried. Then, in Nipmuk, "Friend! Stop!"

The two men circled each other. The Indian was trying to edge around to get at his stone club, with its handle sticking out of the snow, but James kept himself between the Indian and the weapon. He was also trying to get to higher ground on the hillside, but the Indian saw this tactic and kept him away with a series of false lunges. Both men were warriors, both deadly. If she didn't stop this, at least one man would die, perhaps both.

"I'll distract him," James said. "Go for the club."

"You have to listen to me," she said. "If you kill him, we'll never find my daughter."

"But—"

"No!" she said, sharply. "Listen to me. And if he kills you I'll be killed too. Possibly tortured."

This seemed to give him pause. His posture changed to a defensive one. The Indian stiffened as if to charge.

Prudence shifted to Nipmuk. "No fighting. No! We are friends."

The man ignored her and sprang at James. The two men came together in a flurry of flashing blades, and Prudence's heart seemed to stop in her throat. James came out the other side with a shout. He was uninjured. The other man's face contorted with pain, and a bloody gash opened on his bare arm. If not for the leather armband, almost cut in two, it would have been worse.

But he wasn't done yet. He looked as if he were going to drop, but when James moved to attack, he came up with the knife again. James ducked past.

Prudence saw her chance. She sprang for the stone club. She snatched it out of the snow and then looked for a way to come in behind the Indian. Land a blow, if she could. Distract him, if not. He whirled like a cornered animal, his back to the hillside.

"Tell me what to do," Prudence said to James.

No more nonsense about arranging a truce. The other man had understood in spite of the strange dialect. She was sure of that. He'd rejected her pleas and was intent on slaughtering them.

"Wait for my move," he said.

Something crashed on the hillside above them. Three more Indians emerged from the woods on the slope above. They wore snowshoes of bent birch sticks with a lattice of smaller sticks running between them. As they came down into the clearing by the snow cave, they bent and yanked off their snowshoes. These men were dressed much like the first and were all armed with some combination of clubs and knives. One was an older man, and another no more than a boy, but as James came in next to Prudence, she could see from his cornered look that he'd lost faith in their chances.

The men started arguing amongst themselves, even as they encircled the two English with their backs against the snow cave. It was a dialect related to the Nipmuk of Mikmonto's tribe but different enough that she couldn't pick out more than a few words, none of which filled her with confidence: *kill, scalp, enemies.* They seemed to be arguing over who would have the honor of killing James and Prudence.

"Put down the club," James told her. "It's your only chance."

"You too. Drop your knife."

"No, I won't be taken."

"Then I won't, either."

"Think of your daughter."

"*Netomok,*" she tried again in Nipmuk. *Friends.* "Not your enemies. Please, we need a truce. We don't want to fight."

The older man pushed ahead of the wounded man, who snapped something in irritation. The old man thrust his finger toward her. He spoke slowly in his own language. "You *Puda-katan*?" She understood.

"*Nuttisowis, Puda-katan, nux.*" *My name is Puda-katan, yes.*

Relief flooded through her as she turned to James. "They know me. That's my name, that's what they call me. Prudence Cotton. Puda-katan. There is no *r* in their language."

"Don't kill us," she said in Nipmuk. "We're friends. We give no harm. You understand?"

There was more rapid-fire conversation among the Indians. This time, she understood a little more. The injured man wanted to kill them. The older man and the boy did not. The other man seemed ready to follow whoever made the most forceful argument.

These must be Abenaki, she realized. The eastern Abenaki had been decimated in the coastal regions of northern Massachusetts and New Hampshire, but those tribes in Verts Monts and north toward Quebec had stayed neutral. And a good thing, too, or the war might have turned out differently.

The Abenaki spoke an Algonquin dialect, related to the Nipmuk. And if these men had heard of her, then there must indeed be Nipmuk who had taken refuge with them.

"My daughter," she said. "Puda-katan's child. Do you know her? Is she still alive? She is called Mary."

Mary. My dear Mary. Please, Lord, let her be alive.

The Abenaki paid her no attention, being caught up in their own arguments. At last, the injured man turned with a snarl, crossed his arms, and showed the others his back. Prudence felt a flood of relief. He'd capitulated.

James seemed to recognize the signal as well. He put away his dagger in a swift motion and lifted his hands. "I won't fight," he said in English. "No fight."

"Will you take us to the Nipmuk?" she asked them. "You know them, yes?"

They would, yes, or at least they were willing to take James and Prudence somewhere over the next hill. But first, they were demanding a gift, some token of friendship. James reached into his cloak—a move that made the Abenaki stiffen, as if they expected him to come out with his dagger again. Instead, he removed a pewter medallion on a chain, marked with the cross on one side and a shield on the other. He handed it to the older man, who grunted in pleasure and put it around his neck.

"What is that?" Prudence asked.

"A medallion from the captain of a Spanish treasure ship."

"Why do you have that?"

"The pope gave it to him. I took it away. Or do you mean, why do I have it on my person?" James shrugged. "Hard to say. I thought it might come in handy. Not like this, mind you."

While the other Abenaki admired the medallion and its chain, the angry young man looked up from where he'd been rubbing his injury with snow, and a flicker of curiosity and jealousy passed over his face. The old man made to show it to him, but the young man turned away, as if uninterested. The boy grinned at this and met Prudence's gaze. She returned his smile. The boy looked like the younger brother of the older one, taking some delight in seeing his overbearing older sibling's pride trimmed an inch or two.

The older man said his name was Kepnomotok. He introduced the others. The injured man was named Tictok, and was apparently his son, as was the younger one. The other warrior was either a cousin of Kepnomotok, or a brother—she thought the word was the same in their dialect.

"Did he say the injured fellow's name is Tictok?" James said. "Like a clock?"

"Never make sport of a man's name," she said. "They take that very seriously."

"I was only remarking to you."

"We don't know if they speak English. They are good with languages, and not always forthcoming about their knowledge, for the sake of gaining an advantage."

"Yes, of course." He sounded taken aback. "That was a mistake."

They were not at risk of a swift, brutal end, as it had first appeared, but neither were they honored guests. It was soon clear that the Abenaki considered them prisoners. Tictok hacked off part of Prudence's petticoat, which he used as a bandage on his upper arm. Then he and his brother forged ahead on snowshoes while Kepnomotok and the other one brought up the rear, watching Prudence and James with one hand always on a knife or club.

The two English could only make slow progress through the snow, which frustrated the Abenaki. After about ten minutes, Kepnomotok made exasperated noises and ordered them to stop. His older son continued ahead, while the other two trimmed and tied crude snowshoes for their two prisoners.

Prudence had used snowshoes before, but it took James a few minutes to get the feel of them. After that, they made good progress, their only obstacle the softening snow due to the warming air.

Sometime later Tictok rejoined them on the trail. He carried a dead doe draped over his shoulders, already cold and stiffening, its hooves tied off for ease in transport. They must have killed it earlier when one of them had spotted the last trickle of smoke from the campfire and sent Tictok ahead to investigate.

Shortly they came onto a packed trail that led down to the valley between two hills. They crossed a stream, frozen solid on top but still gurgling beneath the ice, then the trail twisted through the woods for another hour before it crested yet another hill and emerged into a larger valley. There, they came onto the banks of a large river.

It was easily a hundred and fifty feet wide, and Prudence guessed it was the Connecticut again. Ice stretched from each bank, but the middle third was unfrozen and still flowed swiftly, carrying its burden of slush and ice south toward the sea.

Moments later came the telltale *thwack, thwack* of someone cutting wood. And not the crisp bite of a metal ax, but the duller thump from one of the sharpened stone adzes used by the natives. Her heart quickened.

The trail led around a granite outcrop that forced a bend into the river, and they came upon an Indian village in a meadow above the riverbank. It was a collection of some thirty dwellings, beginning roughly twenty feet above the water line and abutting the forested hills at its rear. The wigwams were rectangular, built of frames lashed together with vines, the sides made of woven matting. Arched roofs could shed rain but had been hand-scraped clean of snow, as they tended to leak when ice and snow melted during warm stretches. Smoke trailed into the air from squat mud-and-stick chimneys on one end.

The homes were smaller than the Nipmuk dwellings she'd seen in Sachusett, and more tightly clustered. The village was smaller too. A porcupine-like palisade of crossed, sharpened logs enclosed the part that didn't face the river, and a hand-dug moat added to the defense where the trail passed into the village. Even here, where the war had never reached, the fighting seemed to have encouraged the Abenaki to fortify their village.

She glanced at James. "It's strength they value and respect. Try not to look nervous."

"I'm trying, believe me. It isn't easy."

"For me, either."

Tictok broke into a trot and ran ahead to the village, crying out as he passed between the opening in the palisade. Men, women, and children came racing out of their wigwams. The men wore bear and wolf pelts over their deerskin clothing, and both men and women wore wampum bracelets made of shells traded from the coast. Unlike the Nipmuk, only women wore feathers in their hair and on thongs around their upper arms. The Abenaki seemed to prefer blue jay feathers instead of the long black plumes of ravens and crows favored by the Nipmuk.

Younger children came all the way forward to gape and stare unabashedly until the adults—themselves discussing and arguing in a cacophony of people all talking at once—pushed them out of the way. A couple of older boys watched from farther back with practiced nonchalance. The boys were dressed like men, with leather armbands, but no wampum.

When the older boys spotted Tictok's younger brother, they called him over to demand answers. He swaggered to join them, chest puffed, and began to elaborate the story in a proud tone, his hands gesticulating. The younger children gathered there, where the telling was more dramatic. Prudence scrutinized each of them, looking for her daughter. Her stomach fell. There was no sight of Mary or any other English child.

"Puda-katan," a voice said behind her.

She turned and came face-to-face with two Nipmuk women from Sachusett—Hapamag and Laka, mother and daughter. Laka had been Mikmonto's wife. She held an infant who suckled at an exposed breast. It was too young to be Mikmonto's; the sachem's head rested on a pike outside the Winton meetinghouse.

"Laka, Hapamag. You're alive!" Prudence said in Nipmuk. She opened her mouth to ask about the rest of the survivors, then stopped.

A second, older child clung to Laka's leather breeches and peered shyly around her legs.

The child's face was dirty, her clothes a simple hide shift like they put onto children of both genders, with no underclothes, until they learned to go outside to pass water. Her hair was cut high on the scalp, Indian-style, and everything about her mannerisms was no different than that of the other children.

But she had blond hair and blue eyes.

"Mary!" Prudence cried, reaching for the child.

The girl screamed in terror.

CHAPTER TWENTY-SEVEN

The two Nipmuk women blocked Prudence's desperate lunge for her daughter. And Mary showed nothing but complete terror at this strange woman who had come into the village and immediately tried to snatch her up. Because Laka was holding the baby, the older woman swept up Mary and cradled her in her arms.

Mary was screaming, "*Nuken!*" *Mama*.

But she wasn't reaching for Prudence, she was reaching for Laka, who was trying to shuffle the baby and reach for Mary at the same time. The realization of what she was seeing struck Prudence like a fist to the belly.

Abenaki surrounded Prudence and pushed her back. A man grabbed her wrist, while another hefted a stone ax. It was the man who had been chopping firewood when they'd entered the village.

"Unhand her!" James cried. He fought his way toward her.

Prudence was horrified at her blunder. She'd terrified her daughter and turned a tense atmosphere into a dangerous one. The two Nipmuk women had swept Mary away and were disappearing through the crowd.

Tictok dropped the dead doe and drew his stone club as he rushed in to confront James with a look of triumph and joy. Prudence could read Tictok's thoughts. Time to settle the matter left unfinished at the snow cave.

She raised her hands. "No!" she said in Nipmuk, hoping they could understand. "We won't fight. No!"

James reached her side. She broke free of the grasping hands and threw her arms around him to hold him still. "James, please! No!" He stopped struggling.

She braced herself for blows. It was how the Nipmuk had treated captives who misbehaved. Knock them around until they remembered their place. They even did this with other Indians who had become nominal parts of the tribe.

But after some pushing, some shouted arguments, she soon found herself in a circle of Abenaki adults. Kepnomotok and his son argued in loud, angry tones.

"Where is Laka?" she asked. "Where is my daughter? Does anyone speak Nipmuk?"

There was no sign of the dead sachem's wife or her mother, but the Abenaki pushed another woman forward.

"Do you understand me, Puda-katan?" the woman said in Nipmuk.

Prudence said she did, asked if she could speak to all of the surviving Nipmuk.

"We are not Nipmuk," the woman said.

"But you speak it well. You must be Nipmuk, even if it is a different . . ."

Prudence stopped. She couldn't remember how to say the word "dialect." This woman had a strange accent, but there was no question she was a native speaker. From another tribe, then.

"We are not Nipmuk," the woman insisted. "We are adopted. All Abenaki now. We speak it, we live it. We pray to the dead fathers of the Abenaki, honor the spirits of their lands and streams. The Nipmuk are dead."

Now Prudence understood. The Abenaki wouldn't let Nipmuk into their lands, not without shedding their entire identity, even down to their spiritual rituals. Pagan though they may be, she'd seen how deeply those beliefs infused their lives. To surrender them must have been wrenching for the surviving Nipmuk.

Yet how was that so different from what had happened to Peter Church and the other Praying Indians? The small English-style Indian villages that survived on Cape Cod and the outskirts of Plymouth? To live among the English, they must *become* English. Settled, Christian, subject to English law.

"What did she say?" James asked.

Prudence translated for him. At the same time, the other woman spoke to Kepnomotok in Abenaki, no doubt doing the same. He must be the sachem of the village. That was fortunate, as he seemed to be the only thing restraining the younger men from attacking them.

"Ask her how many Nipmuk are still alive," James said.

"How many adopted are you?" she asked the woman.

"Nine still live."

Only nine? The number was stunning after all the hundreds she had met during her captivity. She told James.

"Any men from Sachusett?" he asked.

"Why do you—oh, so we can find out about why they attacked Winton."

She asked the young woman, who grimaced and gave the slight toss of the head that counted among the Nipmuk as a head shake—no. She said she'd fled an English attack with her husband, hoping to gain safety in the north, but the Abenaki had killed him. They had killed two other men too. The only surviving Nipmuk were four women and five children, none of them boys.

"Why would the Abenaki do that?" James asked after Prudence had translated. "What risk are a few men?"

"For the same reason they forced Nipmuk to become Abenaki. First men ask for help, then they form their own village. Then they make war against you. The women and children have value. The men are only a threat."

James's brow furrowed at this. At first she supposed he was troubled by the thought of men being slaughtered simply for being of the wrong tribe, but then he said, "Are they counting Mary as one of the nine?"

"Yes, they must be."

A sick feeling settled into her belly. Mary had cried for Laka as if she were the woman's daughter. And the Abenaki would consider her one of their own.

Kepnomotok pushed through the crowd, gesturing for them to follow. "You come. Come."

Prudence looked around the group of Indians. Every person in the village seemed to have gathered, numbering at least a hundred. Many of the younger men still seemed agitated and were arguing with their elders. No doubt itching for some blood sport.

"I believe," James said, seemingly coming to the same conclusion, "that we'd be safer obeying the chief."

✳

It wasn't the sight of the village that transported Prudence to her captivity. It wasn't the language, so similar to Nipmuk, yet different enough that her hard-fought language skills served her poorly.

No, it was the smell of Kepnomotok's wigwam. The fire in the pit at one end mixed with the smell of dry rushes, the scent of bear fat rubbed over flesh to keep it clean and help the wearer stay warm in the chill of winter.

One of the sachem's wives used two forked sticks to remove a clay pot from the coals on the edge of the fire. She flipped off a flat stone from the top that had been serving as a lid. Steam billowed into the air, smelling of corn and peas and venison, seasoned with wild leeks they collected in spring and then preserved in sea salt. Prudence knew exactly what the pottage would taste like; she'd eaten it many times.

Kepnomotok took a stack of bowls carved from the burls of maple trees and handed them to a second wife, this one older, her thick black hair streaked with gray. She began to fill the bowls. The sachem sat down on a rush mat in the middle of the floor and gestured for Prudence and James to do the same. He pantomimed eating.

The man seemed remarkably calm, given that two English were in his wigwam and the whole village was still in an uproar outside, their many conversations audible through the walls. In addition to his wives, a girl of twelve or thirteen sat quietly on the opposite side of the single-room house, her knees pulled to her chest, watching them with wide eyes. Tictok stood by the doorway, arms folded. Dried blood on his upper arm served as a reminder of the fight between him and James only a few short hours earlier.

Prudence's stomach rumbled with hunger, but she refused to look at the food or obey Kepnomotok's command to sit. James followed her lead.

"Where is my daughter?" she asked in Nipmuk.

"Puda-katan, you sit." Then something else that she couldn't decipher. This was to his son, who scowled but came over, where he sat next to his father.

"Sit," Kepnomotok said, more insistently this time, as if her only objection had been that Tictok had not been seated.

"No. Daughter first."

"Why don't we sit?" James said. "Share a meal. Heaven knows we need it, and it will show that our intent is peaceable."

"Not yet, no. Follow my example." In a lower voice, in case they understood English, she added. "It's strength they respect."

James and Tictok stared at each other. The younger Abenaki gave a boastful appearance, as if taunting his opponent by the very act of sitting. That James didn't sit, that look said, showed he was a coward.

The young man's posture reminded her of the Nipmuk sachem, Mikmonto, and that memory threatened to overwhelm her. Mikmonto had worn that same sneer when he'd come to her with hands stained in Benjamin's blood. Her husband lay dead on the commons, but his screams for mercy still rang in her ears. Her kind, brave husband tortured to death. If not for fear of letting go of her daughter, she'd have fainted. The memory of it left her lightheaded now.

Prudence couldn't let that show. She had to master her emotions.

"Call for Laka," she said to Kepnomotok. Did he catch the tremble in her voice? "Laka." She pantomimed holding a baby at her breast.

The sachem hesitated, but he gave an order to his younger wife, who had finished hauling the pots from the fire. The woman pushed aside the deer hide at the doorway and stepped out. In the moment before the hide swung back in place, Prudence saw a dozen curious faces peering into the wigwam.

The wife returned with Laka. The young Nipmuk woman still had her baby, but Prudence's heart fell that Mary wasn't with her. Prudence nodded at James, and the two English sat. The sachem's other wife put down four bowls of pottage, one in front of each of the two Abenaki men, and the others for the two visitor-captives. She put down a clay pot filled with water for washing their hands, which all four of them used in turn before eating.

James watched Prudence carefully and only picked up the bowl when she did. She waited for Kepnomotok to eat first, then

Tictok, then nodded to James that it was all right to eat. The sachem grunted and looked satisfied that she seemed to understand proper eating behavior.

After that, however, there was little etiquette. Prudence was so hungry that she devoured the food, holding the bowl in one hand and picking out the pieces of meat and vegetables as fast as she could without scalding herself. The natives didn't drink much water—they believed that disease came from the water, not the air, and that cold water was more dangerous than hot—and so their soups and pottages always had a lot of liquid. When the larger bits were gone, everyone lifted the bowls and sipped and slurped until there was nothing left.

The wives had retreated to the far side of the wigwam, together with the girl, who still sat quietly, watching. Laka stood behind Kepnomotok's shoulder. She didn't eat or ask to be fed.

Prudence put down her bowl. One of the wives came forward to refill it, but she told them no, not because she wasn't still hungry, but because she couldn't stand waiting any longer now that she'd satisfied proper behavior.

"Laka," she said.

"Yes, Puda-katan?"

Bring me my daughter. You have no right!

She didn't voice this. "Do the Abenaki treat you kindly? You and the other Nipmuk who survived?"

"There is food in our belly and our burdens are light."

It was the proper answer, yet pain flickered in her eyes. Laka cast a significant glance at Tictok, who was still staring haughtily at James, ignoring the women, unlike his father, who was listening with his brow furrowed. In that look from Laka, Prudence understood. The young widow had become Tictok's wife.

And the baby at her breast? His too, no doubt. Prudence counted months from the time of the Crow Hollow massacre to now. It had been less than a year since Laka's husband had fallen.

Yet here she was, already with a child who must be two months old. No time to mourn her husband's death.

The Abenaki had imposed harsh terms on the desperate Nipmuk survivors. First, the men had been killed. Then the surviving women had been accepted only by becoming Abenaki, by submitting to immediate marriage with the men of the tribe.

Both James and Kepnomotok asked for translations, which the two women did in the respective languages.

"It's a harsh land," James murmured, when Prudence added what she'd surmised about Laka and Tiktok.

"The sachem asks why you have returned," Laka said.

"For my daughter."

"She is Abenaki now. Do you wish to become Abenaki, Puda-katan?"

"You know that I don't. I am English."

"English are killers. They are *moz*."

Moz literally meant "moose" in Nipmuk, but the name for the animal came from the word "strip," because of how moose stripped the bark from trees. And in this case, it didn't mean moose, so much as *despoilers*.

Nipmuk used the word to refer to the way the English would clear fields by girdling the trees so they would die, or how when the English arrived, the fish and game would become scarce. She'd also heard it from a Nipmuk from the coast whose village had been decimated after a Portuguese fishing boat ran aground. The villagers had helped the Portuguese crew, only to discover that the captain was suffering from smallpox. Scarcely a handful of heavily pockmarked villagers had survived the subsequent plague.

"The English are my people," Prudence said. "Like the Nipmuk were your people."

More translations ensued.

"Is Mary well?" Prudence asked.

"Her eyes are bright and her legs grow long."

That was to say, yes.

"Does she remember me?"

Laka hesitated. "She . . . asked about you before. And she was very curious when you returned. But I do not know."

"I must have her back."

"She is Abenaki," Laka repeated, stubbornly, and, Prudence thought, possessively. "Here she will stay."

"You could come with me, Laka."

"No."

"To serve as Mary's maid. Not a slave, not an indentured servant, but to earn a wage. Enough for you and your son."

"I would die."

"You wouldn't die. You could become a Praying Indian."

Laka frowned at this, and Prudence felt a guilty twinge, though she couldn't exactly pinpoint why. Of course Prudence should offer this woman the truth of the gospel of Jesus Christ. There was no path to salvation following false, heathen—some even said satanic—beliefs.

Kepnomotok was still wearing the pewter medallion that James had given him, and now lifted a hand to his throat to fondle it. Now he spoke to Laka, who said, "The sachem asks another gift from the Englishman. Another emblem, this one for his son."

The specific term for "ask" was polite, but it was really more of a demand. Prudence passed this to James.

"I don't have another medallion," James said. "But I do have something else. It is a ring given to me by the great English king. A symbol of royal power." He reached into his cloak and came out with a signet ring.

The sachem stared at the ring with unabashed desire. He held out his hand.

James pulled back his hand. "No. First, I must have information. Tell him, Prudence."

What information? the sachem wanted to know, his expression guarded.

James said he wanted to speak with every surviving Nipmuk. He needed to find out what happened at Winton, at the village of Sachusett, and at Crow Hollow. He had reason to believe that a man named Samuel Knapp—James's enemy, and an Indian killer—had behaved treacherously. When Prudence translated, she used the word "despoiler" to describe Knapp, hoping that Laka would find a similar word in Abenaki.

Kepnomotok seemed pleased at the thought that James might be enemies with Samuel Knapp, whose foul reputation had apparently extended all the way into Abenaki lands. He readily agreed and sent his wives to get the rest of the Nipmuk survivors.

James gave Prudence a significant glance. "Too bad I only have one ring. And no more medallions. A few more trinkets and I could buy anything from the chief that I want."

Yes, anything. Such as the freedom of Prudence's daughter. Instead, he'd used the ring to buy information.

No matter. She had no intention of leaving without Mary. Never.

Chapter Twenty-Eight

It took some time for James to make sense of the jumble of narratives from the surviving Nipmuk. They'd brought in Prudence's daughter, and at first the distraction was so great that Prudence could scarcely maintain the concentration to do the difficult business of passing from English, to Nipmuk, then back again, with delays while Laka translated into Abenaki for the sachem.

Mary was also staring at Prudence, a look of intense concentration on her face, as if she were trying very hard to remember something important. James was afraid that Prudence would lose control and run for the child, so he held her hand tightly. At last, the sachem ordered the children out, and after a moment of distress from Prudence, she seemed to calm down.

There were eight surviving women and girls from three villages that had once totaled perhaps a thousand people, plus Mary, who was counted as the ninth. Of these eight, five were from Sachusett, the other three from a pair of villages that had either been enslaved and sold to the West Indies or been scattered to the north. James asked these three a few questions, but he sent them away when he realized they held no useful information.

From the Sachusett survivors came a horrific story. They were reluctant to tell it, but Kepnomotok was anxious to get the signet ring and prodded them whenever they tried to hold back.

After Knapp had broken the truce at Crow Hollow, cornered the warriors, and slaughtered them without pity—the details of which the women knew less of than James did, having heard the story from Prudence already—the English had come rampaging into the defenseless Indian camp. Only five Nipmuk men had remained behind, these ones either too old, sick, or injured to join the warriors who'd gone to parley at Crow Hollow.

Laka and the other survivors had been washing clothes at the creek when the attack came. They heard the screams and gunfire and came running up through the woods. They entered the clearing to see a force of several dozen English soldiers rampaging through the camp. Half were on foot, half on horse. They set fire to the lean-tos and other temporary shelters, then knocked them over while people screamed inside, burning alive. Other Nipmuk escaped the burning shelters only to be hacked down with swords or shot at close range. The killing was without quarter, an extermination of women, children, the elderly.

Laka had two young sons by Mikmonto. One was a year old; the other had survived three winters, or roughly the same age as Mary Cotton was now. Laka saw an English soldier swinging the babe by its feet and smashing his head repeatedly into the ground. Her other son was running in terror. A man on a horse rode him down and trampled him to death.

Laka screamed and tried to run toward the soldiers, but the other Nipmuk women dragged her back into the woods. One of these women was her mother, Hapamag, who was the one to tell this part of the tale, as no amount of prodding from Prudence or the sachem would get Laka to discuss the death of her children.

The entire story was eerily similar to the brutal Nipmuk attack on Winton. One side murdering practically unopposed, the other burning alive in their homes, or coming out to be slaughtered mercilessly. And yet this was the English doing the murdering, men who professed their faith and worshiped every Sunday.

There are no Christians in war, Prudence had said.

Together, the women hid for three days in the woods until the English finally stopped searching and went away. On the first night the women discovered two boys and an old man in the woods. On the second night, while sneaking out of their hiding place in the woods to check a few of their secret rabbit and squirrel traps, they had discovered little Mary Cotton, hungry and frightened but unharmed. The women took her into their care.

Prudence stopped the translation to proclaim a miracle, a blessing from God.

More likely, James thought, Knapp's brutes had spotted the blond-haired child and been unable to bring themselves to murder her. Then she'd run away and hid. Or, even more darkly, Knapp had left the child to die of hunger and exposure so as to conceal his crimes. Or even to justify them. After all, he would later say, Indians who would murder an English child in their care deserved nothing more than extermination.

The surviving women fled north, encountering a handful of other Nipmuk from different villages as they traveled toward Abenaki lands. These others also had a few men and boys with them. During the initial, confusing encounter with the Abenaki—themselves fearful of English attack as the war engulfed the entirety of New England—there was conflict.

Here Laka and the other Nipmuk women grew vague and fearful. There seemed to have been some argument within the Abenaki, after which the Nipmuk men were killed. The youngest boys they left to die of exposure.

Tiktoc grunted when this was translated into Abenaki. He looked proud, almost smug. Had he been responsible for the murders? No doubt. His father, Kepnomotok, seemed a more reasonable, measured sort. Surely it hadn't been his idea. Yet just as surely the sachem had given in to his son's demands.

Laka continued. Within days of her arrival, and speaking very little Abenaki, she and the other women were given as either wives or servants to members of the Abenaki tribe.

"I must know what happened at Winton," James said to Prudence. "Ask them. Why did the warriors of Sachusett attack after they'd promised peace?"

"I asked them that when I was a captive," she said. "As soon as I'd learned enough Nipmuk to pose the question. They wouldn't answer."

"Ask them again."

Prudence licked her lips. Her right hand was trembling. Of all of the awful, bloody affair, the murder of her husband seemed to trouble her the most.

James put a hand over hers until she stopped trembling. "We must know."

Prudence began speaking again, but the women seemed reluctant. After a moment, Prudence turned to James with a shake of the head.

"They said something about English treachery. They don't want to speak of it."

They didn't, or Prudence didn't? She didn't seem to be pushing very hard.

"Tell them they're Abenaki now. Kepnomotok is their chief. He ordered them to speak plainly."

She prodded them again, then appealed to Kepnomotok, who said something that sounded disinterested. James took out the signet ring that had attracted the sachem's attention.

"I must know everything. If not, I keep the ring."

The sachem didn't need this part translated. He looked displeased, but grumbled something to the Nipmuk women, who whispered amongst themselves. Laka's baby started to fuss, and she put the child at her breast. At last the young woman began to speak, reluctantly at first, but shortly with greater confidence. Prudence translated for James.

A few days before the Indian attack on Winton, Sir Benjamin and two other Englishmen arrived at Sachusett. They brought gifts of beef, a delicacy for the Nipmuk, and a bottle of spirits. The Englishmen smoked pipes with Mikmonto and the elders of the tribe while Laka prepared food. The men ate and smoked together until late into the night, promising that come what may, the village of Winton and the village of Sachusett would not fight in the war.

What's more, Sir Benjamin promised, if Mikmonto would agree to do the same with his fellow Indians, he vowed to keep the colonial militia from encroaching on Sachusett's lands or harassing the members of the tribe in any way. Mikmonto sent the Englishmen away with promises of eternal peace and friendship between the two villages.

The next day, Laka and her sister were harvesting ears of corn when two Englishmen came strolling up the village road. It was a wary time, with the war raging only a few miles away, and Laka's sister was afraid and wanted to run back to the village for safety. But Laka recognized the men from the council her husband had held the previous day. It wasn't Sir Benjamin, but his two confidants. Laka greeted them, saying "Good cheer," one of her few phrases in English.

The men drew swords. Without word or warning, they attacked Laka's sister, hacking her down before Laka could recover her wits enough to scream. Then they threw Laka to the ground, and now she did find her voice. But the fields were in the meadowland nearly a mile distant from Sachusett, and nobody was there to hear. One of the men forced himself on Laka, while the other watched. When they were done, they ran off, leaving one woman dead and the other violated.

Laka ran crying into Sachusett. Soon, the village was in an uproar, with Mikmonto holding a war council and gathering his warriors. He sent runners to the Nipmuk tribes to the east, to tell them he meant to join the war, and ask for help in exterminating the English village of Winton.

James interrupted Prudence's translation, troubled by the story. "It can't be by happenstance."

"How do you mean?"

"They kill a woman without provocation. Then one of the men violates the chief's wife, but leaves her alive. It was a calculated attack."

"What Godly man would do such a thing?" she asked.

"No kind of Godly man at all."

"It wasn't Benjamin who set them to it," she said firmly. "He would never do such a thing. He couldn't have known."

James didn't fully trust Prudence's judgment—there was still the matter of Peter's poisoning in the Stone household to consider, after all—but he believed she was correct in this case.

"Mikmonto must have known Benjamin had no part in it," she continued. Her face was stricken, her voice high and tight. "Why did they torture him? He was innocent. He would never—"

"Tell Laka to describe the men," James said quietly. His heart was thumping. Here it was. Here was the answer to all his questions.

One was tall, with gray hair. He seemed to be the master of the pair, but the other, the man who had done the violating of Laka's virtue, was short, with long blond hair. A violent man with an ugly sneer.

"Samuel Knapp," James hissed. "That villain! I knew it."

Prudence looked horrified. "And the other? Was it Fitz-Simmons?"

"Tall, gray hair. Yes, I think it was."

"They are the cause of this atrocity," she said. "They must be brought to justice."

James sprang to his feet and paced about the room, agitated. Tictok stiffened near the door, but his father waved him back. Kepnomotok wore a calculating expression. He asked Laka something, which came through to Prudence, and then to James.

"He wants to know if you are enemies of these men."

"Aye," James said. "They are traitors of my king, and murderers of both Indians and Englishmen alike. I will see them hanged."

The sachem looked pleased at this, but Prudence gave a confused shake of the head once she'd translated. "How do you mean, murderers of Englishmen?"

James stopped his pacing. He took his seat and calmed his breathing. His mind was galloping.

"Sir Benjamin made peace overtures to Sachusett," he began, "perhaps at Fitz-Simmons's and Knapp's urging. Then he returned to Winton to assure the people that they were safe from their neighbors. That was the plan. That's what Sir Benjamin's enemies intended all along."

"But he had no enemies," she cried. "Why would they do such a thing?"

"Except that rumors put Winton on the run anyway. Knapp, fighting in Springfield, must have heard. He rode back to tell you to turn around and go home."

Prudence was breathing heavily. "Benjamin led us back to Winton. Mikmonto had promised friendship. We were safer there, Benjamin said. But nobody knew the Nipmuk would be on the warpath."

"Except Knapp and Fitz-Simmons."

"I don't understand." Her eyes were wide, her lips trembling. "Bless me, why would they do it? You must tell me!"

He didn't answer. She was a clever woman, she would understand. Soon enough, her eyes narrowed. "The land."

"All the best land, now in their hands. The meadows and forests of Sachusett, plus all of the land they could buy after the people of

Winton were nearly wiped out. Some of it he got from your sister's husband, and no doubt the good reverend sold it to him at a quick and ready price."

"I don't believe it. I can't."

"What kind of man was Knapp before the war?"

"From a family of modest circumstance. His father a wheelwright, his mother arrived from England as an indentured servant."

"And now?"

"Living well, prosperous. Fitz-Simmons too. But some men rise, while others fall—it is the way of the world."

"And often men rise through nefarious means," James said.

"I cannot believe it." Now Prudence was the one rising, pacing the room. "Everything we suffered. My husband—it was like the torments of hell! My captivity, my daughter. All for money?"

"Nothing but wealth. Filthy lucre. It was in their minds all along."

"Where is she?" Prudence said. "Where did they take Mary?"

She fired off a rapid stream of Nipmuk at Laka. The other woman flinched. Her lips came together stubbornly. But Prudence didn't let up.

Kepnomotok had also risen to his feet. His son drew his scalping knife. The Abenaki outside the wigwam raised their voices, having apparently heard the commotion and trying to decide whether to rush in and aid their sachem.

"Prudence, please. Sit down. You'll get us killed."

"And you," Prudence turned on James. "Buying information. What about my daughter? You promised—or are you a liar too?"

"Sit down!"

She blinked at his sharp tone, then looked around the room, seeming to notice for the first time that her outburst had left the Indians agitated. The Nipmuk women, especially, seemed afraid of her. *Puda-katan*, it seemed, had a reputation. Yes, of course she would. A woman did not survive so many months of captivity without drawing on a reserve of steel.

James took her shoulders and gently pulled her down. He was agitated too, but this outburst wouldn't help. The Indians calmed once the two English were seated.

"What about my daughter?" she persisted, stubbornly. "You never meant it, did you?"

"What kind of man do you think I am?"

"A servant of the Crown, as you've told me so many times. You told me what I wanted to hear. You never had any intention of recovering my daughter, not unless they handed her over without complaint."

The accusation left him frustrated and angry, in part because he understood why she believed that very thing. He'd told her so several times. His duty was to the Crown.

"I am a man of honor, Prudence Cotton. And now I will show you."

James took out the signet ring and held it up for all to see. Then he rose slowly and nonthreateningly to his feet and walked toward Kepnomotok with the ring in his outstretched hand. The sachem grunted, his expression pleased. He reached for the ring.

"No, not yet." He turned to Prudence. "Tell him I need more, the information wasn't sufficient."

Her face shining, her eyes bright with expectation, she obeyed. Kepnomotok made displeased sounds.

"We need provisions and guides back to English territory. Go ahead, tell him," he said when she hesitated, her hopeful expression fading into worry.

There was some back and forth, and Kepnomotok agreed. What's more, James said, he didn't want to be led back to the outskirts of Winton. That was too dangerous. He wanted the Abenaki to take them east, through Verts Monts, to emerge in the English colony of New Hampshire. From there, they could make their way safely to Boston. If the sachem could guarantee that, James would give him the great emblem of the English king. Grudgingly, Kepnomoto agreed, but James could tell he was pressing his advantage almost to the breaking point.

"And one more thing," James said. "Return the English girl to her mother. There will be no agreement without the child."

Prudence stared at him. "Thank you."

"He hasn't agreed yet. Tell him."

As soon as she started to speak the words, Laka's eyes widened. She made as if to run for the door, but Tictok blocked her way while his father demanded a translation. Laka wouldn't give it. Instead, one of the other Nipmuk women had to tell him what James had demanded. Kepnomotok grunted his answer.

"He says no," Prudence said, her voice trembling. "Oh, James. We can make our own way back if we must. Rescind the request for a guide, and maybe he'll trade Mary for the ring."

"You said strength, remember?"

"But it isn't enough. He almost didn't accept the other demands."

"We'll never cross Verts Monts alone. We need that guide."

"He won't do this," she said. "You ask too much and offer too little."

James handed Prudence the ring and reached into his cloak for his purse. He loosened the drawstrings and poured the gold and silver coins into the palm of his hand. "Twenty pounds. Enough to buy two cows, eight sheep, a pair of horses, five bottles of rum, and several firearms."

Prudence licked her lips. "Perhaps in England. Here it will buy a good sight more than that."

"Good."

"But they cannot use the money. No Indians will enter the colonies, not at the moment. It's too perilous for them."

"There are French trappers in Quebec. They're not too proud to take English gold, I should imagine."

"Ah, yes." She translated.

Kepnomotok agreed at once. So quickly, in fact, and with his eyes wide and greedy, that it was obvious he'd have agreed to the exchange for far less than that. But James hadn't made such a generous offer for the benefit of convincing the sachem.

He had spent the king's gold to win the confidence of Prudence Cotton.

Chapter Twenty-Nine

Prudence waited, shaking with anticipation and worry as Tictok went for Mary. Laka threw herself to the ground, wailing, while women gathered around her, trying to comfort her. Hapamag held Laka in her arms, keening and rocking back and forth.

The young woman kept crying, "My daughter, my daughter." She clutched her baby to her breast, as if terrified that they would take him too.

Laka didn't appeal to Kepnomotok, who sat with a stony face, refusing to look at her. Among the Nipmuk, at least, tribe members could and did argue with the judgment of the sachem. Even women had that right. Decision-making often had the contentious nature of a New England town meeting, until finally the sachem made his ruling. Even then, the arguing sometimes continued.

But the status of an outsider, an impoverished petitioner seeking refuge in the protection of a tribe, was more akin to that of an indentured servant in the colonies. Laka, for all her claims to have become Abenaki, was still more possession than free member of the tribe.

Instead, Laka begged Prudence. "Do not do this. Do not take my daughter, Puda-katan."

Prudence was moved by the woman's grief. How could she not be? And she understood. Both women had lost husbands, both women had lost young children. Laka's had been killed, while Prudence's had been taken from her and given to the young Nipmuk widow. For ten months Laka had cared for the child, and now Mary was being taken away from her.

"Send her away," James murmured. "You must tell the chief. Laka cannot be here when your child arrives."

"I'm her mother," Prudence said, stubbornly.

"Will these people think so? Will Mary?"

Mary. Yes, of course. That frightened look in her eyes when Prudence had grabbed for her. The attachment went both ways.

Before she could speak to the sachem, Tictok pulled aside the deerskin and stepped into the wigwam. He held Mary in his hands. The child was crying, frightened. She spotted Laka wailing and reached for her. "*Nuken!*" *Mama.*

Prudence, her heart breaking with such a complex mix of emotions she thought she would swoon, moved to the young Abenaki man before her resolve could give out. Mary screamed and grabbed at Tictok. Prudence pried Mary away.

Laka wailed harder. Tictok, showing no mercy for his wife or concern for his adopted daughter, snarled something at her. He jabbed her roughly with his foot.

The Nipmuk women on the ground with Laka snapped at him and pounded his leg with their fists. He withdrew, startled, before the familiar haughty look reasserted itself. James was paying the scene little attention, instead completing the transaction. He handed Kepnomotok his signet ring and his purse, heavy with gold and silver.

Prudence did not allow herself delusions. This terrible scene was her choice, not his, not the sachem's, not anyone else's. Hers.

You have bought her. You have bought a child from another woman.

Her heart pounding, Mary screaming in her ear and flailing to get free, the women wailing, Prudence could only flee the wigwam.

Outside, there was no relief. Dozens of Abenaki stood in tight knots, talking amongst themselves. Their voices hushed as she appeared. Whispers of "Puda-katan, Puda-katan" passed through them like wind shaking the bare branches of the surrounding forest.

Prudence staggered away, pushing through, yelling at them to let her pass. They did. But once she was past, they all fell in behind her, following, their whispers continuing.

She ran to the banks of the river. It was the only place she could get where she wouldn't have to be surrounded on all sides, but from behind came the whispers. "Puda-katan, Puda-katan."

If the river had been frozen all the way through the center she would have stumbled across to the snowy woods on the opposite bank, but as it was she was pinned against the river with the crowd of Abenaki at her back, her wailing daughter in her arms. Mary stopped to take in a huge, sobbing breath.

From beneath the ice came the sound of rocks grinding along the river bottom, the gurgling of water churning through icy fissures and chasms, pushing always to the sea. Mary renewed her screaming.

"Mary, please. I'm your mother. I love you. I came back for you."

She kept talking until her daughter had to stop for another gasp. This time Mary didn't scream, but gave way to a whimper instead. She stared up at Prudence with huge, tear-filled eyes.

So blue, like Prudence's own, but with blond hair like Benjamin's, and his full lips too. Prudence used her thumb to wipe away tears.

"Do you understand me? Do you remember English?"

Mary only stared. She had only just begun to speak in phrases last spring, when she was taken from Prudence's arms, but of course she had understood everything. And at the time, she had already absorbed more Nipmuk than even Prudence had, in spite of the woman's greater concentration. But if a child's mind was wide, quick to swallow any new information, it was also shallow. Memories, even language, it seemed, drained away if abandoned. It was clear that her daughter was struggling to remember, as if she could almost grasp some remembered fragment that remained out of reach.

"I'm your mother. I always meant to come for you. Please, trust me, you will remember me quickly. We will go together, and I will care for you always."

"Where is my mama?" Mary asked in Abenaki. Those particular words were almost identical to the Nipmuk, and Prudence had no difficulty understanding.

Prudence hesitated. She spoke in Nipmuk. "I am right here. I am your mother."

Mary also understood and took up her wailing again. The whispers behind grew.

Prudence ignored them and continued to hold her daughter, trying again in English. Once again, curiosity got the better of the child. She stopped struggling.

"You are so big. Did you know in two weeks you will be three?" Prudence nodded. "I remember when you were born. The midwife felt my belly and said I was carrying you low, and you were going to be a boy. Your papa was going to name you Harold, after your grandfather. Sir Harold was an English baron, a very important man. But when you came, you surprised everyone. You were a girl."

Prudence spit on her thumb and used it to wipe some of the dirt from Mary's cheeks. "I was happy, I had secretly wanted a daughter. We could have our Harold later. But then you wouldn't take to nursing. They worried you wouldn't thrive—sometimes children die when they are wee infants, and everyone told me not to name you. Not for two weeks. Your papa was sick with worry. He wouldn't sleep, he wouldn't even sit down.

"I loved you so much," she continued. "If you passed away, I didn't think I could live. I prayed, I prayed so hard. 'Please, Lord, let this child live. I will teach her to honor thee always. But please, don't take her away.' I knew in my heart that God wouldn't take you from me. And he didn't."

When Prudence stopped, she sensed someone standing right over her shoulder. She turned, expecting to see one of the more bold Abenaki, but it was James. He was watching her with his mouth down-turned and his eyes full of sorrow.

"I can't leave her," she told him, pleading. "Please don't ask me."

"Prudie, no. I would never ask that. She is your daughter. She belongs with you."

"Then why are you looking at me like that? James, you must stop, I cannot bear it. Please, I beg you."

He took her in his arms, with Mary between them. The child was now still. Very, very still, with barely a sniffle. A long, shuddering sob worked its way up from deep inside Prudence's bosom.

"The chief gave away the child," James said. "He didn't hesitate. She is ours to take where we will."

"They are slaves, the Nipmuk women." Her voice shook. "Mary was property."

"How could it be otherwise? They were strangers in a strange land. It is the way of all mankind."

"How do you mean?"

"Where two people live together, only one can rule. French and English, Indian and European, Puritan and Quaker." He was saying this not to her, but almost as if speaking to himself. He pulled away and studied her face. "We must go. Quickly now, before you lose your will."

She found her courage. "I won't lose my will."

A wail sounded from the direction of Kepnomotok's wigwam. They turned to look. Laka threw herself onto the icy ground, surrounded by other women. Soon, the others had blocked the woman from view. Those standing closer to the English, some no more than an arm's length away, studied Prudence with sharp gazes.

She swallowed hard and squeezed Mary to her breast. The child began to cry again.

"Yes," she said. "We must leave at once."

❧

To Prudence's dismay, it was Tictok who was chosen to lead them east through Abenaki lands. The young warrior wore a hard expression as he hoisted a leather satchel on a cord, which he tied around his shoulders. He refused to look at James, and when Prudence tried to speak to him, he only grimaced and turned away.

The Abenaki had fit Prudence with one of the slings women used to carry their young children while they planted corn or plucked caterpillars from their crops. Mary was too big for the sling—normally, a child of three would walk about freely—but they had many miles to travel. She would never be able to walk so far.

At first it seemed as though Mary would settle into the rhythm of the journey. Her wails subsided as they left the tumult of the village. Prudence spoke to her quietly, telling stories about Mary's father, about the child's first year in Winton. Of course Mary wouldn't remember the way she'd run screaming from an overly aggressive rooster, or the time her father had captured a green frog at the millpond and put the squirming thing in her hand.

But she did seem to recognize her mother's voice. And when Prudence sang her the nursery songs that she'd used to soothe her daughter during their captivity, it was as if something was stirring deep in Mary's mind. Old memories, called forth from dusty corners. After a couple of hours, Mary drifted off to sleep.

But she woke a short time later, sobbing in Nipmuk for her mother. And she did not mean the woman now carrying her away from the village. It was enough to break Prudence's heart.

Be patient. Mary has suffered her own traumas.

Prudence fell farther and farther behind the two men as they followed a deer path over hills and through meadows. James offered several times to take a turn carrying the child, but Prudence was reluctant to release her daughter for any reason. Eventually, she had no choice. Her aching back and shoulders took great relief from releasing their burden.

James couldn't figure out the loops and knots of the child sling, so she helped him fix it in place. Tictok tossed down his satchel, crossed his arms, and watched with a look of sneering disbelief. Men did not carry children. Not Nipmuk men, and apparently not Abenaki, either.

They didn't stop for more than a few minutes until evening, when they halted in front of a shallow, rocky cave deep in the hills. The bones of animals and the remains of several fires marked it as a regular way station for travelers.

Tictok disappeared with his bow and arrows to hunt, while the other two lit a fire and gathered wood. The Abenaki returned shortly after dark, empty-handed and disgruntled. He removed three long pieces of pemmican from his satchel—pounded-down venison mixed with bear fat and chokeberries—and handed Prudence and James their own pieces, while he squatted on the opposite side of the fire. Prudence broke off pieces of pemmican and fed some to Mary, eating the rest herself.

When the girl finished, she held out her hand. "More."

Prudence was explaining that there was no more to give, when she stopped, startled.

"What's wrong?" James asked. He'd been staring into the fire but now fixed her with a curious expression.

"She said 'more.' In English."

Prudence hugged her daughter, who did not respond, but stared into the darkness.

When traveling in the winter, the Nipmuk had slept all huddled and shivering together, and she was sure the Abenaki followed the same custom. But Tictok and James wanted nothing to do with each other. The Abenaki wrapped himself in his wolf pelt and curled up next to the fire. James and Prudence lay down wrapped in their cloaks, with Mary between them, their snowshoes serving as pillows of a sort. The girl sniffled and cried, but didn't pull away when Prudence stroked her cheek and sang to her in a quiet voice. Eventually, she fell asleep.

James was still shifting on the hard ground, clearing his throat, swallowing, and making other noises, so she knew he wasn't asleep, but he didn't say anything to her, either. Neither did he reach out and touch her.

Prudence ached with loneliness. She held her daughter again, a miracle after so many years, and she had whispered a dozen prayers of gratitude in her heart since leaving the Abenaki village. Yet it was not enough. Why was James so distant? She wanted to reach over her daughter and take his hand, but she was afraid of being rebuffed.

Perhaps he was thinking of her betrayal, when she'd left a note to send back to Boston, to warn that James was attempting to seize the colonial charters. Or maybe he was regretting the night they'd spent together after fleeing Winton. She had taken a terrible risk in offering herself to him. If he loved her, if he would have her, then surely God would understand.

But what if she meant nothing to him? If he thought of her as a trifle, no more than Lucy Branch and her animal passions? For that matter, how could she be sure he hadn't slept with Lucy and lied about it?

Prudence shouldn't have done it. She had been a maiden on the eve of her marriage to Benjamin, and if she hadn't been married before, she had little doubt that she would have been able to resist offering herself to James. But those passions, once awakened in marriage, were not so easily stilled by widowhood. Even so, she'd managed to convince herself that he loved her, that he would take her to wife. Otherwise, she'd have never done it.

What a fool you are, Widow Cotton.

James had taken what he wanted. Now he would sail back to London, colonial charters in hand, the stolen virtue of his New England conquests a delightful memory.

Stop, she told herself. *You will devour yourself from the inside.*

And then Mary whimpered in her sleep, and Prudence pulled her daughter closer, forgetting any other worries.

Chapter Thirty

By the time they stopped, late on the second day, James was exhausted, and not solely from hiking through hills and dales for mile after mile. He'd barely slept during the night, afraid to relax his vigil against Tictok, who had led them through the wilderness without once shedding his hostile demeanor.

The Indian was an enemy, and make no mistake. His father may have compelled him to guide James, Prudence, and her child, but the farther from his own village he was, the less likely that anyone would notice if a mishap befell the two English and he came back with the child. After all, Mary was the adopted daughter of his wife, and therefore his own property.

This time when they stopped for the evening, Tictok returned victorious from his hunting expedition. He had shot a deer and already had it cleaned and dressed, which surprised James.

"We don't want to attract wolves," Prudence explained. "He left the entrails and pelt in the woods, where 'twould distract them."

They cooked huge chunks of sizzling venison on skewers made of birch saplings. It was well after dark before the food was finally done. They ate like ravenous wolves themselves.

When James lay down, he tried to stay awake until he was sure Tictok was asleep first. Prudence and Mary were already breathing heavily, both snoring softly, but the Indian was still shifting about. To distract himself, James counted the days since he'd arrived in Boston. It had been nine days now. He was startled to realize that today was Christmas. It hadn't occurred to him earlier, and now it was too late to even offer good cheer to Prudence.

Back home in England, his family would be fast asleep, their bellies full of fruitcake and fat Christmas goose. In a few short hours they would wake on Boxing Day and load the carriage or the sleigh and go visit uncles and aunts, friends and cousins. More feasting and merrymaking.

From the time they were young men, James and his brother Thomas had set out on Boxing Day with sprigs of mistletoe. They used it not to seduce girls, but to tease and delight old women. Once, when they were handsome young men of nineteen and seventeen, the brothers leaped from their sleigh to run up behind a crofter's widow from the village. She'd been trudging wearily under a bundle of sticks with her back turned, and she let out a terrified shriek at the unexpected assault. But she giggled like a girl when they held up the mistletoe and kissed her cheeks. As James and Thomas leaped back into the sleigh, she called playfully after them that she was widowed and free to remarry either or the both of them. Thomas turned and blew her kisses, while James threw imaginary flowers in their wake. Every time they saw her after that, the brothers would give her winks while she blushed furiously.

James smiled at the memory. He wondered if the old woman was still alive. If so, he hoped Thomas would pay her a visit tomorrow.

The night was warmer and his belly full. Soon, he could no longer fight sleep. When he woke in the morning, he was momentarily alarmed, but grateful that no harm had come to them at the hands of their reluctant guide.

By the morning of the third full day after leaving the Abenaki village, Mary's first tentative English words had become two words, then three together. She still spoke more Nipmuk and Abenaki than her native tongue, but it was clear that her English was thawing from some deep memory. And she was thawing, too, toward her mother. When they stopped, she wanted to stay in Prudence's arms, and finally called her mother "Mama."

Tears of joy streamed down Prudence's cheeks. It warmed James's heart.

Tictok soon had them traveling in silence, and about an hour after setting out there was a tense standoff with two young Indians, armed with muskets, who met them on the trail and argued for several minutes with Tictok before letting them past. Later, they heard a musket fire in the distance, and Tictok kept them hidden in the woods for almost an hour before they continued on.

A few hours after that, now late afternoon, they came out of the woods and onto a wider trail. It was not much bigger than the one they'd been traveling on for the past three days, but wide enough that James at first supposed that it was a road between two Indian villages. They were still deep in what felt like wilderness.

Here Tictok would go no further. He pointed at the road. "*Postoni.*"

"What does that mean?" James asked.

"Boston people," Prudence said. "It's one of their words for the English. This must be an English road."

James turned to Tictok, but the man was already disappearing into the woods, his snowshoes crunching on the snow. An instant later and he was gone.

It was then that James looked back to the larger trail and saw that it was marked with hoofprints, pressed into the snow and mud and then frozen.

The road was nothing but a sleepy country lane, too narrow even for a full-sized wagon, and they had no idea what lay on the other end. A farmstead? A town?

James and Prudence passed through another wooded stretch that led them up over a gentle hillock. When they came down the other side, the landscape opened into meadows and cleared fields overlaid with a blanket of glistening white. Below the fields sat a tidy English village. Not a large town like Springfield, but larger than Winton. Perhaps the size of Natick, which surely meant there would be an inn.

They stopped to toss aside their snowshoes and Mary's sling but couldn't decide what to do about the child's leather breeches and tunic. They were clearly of Indian manufacture and would raise suspicions. Being strangers on the road, they needed to avoid unwanted attention. Prudence suggested wrapping Mary in her cloak as if she were simply cold. This would serve until they gained lodging, but what then?

"I can sew," Prudence said. "If you venture out to buy fabric, needle, and thread, I can make her some clothes in our room."

James chewed at his lip. "That will take time."

"I'll work every waking minute."

"I'm sure you will. That's not my worry. Let me give it some more thought."

Their paces quickened in anticipation, until soon Mary was flagging. James picked her up and she wrapped her little arms around his neck.

Prudence studied him with a curious expression.

"Thank you, James."

"You're tired. I can carry her the rest of the way."

"For keeping your word. I shouldn't have doubted you. You are a good man, and true."

He shrugged, unused to such compliments and embarrassed as a result. "There's a reason you doubted me."

"If anyone should doubt, it would be you. You promised to help me find my daughter, and I betrayed you when I left the letter for Cooper's confederate. It might have sabotaged our entire journey."

This much was true. It might still sabotage them, depending on where that letter had landed.

They continued into town, drawing a few curious stares at their bedraggled appearance, but no comments. When they reached the inn, a small place named The Goose and Turkey, James went in first to secure lodging, being wary of who might be waiting inside. They were so far east from Winton and Springfield that they were unlikely to meet enemies, but he'd committed several errors in judgment already and wasn't keen to commit another.

The proprietor was a red-faced fellow, as stout as a Dutch burgher, with shiny brass buttons on his jerkin. His hair had receded to a fringe around his uncovered head, but he didn't look older than forty, and the sound of children, ever present in New England, came from a back room.

James paid for lodging and supper for two people and a child, making up a story as to why they didn't need stabling for animals (he had lost his team and wagon and intended to hire transport in the morning), and then hesitated when the innkeeper asked if he needed any special considerations.

James had emptied the contents of his purse in Kepnomotok's hand, but he now retrieved several silver pennies and a half crown tucked into hidden pockets in his cloak, worth thirty shillings in total. He still had more than enough to get them back to Boston, if he were frugal. But there was one indulgence that he was craving.

"Can your mistress draw up a hot bath?"

"Of course. Piping hot water." The innkeeper made a note in his ledger. "That'll be an extra nine pence."

"Wait, make that two baths. One for me, and one for the missus. We've been too long on the road. And some hard soap—do you have it?"

The innkeeper looked up from his abacus where he'd been tallying the expenses. He raised his eyebrows. One bath was a luxury, two an extravagance. The act of emptying the tub and refilling it with clean hot water would cost. And hard soap, too, not the soft tallow soap that could be made in any home.

"Yes, of course." His expression sharpened. "What did you say your name was, good sir?"

"Pray pardon me, I didn't give it. My name is John Clyde." Clyde was the name of his maternal grandfather.

"And how is it that you travel in such bedraggled circumstances?" He glanced over James's shoulder at the door. "And where are the missus and the child?"

"We are emigrating from Hartford to Gloucester, but we lost the wagon crossing the river when it broke through thin ice. And two good mules, besides. One drowned and the other broke his leg on the ice. Very nearly lost our own lives. Had a rough scramble of it these last two days. The good wife is ashamed of her appearance. We haven't much in the way of possessions, or even clothing for the little one."

"Yes, well. For a man who has lost so much, you have resources and to spare. *Two* baths." The innkeeper rang the bell for one of the servants. "You must love your wife dearly."

"Aye, that I do."

⚜

James unfolded a map of the Bay Colony and spread it on the bed while Prudence settled Mary in the little cot and covered her with wool blankets. To Prudence's relief, her daughter fell asleep almost at once. The room was warm from a crackling fire, and their bellies gloriously full from the meal. And they were clean. The bath had been almost scalding, with fine Castilian soap made of olive oil. The water had been dirty when she finished, but by the time Mary was through, it looked like someone had poured in a bucket of mud. James had bathed in a separate tub of water.

Upon hearing of their supposed catastrophe on the frozen river, the innkeeper's wife sprang into action. By the time the servant girl had drawn up the first bath, the goodwife had collected spare outfits from the village for the lot of them, and she gave Prudence a bundle of clothing in Mary's size, tied in twine.

The charity made Prudence sting with guilt. Soon enough, the scandal would reach every corner of New England, and the woman would realize that she had been hoodwinked. Her guilt increased when the goodwife personally served a delicious supper of beef stew, dark bread, and the ever-present corn pudding.

Now upstairs, Prudence stroked Mary's face for several minutes after the child was asleep. She was so sweet and innocent and clean, her cheeks rosy and fair. Again, Prudence was struck by how much she looked like her father. So much the child had lost. No life was ever spared tragedy, Prudence reminded herself, and at least the two of them were reunited. That was a blessing.

"I didn't realize how far east Gloucester is," James said, still studying the map. "Well out on Cape Ann. We'd be better off traveling to Salem instead."

She came over to look at the map James had borrowed from the innkeeper. Crosses marked the English settlements, widely spaced here on the frontier, more numerous near the coast. Even there, many of those settlements had been destroyed during the war.

"Why not go straight to Boston?" Prudence traced her finger down the east highway cutting through Concord and Woburn. "Here, where they're not expecting us."

"You must think like our enemies. Knapp will hope that we've perished in the wilderness. Perhaps he's still searching for us on the Winton and Springfield road. But maybe he captured Cooper. Under torture, Cooper would give up everything."

That was a horrifying thought. "You think it likely?"

"Nay, I think Cooper escaped toward Hartford. With a bit of good fortune, he has reached New York by now and has made contact with the king's agents." James wiped the side of the candle to smooth out the hot wax that was threatening to drip onto the map. "By now Knapp and his devils know that I'm relentless. They must know I'll return to Boston and press matters with the General Court, or perhaps regain the *Vigilant* and flee for England. From there to return in greater force."

"Either way, they must stop you," she said.

"Quite."

Prudence found this glimpse into the minds of their enemies a fascinating exercise. Those villains would be scheming to keep their crimes hidden. What would they do?

"Knapp has had plenty of time to guard the main highways," she said. "We'll face certain ambush if we go back on either one. So you mean to travel to Gloucester and take the coastal road south?"

James smiled. "We're not taking the road. We're going to hire fishermen to sail us into Boston Harbor from behind."

"Oh. Yes, I see."

"I told the innkeeper we were moving to Gloucester to live near your elderly father. So he has hired me a coach. Would it raise suspicions if we had him drop us in Salem instead? We'll sail from Marblehead."

He tapped his finger on the map at the town of Salem, which was midway between Boston and Gloucester up the coast. Marblehead was only a few miles east on its own small peninsula. And it was, indeed, a fishing town. The rules were lax in such places, the men a mix of English, Scottish, and even Portuguese and Irish. Often single young men, quick to do shifty work for a bit of silver.

There was only one problem.

"Reverend Stone's brother is the minister in Salem."

James frowned. "Oh?"

"They are a stiff, dour-faced congregation. They will take note of strangers, and if I'm spotted, I'll be recognized. I'm well known in Salem. And when the minister hears, he'll send word to his brother in Boston."

James studied her face. "You're no longer certain, are you?"

"My brother-in-law is an honorable man. My sister is forever true. They would never betray me."

"Then explain your predicament. If you are correct, either reverend will be quick to offer us aid."

How certain was she? At the moment, not very. To imagine her own family, the husband of her flesh-and-blood sister, turning on her was sickening. And Stone was a man of God. Surely, he could not be implicated in this wickedness.

"I am not certain," she admitted at last.

His expression was sympathetic, but neither did he seek to change her mind. "Then we'll ride straight for Gloucester and leave aside Salem and Marblehead. 'Twill give Cooper an extra day to raise help, if it is coming."

"James," she said. "Are all men false at heart?"

"No," he said. "Most men are honorable."

⁂

There was no room in Mary's undersized cot, so Prudence slept in the bed with James, once more with her body against his. He put his arms around her but didn't touch her intimately. She was glad he did not. She was confused already, and under his strong touch, his skin and clothing smelling of soap, his face freshly shaved, she would have given herself to him again. And that would only confuse her more.

James soon fell asleep, but Prudence's own thoughts wouldn't stop churning. To get her mind off Laka and her awful wailing when Mary had been wrenched from her arms, Prudence imagined what Knapp would do, worked through his stratagems for ensnaring them before they reached Boston.

But even supposing they reached Boston safely, what then?

She'd spent so much time working through what their enemies might do that she'd given little thought to how James intended to bring justice to Knapp and Fitz-Simmons. And her brother-in-law, too, she thought gloomily. Anne would be destroyed.

Why would the reverend do it? He was a Godly man, one of the most prominent and honored ministers in New England. Perhaps only Increase Mather was more respected. And Stone received a just income from the congregation. He had no need of money. Knapp and Fitz-Simmons, yes; they had emerged from the war with newfound wealth and power, and now she knew how they'd done it. But Reverend Stone?

But what other explanation could she find for him poisoning Peter Church? There was nobody else in the house with the means or the motive. Neither Knapp nor Fitz-Simmons had access to the house or its food supplies. Not to mention that whoever did it must have poisoned a single meal at a time, not the entire food stock of the family, because nobody else had fallen ill.

Suddenly, she knew.

Prudence shook James. "Wake up. I know."

"Hmm? What?" He sounded groggy, not yet fully awake, but he sat up, yawning. "What do you know?"

"I know how Peter was poisoned."

CHAPTER THIRTY-ONE

Every muscle in James's body tensed as the ship eased into Boston Harbor. He half expected to see Samuel Knapp at the head of an armed militia, waiting to slap him in irons and carry him swiftly to the gallows. That was if the little beast didn't simply gun James down as soon as he set foot on the wharfs. But there was no suspicious gathering along the waterfront, only men about their work.

The captain, a one-eyed man named Blunt, gave the orders to brail up the gaff mainsail to cut their speed as they maneuvered through the taller ships at anchor.

Blunt's was a stout little dogger with a square rig on the mainmast and a long bowsprit out front, displacing perhaps a dozen tons. It had a crew of six and had been readying to head out to Georges Bank for an extended fishing trip when James hired her to take a detour south to Boston. The ship was small enough to hide among the larger pinnaces and brigantines in the harbor, yet not so small so as to look out of place coming in off the open sea.

It had been three nights and four days since Tictok had left them north of Haverhill and only two weeks since James had first eased into Boston harbor aboard the *Vigilant* with Peter Church. Yet so much had changed.

"Do you have enough to pay Blunt the rest of your debt?" Prudence asked. She held Mary in her arms, the girl staring wide-eyed at the town rising above them.

Before leaving Gloucester, Prudence had dyed her raven hair with henna, leaving it a reddish auburn. Such disguises were readily available among the smugglers of Cape Ann. With her hood up and most of her hair covered with a head rail, dressed in different clothing, and carrying a child, he doubted she'd be recognized if she kept her eyes averted. James was another story—he expected that there were men in Boston with his description in their heads and a few pieces of silver in their filthy palms.

"Aye, and two shillings to spare," he said.

A few minutes later, when they'd paid Blunt and the dogger had been tied against the pier, James and Prudence came warily down the gangplank. Still nothing to arouse suspicion. James forced the tension from his body as he led Prudence and her child off the pier to solid ground.

Mary buried her head in her mother's shoulder. She wouldn't yet talk to James, but she had succumbed to Prudence's patience and tender caresses. Her English was improving day by day. He guessed she would forget her Abenaki and Nipmuk just as quickly, which was a shame.

"You're sure the General Court will be in session?" he asked Prudence. "It is still Christmastide."

"Popery and pagan festivals do not put aside the General Court. The committee of land and deeds meets on the final Friday of the month, whether the governor is present or not."

"With good fortune, Governor Leverett will have returned from Hartford. If not, if the deputy governor is holding court in his stead, it will be a good sight more difficult. Fitz-Simmons will not surrender without a fight."

"Be careful, James."

"I am a very careful man."

"You won't confront them alone. You must not."

"I will do my duty to my sovereign. If Cooper has fallen, or is false, I'll have no other choice."

She opened her mouth as if she were going to argue, but then she nodded. "You do your duty, and I shall do mine."

They looked at each other for a long moment, then Prudence glanced around, as if afraid of prying eyes, before leaning in to kiss him quickly on the mouth. When she came away, she was blushing in a way that was all the more endearing.

Holding Mary in her cloak, Prudence made her way swiftly up the dirt alleyway into Boston Town, toward her home. When she was out of sight, James gathered himself and moved down the muddy alley that led to the shanties, fishmongers, and alehouses along the waterfront. Now that the coast had thawed with the shift in the weather, it smelled damp, of rotting piers and fish guts.

The Windlass and Anchor was a disreputable-looking place, the green paint on the door battered and flaking, the windows few and tiny. Greasy smoke trailed up from the chimney, and two bearded fellows with bad teeth stood out front with tankards of grog in hand. They eyed him through narrowed eyes, as if sizing him up for a quick knockdown and purse grab.

James returned a steely gaze and swept back his cloak to show his dagger, now at his belt. The men stepped aside and let him in.

The interior was dark, smoky, and cramped. It smelled of cheap pipe smoke and stale body odor. There were furtive glances from the sailors and stevedores crowding around tables, but as soon as they got a good look at him they turned back to their business, which seemed to be dice and cards. Those men out front, he realized, had not been considering robbing him. They were lookouts, ready to give the warning should the city watch of Boston come aiming to crack down on gambling.

You couldn't turn seafaring types into good Puritans—that much was universally true. Although James noted, looking around, that other constant of such places—women showing too much skin and too much interest in strange men—was notably absent from the Windlass and Anchor.

"You have a sharp look about you, friend," a man said in a low voice.

James turned, resisting the urge to snatch out his dagger. A short man with a piercing gaze and blackened teeth grinned up at him from the rough chair in which he slouched.

"Perhaps you are searching for something," the man continued. "Company, perchance, in this dark place. The winter nights are long and cold."

Ah, here it was. They kept the women in the back rooms, out of sight of the enforcers of morality. You could sweep cards into your cloak quickly enough, palm your dice and coins, but hiding women was another matter. That men still managed to smuggle in and hide strumpets in this dangerous corner of Christendom must have taken imagination. But he supposed the rewards equaled the risks.

"No. I come for ale and a pipe. Nothing more."

"I see." The man sounded disappointed.

James was fighting his own disappointment. There was no sign of Cooper, or of Joseph McMurdle, the Scotsman who was head of His Majesty's service in New York. Assuming James could recognize the man—it had been several years now.

That meant he was alone. He grabbed an empty chair and dragged it into the corner farthest from the hearth. There, he hoped to stay unnoticed for a stretch while he turned over matters in his head. Better to save his last few precious coins than waste them in a place such as this. But the barman found him at once, and shortly he ended up changing one of his last two shillings for small coins and ended up with a tankard of beer.

The weaselly fellow with the bad teeth hadn't stopped watching him. A few minutes later, the man came up, grinning, and stood there while James stared off in the other direction.

"Well, then?" James asked sharply at last, without turning. "What do you want, man?"

"She's a pretty half-breed lady from Martinique. Good teeth and a nice bottom."

"I don't want your confounded, poxy whore. Now leave me alone."

The man's grin spread. "Why, Master Bailey, I'd heard you were a man of healthy appetites."

The fellow had put him off his guard, and James whipped his head around at the sound of his name before he recognized the feint for what it was. He smoothed over his face, but too late.

"I don't know that name. My name is Clyde."

"I thought it was you. Quickly, now. Your friends are waiting in the back room."

"Friends?"

"From New York. Come, there are others watching this place."

James rose to his feet and followed the man toward the back door. The man winked at one of the tables of dice players, and the men sneered at James with knowing looks and lewd suggestions. One man cupped a hand and thrust his index finger in and out. Laughter.

James didn't trust the shifty man who led him out of the room, so he kept his hand inside his cloak as he followed him down a hallway and then up a set of rotting, half-broken stairs. If this was a trap, if they'd tortured Cooper and now meant to murder James in a back room, he swore he'd sell his life dearly. First the pistols, then the knife.

The man threw open the door. There, to James's surprise, was a comely young mulatto woman. She wore kohl around her eyes and a beeswax lipstick so scarlet that it gave her mouth a wide, obscene appearance.

"What the devil?" he started to say, turning toward the shifty fellow to demand he be let back downstairs.

Laughter came from the far corner of the room. Two men sat on a long sea trunk holding pistols, which they were swabbing out and cleaning. One was Cooper. The other, he recognized after a moment, was McMurdle.

"Why, you ruddy scoundrels," James said, but he was delighted.

The two men shook his hand heartily, and Cooper slapped him on the back. James glanced again at the woman.

"That is Marianne," Cooper said.

"Pleased to meet you, *monsieur*," she said in a French-tinged accent and held her hand out in the dainty fashion of a fine lady.

"She isn't a whore," McMurdle added quickly.

"Not when I can help matters, no," she said.

McMurdle explained. Marianne was a spy in the West Indies, where England had long cast a covetous eye on rich colonies like Guadelupe and Martinique. They were more valuable, in their way, than the whole of New England. And the French were notoriously loose-lipped when it came to boasting to beautiful women, which Marianne most assuredly was.

The shorter man with the bad teeth was named Vandermeer, a Dutchman with an English mother, who worked carrying goods up the Hudson River between Manhattan and Fort Frederick and spying on the Dutch towns along the way. Now that New York was firmly in English control yet again, his was a sleepy post.

Cooper told of his own adventures. After escaping the woods, he'd nearly been ensnared on the road south from Springfield. Only a warning from a friend when he reached Windsor told him that riders were searching for him on the road ahead. His friend loaned him a horse, and Cooper bypassed the highway and arrived in Hartford, where he made contact with their other spy. This was an old man named Patterson, who provided resupply and information but nothing more. Cooper was almost to New York when two men tried to ride him down. They'd chased him for nearly twenty miles before he came into Dutch country, and here the two men giving pursuit had turned around. From there, it was a simple matter of making contact with McMurdle in Manhattan and arranging for a return to Boston.

As Cooper told his story, and James in turn relayed his own tale of time among the Abenaki, Marianne scooted the men from the sea trunk and changed her clothing, seemingly unashamed to be doing so in front of four men. She stripped out of her petticoats until she stood in her small clothes, then took a long linen strip and used it to bind her breasts flat. She pulled on a man's shirt, a jerkin, breeches, and a cloak. She pinned her hair up and pulled a cap over it. Finally, she used a rag to wipe the face paint away, and with a change to her posture she had somehow transitioned from a beautiful woman to a dusky, smooth-faced young man.

If one got too close, or spotted her in daylight, one would see through the ruse. But at night, she could pass for a fifth man.

Even so, five people did not seem enough to confront Knapp and Fitz-Simmons as they met with the General Court. James had hoped for eight, maybe even a dozen men in total, but according to McMurdle, the old New Amsterdam spy apparatus had been almost completely dismantled. The Dutch were more concerned with their profits than with resuming control of the colony, and England had proven happy to continue the existing trade. As a result, the other men in His Majesty's service had been sent to Quebec, Florida, the West Indies, even Mexico. They'd been fortunate in their timing as Marianne's ship was in port, resupplied and ready to sail. Otherwise, they'd have been only four.

"It took little persuading for Captain Dupont to stop in Boston instead of sailing back to France," Marianne said. "The justification to his crew is to add furs to the indigo we're smuggling from

Martinique back to England, but really it was because I wanted to see Boston on a whim. Or so Dupont believes."

Marianne had a charming accent, and McMurdle seemed enamored of her. Indeed, James had caught his old confederate stealing glances at the young woman while she dressed. Something Cooper had said about the operation in Manhattan caught James's attention.

"Then there were only the two of you in the whole of New York?" he asked.

"Soon to be only one," McMurdle said. "Vandermeer will stay. Marianne and I will continue north to Quebec. The Crown has designs on Canada."

James had his doubts about McMurdle's motives. It took so long for information to pass back and forth across the ocean that agents of the Crown had a certain autonomy, following their own instincts until called on for specific purposes. Yet how much of this Quebec scheme was in service of the Crown, and how much in service of a beautiful woman? Rather more of the latter than the former, James suspected.

"I am glad to hear it," James said, "but there are other reasons to maintain strength in New York besides the Dutch. It's a den of smuggling. Ships of every nation pass through her port. And a good deal of information comes with it."

"Aye, if you care for that sort of tedious business. No adventure, no excitement."

A little less excitement sounded like a welcome change at the moment, James thought. Still, he was captain of these men until given instructions to the contrary, and he wanted McMurdle in Manhattan until he had a chance to return to London to clarify. The man wouldn't like the orders; James determined to wait until this business was finished before delivering them.

"It must be nigh on sunset," James said. "You have a sword for me too? Good. Let's get prepared."

"Clarify your intentions," Cooper said.

"The moment it's dark, we move on the General Court."

A worried look passed over the man's face. "And then?"

"And then I intend to arrest the seditious government of the Massachusetts Bay Colony."

CHAPTER THIRTY-TWO

Prudence came quietly up the side street to the Stone household. She kept her head low, her daughter against her breast. It was dusk, the light failing, but she was cautious nonetheless. She couldn't risk getting recognized by Goody Brockett or one of the other gossips of the Third Church. Word would spread, alerting the enemies already searching for her.

She slipped down the alley between the Stone house and Goodman Upton's home to its north. The passage was barely wide enough to pull a handcart loaded with firewood, and she took comfort in the deep shadows between the two houses.

Prudence slipped through the gate and into the backyard, where the woodshed and snow-covered vegetable garden lay. It was quiet except for the sound of softly clucking chickens roosting inside their coop, safe for the evening against raccoons and weasels.

The back side of the house had no windows, and when she came up to the door she could hear nothing. Who was inside? The reverend, his family, and their servants? Or Knapp's men, waiting to seize her? Her heart quickened.

Prudence thought briefly about trying a ruse, perhaps letting the door bang open, as if left ajar and caught by the wind. Then she could see who came to latch it up tight. If it was her sister, Prudence could test the situation, voice her suspicions, see if Anne dismissed them. Could this all be a fantasy spun in her own head? No, she wouldn't do it.

She'd hid herself too long under this roof. Writing her narrative, begging her sister and the reverend for aid while they soothed her with meaningless assurances. She'd convinced herself there was no alternative. What more could she have done? She couldn't venture into the wilderness alone, and she lacked the strength to compel others to assist her.

It was a feeble effort, and it had cost her dearly. The injured child in her arms attested to that: torn between two mothers, two peoples. Only gradually would those wounds heal.

"Find your courage," she whispered. "Do it now."

Mary lifted her head from where it was buried against Prudence's breast. "What, Mama?"

"Shh. You must keep very still."

Prudence climbed the three steps, her boots loud on the wood. She swung open the door and entered the back pantry. Old John Porter was there, back turned, latching the oatmeal bin and checking the other barrels and boxes containing the dry foodstuffs to make sure they were sealed against mice. The smell of the room—the flour, the corn, the dried sage and thyme on the shelf—sent a wave of longing washing through her. This was her home. Her family, her people. Yet she had come to denounce them.

She tried to sneak past Old John, but he must have caught her movement from the side of his vision, for he turned before she could get through the door.

"Bless, what is this?" he said. "Prudence?" His eyes opened wide when he spotted Mary, and they began to fill with tears as a wide smile broke his face. "Can it be? Praise the Lord, it is!"

As of yet there was no stirring from the rest of the house. Prudence put her hand against Old John's wrinkled cheek.

"Bless you, John. I always knew you were true."

"GOODY STONE, REVEREND!" he boomed. "OUR PRUDIE HAS RETURNED! AND SHE CARRIES A MIRACLE!"

Prudence didn't wait to hear what this shouted pronouncement would bring, instead pushing into the keeping room. A fire crackled in the hearth, where Alice Branch slid a loaf of dough into the brick oven while Anne tended to the soup kettle. The reverend sat at the table, writing, his fingers stained with ink. Several of the children read their primers or mended socks.

For a moment, nobody moved, even as Prudence stood in front of them, holding her daughter, and Old John burst into the room behind her, waving his hands and shouting in excitement.

Anne dropped the ladle into the soup and came running. Her eyes were shining, her face aglow. Yet her tone was disapproving. "Oh, Prudie. What trouble you have caused. What trouble! Is this—is it . . . ?"

"Mary. My daughter. Sit down. Hold her. I have matters to attend to."

Anne seemed taken aback by Prudence's hard tone. But she obeyed at once. She stared at Mary, who barely squirmed but looked back with her wide, innocent expression.

By now, the rest of the Stone children had come racing down the stairs to stand gawking. Lucy Branch was there too, her mouth forming a surprised little circle. The reverend rose from the table, blinking, as if still unable to understand what he was looking at. His quill dropped on the paper, where a blotch of ink spread over his letters.

"Children, servants," he said. "Leave us now."

"The children, yes," Prudence said. "But not the servants. They stay."

Stone's face darkened. "Hold your tongue, woman. I am the master of this house, not you."

Prudence hardened her heart, forced herself to stand upright. "You have surrendered your moral authority, Reverend. A terrible and wicked sin has taken place under your roof, and as God is my witness, I will have it out."

"How dare you?" His voice shook.

"Henry," Anne said in a quiet voice. "They said Prudie was dead, yet here she is. And she brings her daughter. Something momentous has come to pass. I want to know what."

Stone opened his mouth, then closed it abruptly. He turned to the others, who were still gawking. "Children, go. Servants, remain."

Prudence waited until the children had left, then said, "Everyone sit down."

The Branch sisters took seats at the table, together with Old John Porter, who looked confused. He cupped his hands to his ears. The reverend came past Prudence, studied her face, and sat in the double-wide bench next to his wife, who still held Mary. Only Prudence remained standing.

"Anne, who said I was dead?"

"Samuel Knapp." Anne licked her lips. "Truth, it was Goodman Walker, but Knapp sent him."

"Walker, hmm? Of the General Court?"

"Aye." Anne frowned. "What is this about? What happened? And why did you leave with those men? Where are they now?"

Prudence ignored the questions. She turned to the reverend. "Where is my money?"

"Money?"

"My inheritance. Have you spent it?"

"Of course not. You think I have robbed you?" He sounded shocked. "I have been keeping it in trust to give your husband when you remarry."

"Prove your words."

"Why, I scarcely think that now—"

"Prove them," Prudence interrupted, her tone sharp.

Stone rose to his feet and went to the chest on the far side of the room where he kept his papers. He opened it with a brass key taken from a pocket of his jerkin, and after rummaging around for a minute came up with a piece of parchment with figures scratched on it, together with names and transactions, filed in double columns.

Prudence studied it for a moment, trying to make sense of the names and figures. "You sold six hundred acres to Knapp for thirty-seven pounds?"

"Poor land, rocky soil. It needs to be cleared of trees, manured for many years before it can give forth a good yield."

"That is a lie. This land is rich soil, with a stream and a mill."

Stone blinked. "But I saw Knapp's appraisal. It was only worth thirty-nine. He offered to buy it at a small discount to save me the discomfort of becoming embroiled in land speculation. Now, I confess that I did not see the land myself, but—"

"You trusted Knapp's appraisal of land he wished to buy himself?"

"He is a Godly man. And the appraisal was countersigned by the deputy governor."

"He is no Godly man," Prudence spat. "He is a murderer. And William Fitz-Simmons is his confederate in wickedness."

She paced back and forth across the room, while the others stared. Old John Porter asked for clarification, but the others hushed him.

Some of her anger was at herself. In her grief, she had abrogated the settling of Benjamin's estate to Reverend Stone, thinking he could be trusted. According to the paper held in her hand, the sum total of her possessions amounted to a shade under three hundred pounds, less than a third of what she had supposed.

Still, three hundred was no small sum, when a handsomely paid minister like Stone maintained a fine house and family on the hundred and twenty a year paid by the congregation. That was, if her brother-in-law truly was living on his salary, and not her own inheritance.

"Do you swear before God that you made these transactions in all good faith?"

"What reason have you to doubt it?"

"Answer the question, Henry," Anne said quietly.

He turned to her with a hurt look. "Surely, you don't think—"

"Henry, for the love of God," Anne said.

"Yes, I did in good faith. Perhaps I was overly hasty to settle matters, that I freely confess. But I swear before my Father in Heaven that I did not cheat Prudence. I have not spent a tuppence of her wealth, and have not sent it pursuing foolish, speculative ventures. It is safely concealed along with our own modest savings. When she remarries, I will turn it over with all good pleasure to her new husband."

"You will surrender the money when I tell you to," Prudence said coldly. "That is the law, if not the custom."

The reverend blinked, opened his mouth, and shut it again.

"Knapp is a murderer, you say?" Anne asked.

"She is speaking of how he put down the savages," Stone said. His tone was dismissive, and he seemed to have recovered from his surprise at Prudence's defiance. "You know her sympathies."

"No, I am not," Prudence said. "Though certainly Knapp is guilty enough of wicked crimes against those people as well. But Knapp's murders disturb the king's peace as well."

Briefly, she told of what had happened on the road to Winton, starting with her desperate meeting with James and Peter on the road near the Common. Peter had been poisoned and would later die at Knapp's hands. Here, the reverend interrupted to point out that Prudence didn't know this, couldn't know it, since the highwaymen had been masked. He dropped this objection when she told of their escape from Winton and the hunt and narrow escape in the woods. She had seen the man's uncovered face with her own eyes. Stone's own face settled into a look of deep despair.

She told them what she'd learned from the Nipmuk. Knapp and Fitz-Simmons had murdered one Nipmuk woman and committed an outrage against Mikmonto's wife, whom they left free to return to her people. Then Knapp had tricked Benjamin and the other English into returning to the supposed safety of Winton, where so many were then slaughtered by the enraged, formerly peaceable Nipmuk of Sachusett.

The reverend buried his face in his hands. Anne sat stiffly, her mouth a line. Lucy and Alice Branch looked dumbstruck, casting their glances to the door as if they wished to be sent away from this madness. Old John Porter wore a look of deep confusion; he had apparently followed none of it.

"These evildoers will be brought to justice," Anne said. Her voice shook.

"Perhaps," Prudence said. "They have powerful friends." She cast a hard look at Stone, who was raising his slack face from his hands. "And many who would sooner see the problem disappear."

"There is one thing that troubles me, that cannot be true," Anne said. "This conjecture about the Praying Indian. You say he was poisoned?"

"I do. Master Bailey is certain of it. And when Peter was beyond the gates of Boston, he began to recover at once."

"But Henry led the two men directly to our house," Anne said. "They ate nowhere else before the three of you fled into the wilderness."

"Yes, so you see. It was food or drink consumed under this very roof."

"Impossible," Stone said. "It simply cannot be. Neither Knapp nor Fitz-Simmons, nor any other man in this supposed conspiracy, had any access to the Quaker's meals."

"No, they did not," Prudence said. "But they didn't need to, either. That is because the poisoner lives under this roof. And I know who it is."

CHAPTER THIRTY-THREE

Prudence let those words float in the air, thick and pungent as pipe smoke. The room was quiet except for the crackle of the fire and Mary squirming in Anne's arms.

The power Prudence held left her almost giddy. Here she stood, standing over them, ready to pronounce judgment while they waited in fear and anticipation.

This was what Reverend Stone must feel every Sabbath while his deacons called sinners to repentance. This man would get flogged, this woman put in the pillories. At one time she herself had waited, trembling in the pews, afraid that the men of God could stare into her soul and grasp the secret, wicked thoughts there: envy, doubt, and, of course, lust. That same fear was in the faces of the others now. Enjoying their fear was a wicked, unholy feeling, and she put it down. This was for justice.

"Prudie," Anne said quietly. "For the love of all that is holy. It is torment."

Prudence turned to the servants. She fixed on Lucy Branch. "Tell us, Lucy. What did you do on the evening our two guests arrived from England?"

"Nothing untoward, Goody Cotton. We spoke of the two men, of course. It isn't often we have strangers under our roof. But we didn't gossip!" Lucy cast an anxious glance at her sister.

"That be truth," Alice agreed with a vigorous nod of the head. "We didn't gossip."

"I am not speaking of gossip, Lucy. You warmed Master Bailey's bed."

Her eyes widened. "With the pan, mistress," she squeaked. "With the pan!"

"Don't tell me lies, Lucy. Your soul is in jeopardy. And your life."

"My life?"

"What are you driving at?" the reverend asked. "Are you accusing this girl of fornication?"

Prudence gave him another look, and he fell silent. She turned back to Lucy.

"Tell me what happened. I know it already from Master Bailey's own lips. If you lie to me, I will see that you are hanged."

Lucy was trembling, and if Prudence weren't very nearly certain of the girl's crimes, she would have felt sorry for her. Lustful behavior toward a handsome single man was not the issue—if so, Prudence herself would stand condemned by her own behavior.

"I—I didn't resist. Not as I should have. But I didn't lie with him, I swear it. We kissed, he put his hands on my body, then he opened the door and sent me on my way. I wouldn't have given myself to him, and he didn't ask. I had hoped . . ." Her voice trailed off.

"Hoped what?" Prudence said.

"I had hoped he would speak to Goody Stone," Lucy said, "and she would ask permission of the reverend."

Anne and her husband exchanged scowls at this. "You had scarcely met the man," Anne said. "And you would marry him?"

Lucy stuttered, then shook her head and closed her mouth.

"You are anxious to marry, is that right?" Prudence asked.

Lucy looked more frightened than ever, though the reverend seemed more annoyed than angry at the revelation that there had been light sinning taking place under his roof. Were this the extent of Lucy's crimes, he would no doubt scold the girl but would hardly put her name in front of the congregation, or worse, turn her out into the street.

"Answer the question," Prudence said. "Are you anxious to marry?"

"I have four more years of indentured servitude. But I am nineteen, and old enough to marry. If a man of means, like Master Bailey, were to take my hand, he could buy my freedom."

"Is your life so hard, child?" Reverend Stone asked. "Do we not feed you and keep you clothed?"

Lucy turned to him, her eyes flashing. "Would you trade places with me, Reverend?"

"John Porter serves, and willingly, though his indenturehood is over these twenty years." He gestured at the old man, who still looked bewildered.

"He serves for money, Reverend. For money. And where would he go, anyway?" Lucy clenched her fists in her lap. "I am young. I have a life to live. And I don't want to spend it here. I am not like my sister. I do not take to slavery."

Stone looked aghast. "It is not slavery! Alice, tell her, explain."

The conversation was running away from Prudence, so she jumped in before either Lucy or Alice could respond. "How many other men have you attempted to seduce?"

"I do not seduce, Goody Cotton. I let known my interest."

"How many have you fornicated with?"

Lucy thrust out her chin. "How many have you?"

"Mind your tongue," Anne said sharply. "Prudence is a virtuous woman."

"One of your lovers will soon have his head in a noose," Prudence told Lucy quickly, before anyone could see her blush at Anne's misguided defense. "You had better confess before he blames you to save his own neck."

"You know the answer already, don't you?" Lucy was speaking with real fire now. "So why don't you say it yourself?"

"Prudence, tell us," Anne said.

"One of her lovers gave her poison, which she placed in Peter Church's food."

The others looked at Lucy. The girl refused to answer or confess, but her silence was enough that this allegation was quickly confirmed in the shocked expression on the faces of Anne, Reverend Stone, and even Lucy's sister, Alice.

"He said 'twould make him sick," Lucy said at last. "He didn't say it would kill him. They wished to keep the Indian in Boston. I don't know why."

"They meant to kill him," Prudence said. She walked over to Lucy and stared her in the eye. "They *did* kill him. Cut him down on the road like a diseased dog."

Lucy stared back. "That's what he was. A savage. A Quaker."

Prudence slapped Lucy, hard. The girl cried out and put her hand over her cheek. Her eyes watered and her lips trembled with rage. Prudence turned away.

"Indian lover," Lucy spat. "We all know what you did with the savages. It's no wonder you went back. To fornicate with your Indian lovers."

This brought horrified gasps from the others. Alice begged her sister to hold her tongue, while Anne and the reverend angrily denounced Lucy. Old John Porter seemed almost in tears as he turned from one party to the other, trying to figure out what was happening.

"Enough," Prudence said. "Tell us why you did it."

"I told you," Lucy said. "I didn't think it would kill him, only make him sick. He gave me a powder—"

"Who gave it to you?"

"You know. Samuel Knapp."

"Go on."

"And I put it in Peter Church's beer. I did it three times."

"But why?" Prudence asked. "Had Knapp promised to marry you?"

"Aye, he promised to marry me. Then I gave myself to him and he refused to speak to the reverend. When I pressed him, he laughed, goaded me, told me to confess my sins to the reverend. I knew what that meant."

"Knapp would have been punished too," Stone said, "if he seduced you and then refused to honorably marry you."

"No, Reverend," Lucy said. "Knapp would have accused me. He'd claim that I bewitched *him,* came to him in the night as a succubus. He would have been whipped for giving in to temptation, but I would have been put to death as a witch." She gave a hard look at Prudence. "That was his threat. That's why I did it, Goody Cotton. He told me if I didn't feed his powder to the Indian, I'd be accused of witchcraft."

Prudence turned away. She walked to her sister and picked up Mary. The girl seemed frightened by all the raised voices, and Prudence kissed her and gently stroked her hair.

There was no absolving Lucy from her sins. She could have made a different choice at every step. Not to lie with Knapp, not to poison Peter even though she did so under duress. And she had suffered little guilt, only admitting it under hard questioning.

But Prudence had made her own mistakes. She had been too weak for too long to hate others for their weaknesses.

"Now you have me," Lucy said. "My sister is innocent—I swear that much. She knew nothing of any of this. But I confess my own guilt, my own sins. What will you do with me now?"

Stone cleared his throat. He began tentatively. "This is a hard thing. You attempted to poison an agent of the king. If Bailey wants your head, I'm afraid you'll hang."

Alice gasped. Lucy hung her head.

"And if he doesn't?" Prudence asked. "If I speak to him?"

"There is still the matter of fornication," Stone said. "Although it has been freely confessed, which counts in the ledger. And I, too, have been guilty of poor judgment, so I am loath to cast stones in this matter. Perhaps a light sentence. I'll make a recommendation to the deacons, let them decide. You live under the reverend's roof—this matter cannot simply be ignored."

The talk of ledgers and Stone's own mistakes gave Prudence an idea.

"How much is the value of Lucy's indenturehood?"

"Fifteen pounds per annum. Nigh four years remain."

"I will pay you thirty from my estate," Prudence said. "The other thirty will erase your debts in the mishandling of Sir Benjamin's lands."

"What will you do with a servant?" Anne asked. "You already enjoy her services to the family."

"I don't intend to hire her as a servant. I intend to set her free." Prudence turned to Lucy, who was staring, mouth open. "Is that acceptable to you?"

"Thank you," Lucy gasped.

"Upon one condition."

"Anything."

"You testify against Samuel Knapp and his evil confederates. If you lie, if you try to protect yourself, you will die in this world and burn in the world to come."

Chapter Thirty-Four

James pushed open the doors of Boston's First Church. The iron hinges groaned. Warm air came flowing out, smelling of birch logs and burning tallow. On the far end, the candles on the table flickered. The men sitting there all looked up.

There were more than a dozen in all, their table near a roaring fire. Papers and maps lay spread in front of them, with a large, open Bible in the middle. One man was on his feet already and had been addressing the others. He froze. Another man had been taking notes, and paused with his quill pinched between ink-stained fingers.

James strode down the aisle with his sword in hand. Cooper and McMurdle followed, each man armed with a musket. The other two—the little Dutchman Vandermeer, and the mulatto woman Marianne (still dressed as a man)—closed the doors and remained there with drawn pistols. Neither of them would impress if given serious scrutiny. But standing as sentries, they looked more formidable.

"What is this?" said the man who'd been standing when they entered.

He had a strong, beardless face and gray, shoulder-length hair. He wore a fine cloak with brass buttons. When the interlopers came striding toward him, he put his long, bony hands on his hips as he stared at them with a haughty, patrician air.

"This is Bailey," another man said. It was Knapp, the bloody villain.

"Yes, I thought so," said the first man.

"Governor Leverett?" James guessed.

"And you must be the imposter from London, sirrah," the man said.

McMurdle lifted his pistol. "Don't you 'sirrah' him, you traitor. This man is the ultimate authority in New England, and you will show him respect or I will put a ball in your damned skull."

If the governor had denigrated James with his 'sirrah,' as one might speak to a boy or a servant, McMurdle's insolence and profane language served the same insult to the other side. Several men shoved back chairs and sprang to their feet with angry retorts. A bottle of ink overturned. Two men produced daggers.

Knapp and a few others remained seated. Among them was the deputy governor, William Fitz-Simmons. Neither man looked worried—they looked triumphant. A niggle of doubt burrowed into James's confidence.

"According to forged papers," Leverett said, his voice booming over the other voices. "Did you think your deception would carry?"

John Leverett was no Puritan fanatic, although he had returned to England during the Civil War to fight with Cromwell. But he held to the seditious position that the Bay Colony did not answer to the Crown and Parliament. It was his impudent comments, dutifully recorded by a loyal Boston merchant, that had precipitated James's voyage to New England.

Nevertheless, James didn't know yet if Leverett were a party to the conspiracy, or if Knapp and Fitz-Simmons had whispered tales into his ears. Either way, he guessed the king's commission would change no minds. Leaving aside the vague words, the king's seal was broken, had fallen completely away during his travels.

"Whatever you know or think you know about me is a lie," James said. "I was sent by His Majesty to investigate the death of Sir Benjamin."

"You were sent by Sir Benjamin's creditors," Leverett said. "They wish to recover the man's gambling debts in London and to rob the widow of her inheritance."

"That is a damned lie."

"You profane at your peril, sirrah."

"Who told you this?" James pointed his sword at Knapp. "This man?"

Leverett smiled. "A warning letter arrived by boat from England. It arrived two days after you fled Boston to avoid arrest for disturbing the peace. It warned of your ruse. Where is the Praying Indian?"

"Murdered on the road by Samuel Knapp and his confederates."

"Then you have many crimes to answer for," Leverett said. "If you have caused the death of your companion, as well."

James had been knocked off balance by the confidence of this man. He'd expected to face Knapp and Fitz-Simmons, had been ready to answer their lies. He hadn't prepared himself for this confident, self-assured governor, used to commanding and being obeyed. Another moment and the last remnants of James's authority would fall away.

"Let me tell you what these men did," James said. "Knapp is responsible for the destruction of Winton, the murder of Sir Benjamin and many other innocents, English and Indian alike. He and Fitz-Simmons—"

Leverett waved a hand, a look of disdain on his face. "I know all about your allegations. I received warning from London, I tell you. From one of your confederates. You have been betrayed, sirrah."

James lifted his sword tip and pressed it against the governor's chest. He used it to force the surprised man back.

Then, to Cooper and McMurdle, "Arrest those two. The short ugly one. The gray-haired fellow next to him too. We'll question them in private. Then we'll return to arrest the other conspirators."

James's fellow agents moved around the table with their pistols drawn while Knapp and Fitz-Simmons sat calmly. The mood was ugly among the other members of the General Court, but most were older, prosperous-looking men; if a few resisted, he had little doubt that the three king's agents, plus the two at the door, would cut down any opposition.

There would be hell to answer for back in London, though, if it came to bloodshed. He'd been tasked with creating a disturbance, perhaps even seizing the charter of the Bay Colony, but overthrowing the entire colonial government through violent means was likely to cause trouble among the restive New Englanders.

All of this went through James's head in an instant, and he scarcely had a chance to question why Knapp and Fitz-Simmons were sitting so placidly. Knapp even managed a sneer.

Then the doors behind the chapel opened, and pouring from the reverend's personal chambers came several men armed with muskets. Many of them were the same men who'd met James and Peter on the wharf.

"Stand back, you dogs!" one of them yelled.

Cooper was reaching for Knapp's shoulder as if to drag him to his feet, but now he froze. McMurdle's confidence vanished in an instant. The militia members came at them, but the two men had the presence of mind to stand back with their pistols aimed at their would-be attackers.

James still had his sword pressed against the governor's chest. Three muskets aimed at him, the rest at his companions.

"Now listen to me," James said to the governor. "You're making a terrible mistake. I'll give you a chance to step back and reconsider, but call off these men first. If not, you will sow the wind and reap the whirlwind, I swear before God."

Leverett's jaw clenched, and he met James's gaze and held it. "Put down your sword, sirrah."

They wouldn't take James without a struggle. Could he count on Cooper and McMurdle, or would they throw down their weapons and beg mercy? How about the two at the door? If they came rushing down the aisle, the five of them stood a slim chance of fighting their way clear. A very slim chance. These men would be veterans of the war, hardened by battle and bloodshed. They wouldn't panic and run. And even if James did break free, what then? Flee through the streets of Boston while they were hunted down like vermin?

He cast a glance to the doors to see them wide open and Marianne and Vandermeer with their backs to him. The cowards meant to run.

No, damn you.

But then he saw that they'd opened the doors not to flee, but to admit newcomers to the meetinghouse. The first one in was Prudence Cotton. Behind her came her sister, holding Mary, followed by Reverend Stone and Lucy Branch.

Thinking quickly now, James grabbed the governor and held the sword up to his throat, using the man's body to shield himself from the men with muskets, who were trying to flank him but finding it difficult to maneuver around the pews.

"Everybody stop!" Prudence cried. "Put down your weapons. James, please!"

"Are you a traitor, sir?" James asked the governor in a low voice.

Leverett stared back at him. His jaw was set, a vein throbbing at his temple. He did not look afraid.

"If I release you, will you listen to the widow?" James asked.

"You make no demands here."

"I demand that you listen. Or are you too proud for that?"

"Very well. I will listen. Then you will hang for your crimes."

"We shall see," James said.

He pushed the man away and took two steps backward. Vandermeer and Marianne came down the aisle ahead of Prudence and the others, and James fell back until he stood with them. Cooper and McMurdle were in the grasp of the militia, disarmed and glaring. Knapp was on his feet now and standing defiantly with the militia. Fitz-Simmons remained seated. For the first time he looked troubled.

Prudence strode up to the governor. "I denounce Samuel Knapp and William Fitz-Simmons for murder, for treason, and for the violation of a woman's virtue. For the killing of unarmed prisoners, including children. For theft of property through deception."

The men in the room had quieted to hear what she was going to say, and now murmurs of disbelief passed from one man to the next.

"Whatever lies Bailey told you," Leverett told her, his voice measured, patient, "rest assured that you will be offered leniency for your role in this matter. You acted under duress. You were deceived. Trust me, Widow Cotton, we have the truth of it."

"No, Governor. You are wrong." Prudence waved her hand. "Lucy, come. Now."

The servant girl stepped forward from where she'd been cowering next to Prudence's sister and the child. She stared at the floor as if she could bore holes in the planks with her gaze. Prudence had to take her elbow, she was trembling so violently.

"Tell us," Prudence said.

"I poisoned the Praying Indian," Lucy said.

"What?" Leverett blurted. The room exploded in shouts of disbelief. The governor quieted them with a gesture. "Tell the truth, child."

Lucy pointed her finger, lifting her gaze for the first time to stare at Samuel Knapp. "This man forced himself upon me. Then he threatened to accuse me of witchcraft and whoredom if I did not adulterate the drink of the Praying Indian."

James kept his gaze steady, but he was surprised. This was not what Prudence had surmised before. She had been certain that Lucy had offered herself freely, to try to attract the prosperous, powerful man's interest in marriage. Was this a lie to protect the girl?

The certainty faded from the governor's face. He cast a glance at the two accused men.

"She's lying," Knapp snarled. "She wants to protect her lover, this knave from London who seduced her."

Leverett turned away and looked at James, then Prudence. "I cannot believe it. Knapp, perhaps, but Goodman Fitz-Simmons is my deputy. There's no man I trust more in Boston."

Prudence lifted Mary from the arms of her sister. "This is my daughter. Kept by the Indians these nine months. I heard the truth of the matter from the mouth of the surviving Nipmuk. Knapp and Fitz-Simmons murdered a woman and committed an outrage against the sachem's wife. They did this so the Indians would attack Winton and slaughter its inhabitants. My husband had promised peace, and his two associates grossly violated it. When the Indians caught Benjamin, they subjected him to special torture."

"More lies!" Knapp cried. "Tell them," he urged Fitz-Simmons.

But the deputy-governor remained silent. Anguish broke across his face.

"Reverend?" Governor Leverett said, turning to Stone, who stood with his wife. "What is this? Is any of this truth? I feel as though I'm being deceived by Satan."

"There is deception here, Governor," Stone said. "But not by Widow Cotton, and not by Master Bailey."

"How can this be? The Praying Indian was poisoned under your very roof?"

"Mistakes were made, eyes closed in blindness. Knapp acquired the richest lands left by Sir Benjamin. He told me the land was worth little. This was a lie."

"But the rest of it?" Leverett said. "Can you vouch for this story?"

"Aye, that I can," the reverend said. "Lucy already confessed to poisoning the Praying Indian under command of Captain Knapp. As for the rest, I believe it all. So does my wife, and she has never led me astray. I do not believe that Prudence is deceived, and neither does Anne."

A tremble hit the reverend's voice, and James almost felt sorry for him, even though his words were slippery even now. Mistakes made, eyes closed in blindness? Was he incapable of accepting responsibility?

"Goodman Fitz-Simmons," Leverett said. Some of his confidence had returned, the iron morality of his tone, but it was no longer leveled toward James, but toward the deputy governor. "Answer these charges. Are you in league with Knapp?"

Knapp sputtered. "Nobody is in league with me. It is all a lie!"

Fitz-Simmons was shaking worse than Lucy Branch as the governor came over to him.

"Tell me the truth," Leverett said. "It is your only hope to avoid the hellfire and damnation that surely await on the other side."

The room had fallen silent. The only sound was the crackling fire. James held his tongue. Cooper and McMurdle had freed themselves and made their way quietly to his side.

"It is true," Fitz-Simmons said at last. "All of it, even the attack on the highway and the murder of Robert Woory and Peter Church."

"May the Lord have mercy on your soul," Reverend Stone murmured.

James had been studying the other men, both those armed with muskets and the members of the General Court. Watching for guilty reactions. Knapp was edging away from the table, his body tense, casting furtive glances toward the back door from which the militia members had materialized earlier. Getting ready to flee.

James sprang after him before he could move. All attention was on Fitz-Simmons, and nobody moved to block him until it was too late and he was at Knapp's side. He swung with his sword hilt and smashed Knapp on the head. The man staggered back with a cry, and James punched him in the gut. Knapp doubled over and fell. He reached for something in his cloak as he tried to rise, but James straddled him and pressed the sword tip against his throat, and Knapp went limp as a dead snake.

For a moment there was stunned silence, then the rest of the king's agents rallied around him. Cooper plucked away muskets, and McMurdle snarled threats at those who resisted. One of the older men from the court pleaded for peace, for the New Englanders to obey the king's agents.

In a moment, Cooper and McMurdle had disarmed the militia and tossed all the weapons to the floor. Vandermeer hauled Knapp to his feet while Marianne covered him with a pistol. Blood trickled from his forehead, and he could scarcely remain standing without assistance.

Leverett crossed his arms and stared at Fitz-Simmons, who was still trembling. "Will you name your accomplices in sin?"

"Some died on the highway west of Boston."

"And the rest? Name them."

The deputy governor swallowed hard and nodded. "John Johnson. Harold Kitely. William—"

A gun fired. Men startled. Mary cried out in Prudence's arms.

One of the older men slumped across the table, dropping a pistol that clattered on the floor. Blood gushed from his ruined head, spreading across the papers and maps on the table. He'd blown out his brains.

Prudence turned away with her daughter, covering the child's eyes. James moved to her side, almost put an arm around her before remembering where they were.

Leverett cast an unforgiving glance at the dead man. "William Crispin, you were going to say?"

Fitz-Simmons swallowed hard and nodded. "Aye, Goodman Crispin."

James was angry at himself for not checking all of the men for hidden weapons. He ordered Cooper and McMurdle to search the rest of the members of the General Court.

"Continue," Governor Leverett told his deputy when that was accomplished. "Name the rest of the condemned."

"Matthias Walker. Joseph Nance. Henry Edwins. And Samuel Knapp, our leader. That is all. May the Lord forgive me my wickedness." Fitz-Simmons buried his face in his hands.

"The Lord may," James said. "But His Majesty, Charles the Second, will not."

Chapter Thirty-Five

A mob loved a hanging, and the good Puritans of Boston were no exception. By the time James and Cooper arrived at the frozen Common on horseback, several hundred people were milling about the large, open field around the gallows.

A small group of officials, wealthy merchants, and ministers gathered in a somber knot. Stone was up there, speaking to the governor in quiet tones. There were several women in the governor's coterie; perhaps Prudence was among them. He hadn't seen her since the trial three days earlier, when she'd testified against Knapp and his confederates. Since then, he'd been busy writing letters, negotiating with the colonial government, and arranging credit to finance the expenses of his final days in Boston before his return to England.

"McMurdle is on the *Vigilant,* guarding the prisoner?" James asked Cooper.

"Aye, with the mulatto. McMurdle will sail to London, if you'll allow him. There will be honors. This could be his opportunity."

"And you? This could be your opportunity as well."

"With your permission, I will return to my family in Springfield."

James considered. It would be a cruel thing to force Cooper back to London.

"Stay in the Bay Colony, if you must, but you will settle in Boston. I need a man in the city."

Cooper nodded, looking relieved. "You could stay too. 'Twould be good to have a friend among these stiff-necked fellows."

"No, I am leaving as soon as I settle affairs here."

"Nothing could make you stay?" Cooper gave him a sharp look. "Not even the love of a good woman?"

"As for McMurdle," James said, ignoring the question, "I have half a mind to order him back to New York. Vandermeer isn't enough—I need someone with more cunning and force of will. The Dutch came back once—who can say they won't try again? Moreover, if he's enamored of Marianne, and she of him, they'd fare better in Manhattan than London."

"Aye, that they would. What about the colonial charter? Will you seize it?"

"No. I made promises to Governor Leverett in order to secure his cooperation. Betraying that promise now would only incite more sedition. But I'll make my recommendation to the king. Know this, the Crown will be exerting more control of New England. Soon enough, we will have those charters and these will be royal colonies."

The two men ignored the stares as they came up front and dismounted. They tied their animals to the side of the scaffolding. The long arm of the gallows creaked in the wind. Six nooses waved back and forth, glistening in the morning sun, the rope coated with ice. The hanging was to have taken place the previous evening, but Leverett had asked James to grant a temporary stay. The wife of one of the condemned men had given birth the previous day, and the man wished to hold his child first. James granted the stay. Freezing rain had fallen during the night. The last thing the men would feel before the swinging was an icy collar tightened around their necks.

Eight conspirators. One was dead, having blown his own brains to kingdom come when his name was spoken. He would receive his reward in the next world. Another man was in chains in the hold of the *Vigilant,* on his way to England to face the king's wrath in person. The other six would hang.

As James and Cooper stepped up front, Leverett and the other men with him turned away, refusing to look at the king's agents. Only Reverend Stone approached.

"The widow is not here," Stone said. "She is with her child and my wife at the house."

James had been looking around for Prudence; now he turned to the reverend, attempting to keep the disappointment from his face. "It is for the best. A hanging is an ugly thing. One should not delight in the death of one's fellow man."

"How very true," Stone said. "There has been altogether too much delighting in these parts as of late. We defeated our enemies in battle, but at a terrible cost."

"It was a war. War is brutal."

"Do you remember what Peter Church said when he denounced me during my sermon?"

"He was denouncing all of Boston," James said, "not you in particular."

"Instead of spreading the gospel to the native sons of this land, those who hungered for truth were given gall and hot lead. Their blood cried up from the soil for justice. And this," Stone added with a nod toward the gallows, "is a taste of the punishment the Lord will deliver this land if we do not repent."

"Here they come," Cooper said.

In England, a beating drum would have announced the arrival of the condemned as they were marched up to the gallows. The hollow booms seemed to mark the footsteps of the men being led to their doom. But here, there was no drum, no crier. The crowd merely parted and five men came shuffling through the crowd with their hands bound behind their backs. The sixth would arrive later.

Stone took James's arm, cast a glance at Cooper, then led him a few paces away. "Tell me, Master Bailey. Have you betrayed your trust?"

"How do you mean?"

"With Prudence. Did you form an understanding?"

A dull ache worked at James's stomach. "We formed no understanding. I have betrayed nothing."

"You were alone with her and wandering the wilderness, hiding from the savages and falsely claiming to be man and wife while you spent nights together in inns and country houses. I want to know if you respected her chastity."

"Why are you asking me?" James pulled free and turned his attention to the five men trudging forward. "Put the question to Prudence if you'd like to know."

"She refuses to answer, says the question is an insult."

"Aye, and that it is."

The five men reached the front of the gallows: John Johnson, Matthias Walker, Henry Edwins, Harold Kitely, and Joseph Nance. William Crispin was dead. Only Fitz-Simmons and Knapp were not present.

"But if you led her to believe something . . ." Stone continued. "Look at me, Bailey!"

"What?" He turned, annoyed.

"Prudence doesn't understand the worldly ways of a man like you. She is a simple girl at heart."

James scoffed at this. "She is a strong, sharp-witted woman. Confident and clever."

"Aye, that she is, and I underestimated her all along. That isn't what I meant. But if she is all of those things, Master Bailey—"

"If you'll excuse me. I must attend to the king's business."

Cooper fell in next to James as he stepped up to the front. Leverett stood there, grim-faced, together with two armed men. Three of the condemned were trembling with fear. Another, this one the oldest of the conspirators and a former member of the General Court, stared at the ground with such a look of shame it was as if he wished a hole would open and carry him straight to hell rather than face the good people of Boston.

The final man was Henry Edwins, the man whose newborn baby had caused the delay of execution. Edwins stared straight ahead with tears filling his eyes. Never once had any of the men begged for mercy, and except for Knapp, who had remained defiant, all had confessed their guilt. Even so, James had wished someone would ask clemency on behalf of Henry Edwins.

According to the other men, Edwins had come into the conspiracy only after the war was over, and he had not been present during the attack that left Woory and Peter dead. He'd had no knowledge of these things, but he *had* been among the men who chased James, Prudence, and Cooper into the woods outside Winton. And he had attempted to hunt down Cooper on the road to Hartford. That made him a traitor.

"Tell your man to fire his musket," James said to the governor.

"It is a hard thing you ask, Bailey."

"It is a mercy compared to Samuel Knapp's crimes. Fire the gun."

The governor gave the order. A man lifted his musket and fired into the sky. The hollow shot rolled through the winter air.

For a long minute there was silence, then the sound of horse hooves came clumping from the direction of High Street. The crowd parted, and in trotted a horse without a rider, being driven by two men. One of them was Vandermeer. The horse dragged a naked man by his feet; the man groaned as the frozen ground battered him. When the horse stopped, they untied the man and hauled him to his feet. It was Samuel Knapp.

The drawing had torn the skin on Knapp's back to ribbons, and blood streamed down his buttocks and legs. His shoulder hung crooked in its socket. He groaned when it shifted.

"Murderer!" someone shouted, and then dozens of voices were jeering and calling. People pelted the naked man with snowballs and rotten turnips.

"You have had your pleasure," Leverett said. "Finish this business and send the people home."

In truth, James gained no pleasure from seeing his enemy abused. These people had once hailed Knapp as a hero. Had Prudence failed, had Stone proven a coward, had Leverett believed Knapp, they would be cheering Knapp instead. James would be the one on the way to the gallows.

"Drawing was a courtesy," James told the governor. "When the *Vigilant* arrives in London, Fitz-Simmons will be drawn to the gallows, then hanged until he is almost dead, then he will be disemboweled and emasculated. Only then will they kill him."

"How is that justice?" Leverett demanded. "He was not even the leader of the conspiracy. Why should he suffer more than the others?"

"He was a high official, which makes his treason more severe. But what you should be asking is whether Knapp should receive leniency when your deputy governor will not."

When Leverett didn't answer, James told him to order the condemned men to the gallows. The governor gave the command.

Leverett's militia led the men up and fit the icy nooses around their necks. Edwins fainted and had to be held up, and one of the other men cried out a woman's name, presumably his wife's. James stepped up to the gallows. His heart had sunk like lead to his bowels.

"Mercy!" one of the condemned cried when he saw him.

Knapp, still naked and bleeding, fixed James with pleading eyes. "For the love of God, mercy."

At last, contrition. Fear.

"Like the mercy you showed Peter Church?" James asked in a quiet voice. "Or Sir Benjamin? Or the sachem's wife, whom you violated in defiance of God and common decency? No, you will hang."

James turned to face the crowd. People were shouting, many eager, or even angry. Others clenched each other; these, James counted as family members of the accused. There would be widows in Boston tonight. It was an ugly, terrible thing he was about to do.

He spotted Lucy and Alice Branch. Old John Porter. Men from the General Court or militia. Some of the men, he suspected, could as easily be up here on the gallows if not for a twinge of conscience at the right moment, the wise voice whispering that they stay away from the filthy bargain being offered them.

"People of Boston!" James cried. He had a loud voice, and it carried through the crowd, but he had to repeat it two more times until they quieted. "English subjects of His Majesty, Charles the Second, by the grace of God, King of England, Scotland, France, and Ireland, Defender of the Faith, etcetera. These men are accused of high treason and shall be hanged by the neck until dead: Samuel Knapp, Matthias Walker, Joseph Nance, Harold Kitely, John Johnson, and Henry Edwins."

A woman's high wail came above the whispers and crying children. It came from a young woman standing near the front, a bundle in her arms that could only be a baby. Who was she, Edwins's wife?

As James spoke, men had put hoods over the heads of all of the men except Knapp. Some of them were openly weeping or still begging for mercy. Now the militia tied sand-filled bags to the feet of all of the men except for Knapp. Reverend Stone came trudging slowly up onto the scaffolding.

The reverend was a portrait of dejection, his brow low, mouth down-turned, his gaze fixed on his boots. Every ponderous step was as if he, not the condemned, were the one with bags of sand dragging on his feet. When he reached the top, he recited a scripture and uttered a prayer to God, thanking Him for His mercy, honoring His righteous anger. But Stone's voice was weak, desultory. Nothing like the man who had thundered his sermon in the Third Church meetinghouse.

This might be Reverend Stone's last sermon and prayer. During recesses in the trial, James had heard from more than one person that the Third Church was moving to strip Stone of his position. Stone may not have been guilty of conspiracy, but he had been spiritually blind, and for that he would pay.

When Stone was finished, he stood there, stunned, until James took his arm and nudged him toward the steps down from the gallows. The militia had descended as well, and now it was just James and the hangman, who came up the stairs when the reverend had descended. The man wore a scarf around his face, his head beneath a hooded cloak, but James had hired the hangman himself and knew his identity. He was a sailor and drunk who had been milling around The Windlass and Anchor, and who had been willing to do the killing in return for fifteen shillings and two bottles of Barbados rum.

James looked down at the expectant faces, the weeping women, and then back at the condemned men. Knapp looked gray. His hooded companions trembled as if they would fall before the platform was pulled away. The man on the end—Edwins—was still weeping.

And James's resolve broke. Quickly, before he could reconsider, he made his way to Henry Edwins and cut the rope with his sword. He plucked off the hood, and the man stood gaping at him.

James lifted his hands until the crowd quieted. "These men have been condemned to death. But His Majesty is a merciful sovereign. This man's punishment shall be commuted to a lesser sentence."

"Bless you!" Edwins gasped as James cut the rope binding his hands.

But he couldn't simply pardon the man and send him on his way. "Henry Edwins, your life is spared, but you will lose your freedom." He spoke as loudly as he could over the sudden tumult of the crowd. "You will sell yourself into indenturehood for three years, the sum to be donated to the care of widows and orphans from the war. You may continue to live in your own house with your wife and child."

Edwins fell to his knees, kissing James's boots. "You are merciful, good sir. Bless you!"

It still wasn't enough. The king's peace must be maintained. Let no one leave this hanging thinking that royal power was weak. That would embolden His Majesty's enemies, both here and in foreign courts.

James took his sword, grabbed Edwins's left ear and hacked off a big chunk. The man screamed and fell on his face. James lifted up the bloody chunk of ear for the jostling, craning crowd to see. Then he threw it down, where it landed at the feet of Governor Leverett.

"That your crime will be marked forever."

"Mercy!" the other condemned men cried from beneath their hoods. "Pardon me too, for the love of God."

"And me!"

"Please, good sir."

Only Knapp, who had seen James sever Edwins's ear, didn't take up the cry. He met James's gaze and then clenched his eyes shut. He must surely have seen the hard look in James's eyes. He knew.

James turned to the hangman. "Now."

The hangman kicked at the peg and the trapdoor fell open, even while the hooded men were still begging to be pardoned. The sandbags fell first, jerking down on the men's feet as they kicked suddenly at the air. Their words died with a squeak, and they twisted silently as their necks snapped in the fall.

All except Samuel Knapp. On James's instructions, the hangman had grabbed the man around the waist as he kicked the lever. Instead of plummeting through the trapdoor, he sagged slowly. The noose tightened, but not so suddenly that it would break his neck. Instead, he gurgled, his eyes bulging, his mouth opening and closing like a fish tossed onto the bank. His feet kicked.

The crowd was silent but for a few crying babies. The rope creaked as Knapp swung back and forth, bumping into the dead men on either side of him. All the while his face contorted in pain and fear.

James forced himself to watch. He couldn't show weakness. Not now.

At last Knapp stopped kicking. His bound hands kept twitching behind his back for a long moment, and his lips, now turning blue, moved as if still begging for mercy, or maybe praying for his own wretched soul. At last, this, too, stopped. Knapp stared ahead through unblinking, glassy eyes.

James stepped over Edwins, who was still on his knees, clutching his bloody, half-severed ear and looking down at the pool of blood in front of his face instead of up at the dead men. James nearly stumbled coming down the stairs from the gallows. Cooper and Vandermeer came to his side, but he pushed them away.

Two women came rushing up onto the gallows. One wrapped her arms around one of the dead men, burying her face into his chest and sobbing. The other, also crying, but with joy, came to kneel next to Edwins. She was a plain but gentle-faced young woman, a swaddled baby in her arms. She shuffled the child so she could press a handkerchief to Edwins's ear. She kissed him repeatedly on top of the head.

James looked down at his hand, still bloody from the man's ear, then bent and wiped his hand on the ground. A stain remained in the snow, which he kicked over with his boot until it was hidden.

Chapter Thirty-Six

Prudence waited at home in front of the fire, reading to Mary from a book of Aesop's Fables. When feet stomped outside the door to kick snow from their shoes, Prudence sprang to her feet. The Stone children came running. They had not been allowed to attend the hangings. The front door swung open.

It was Anne and the reverend. "What cheer," they said, but there was, in fact, no cheer in their greetings.

The two parents put off the eager questions of their children and sent them back to their lessons and chores. The reverend went up to his room while Anne set about preparing supper.

Prudence sent Mary off with the other children, then rose to help her sister. Lucy and Alice Branch were no longer living with the Stones. The reverend had sold Alice's indenturehood, and he had freed Lucy as promised. Lucy had moved to Cambridge to live with a cousin and his wife. The reverend had sold Alice for practical reasons. He was shortly to lose his position and salary at the Third Church; they could no longer afford anyone but Old John Porter.

The sisters worked in silence for a few minutes, mixing the corn meal, peeling turnips, plucking a chicken, chopping its innards to make a broth.

"You don't have to leave," Anne said at last. "There is always room in our home for you and Mary."

And Prudence's labor, as well. It would be difficult for Anne to manage without the Branch sisters. Prudence felt guilty, but she could not stay.

"Nay, I've cowered for too long."

"People will talk. You know what they say about a woman who lives alone."

"Let them."

Anne looked disappointed at this but said nothing.

"Has the reverend secured another position?" Prudence asked when the silence grew uncomfortable.

"No responses yet to his letters, but we have hopes. There is a small congregation in Warwick, Rhode Island, that is anxious to secure a minister. The sum is modest, but they are theologically sound."

"You'll move to Rhode Island?" Prudence managed a smile. "The cesspool of New England? Times are indeed desperate."

"Please, Prudie. Come with us."

"I already said—"

"I know what you said, and I know what you're hoping for."

"Do you?" Prudence asked, surprised. "Am I a window that you can see through me so easily?"

"You were on your feet when we entered, but you were hoping for someone else. Do you deny it?"

"I was hoping," she admitted, "but with little expectation. He is probably gone already." To distract herself, she changed course. "Were there many people at the hangings?"

"Most of the town," Anne said. "Knapp died badly. Drawn across the Common by a horse, left unhooded during the hanging.

The hangman held him up as the trapdoor sprang, so he wouldn't fall and break his neck. He writhed in torment."

The image did not give Prudence pleasure. She had chosen to stay away, not wishing to feed her hunger for vengeance. Now she understood that she needn't have worried. Knapp was responsible for the death of her husband and many other murders besides, yet she felt only sickened at the thought of more killing.

"It was no more than he deserved," Anne added. "And only a taste of what awaits him in the eternal torment of hell."

"Only God can make that judgment."

"Pray pardon me, I spoke in error."

Prudence put a corn meal–dusted hand over her sister's wrist. Anne gave her a tired smile.

"The others died quickly enough," Anne continued. "There was some pleading, some cries from family members, but they knew it was just. They all knew. Except James pardoned one man."

"Pray tell. Which one?"

"Henry Edwins. Docked his ear and sold him into servitude for three years, with the sum to be donated for the care of those who lost husbands and fathers in the war."

"My heart is glad," Prudence said. "There has been enough killing. I only wish there had been another way."

"It isn't Master Bailey's fault. The guilt lies here, in the sins of New England. Men fell to greed and avarice. The Lord has scourged us. First, by the hand of the savages, then by the Crown."

Just then, Mary came running through with one of her cousins, who was carrying a rag doll with broken buttons for eyes and a mouth. Mary still wasn't talking very much, but she seemed to be absorbing every word out of the chattering older girl's mouth, understanding it all. It brought a smile to Prudence's lips.

"You could follow him to England," Anne said, unexpectedly.

"He hasn't asked me."

Anne picked up a turnip and trimmed away the wilted greens. "Have you given him an opportunity?"

"He had plenty."

"When his mind was engaged elsewhere," Anne said. "It isn't now."

Prudence carried the corn pudding to the hearth. When she returned, Anne studied her with a serious expression.

"Go to the *Vigilant*," Anne said. "Find him. Ask him to stay. I'll accompany you to give you courage."

Prudence stifled a laugh at the earnest look on her sister's face. "You are serious?"

"I am!"

Prudence's pulse quickened at the possibility, but then she gave a sad shake of the head. "By now it's too late. He meant to sail as soon as the execution was done. I won't chase him to London. That is too much." She sighed. "I couldn't do it. Imagine the humiliation when I arrived and he turned me away."

"He wants you, Prudence. How could he not?"

"You say that because you're my sister. You have hopes for me, you want to see me healed. You want me to start a new family, to have more children."

"Is it a sin to wish happiness for my sister?"

"It won't happen," Prudence said. "Not with James. You don't know him. We spoke about many things on our journeys. He's a good man at heart, but he is young, and hot blood runs through his veins."

"James turned away Lucy when he could have had her." Anne picked up the paring knife and returned to cutting turnips. "That is an honorable man."

How could she explain without making him seem like a scoundrel? If Anne knew how she had given herself to him, she would be disappointed in Prudence and outraged at the liberties James had taken.

"Would he have turned Lucy away under other circumstances? When he was in Paris, and the licentious French girls threw themselves at him, did he turn *them* away?" Prudence lifted a hand to stop Anne's sputtered protest. "I'm not questioning his character. I know he is a good man. But he isn't interested in a wife, and I have no intention of following him to be his mistress."

"Heavens, no!"

"Then we're agreed," Prudence said firmly. "It was a fool's hope all along."

They returned to silence for several minutes while they got the chicken and vegetables into the Dutch oven and carried it between them to the hearth. Then they returned to clean up the mess left by their preparations.

"Time is running short," Anne said. "You need to settle this before the *Vigilant* sails."

"What makes you think she hasn't already?"

"Because I asked about the tides. They sail at high tide, when they can get over the sandbars."

Prudence stopped and took her sister by the shoulders. "Why are you so determined? You thought very little of him when he arrived."

"Because I see what he's done to you. You left frightened and wracked by evil memories. Since you returned, you've changed. You no longer wake at night crying out in terror."

"Because of Mary."

"*And* Master Bailey," Anne insisted. "He healed you, gave you confidence. I was so proud—you'll never know how much—when you pried out the truth from Lucy, and then when you denounced Knapp. And in front of all of those men. Even the governor. I am honored to call you my sister."

"But, Anne—" Prudence began.

"Then when James pardoned Goodman Edwins, I saw what kind of man he was. Strong, but merciful. With principles, but not so rigid that he becomes a tyrant. That is the sort of man my sister should marry. He could be a father for your daughter, and a fine one too."

Prudence turned away. Her heart was bursting. She didn't want Anne to see her lip quivering, or the tears springing to her eyes.

"Prudie?"

"What?"

Anne turned her around and lifted her chin. "Tell me truthfully, do you have feelings for him?"

"I love him, Anne. With all of my heart."

Anne embraced her and whispered in Prudence's ear, "It takes great courage to earn a great reward."

She was right. Of course she was. And if Prudence marched down to the wharves, only to be laughed at by the dockers and sailors, even if James were to rebuff her in front of them all, what shame was there in that? There were few in New England who didn't already know her name. Those who didn't yet, soon would. If she couldn't handle the scorn, she could always leave.

Still, she was not so brave as to go alone. "And you will come with me?"

"Of course." Anne cast a glance toward the stairs. "Quickly, before Henry asks me to explain myself."

The two women took off their aprons on their way to the front door and exchanged them for their cloaks, which hung on pegs. But before they could put them on, the door swung open. James stood in front of the house, cheeks red from the cold, breath billowing. Prudence stood gaping.

"Master James," Anne said smoothly. She put her cloak on the hook as if she had only just arrived herself, then took Prudence's and did the same. "What cheer! Pray come in."

He kicked the snow from his boots and stepped inside.

"Will you be joining us for supper, then?" Anne asked.

"The *Vigilant* sails in thirty minutes. I'm afraid I don't have time."

"I see. Well, that is a disappointment. Come in, anyway." She nudged Prudence.

Prudence caught her breath at last. Her heart was pounding, but she managed to smooth what must have been a dumbfounded expression, slack-jawed and foolish. She took James's cloak and hung it on the hook.

Anne hurried to feed more wood into the fire, then scooted children away and sent them upstairs. Prudence caught whispered threats from her sister should they dare to return. Old John Porter came in from the back with an armful of kindling, and Anne took this and seated him firmly on the far end of the table, out of the way. Old John took one look at James and sighed, as if knowing that interesting happenings were afoot once more and he would not be able to follow a word of it.

"Pray have a seat," Prudence told James, pointing to the bench in front of the fire.

When he obeyed, Prudence took a chance and sat next to him, instead of on the opposite side with her sister. Anne looked pleased.

James cleared his throat. "You weren't at the hanging."

"I had seen enough death."

"Yes, of course—I didn't mean that. Only I wanted to speak with you before I leave."

"Yes?" She tried not to sound too eager.

"To give thanks. You saved my life. And you did your duty to your king and country."

"I am the one who should be grateful. I wouldn't have my daughter if you hadn't—"

Anne interrupted with an exaggerated sigh, and they both looked at her. "Thirty minutes until the *Vigilant* sets sail. That means Master Bailey has fifteen minutes until he must leave. Is this how you want to spend your conversation?"

"Anne!" Prudence said.

"At least one of you has something to say. I hope both of you."

"Then why are you interrupting?" Prudence asked. "Couldn't you go upstairs for a moment?"

"I'm your sister. That wouldn't be proper."

"Heavens, what a gossip. You're as bad as Goody Brockett."

James laughed, and Anne gave a look of false shock at the accusation. Nevertheless, the awkwardness of the situation was broken, and Prudence no longer felt like she wanted to dissolve through a crack in the floorboards and disappear.

"Tell me why you came," she said.

"The truth is I—" He smiled awkwardly and rubbed the back of his neck.

"Yes?"

"Two hours ago I was speaking in front of a thousand people, and now I can't seem to summon the words."

Prudence took his hand. "I hope we desire the same thing. But if not, I would rather we part having spoken everything in our hearts. So if you have returned so you could apologize for your behavior, let me assure you there is no need. I understand you have duties to your king."

"No, Prudie. That isn't why I've come. But I don't know how to ask you. I cannot stay in New England."

"No, you cannot. I knew that all along. How could you become the king's chancellor if you stayed in Boston?"

"But you swore you would never leave New England, and I would never ask you to go with me to London. It's a cesspool of sin and vice. The air itself is so filled with miasma that a child like Mary should never breathe it."

She wanted to protest that she would go with him if only he would ask. Many people raised their children in London, didn't they? Couldn't they find a healthy spot away from the river and its sewage, a place where the breezes blew away the soot and the disease? And weren't there churches, ministers, Godly people to be found?

But maybe that wasn't what he was saying. Maybe this was his excuse. She glanced at Anne, who wore a worried expression.

"I spoke with Joseph McMurdle," James said. "Gave him the privilege to deliver my report to London, offer up Fitz-Simmons for the king's justice. I have no stomach to see the man tortured and killed. McMurdle was to travel to Quebec, but he is eager to take this opportunity."

She was confused. "Then what, you will travel to Quebec in his place?"

"No, I'm on my way to New York. It is a troublesome little colony, pacified, but the Dutch returned once, and might again. Not as important as combating the French, but I cannot trust it to one man. Vandermeer has his uses, but we need more."

"But if McMurdle claims your victory in London, and you remain in the colonies, won't that mean—?"

"Aye. I will surrender my chance at the position of king's chancellor."

"Isn't that your heart's desire?" she asked.

"Nay, that is not my heart's desire. Not any longer."

She swallowed hard and nodded.

"New York isn't the Bay Colony," he continued, "but McMurdle says there's energy in Manhattan, and a growing colony of English, many of them original settlers of Plymouth, Connecticut, and Massachusetts. You might be comfortable there."

And it would be relatively close to Rhode Island, too, if her sister settled there. And she had two brothers living along the Connecticut coast, as well, plus another sister living across the sound on Long Island.

Prudence's heart pounded. Her stomach turned over.

Anne rose to her feet. "This is the part of the conversation where I can slip away. Besides, I should have my own conversation with Henry. I must prepare him for this happy news."

There was a commotion when Anne reached the stairs, as apparently children had crept down to listen. Mild scolding chased them back upstairs.

When Anne and her children were gone, James turned back to Prudence. "I told McMurdle I would send him to England in my stead, but only if you would come with me to New York."

Her heart was pounding and her mouth dry. "Please, be clear. Under what terms, as your mistress? You know I couldn't do that."

James took her hand. "As my wife. If you would have me."

"I—I would do that. Yes."

He apparently took her stuttering as hesitation, because he pressed on. "And as my partner. My lover. You are a beautiful and clever woman, strong-willed and stubborn, but tender enough to be a good wife and mother at the same time. I will be your husband and the father of your child if you let me—*our* child. That is, our *children*. Please be my wife, Prudie, I love you."

She threw her arms around his neck and then they were kissing, locked for a long moment in each other's embrace. When she opened her eyes, there was Anne, standing on the stairs, peering around the corner, a broad grin on her face.

"Well then," Prudence said, pulling away and rising to her feet. She took James's hand and urged him to stand. "We had better hurry down to the docks if we are to wave good-bye to the *Vigilant* before she sails."

They went for their cloaks. As they passed the stairs, James smiled at Anne, now with several gawking children pressed around her as well. No sign yet of the reverend. Of course Prudence would prefer that he be happy to hear the news, but she found herself not particularly concerned if he wasn't.

"Goody Stone," James said. "On second thought, I *will* stay for supper. If the offer stands, that is, and if it will hold until we return from the harbor."

"Aye, Master Bailey. We would be happy to have you." Anne reached out and gave Prudence a little pinch above her hip as she passed.

Prudence slapped away Anne's hand and gave her a raised eyebrow, then playfully stuck out her tongue at the sniggering children when James wasn't looking.

Then she followed James outside and into the cold winter air.

About the Author

Photo © 2011 David Garten

Michael Wallace was born in California and raised in a small religious community in Utah, eventually heading east to live in Rhode Island and Vermont. In addition to working as a literary agent and innkeeper, he previously worked as a software engineer for a Department of Defense contractor, programming simulators for nuclear submarines. He is the author of more than twenty novels, including the *Wall Street Journal* bestselling series The Righteous, set in a polygamist enclave in the desert.